# Praise for
# The Death Wizard Chronicles

Melvin shows his literary mastery as he weaves elements of potential and transformation; his tale dances among literal shape shifters and more subtle powers of mind.
—*Ann Allen, Charlotte Observer*

"Adult Harry Potter and Eragon fans can get their next fix with Jim Melvin's six-book epic The Death Wizard Chronicles . . . Melvin's imagination and writing equal that of J.K. Rowling, author of the fantastically popular Harry Potter series, and Christopher Paolini, author of Eragon and Eldest. Some of his descriptions—and creatures—even surpass theirs."
—*The Tampa Tribune*

"Jim Melvin's Death Wizard Chronicles crackle with non-stop action and serious literary ambition. He has succeeded in creating an entire universe of interlocking characters—and creatures—that will undoubtedly captivate fans of the fantasy genre. It's a hell of a story . . . a hell of a series . . ."
—*Bob Andelman, author of* Will Eisner: A Spirited Life

"Jim Melvin is a fresh voice in fantasy writing with a bold, inventive vision and seasoned literary style that vaults him immediately into the top tier of his genre. The Death Wizard Chronicles . . . is scary, action-packed and imaginative—a mythic world vividly entwining heroes, villains and sex that leaves the reader with the impression that this breakthrough author has truly arrived."
—*Dave Scheiber, co-author of Covert: My Years Infiltrating the Mob and Surviving the Shadows: A Journey of Hope into Post-Traumatic Stress*

"Action-packed and yet profound, The DW Chronicles will take your breath away. This is epic fantasy at its best."
—*Chris Stevenson, author of* Planet Janitor: Custodian of the Stars *and* The Wolfen Strain

"Triken truly comes alive for the reader and is filled with mysteries and places that even the most powerful characters in the book are unaware of. That gives the reader the opportunity to discover and learn with the characters . . . Melvin has added to the texture of the world by integrating Eastern philosophies, giving the magic not only consistency but depth. He has worked out the details of his magical system so readers can understand where it comes from and how it works."
—*Jaime McDougall, the bookstacks.com*

# The Series, Thus Far

## Book 1: *Forged in Death*

## Book 2: *Chained by Fear*

## Book 3: *Shadowed by Demons*

## Death Wizard Shorts by Jim Melvin

### *Torg's First Death*

### *The Black Fortress*

# Shadowed by Demons

## The Death Wizard Chronicles
## Book Three

by

# Jim Melvin

Ann.

May you be
happy, healthy
and peaceful.

Bell Bridge Books

This is a work of fiction. Names, characters, places and incidents are either the products of the author's imagination or are used fictitiously. Any resemblance to actual persons (living or dead), events or locations is entirely coincidental.

Bell Bridge Books
PO BOX 300921
Memphis, TN 38130
Print ISBN: 978-1-61194-287-3

Bell Bridge Books is an Imprint of BelleBooks, Inc.

We at BelleBooks enjoy hearing from readers.
Visit our websites – www.BelleBooks.com and www.BellBridgeBooks.com.

10 9 8 7 6 5 4 3 2 1

Cover design: Debra Dixon
Interior design: Hank Smith
Photo credits:
Woman (manipulated) © Konradbak | Dreamstime.com
Castle (manipulated) © Javarman | Dreamstime.com
Raven (manipulated) © Antaratma Microstock Images © Elena Ray | Dreamstime.com
Background (manipulated) © Bolotov | Dreamstime.com

:Ldsz:01:

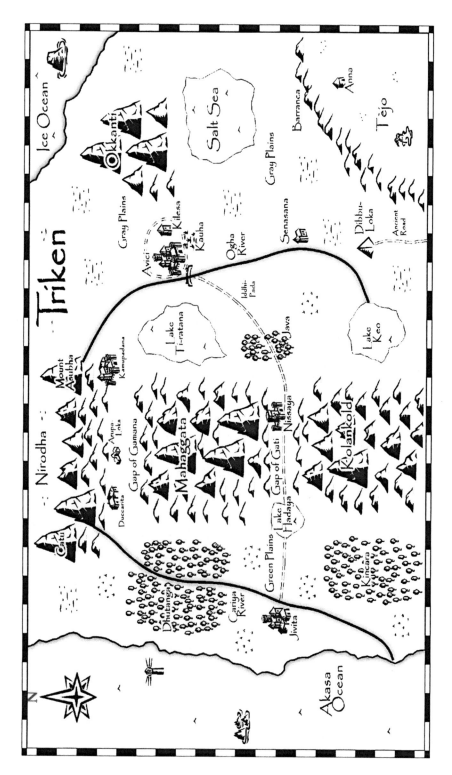

# Author's Note

In Book 1 of *The Death Wizard Chronicles*, the sorcerer Invictus imprisons Torg in a pit bored into the frozen heights of Mount Asubha. After his escape, Torg and several new friends make their way toward Kamupadana, commonly known as the Whore City, where Torg hopes to learn more about Invictus' plans.

Meanwhile, Laylah, the sister of Invictus, appears briefly as a sorceress whom Invictus also has imprisoned. Unlike Torg, she has not yet managed to escape. In fact, she has been her brother's captive for more than seventy years.

In Book 2, the tale is told of Laylah's escape. Under the guidance of the demon Vedana, she flees to Kamupadana, where she eventually meets and is healed by Torg. Along with the Asēkhas, Torg and his companions flee into the wilderness, with Mala, a.k.a. the Chain Man, and an army of monsters in hot pursuit.

Book 3 continues to chronicle their desperate plight.

# Table of Contents

# Dedication

To Jill, who came next.

"Does life matter?

Only if you don't let it."

—*Sister Tathagata, in a lecture to the monks and nuns of Dibbu-Loka*

# Prologue

WHEN SHE RAN like this, all she knew was joy. Her hooves thundered, her white mane fluttered, her green eyes glowed with delight. The Faerie called Bhojja, Jord, and Sakuna, among other names, galloped eastward faster than the wind.

During Triken's long winter, *Vijjaadharaa* (which means Faerie in the ancient tongue) had strayed from the mortal world. After removing the demon's poison from Torg beneath the magical pine trees in the frozen wilderness, she had wandered far in the north, shape-shifting between horse, eagle, woman, and lesser creatures. However, spring had arrived, and now she was needed again.

Like the ghost-child Peta and the demon Vedana, the Faerie had the gift of foreknowledge, though not as superbly developed. However, her superiors kept her informed in ways that were almost as efficient. They were always alert, always watching. And when they saw things that concerned them, they took steps to correct the problem.

The Faerie heeded their call. In the form of Bhojja, she galloped across the Gray Plains and was fewer than ten leagues north of the Golden Wall that encircled Avici and Kilesa. Avici is where the evil sorcerer dwelled. Could Invictus sense her out here, so close to his stronghold? If so, he issued no challenge.

When Bhojja passed farther eastward and eventually reached the foothills of Okkanti, she came to a halt and rested. In two days she had galloped two hundred leagues. Now she fed on sprigs of rye and drank from crystal streams as cold as the cosmos. Bony mountains towered before her. Somewhere in their treacherous heights lay Triken's salvation.

After her strength returned, Bhojja transformed into Sakuna and took flight, rising toward the peak of a mountain several thousand cubits taller than Asubha, its sides sheer and slippery. The eagle was at home in the heights, taking pleasure in the vertiginous surroundings. Finally she landed on a narrow ledge near the summit and waited there, instinctively comfortable in her choice of location. Though it was early spring, falling snow gathered on her plumage. She plucked out several enormous feathers with her beak and laid them gently on the icy stone. Then she changed into Jord, the green-eyed, white-haired woman, and used the feathers as a blanket.

The first snow giant approached within ten paces before Jord even saw her. Jord had existed on Triken in her current forms for more than ninety millennia, but amazingly this was the first time she had journeyed to Okkanti and seen a snow giant. The creature's elegant beauty amazed Jord. Like her own Faerie eyes, the snow giant's were green—but a richer, more luxuriant shade—and her mane was white. This female stood nine cubits tall, slightly shorter than a male. A surprisingly thin coat of fur covered her thick gray hide. Regardless, the cold did not seem to affect the huge beast.

"Are you a sorceress?" the snow giant asked curiously. "We watched from afar as you changed from eagle to human—and were impressed."

"We?"

"Others of my kind are nearby. But neither they nor I will harm you. I sense no evil in your nature."

"Nor I in yours," Jord said. "And I have certainly not come to assault you. Quite the contrary: I am here to beg your aid. Before I say more, allow me to introduce myself. I am known as Jord." She held out her hand, and the snow giant smiled tenderly. Long fangs were exposed, but Jord did not find them threatening.

"I am Yama-Bhari, wife to Yama-Utu."

"Could you ask the others to join us?" Jord said. "Time is of the essence, and I would prefer to not have to repeat myself."

"You have aroused my curiosity," Bhari said. "There is rarely harm in listening."

The snow giant raised her massive arms and let out a howl that echoed eerily among the frozen peaks. Immediately, seven other snow giants appeared. Most of them had been standing nearby, but their colorings blended so well with the ice and stone, it was as if they had been invisible. Even to Jord.

They sat in a circle around her, and though Jord remained standing, they still looked down upon her. One by one, they introduced themselves, including Yama-Utu, who proudly announced that he was the brother of Yama-Deva, the wanderer.

"Have you seen my brother?" Utu said with pleading eyes. "He has been missing for many years, and I have begun to worry. Is it possible he has found mountains even colder and more beautiful than these?"

Jord was stunned. Were these creatures unaware that Yama-Deva had become perverted by Invictus into a creature of malice and was now known as Mala? Then Jord noticed Bhari's green eyes welling with tears.

"It's not enough that we've lost Yama-Deva to the Sun God," she wailed. "Now we are losing my husband, Yama-Utu, as well. His grief ruins his mind, and he forgets about his brother's terrible transformation. Do you wield enough magic to heal Utu?"

"I am a healer," Jord said, "but I have not that level of strength. Perhaps not even the Death-Knower, known as The Torgon, could perform such a feat."

"Maranavidu (Death-Knower) . . ." Bhari said in a tone of awe. "Can you bring Torg to us? We would be most grateful."

"I cannot," Jord said regretfully. "At the moment, I'm not even certain where he is. But I can offer you something else. An opportunity for revenge. If you would come with me, you could strike a blow against the sorcerer who has caused your kind so much torment."

Bhari arched a bushy eyebrow. "And this revenge you offer would heal my husband and his brother?"

"I cannot make such a promise," Jord said. "But what I have to offer would be well worth the effort, I promise you."

Bhari sighed and then slowly lowered her huge head. Tears slipped from her eyes, freezing as they fell and clicking against the stone like fallen baubles.

"You do not comprehend us . . ." the snow giant whispered. "Mayhem is not in our nature. We are not capable of it. Nothing can result from violence but more violence. If you are asking us to fight on your behalf, then our answer is no. Besides, if we left these mountains, we could not survive for more than a few months. Of all our kind, only Yama-Deva strayed from the peaks, and even he never left the foothills—until the day Invictus stole him from us forever."

"If you do not help me, the world as you know it will fall," Jord said. "And the evil that destroyed Yama-Deva will rejoice. I admire your pacifism, but it's obvious you also possess great strength. Will you not wield it?"

"Violence begets violence," Bhari said. "This is the law . . . immutable. All of my kind would prefer to perish than to live with another's blood on our hands."

Jord grunted. Her superiors had sent her to enlist help for the forces of good, but she saw no help here. What did the Vijjaadharaa know that she did not?

"Do you need food . . . or a place to rest?" Bhari said. "We can provide comfort, if nothing else."

"I have neither the need nor the time. My mission is urgent. If you cannot help me, then we must part ways now."

"We cannot help you," Bhari said.

Soon after, the snow giants vanished into their surroundings. But when Jord stepped to the edge of the ledge and prepared to transform back into an eagle, a massive hand grasped her thin shoulder. She turned and looked up into the broad face of Yama-Utu.

"I will come with you," the snow giant said, his voice as resonant as tumbling boulders. Apparently, his earlier confusion had been short-lived.

"My wife fears my madness, but in truth I have never been saner. You offer revenge? I thirst for it. I want to destroy the thing that Yama-Deva has become. Will you help me find Mala?"

"I know those who can," Jord said. "And I will take you to them."

Utu smiled, but not nearly as pleasantly as his wife. Now the fangs looked deadly.

"Climb onto my back, and I will carry you down," he said. "We will journey together. And when the need for violence arises, I will be more than equal to the task."

ON THE SAME day that Jord first met the snow giants, the brother of Yama-Utu—now known as the monster Mala—lay shivering and incoherent in a cave behind a waterfall. It was the morning after his vicious battle with the great dragon Bhayatupa, and Mala was near death.

But he would not succumb on this day. Invictus would see to that.

A band of Mogol warriors found Mala and began his rescue. Blood as foul as poison oozed from a gash on the side of his head and from a dozen other places on his huge frame. His chain glowed sporadically, spewing globules of molten liquid that killed several Mogols trying to rescue him. But the warriors were not deterred, for Invictus had given them orders, and they knew he was watching them even now. They finally managed to drag Mala through a tunnel that led out the back of the cave. Afterward, they built a great litter. It took ten men to hoist him onto it.

Bhayatupa had slaughtered the dracools and the Sampati that had been summoned to aid Mala during his search for Torg and Laylah, but several hundred ravens had survived the assault. Some of these had returned to Avici and alerted Invictus of his general's dire situation. Some flew back and forth, reporting all that they saw from the skies.

The rescue of Mala was slow, even with a team of wolves dragging the litter. All the rest of that day and night, they managed only two leagues. At that rate, Mala would be long dead before they reached the Golden City. But the next day around noon, another Sampati and a dracool landed nearby. Invictus climbed off the dracool. A thin, muscular pilot leapt off the crossbred condor and quickly roped one of its massive legs to the stump of a tree.

As Invictus approached, the Mogols fell to the ground and buried their faces in the grass, not daring to move. A happy band of crickets stopped chirping, a bubbling spring slowed to a crawl, and a frisky breeze lost its way, no longer rustling the spring leaves, as if Invictus' mere presence turned off even nature's sound effects.

With surprising tenderness, Invictus climbed onto the litter and placed his hand on Mala's boulder-sized forehead. "My dear, loyal pet. I'm sorry you've been through so much and that it took me so long to come to you. But do not doubt that I will avenge you. Bhayatupa will become my puppet, before all is said and done."

The Chain Man moaned but did not open his eyes.

Invictus turned to the Mogols. "You have done well, and you will be rewarded. But you are no longer needed here. Return to Avici and await further orders."

As if in relief, the wolves and Mogols fled. Only the dracool, the Sampati, and the pilot remained. The man came forward, his wiry limbs trembling.

"Do you wish me to leave?"

"I have need of you," Invictus said. "Come here now."

"My liege?"

"I have need of you."

The pilot hesitated. "I should stay near the Sampati, my liege. It has a wild temperament."

"Do you disobey me?"

"No, my liege. I would never dare such a thing. It's just that . . ."

"Come here."

"Yes, my liege."

The pilot stumbled forward, finally clambering onto the litter and staring into Invictus' brown eyes.

"Give me your hand," Invictus said.

"Yes, my liege." The pilot held out his right arm.

"You must have misunderstood my command," Invictus said. "Must I repeat it?"

"My liege?"

Invictus sighed. Then he grabbed the pilot's forearm and spat a ball of yellow mucus onto his wrist. The flesh sizzled, and the hand fell onto Mala's chest, its fingers still wiggling.

While the pilot howled in agony, Invictus calmly said, "If you wish to live, give me your hand."

"Yes . . . yes . . ." the pilot managed to mumble. He reached down with his remaining hand, picked up the severed one, and gave it to Invictus.

"Very good," Invictus said. "Now you are free to go."

The pilot scrambled off the litter and ran, disappearing into the woods. Invictus could hear him emptying the contents of his stomach somewhere beyond the trees. He returned his attention to his prized servant.

"Everything's going to be all right, my general. You saved my life. Now I'll save yours."

Invictus' body glowed. In a slow and controlled fashion, the severed hand began to melt, dripping liquid globs of flesh, blood, and bone. Invictus held it over Mala, allowing the steamy goo to ooze into the Chain Man's wounds.

"My most loyal servant deserves nothing but the best," Invictus whispered tenderly.

Mala groaned, and his eyelids fluttered. Suddenly the ruined snow giant tore away the restraints that bound him to the litter and sat upright. Even in a seated position, he towered over Invictus.

"Where am I? What's happening?"

"You are with me. I am healing you."

Deep within Mala's tortured subconscious, did Yama-Deva briefly emerge? The once-beautiful creature looked down at Invictus and seemed to recoil. Then tears sprang from his eyes.

Invictus didn't care. "Tears of joy, my general? Yes, I have healed you. You and I have much to celebrate."

The Chain Man smiled broadly, his blood-red fangs glistening in the sunlight, his black tongue stabbing the air like a serpent's. "My king. You have not forsaken me. I feared you would be angry over my failure."

"Angry? Never. I love you. You did your best, my pet. Rejoice! Your dreams will come true, I promise you."

Mala stood shakily.

Invictus reached up and clasped one of the Chain Man's fingers. Like a tiny father with a colossus for a son, they walked through the field toward their mounts. The Chain Man climbed aboard the Sampati, Invictus the dracool, and side by side they flew back to Avici.

# Laylah's Recovery

# 1

IN HER LONG life, Laylah had known a lot of pain. But nothing compared to this.

With methodical precision, a million tiny mouths devoured her body with thorny teeth. She felt as if she were being skinned alive, but it was her essence being peeled away, not her flesh.

The only thing that kept her sane was the man who held her close. Where his body touched hers, she experienced a semblance of relief. Through the hysteria of her agony, she could sense his strength providing just enough succor for her to survive one more moment.

And another . . . another . . . another . . .

Laylah's back arched. White flames sprang from every pore, flaring inside the cramped chamber. She cried out. He screamed in response. She was hurting him, and she cursed herself. In such a short time, she had grown to love him. She wanted to give him pleasure, not pain. She tried to push him away, but her arms lacked the strength. He was strapped to her like a chain. For better or worse, they would endure this nightmare together.

In some ways her senses were blunted. When she opened her eyes, she saw nothing but white. When she tried to listen, she heard nothing but dissonance. She could barely feel the sweat on her skin. Or the blanket on which she lay.

In other ways her senses were heightened. She could smell Torg's sweet breath and feel the beating of his heart. And somehow, when her eyes were closed, she could see through the stone to where Lucius and the others lay sobbing outside the cave. She wanted to tell them that the pain belonged to her alone. But she didn't know how.

Laylah's body went into a spasm, her legs kicking like a pair of insane scissors, her arms flailing against the stone floor with wicked thuds, her eyes opening and closing frenetically, casting beams of molten light that smote the walls and ceiling. In the midst of this chaos, the *efrit* slept peacefully within her abdomen, perceiving no threat.

She felt Torg hold her even tighter, attempting to corral her white rages with his blue-green might. Part of her wanted to embrace his magic, part of her expel it. But he did not ask for permission. Instead, he rode her waves of agony like a leaf on the surface of a raging river. The worst of her pain went on for almost half the night. Without him, she would have perished.

Just before dawn, the pain finally lessened, allowing her to regain full consciousness and to realize where she lay. Now she *could* feel the sweat on her body and the chill of the stone. When she opened her eyes, she was relieved to see darkness; the all-consuming white had fled. Even better, the voracious mouths that had tormented her seemed to have lost their hunger and blessedly departed. She shivered in her nakedness. In response, large arms held her. It had not been just a dream amid nightmare. Torg was truly here.

"The tide has turned," she heard him whisper.

She tried to respond but could manage nothing intelligible.

"Shhhhh . . . quiet now," he soothed. "Try to sleep. You need to rebuild your strength. And when you wake, we'll try a sip of water."

In the silence of the cave, they lay entwined.

And for a time she knew no more.

WHEN THE FINAL shreds of the murky shroud slipped off the surface of the moon, the explosions of light emanating from the cave ceased. One last puff of smoke issued from the maw, as if the den were burping after a spicy meal. Lucius sat up, wiped tears from his eyes, and stared at the narrow entrance distrustfully, not allowing himself to believe that the dreadful cacophony had ended.

He turned to his companions and was surprised to see that all had fallen asleep. Just a moment before, they had been sobbing and moaning, but now Ugga, Bard, Rathburt, and Elu slept beneath the setting moon as silently as corpses. Even their usual harmonic cascade of snoring was surprisingly absent. But nature's chorus returned from its temporary absence. Lucius could hear the songs of crickets and the hooting of an owl.

On hands and knees, he crawled to the mouth of the cave and peered inside. He could see only darkness, but could smell the wispy remnants of smoke swirling in the air. For reasons he could not define, his heart pounded like a frightened child's. Part of him wanted to scramble into the cave and rush to Laylah's side. But another part knew that she no longer belonged to him, if she ever had. The sorceress was beyond him, in power and scope. Denying this would only cause more anguish.

While the owl continued its lonesome call, Lucius sat outside the cave, his face flushed and swollen. He felt disoriented, as if his body were not his own. He stayed there as the moon plunged hurriedly behind a line of trees.

Even as dawn took hold of the day, the cave remained silent. But it beckoned him, nonetheless. The realization that Laylah was lost to him did not lessen his feelings for her. If he could not be her lover, he still could protect her as a friend. That wouldn't be so bad. In fact, considering he was little more than a freak born of a madman, being Laylah's friend was more than he deserved.

With the onset of morning, the tunnel leading to the interior of the cave became partially illuminated, but darkness still obscured Torg and Laylah's whereabouts. If Lucius were to find the courage to crawl inside, he would need to bring a torch of some kind with him.

"Elu made this for you," a high-pitched voice proclaimed.

Lucius yelped and sprang to his feet so fast he grew dizzy, staggering sideways against a boulder that fronted the cave. Elu stood nearby, holding a torch—not yet lighted—that he had constructed using bark stripped from a birch tree and rolled into a tube.

"Elu, you scared me half to death," Lucius said, his cheeks stained with crimson shame.

Rathburt sat up and rubbed his eyes. "What's all the shouting about? Isn't it a little early for fussing?"

Bard and Ugga continued to sleep, but now they snored loudly.

"Well, I can see everything has returned to normal around here," Lucius huffed.

Elu shook his head. "Not yet," the Svakaran said, handing him the torch. "You must go to the great one and his pretty lady."

"*I* must go?" Lucius said. "What's so special about me? Why don't you go? You can squeeze in there better than I. Or how about Master Rathburt? He's the only one of us out here who wields any magic to speak of. I have no desire to go in there, believe me."

"Elu does *not* believe you. We all know that you love the pretty lady. And you are stronger than you look. Go to them. They need you."

Groaning, Rathburt stood and walked to Lucius' side. "For once Elu is right. Someone needs to go inside, and you make the most sense. But hurry up. As much as The Torgon annoys me, I have to admit that I'm worried about him . . . and your sweetling, too."

"She's not mine," Lucius said, motioning toward the cave. "She belongs to *him*."

"This is hard enough on all of us without you causing more problems," Elu said to Rathburt. Then the Svakaran swung toward Lucius. "There are many ways to love someone—and be loved. She might be lost to you in the way you most desire. But she does not have to be lost to you entirely."

Elu pulled a sliver of flint from a pouch tied to his breeches and held it close to the torch, striking it against the blade of his Tugarian dagger. Instantly the birch bark caught fire.

"Beyond belief, Elu is right twice in the same day," Rathburt said, but this time his voice was kind rather than derisive. "Lucius, you must go to her . . . to *them*. You are connected to her in ways that we are not. And you say I have magic? Maybe so. But I don't have your courage or strength."

Lucius didn't feel the least bit courageous, but it was obvious that none of his companions were in the mood to make things easy for him. Finally, his love for Laylah—along with an ever-growing curiosity—compelled him to slither inside the mouth of the cave. Elu and Rathburt huddled by the opening, while Bard and Ugga continued to snore, heedless of anything but their dreams.

Lucius crawled deeper into the tunnel, sliding the torch along the floor of the cave with his left hand. The flames crackled merrily, but cast only enough light to see about two body lengths ahead. Again Lucius' heart pounded erratically. He could not pinpoint why he was so frightened, but he felt as if he were on the verge of entering a place he did not belong, interrupting the reverie of a pair of divine beings who might smite him for his insolence. After the previous night's display of power, Laylah no longer seemed like a mortal. Instead, she felt more like a creature of supernatural magnificence—and not necessarily safe for someone lesser to be around.

Suddenly the chamber before him was illuminated, revealing a pale mass pressed against the stone. His first glimpse of flesh did not look human, resembling a grotesque blob. Had Laylah blown herself and Torg to pieces?

Lucius gasped. But then he realized that what he had seen was a trick of perception. The longer he stared, the more he began to recognize the sorceress and wizard, wrapped in each other's arms, naked and shivering. Obhasa lay next to them, glowing ever so slightly. Amid his fear and confusion, Lucius felt a surge of jealousy. Then he heard Torg's voice.

"Lucius . . ." the wizard whispered. "Bring . . . bring our clothes. I tossed them out there . . . somewhere. And get the rest of the blankets. Now that it's over, she's . . . so . . . cold."

For a treacherous moment, Lucius considered sneaking over to Torg and throttling him. He could not match the Death-Knower under ordinary circumstances, but with the wizard so weak, could Lucius kill him now? The fantasy was fleeting. Instead of attempting murder, he found himself obeying the wizard's commands. He leaned the torch against the wall near Torg and hustled back out, barking orders to Elu and Rathburt.

The Svakaran gathered their clothes and blankets while Rathburt rushed to Ugga and nudged him with his staff. The giant crossbreed, who had been sleeping with the Silver Sword protectively at his side, leapt up and waved the weapon in front of him, unsteady on his feet but determined to fight. The commotion woke Bard, who screamed like a jittery child. Despite his own distress, Lucius couldn't help but chuckle. For the first time, he realized that he considered his companions to be friends.

"Get up, you sleepyheads!" he heard Rathburt saying. "Torg and Laylah are still alive, but they need our help. Do you expect me to do *everything?*"

"Master Hah-nah is alive? And the pretty lady too?" said Ugga, his deep voice still raspy. "That is very great news! I loves them so much."

"If you love them so much, then start a fire and make them—and *us*—something to warm our bellies," Rathburt said. "Can't you see that I'm busy with more important matters?"

Ugga and Bard complied, hastily arranging a pile of deadwood. Elu handed Lucius several blankets, along with Laylah's shawls and Torg's tunic and breeches. Lucius crawled back inside the cave and returned to the chamber, where he found the wizard cradling Laylah. Though she appeared to be deeply asleep, she continued to shiver. Both were filthy, as if they had rolled in ashes. The chamber smelled like a hearth gone cold.

"I believe she's going to survive," Torg whispered. The wizard wrapped Laylah in her shawls before dressing himself. "She was near death last night, but she fought so hard." He paused, and then said, "Are the rest of you all right?"

Lucius was amazed that Torg would even ask.

"Other than being worried, we're fine," he said, also in a whisper. "Ugga and Bard are starting a fire. I'm sure Elu will prepare a nice breakfast. Are you hungry? Will Laylah be able to eat? When will she wake up?"

Torg chuckled. "You always ask a lot of questions, though I'm beginning to find them endearing. Am I hungry? Famished is a better word. Will Laylah be able to eat? Probably not for another day or so, but we need to force her to drink some water. When will she wake up? As my Vasi master used to say, 'Your guess is as good as mine.' And allow me to answer your next question before you even ask it. Is she healed? She'll be weak for a while, but otherwise healthy, I believe. The worst is over, my friend."

Despite his envy, Lucius was touched. "I'll get water," he said softly.

"Let me get it," Torg said. "I need to stretch my limbs and breathe some fresh air. Will you stay with her for a short while?"

At first Lucius wasn't sure what to say. He was no longer frightened, but he felt even more like an outsider. Still, an opportunity to be alone with Laylah was too precious to decline.

"I'd be honored."

When Torg was gone, Lucius crawled next to Laylah, wrapped the blankets more securely, and took her in his arms. The side of her face pressed against the fabric of his tunic near his heart. She breathed slowly but with occasional gasps, as if something in her dreams startled her. He stroked her cheek. Her skin felt clammy, and there were lines of dirt encrusted on her lips. He wet his index finger with his own saliva and wiped some of the dirt away, then continued to cleanse her with his tears. Since his encounter with the Hornbeam, he seemed able to cry at a moment's notice. Was he losing his mind? Did he even have a mind?

One of Laylah's legs jerked.

Lucius stroked her face again and tried to soothe her by humming, though he wasn't much of a singer. His love for her filled him with bittersweet pain. If Laylah could not be his, it was better to learn it sooner than later. His mind pondered a life without her as his wife, and an entirely new future was unveiled. If Invictus were somehow defeated and they were all made safe, who was to say that he could not find a love of his own?

"How's she doing?"

Lucius jumped.

"I'm sorry. I didn't mean to startle you," Torg said.

"I scare easily nowadays. And I can't seem to stop crying."

Torg chuckled wearily. "Ah, Lucius . . . I know what you mean. I've been the same way. For so-called fighting men, we must appear rather fragile."

Lucius grunted. Then he stared hard at Laylah's lovely face. "I've known her for more than seventy years. I've grown to love her so much. It's . . . *painful* . . . to have to let her go."

Without warning, Laylah flailed her arm. Both Lucius and Torg squealed. Afterward they laughed.

"Then again, if she moves around like that in her sleep, maybe I *don't* want to be with her," Lucius said.

They laughed even louder.

The sorceress lay still, as if silently pleased to witness the beginning of a friendship.

With tenderness, Lucius relinquished his hold on Laylah and allowed Torg to take her back. The wizard sat next to her and rested her head in his lap. He had brought a skin filled with water, which he drizzled onto her lips. Though she never opened her eyes, she managed to take some in her mouth and swallow. Torg gave her more. She swallowed again.

"A good sign," he said to Lucius.

They sat for a while without speaking. Lucius was the first to break the silence.

"What was it like being in here with her last night? From outside the cave, it looked like a volcano. How did you manage to survive? I tried to crawl inside, but was nearly burned alive. And why was the eclipse so painful to her?"

"There you go again with your questions, Lucius. As for how I was able to survive? I am a Tugar by birth, and my body is not easily damaged. But the powers that I wield as a Death-Knower are what truly protected me. Your describing what happened in here as resembling a volcano is not so off the mark. Indeed, the white fire that burst from Laylah during her distress was every bit as lethal as an eruption. Still, I was able to contain it, with minimal damage to us—*and* the interior of the cave—though Obhasa and I were sorely tested.

"As to why the eclipse was so painful to her? I can only guess. There must have been dozens of times in her life when the moon became enshrouded with shadow, and it's obvious she survived those occurrences with little harm. But this was the first time that a lunar eclipse followed a total eclipse of the sun. The two together proved too much . . . almost."

Torg looked down at Laylah's face and smiled. "Despite the near disaster, I am hopeful. Invictus was also weakened, which proves that the sorcerer is not impervious to harm. Perhaps, before all is said and done, we can devise a way to defeat him."

A voice from outside interrupted their conversation.

"Breakfast is ready," Ugga shouted. "Little Elu has cooked up a dee-lish-us stew! Is the pretty lady hungry?"

The wizard and Lucius laughed heartily.

But then Torg grew serious again. "I would take Laylah outside, but I'm not sure how she'll react to the sunlight. And right now, she's too fragile to take unnecessary risks. Go and eat, Lucius—and when you're finished, please bring a little for me."

Once again, Lucius didn't argue.


AFTER LUCIUS left the cave, Torg grasped the thick ivory shaft of Obhasa and positioned its round head a finger-length above Laylah's eyes. A sheet of blue-green flame fell upon her face, tenderly cleansing her skin and working its way into her hair, ruffling it like a warm breeze as it subtly vaporized filth and oils. Then Torg slid Obhasa downward, cleansing her breasts, underarms, abdomen, and legs. He gently rolled her onto her stomach and swept the staff along her back and buttocks. Eventually she was as clean as if she had taken a soapy bath.

"I adore you, my love," he whispered. "If it is within my power, you and I will never be parted. Do you doubt it?"

She moaned in response, but did not awaken. For the rest of that day and night, she slept soundly. The others remained outside. Bard and Ugga scouted the surrounding terrain, searching for signs of the enemy. Finally Elu dared an appearance in the chamber, and when that went well, Rathburt came next. When Bard and Ugga returned, each also squeezed in for separate visits. Torg gave Laylah more water, and she even swallowed a sip of wine and a bit of broth from the stew.

Early the next morning, the sorceress finally opened her eyes. At first, Torg didn't believe what he was seeing, but then a pale light emanated from her pupils.

"Beloved," he heard her say, "is this another dream?"

"Laylah, Laylah, Laylah," was all he could manage. She closed her eyes again and slept. Around noon she sprang awake and announced she was hungry.

Torg called for Elu, and the Svakaran reacted quickly with a bowl of soup made from wild onions and chitterlings.

Laylah managed a few spoonfuls and then fell asleep again, as if drugged. When she woke later that afternoon, she became eager to leave the cave, needing to relieve herself somewhere in private. She managed to crawl shakily through the tunnel without aid. When she emerged, Lucius and the others applauded.

Luckily, the sky was heavily overcast, so bright sunlight wasn't a problem. Torg led Laylah to a nearby copse and left her there alone except for Obhasa, which thrummed and glowed as if pleased to assist her. Eventually she emerged on her own, using the staff as a walking stick. A cool breeze swirled through her silky hair. Her beauty nearly caused Torg to swoon.

"You're all staring at me like I'm an invalid," Laylah said. But then she laughed. And they laughed with her.

"Elu's soup was good, but I didn't get nearly enough. What else is there to eat? I'm starving."

As it turned out, there was plenty. Bard had slain a pair of geese with Mogol arrows loosed from Jord's bow, and their bare carcasses were already roasting over a fire. They also had berries, nuts, and edible leaves and roots, which they found in abundance near the camp. When evening came, they sat together and feasted like royalty. For the first time in days, the rising of the moon did not seem to perturb Laylah, though she never released her grip on Obhasa.

By the time they finished their meal, the sky had cleared. Laylah wandered from their camp, all the while staring at the moon. Torg nestled beside her. She wrapped an arm around his waist.

"I was hoping you'd join me, beloved."

"You're not worried about Lucius?"

"When you're with me, I don't worry about anything."

Torg squeezed her shoulder. "What do you feel?"

"Hmmm? I don't understand."

"When you look at the moon . . . what do you *feel?*"

"Aaaah. I thought you were asking how I felt about you. But that's obvious, isn't it?" She laughed softly. "As for the moon, the *wrongness* is gone. It feels friendly to me. Replenishing. Like it used to."

"I'm so pleased. Do you remember anything that happened the night of the eclipse?"

"Not much, I'm afraid. But somehow I knew you were there. You saved my life."

"You saved yourself. I was humbled by your strength."

"Don't be foolish, Torgon. I'm the one who's humbled. I've done nothing in my life to deserve you."

"Now whose words are foolish? Let's not waste our time on such talk. Instead, let's discuss our future. If we're to spend it together, we must find a way to survive the present. Though we've evaded the enemy for now, we remain in danger. The worst thing we can do is stay in one place too long. We've risked much with all these cook-fires. I hate to ask you this so soon, but I must. Do you feel strong enough to travel?"

"To be honest, I'm looking forward to doing some walking, especially if you allow me to carry Obhasa. Just don't be in too much of a hurry and leave me behind."

"Invictus himself could not force me to do that. What you really need is a month's worth of pampering, but sadly we are not permitted such luxury. Let's tell the others that it's time to move on."

Lucius was incensed. "Are you insane? She's barely able to stand, much less walk. How can you expect her to trek through these mountains in the dark? It's too much to ask of a person who is well, much less Laylah, who's barely recovered from her ordeal."

"Nonetheless, it must be done," Torg said. "Thanks to Rathburt and Laylah, we escaped Mala and the wolves. But Invictus will not rest until we are captured. These mountains will soon be swarming with his minions. We must pass north of Duccarita and reach Dhutanga as soon as possible. Once there, we can decide whether to skirt the forest or venture on to Cariya. Either way leads to the White City."

"And if she drops dead of exhaustion?"

Torg was about to say more, but Laylah interrupted. "Torg is not forcing me," she said. "But I will do whatever he asks, without question. Against the threat of Invictus, he is my only hope—*our* only hope. For my sake and yours, you need to stop arguing with Torg and start doing what he says. He wants the best for all of us. Surely you can see that by now. He loves us."

"And we love ya too, Master Ogre . . . er . . . Hah-nah . . . er . . . what do we call ya, again?" Ugga said. "I gets confused."

"Call him Master Showoff," Rathburt said.

They laughed, loud and hard.

Even Lucius.

# 2

TO THE OTHERS the moon was a nuisance, providing too much light for prying eyes. But to Laylah the golden orb had returned to its former glory, nourishing her with strength and vitality. The wrongness she felt before the onset of the eclipse had vanished. For the first time in a long while, she felt whole.

Thanks to the combined magic of the moon and Obhasa, Laylah grew steadier with each step. As Lucius had claimed, the mountain trails *were* treacherous, blanketed with exposed roots, jagged rocks, and muddy bogs. Low-hanging branches slapped at their faces. Sudden drop-offs appeared without warning. But Laylah thrived in this environment. Her years with the Ropakans had taught her how to survive in the mountains, whether day or night. And she still remembered these skills instinctively.

Torg led the way. Elu also was capable—the diminutive Svakaran had proven to be a master of the wilderness—but the wizard was the only one among them who had wandered in the mountains this near Duccarita. Ugga and Bard appeared comfortable in any setting, and even whiny Rathburt was a capable woodsman. But Lucius encountered all kinds of problems. He was an army general used to open terrain. In this bony and vertiginous world, he was out of his element. Laylah felt sorry for him.

When they reached a dip in the trail sheltered by tall pines, Torg suddenly stopped. In the oppressive darkness, the wizard's eyes glowed like coals.

"Do you hear them?" he whispered to his companions.

Rathburt, of course, was the first to respond, his voice overly loud. "What are you babbling about now, Torgon? Hear what?"

"The taunts of the demons."

"I doesn't hear any demons," Ugga said worriedly. "And I doesn't want to. Where are the demons, Master Hah-nah? Are they somewhere near?"

Laylah grasped Torg's arm. "I don't hear them, either."

To her surprise, Lucius spoke next. "Arupa-Loka is not far from where we stand. If we turned south, we could reach the Ghost City before dawn. Is that why you hear them, Torg?"

But the wizard didn't answer.

Which, of course, annoyed Rathburt.

"For Anna's sake, someone *please* slap him!"

"Be quiet, Rad-burt!" Bard said. "If Master Hah-nah needs to think, let him think."

"I *think* he's gone crazy," Rathburt responded.

"She watches us," said Torg, in a voice so deeply eerie that Ugga yelped.

Elu tapped the wizard on the leg. "Who watches us, great one?"

Torg's facial muscles contorted. Laylah stroked his back to try to calm him, but he didn't respond.

"Beloved," Laylah whispered. "You're frightening us. Come back."

Not knowing what else to do, she gently touched the side of his face with Obhasa's rounded head. Unexpectedly, a burst of energy leapt from the staff and sizzled between Torg's eyes.

The wizard tore the shaft from her hand with frightening strength.

Lucius drew his *uttara* from its scabbard, but Laylah said, "No!"

The wizard held the staff aloft and shouted words from the ancient tongue.

"*Dhiite! Dhiitaake!*"

Blue-green energy spiraled skyward, crackling as it ascended and leaving a column of smoke in its wake. A flock of bats sprang from the trees and flew in wild circles around the smoke, which resisted dissipation despite a strong breeze.

Torg froze again, but his strange facial contortions continued.

"He'll kill us all," Laylah heard Rathburt whisper.

She couldn't bear to see the wizard in such distress. Despite his fey mood, she flung herself against his chest. "Torg, I'm here. Come back to me!"

The others watched with relief as Torg lowered the staff and gazed at her face. His body relaxed, and his expression softened. "I'm sorry, my love . . ."

"Beloved . . ." she purred.

Elu hugged Torg's calf. "If the demons are hurting you, Elu will kill them all."

"You can't kill a demon," Rathburt said, his voice quivering. "They're already dead. Well, sort of." Then his characteristic annoyance again took hold. "Oh, forget it. Torgon, if you've finished terrifying us, would you mind telling us what just happened?"

Torg seemed to take extra time to absorb the meaning of the question.

"Let's just say that I'm not as strong as I thought," the wizard finally whispered. "For a moment, the demons were able to take hold of my mind. They are better . . . *organized* . . . than they used to be."

"Are the nasty demons going to get into *my* mind?" Ugga said.

"We need to keep moving," Lucius said with renewed annoyance in his voice. "We're too near their stronghold."

"I agrees with Loo-shus," Bard said. "Let's run . . . far, far away."

Laylah listened in silence, then spoke directly to Torg. "You shouted words from the ancient tongue. I don't know what they meant. What did the demons say that upset you so?"

Torg shook his head. "Not now." Then he turned to the rest of them. "Lucius is right. We need to get away. If the demons were to attack us here in the middle of the night . . ."

After that, Torg would say no more, which seemed to annoy Rathburt, per usual. Instead, Torg handed Obhasa back to Laylah and led them hurriedly down the path, setting a pace that even Elu found difficult to match. Despite her newfound strength, Laylah struggled to catch her breath, her thighs burning from the exertion. Lucius fell almost out of sight. They went on this way for three torturous leagues.

As much for the firstborn's benefit as her own, Laylah finally said, "Torg, you must slow down. I'm too weak."

Torg halted. "Sometimes I forget who I am with," he said apologetically. "The Asēkhas can march like this for days."

"Now he insults us," snapped Rathburt, leaning heavily on his staff. "Not everyone is as robust as one of your precious Asēkhas, you know."

By now, Lucius had caught up. "Don't slow down because of me," he said, dripping with sweat despite the chilly night.

"Dawn approaches," Torg said. "Soon we'll reach an area of flatland that will be easier to traverse. But also more dangerous. We've had a respite from the eyes of the enemy. They will be upon us again."

"If we continue in this direction, won't it take us directly to Duccarita?" Lucius said between heaving gulps of air. "I thought you wanted to pass north of the city."

"You must trust my instincts," Torg said. "Follow me just a little while longer. Then we can eat and rest up for tomorrow night."

"What happens then?" Lucius said.

"We shall see what we shall see."


WHEN DAYLIGHT arrived, they settled in a rock shelter behind a small but robust waterfall. Once inside the stone chamber, Torg permitted them to dare a small fire, knowing the running water would filter out most of the smoke.

Elu hurriedly made a wild vegetable stew that was not nearly to his usual standards, but at least it put something hot in their stomachs. After eating, they cast themselves onto their blankets and fell into deep sleep—except for Torg, who remained seated with his back against the sweating stone. Laylah lay with her head in his lap. He stroked her hair, admiring her beautiful face and flawless skin.

*One day, my love, all of this will be behind us . . .*

Torg closed his eyes and tried to rest, but his mind remained overly active, replaying the previous night's encounter with the demons. Somehow they had homed in on his presence, bombarding his mind with an ugly torrent of threats and obscenities. The demons had remembered his previous visits to the Ghost City—but not fondly—and they had invited him to return and face them again.

*Do you dare, Death-Knower?*

Even as Torg struggled to thwart their assault, another voice rose above the tumult, causing him a different kind of pain.

"*Dhiite! Dhiitaake!*" he had cried in response to the voice, unwittingly unleashing a powerful blast of chaotic energy from Obhasa. Without Laylah's assistance, he might have put on a display that would have alerted anyone within ten leagues. Just in time, she had brought him back.

During his psychic battle with the demons, a terrible secret was unveiled, staggering Torg with its ramifications. When and how he would reveal what he knew to Laylah and the others was unclear. He wished he could speak to Sister Tathagata, whose insights always aided him.

Movement outside the chamber interrupted Torg's thoughts.

Ugga and Bard murmured in their sleep, as if a ghostly visitor disturbed them. It took Torg a moment to realize that someone—or something—was standing on the other side of the waterfall, just a few cubits from where he sat. The large figure cast a wobbling shadow. Torg believed the being contained formidable power, but he did not sense evil.

He rested Laylah's head on a rolled-up blanket and placed Obhasa in the crook of her arm. Then he strapped the Silver Sword to his back and left the shelter with the silent grace of a Tugar.

Torg stepped through the sheet of water. Temporarily he was soaked, but he dried his hair and clothes with blue-green flames. To his right was an odd-shaped boulder, with a curved finger of rock protruding from its side. Perched upon it was the largest mountain eagle Torg had ever seen. Other than its extraordinary size, its appearance was not unusual: dark-brown plumage with a golden wash over its head and neck. But then he noticed that its glowing eyes were the color of pine needles, and they gazed at Torg with a fierce intelligence. Torg recognized those eyes. They belonged to the white-haired woman named Jord who had watched—for centuries—over Ugga and Bard in the foothills of the northern mountains.

"Jord?" he whispered. Then he approached within a single pace. The eagle lowered its hooked beak until it touched the tip of his nose.

"Why have you come? Have you something to say? Or show?"

The eagle hopped onto the ground, turned away from Torg, and offered him its broad back.

"Will the others be safe while I'm gone? Will *she* be safe?"

As if in response, another eagle landed nearby. It was smaller than the first, with black eyes instead of green, but even so it was a formidable beast fully capable of protecting his friends. Torg nodded and then climbed onto the back of the larger bird, which sprang into the air and gracefully climbed several thousand cubits before banking southwest.

Torg caught a glimpse of Duccarita before the eagle carried him over the western maw of the Gap of Gamana. Wolves and other creatures patrolled the open plains. As he already had surmised, it would be nearly impossible for him and his companions to cross this portion of the gap on foot without encountering the enemy.

The eagle surged farther southwest, quickly approaching the eastern border of Dhutanga. From this height, the largest forest in the known world looked like an immense green blanket, its towering canopy unbroken as far as he could see—except for the Cariya River, which ran through its middle like a blue spine.

The eagle flew faster than the prevailing winds, covering vast distances. They passed over the heart of the forest and then spiraled downward until they skimmed the tallest trees, which towered four hundred cubits above the floor of the forest. The great bird of prey found a perch on the canopy.

Torg climbed off its back and knelt on a branch. Far below was a mile-wide clearing, within which clustered an army of druids as thick as swarming termites. Tens of thousands hummed in unison, torturing Torg's ears. In the center of the clearing stood a single tree, taller than any he had ever seen. Druids poured in and out of an opening in its hollow base. It was obvious that this was the home of the druid queen, a bulbous egg-layer that ruled her vicious army with her psychic will. But it appeared she would not make the same mistake as her predecessor, whom Torg had slaughtered almost a millennium before. This queen was well protected.

Now Torg knew what many had long suspected. The druids had replenished their numbers—and then some. Jivita was in as much danger from Dhutanga as Nissaya from Avici.

The eagle let out a shrill twitter.

Torg climbed onto its back, and they headed southward, following the winding, frothy course of Cariya. They eventually left the forest behind and flew high over Jivita, where Torg could see a long line of civilians abandoning the White City on its way to the cliffs that lined the Akasa Ocean. The city's guardians had prepared hidden havens on the rocky coast. Obviously the Jivitans believed war was at hand.

Then the eagle veered to the east and flew along the ancient road called Iddhi-Pada. When they reached Lake Hadaya, Torg could see a Tugar encampment on its shores. The sight filled him with hope.

From there, they sailed over Nissaya. The black knights, some two thousand Tugars, and the rest of the occupants of the immense fortress were hard at work in the fields outside the concentric bulwarks, harvesting lettuce, cabbage, carrots, and turnips in an obvious attempt to further stock their provisions. Instead of leading away from Nissaya, a procession of people, wagons, and pack animals moved ponderously toward the fortress, some already funneling into the first entryway. In addition to its army and citizenry, Nissaya could house, on a temporary basis, more than one hundred thousand within its walls.

The eagle turned northward, soaring over the eastern border of Java and eventually over Avici itself. To avoid Invictus spotting them, the eagle flew higher than a dracool, but even from this great height Torg could recognize the immense stone city and also the tower of Uccheda, which gleamed like a golden spear. With sadness, he saw that the army of Invictus—more than two hundred thousand strong and five leagues from head to tail—had already begun its plodding march down Iddhi-Pada. Torg guessed it would take nearly three weeks for the entire host to journey from Avici to Nissaya.

The eagle soared westward, passing over Lake Ti-ratana and then the snow-covered peaks of Mahaggata before landing on a frozen summit as desolate as Asubha. Crimson smoke drifted from the maw of a cave. Torg knew, without being told, that Bhayatupa lurked within.

They continued on, and for a brief moment a raven accompanied them, squawking and fluttering, but it was unable to match their speed. It dove away and vanished.

Soon they returned to the waterfall, but before landing, the eagle made one last sweep over Duccarita, which lay just a few leagues to the west. Three sides of natural granite bulwarks a thousand cubits tall encased the City of Thieves. The eagle landed on top of one of the walls.

Torg climbed off the eagle's back and knelt to watch the activity far below. A new batch of slaves had arrived from the west, carried over the ocean by sea-masters who served the pirates. Odd-looking, pink-skinned creatures were being forced to hobble down into roofless pens that offered little protection from the elements.

A familiar voice startled Torg.

"There is help for you there."

He turned slowly, and what he saw did not surprise him. The eagle had transformed into Jord, whose long white hair swirled in the winds that swept along the battlement of the granite bulwark. She looked beautiful in a white gown conceived of magic.

"Who are you, really?" he said. "*What* are you, really?"

"Have you not already surmised, Torgon?" she replied, her expression momentarily mischievous. But then she grew serious. "I have traveled far and wide. Not long ago, I even visited the snow giants, of whom you are familiar. But as to who or what I am, I am best described—in your comprehension—as a watcher, though some call me Faerie."

"Why do you watch? And for whom?"

"I am not permitted to elaborate. It must suffice to say that the ascendance of Invictus has raised concerns among my kind."

"If Invictus worries you so much, why don't you and your kind destroy him?"

"I cannot. We cannot . . . that's why we're concerned."

"If he's too great for you, he's too great for me."

"Do not underestimate yourself, Torgon," Jord said, and then to his surprise, she leaned over and kissed him on the cheek. "I . . . we . . . surpass you in some ways. But our ability to destroy might not be as great."

"Do I take that as a compliment?"

"You are admired . . . in high circles. You can take *that* as a compliment."

Torg smiled and then looked down at Duccarita, pointing a finger toward the pink-skinned slaves. "*They* can help? Tell me how."

"The slaves are not as weak as they appear. But there is an evil within the city that holds great sway over them, rendering them impotent. Eliminate that evil, and you will have a powerful army at your disposal—with a general already in place."

"A general?" Torg said, but when he turned back to Jord, the eagle had reappeared and again beckoned him to climb onto its back.

At dusk, they landed at the waterfall just in time to witness a commotion. In addition to the eagle that had remained to guard Torg's companions, six others were perched in various places near the overhang. Ugga and Bard—their hair, beards, and clothes dripping wet—stood outside the rock shelter and eyed the birds distrustfully. The crossbreed bore his axe and Bard his bow, an arrow nocked in place. Laylah and the rest were a few paces behind.

Torg dismounted and strode toward them. "Desist! These creatures are our friends."

Rathburt was the first to respond. "Nice of you to drop in, Master

Showoff. I'm glad to see you've finally chosen to return from your latest round of gallivanting. Did you have fun while you were gone?"

THE RAVEN huddled in the rotting trunk of a dead tree, watching the proceedings with interest. Just a short time ago, she had caught a glimpse of Torg and the Faerie as they flew. Then she'd briefly winked out of the physical world before appearing near the waterfall to await the wizard's return. From her hidey-hole, Vedana had watched six of the mountain eagles—longtime allies of the Faerie—land on the tumbled boulders and join the one who guarded Laylah and the others.

While the goody-goody wizard talked to his companions, the Faerie had stood off to the side, choosing to remain in the form of a mountain eagle, but not bothering to conceal the unusual color of her eyes. As a fellow shape-shifter, Vedana slyly noticed this faux pas. When Vedana assumed an identity—whether human, animal, or plant—she tried to get it just right, out of pride if nothing else, though she admitted to herself that she hadn't fully mastered the raven incarnation. Her beak still moved woodenly when she spoke.

The presence of the Faerie made Vedana uneasy. No matter what it called itself—Bhojja, Jord, Sakuna, or a host of other names—it always seemed to cause some sort of trouble. Vedana's carefully laid plans to dethrone Invictus and crown a new Sun God were anything but certain to succeed. If she made the slightest mistake, her schemes would collapse. To make matters worse, the Faerie kept poking her nose, muzzle, or beak where it didn't belong.

Though the Faerie had roamed the wilds of Triken even before Bhayatupa was born, Vedana didn't believe that Jord's powers were any greater than hers. But her persistence was wearisome, to say the least. Whenever Vedana ventured into the physical world, the Faerie seemed to be there . . . watching intently. Over the eons, Vedana had found this extremely annoying, especially when she had so recently learned that it was the Faerie who had removed her demon poisons from Torg's body.

When Vedana attempted to pinpoint the source of the Faerie's magic, the only thing she could discern was a strange kind of buzzing—as if its powers originated from an invisible place beyond even Vedana's awareness. Still, the Faerie seemed able to tap only small amounts of this mysterious energy, which suited Vedana just fine. One Invictus was enough, thank you very much.

For Vedana's plan to succeed, several things needed to occur. The most important was making sure that Torg and Laylah remained alive and free. Another was arranging matters in such a way that the armies of Avici, Jivita, Nissaya, and Anna were decimated.

Sigh. It was so difficult to keep everything in order.

Vedana watched the Faerie shift shapes and become the white-haired woman, robes of woven magic covering her body. The bear-man rushed over and hugged her, tears bursting from his beady eyes.

Several times over the past few days, Vedana had attempted to enter the minds of Torg's companions. As expected, Laylah was far too strong. Unexpectedly, so were the others. But Vedana wasn't overly concerned. Possession demanded too much energy to make it worthwhile, anyway. Even the obese Kamupadanan innkeeper had put up a respectable fight.

A commotion below caught her attention. Vedana cocked her head and listened.

"Jord, ya have come back," the bear-man was shouting. "Me love, where have ya been? I has missed ya so much." And then he dropped to his knees and wailed like a baby.

"I missed ya too," the handsome one named Bard said. "I loves ya, I does."

"I'm sorry I left ya for so long," Jord said, mimicking the dialect of northern folk, which some of the the pirates and slave traders of Duccarita also spoke. Then, much to Vedana's relief, Jord reverted to the common tongue. "But I had important things to do."

"Are ya going to stay with us now?" the crossbreed said.

"I will stay for a while," Jord said. "There's something that needs to be done, and you will need my help."

*What are you cooking up now, you meddlesome bitch? You are such a pain in the . . .*

Suddenly, Vedana noticed a subtle but invasive surge of magic floating down from above, like a shimmering blanket. Invictus was at it again, using the art of scrying in an attempt to locate Laylah. Vedana quickly spread a shroud of mist over all of them, clouding the sorcerer's vision. Though her grandson was supremely powerful in most ways, some of his psychic abilities remained relatively crude, making it possible for her to deflect his scattered searches. She had veiled Mala's battle with Bhayatupa, as well. But the sorcerer was improving, which made it more and more difficult to delude him.

Must she do everything for everyone? If not for her, Invictus would have found Torg and Laylah already. And if that happened too soon, Vedana would be doomed.

Then she had another frightening thought. What if Jord and the pesky eagles offered to fly Torg and Laylah to some far-off hiding place? That would foul up Vedana's schemes. Maybe even ruin them for good. What should she do?

Hmmmmm. Bhayatupa might prove useful. The great dragon enjoyed eating mountain eagles almost as much as dracools.

# 3

BY THE TIME they were prepared for flight, the rising moon waned gibbous in the evening sky. Just before dusk they had eaten a cold meal, finishing off what remained of their meager provisions while listening to the white-haired woman discuss her plan to enter the City of Thieves. At first, the others had been stunned. But Jord insisted that the fate of Triken hung in the balance.

Laylah paid close attention to everything the woman said. Though she felt stronger than she had in weeks, she continued to depend on Obhasa to feed her a consistent supply of energy. With Torg wielding the Silver Sword, it made sense for her to retain possession of the wizard's ivory staff.

During what remained of the afternoon, they sat in the rock shelter and listened to Torg describe what he had witnessed earlier that day during his flight with Jord. While Jivita and Nissaya prepared for siege, the vast army of Avici had begun its march. By mid-spring, the world would be at war. No ordinary army could breach the walls of Nissaya, but the army Mala led was anything but ordinary. And with the druids gathering to assail Jivita, the White City would be in no position to aid the black fortress.

Amid the gloom were tidbits of hope.

Jord leaned forward and told them a story that even Laylah found fascinating. The white-haired woman—whomever or whatever she was—claimed to have been many places, including the other side of the Akasa Ocean, where she said there was a forest that dwarfed even Dhutanga in scope. Within this behemoth of trees lived a peace-loving community of intelligent creatures called the Daasa, which communicated with barks, squeals, and whistles instead of words. The trees in this strange land were a different species than any east of the ocean, bearing fleshy nuts and fruits that were the Daasa's main source of food. Like the druids of Dhutanga, the Daasa were shepherds of the woods. They also resembled the druids in the way they interrelated, moving about in massive, single-minded droves. But unlike the murderous druids, they were kind and gentle.

"I don't mean to sound crude," Rathburt said, "but if they are so kind and gentle, how can they help us?"

"That's only part of their story," Jord responded. "When they get angry or scared, they can wield great power."

"What kind of power?" Laylah said with a touch of irritation, not appreciating how near the woman sat to Torg.

If Jord sensed Laylah's jealousy, she didn't show it. "When they get angry . . . they change."

"Huh?" Rathburt said.

"They become the opposite of what they are," Lucius said, surprising Laylah and the others.

"How do you know this, firstborn?" Torg said.

"I've seen it myself, in the torture chambers of Invictus. Whenever he scheduled one of his infamous bloodbaths in the stone arena beneath Uccheda, the king loved to include the Daasa among the victims. When tortured, they made heartrending sounds, which tantalized Invictus and the monsters.

"Most often, the Daasa put up little fight. But one time, I witnessed a much different occurrence. One of the pitiful creatures began to change in a way that reminded me of a Warlish witch. But instead of transforming from beautiful to ugly, the Daasa changed from harmless to monstrous. Thorny spikes rose from its soft flesh; fangs erupted from its mouth; claws sprang from its toes. The beast growled like a rabid wolf and then leapt upon a vampire, ripping it to shreds. Several more monsters were slain, including a cave troll, before Mala managed to kick it to death.

"I have never seen Invictus laugh so hard. But no one else was amused. Including me."

Lucius' story amazed Laylah. She remembered him saying once that he'd seen things beneath Uccheda that were every bit as terrible as what she'd suffered above. Now she understood a little better what he'd meant.

Rathburt spoke next. "If these Daasa are so dangerous, why would they help us? It sounds as if their transformations turn them into mindless beasts."

"Like the druids, the Daasa are of a single mind and can be commanded by a single will," Jord said. "An evil resides within the City of Thieves that renders them impotent. The Daasa consider this being an abomination, but its psychic power is too great to resist, reaching across the ocean itself. If this evil is eliminated, the Daasa's long-suppressed rage will rise to the surface, eager for vengeance."

"These Dah-sah are very scary," Ugga said. "I is not sure I likes them one bitsy."

"In these dire times, we must seek allies wherever they might be," Torg said. "If Jord says this venture is crucial, I believe her. Tonight we must fly to Duccarita on the wings of eagles and slip over its stone walls like shadows. Even within the city, we are not without friends. Jord knows of a haven.

Once there, I will seek to destroy the evil of Duccarita."

Laylah squeezed Torg's thigh. "You won't be alone," she said, looking at Jord to make sure she knew to whom the wizard belonged. "I'll be with you."

"So will Elu," the Svakaran said.

Ugga and Bard agreed. Even Lucius nodded.

Rathburt only rolled his eyes.


LUCIUS FOUND flying on the back of a mountain eagle far more peaceful than clinging to a dracool. The birds of prey, though not quite as large as *baby dragons*, carried their riders with more grace. All in all, it was a pleasant experience. He wondered if the eagles enjoyed it as much as he. Or did flying become as mundane as walking to such creatures?

With the bright moonlight providing visibility, Lucius could see six other eagles soaring around him. The one that bore Ugga had fallen slightly behind, the crossbreed's girth and the weight of his axe overburdening it. Surprisingly, Jord had remained in her human form and chosen to ride, her streaming white hair even longer than Laylah's blond locks.

Eventually they approached Duccarita.

Like the walls of Nissaya, the stone bulwarks that guarded the City of Thieves had been created almost entirely by natural forces, constructed underground and then vomited skyward. The eagles skimmed the top of the eastern wall, then dove steeply down its side. Lucius could see the immense city looming below, broad and glittering. From his previous visits as an emissary of Invictus, he remembered Duccarita as a conglomeration of warped and weathered buildings. In the congested heart of the city, most of the streets were barely wide enough for a wagon, and the alleyways were even narrower. Stories of horrors in the darkness made even a hardened soldier shudder.

With Jord's mount leading the way, they flew over a grotesque mishmash of shingled rooftops. The eagles skimmed above them with surprising delicacy, making less sound than a breath of breeze. From the ground, they would have been invisible to all but the wariest eyes, though it mattered little. At this time of night, hard drinking, whoring, and gambling would eliminate most attempts at wariness. Besides, what few guards Duccarita kept on hand were stationed at the southern entrance of the city, where the natural stone bulwark opened into the Gap of Gamana like a dam burst asunder. Once within the city, there were no guards—only pirates, thieves, and a variety of other rascally types, who would slit your throat for a mug of ale or a pair of worn boots.

They landed on a rooftop that looked no different to Lucius than any of the others. How Jord and the eagles were able to distinguish this particular place was beyond his comprehension. The white-haired woman opened a pair of shutters set into a dormer and climbed inside. Lucius was the last to follow. Before entering, he turned and watched the eagles launch into the sky. For better or worse, he and Laylah were trapped within the most wicked city in the world.

Once inside, Lucius squinted to make out his surroundings. He and his companions stood in a dark room barely large enough to contain them. He hunched over to avoid banging his head on the angled ceiling. A large man stood at the head of a stairway, whispering to Jord in a conspiratorial tone. Then he started downward. Jord followed, motioning for the others to do the same.

Torg went next, and then Laylah. The pair were holding hands. Lucius felt a surge of jealousy, his hundredth of the day, but he noticed that each occurrence was becoming a little less intense. Somehow he was growing accustomed to the fact that the wizard and his queen were inseparable. At the same time that it broke his heart, it also warmed it. Seeing Laylah so happy wasn't such a bad thing, even if he weren't the reason for it. And he had to admit that, despite his best efforts to the contrary, he was starting to admire the Death-Knower.

The stairway was claustrophobically narrow, with wooden steps that creaked and complained. The stairs spilled onto the second floor of a small inn. The group filed into a bedchamber as cramped as the room they'd first entered. The large man bowed to Jord and then slipped away to attend to other business. A foul-smelling oil lamp provided the only light. They huddled together between a pair of lumpy beds and waited for Jord to speak.

"This floor of the inn belongs to us," she said in a low voice. "There are three other bedrooms, so we can spread out some. The innkeeper will bring us a meal shortly."

"Who *is* the innkeeper?" Laylah said. "Why should we trust him?"

Torg answered, instead of Jord. "His name is Ditthi-Rakkhati, and he owns this inn. But in truth, he is a Jivitan spy. In the past, the White City has paid scant attention to Duccarita, because the pirates and slave traders rarely ventured south of the gap. But in these dire times, Jivita has found it necessary to broaden its horizons. Despite his appearance, Rakkhati can be trusted."

"How do you know this?" Laylah said in a wounded tone.

Lucius realized he wasn't the only one struggling with jealousy. But the wizard's response surprised him. "The eagle told me, as we flew over the walls."

"Not Jord? You mean, a real eagle told you this?" Rathburt said, rolling his eyes. "So now you can speak with birds?"

"You talk to plants," Torg said. "Why can't I talk to animals?"

"Hmmph!"

"My eagle spoke to me too," Ugga bellowed proudly. "He said, 'Ya are one heavy booger!'"

They all laughed, Jord the loudest.

But a moment later, the white-haired woman's countenance changed dramatically and her face contorted. "Why didn't you warn me?" she cried, as if to an invisible presence. Then: "Noooo! *NO!*" She raced up the stairway.

Torg and the others followed. When Lucius finally clambered onto the roof, he heard screams coming from the street.

"The dragon comes," a stranger was shouting from below. "Lord Bhayatupa is upon us!"

A crackling explosion caused the night sky to erupt. Lucius cowered, but another blast jerked his attention upward.

"Kwahu!" he heard Jord scream as she transformed into a mountain eagle and sprang into the air, leaving shreds of her magical robe sparkling in her wake.

"*Stop!*" Torg cried.

The wizard leapt after her, but he was too late. In her new incarnation, Jord hurtled toward the dragon, whose hovering silhouette was clearly visible on the moonlit horizon. A pair of black specks circled the dragon's head, and he realized with a gasp that these were the mountain eagles, doing battle with the monstrous serpent, which was thirty times their size, at least. Even more frightening, several balls of fire—the burning carcasses of eagles already fallen—clung to the crest of the eastern wall, as if someone had lighted bonfires on ledges a thousand cubits off the ground.

"You are not his match. Not like this!" Torg yelled, but the hooting and cursing that came from the streets below drowned out his voice.

The black speck nearest Bhayatupa's snout burst into flame. The other appeared to flee, but it too succumbed to crimson fire. Then another silhouette rose in challenge, expanding in size until it rivaled the dragon, though more bird-like in appearance. Green torrents surged from its open beak, engulfing Bhayatupa in a barrage of energy. But the dragon spewed a ball of crimson vomit at his attacker, and the eagle incarnation caught fire and fell from the sky, dropping somewhere beyond the wall. Soon after, a blast as hot and angry as a desert windstorm collapsed upon the city.

Horrified, Lucius turned to Torg for some kind of comfort, but the wizard stood still as stone, staring at the smoky night sky. Things had happened so fast the others were still peering at the carnage from inside the window. Just then, Bhayatupa plunged upon them, soaring over the rooftops like a mountain with wings, the wind of their wake knocking Lucius off his feet. When Bhayatupa passed by again, Lucius looked up and saw one of the dragon's massive round eyes, glowing with ancient might.

"*Abhisambodhi!* (Highest enlightenment!)" Bhayatupa howled, so loud that all who dwelled in Duccarita must have been able to hear—and then the greatest of all dragons, past or present, sped away beyond the walls.

"*Andhabaala* (Fool of fools)," Torg shouted back. "*Abhisambodhi* is beyond you."

Lucius had little idea what either of them had meant.

# Demon and Dragon

# 4

A FEW HOURS before Bhayatupa would fly to Duccarita to do battle with Jord, a pair of beings as wicked as the great dragon huddled together on the second floor of the ziggurat. Vedana's grandmotherly incarnation leaned over the glass basin that contained a magical silver liquid. The mother of all demons was Triken's unquestioned master of scrying, and when she waved her translucent hands, the contents of the basin came colorfully to life.

Jākita-Abhinno, queen of the Warlish witches, stood beside her demon creator, in awe of her but also afraid of her.

"Does Torg have the strength to destroy something as great as the *Mahanta pEpa*?" asked Jākita, at that moment choosing to be in her beautiful state. "I haaaate to admit it, but I would be impressssed. That creature is as deadly as a druid queen."

"*They* can destroy the Great Evil," Vedana corrected. "Without Laylah's . . . uh . . . *assistance*, it might not get done."

Both of them cackled.

"Things are going well," Vedana said, "but I must keep *The Torgon* and his cutesy little girlfriend out of trouble for a while longer yet."

"Do you think Invictus will go after them himsssself?"

"I doubt my grandson will leave Uccheda until the wars are almost over, except maybe just to sneak a few peeks at the goings-on. If he were to engage in the actual fighting, he would win too easily. He'll much prefer to sit back and watch the rest of us tear each other apart. Only if his army is on the verge of defeat would he deign to save the day. Invictus has a flair for the dramatic. It helps to relieve his boredom. But I am smarter—and more dangerous—than he gives me credit."

"Issss he not invincible?" Jākita believed he was.

"That depends . . ." Vedana said.

Jākita always felt uneasy when Vedana said something like that. She quickly looked back at the basin, hoping to distract the demon from further musings. "Shouldn't we do *sssomething* to thwart the wizard's movements?" Jākita said, trying to sound helpful. "I could send witches to harassss him."

"You'll do no such thing!" Vedana snarled with enough force to knock Jākita onto her haunches. "You always want to stick your noses into things, and yet you have no idea what's really at stake. Perhaps I should dispose of you and promote someone a little more compliant."

Jākita buried her face between her own spread legs and began to moan. As she transformed, rancid smoke oozed from her hair. Crackling explosions followed. Vedana, of course, would be unaffected. Beauty is in the eye of the beholder.

"I meant no offense, Mistress," the now-ugly Jākita said. "Please do not punissssh me. I am your most loyal sssservant."

"Stop whining. I'll allow you to exist another day. Besides, I have business with the dragon that is more important than any I might have with you."

Jākita continued to sob and cough, filling the chamber with her foul-smelling breath. But Vedana paid her no heed. A dark hole opened in the ceiling above Vedana's head, and she leapt inside, vanishing in an instant.

# 5

LATER THAT DAY, the great dragon Bhayatupa mused and smoldered in his lair. Though more than a week had passed since his battle with Mala, Bhayatupa's wounds still caused him pain. The molten liquid that gushed from Mala's chain had scorched Bhayatupa's snout and the inside of his mouth. Already bearing previous injuries suffered during his escape from Avici, the dragon now had a swollen tongue, charred fangs, and a broken bone in his right front foot—all the fault of the most despicable *low one* ever to exist.

To make matters even worse, Bhayatupa suddenly realized that an unwelcomed guest had unexpectedly arrived. Vedana, the mother of all demons—of which she bragged endlessly—slipped into his lair and appeared before him as a raven. As an added touch, the demon perched on the erect penis of one of his marble statues, this one a gift from King Lobha just before Bhayatupa had gone into hibernation ten millennia ago.

"Why does it not surprise me that you would choose this place to rest?" Bhayatupa said. "Vedana, you have become too predictable in your old age."

"I thought my little joke might cheer you up. You look terrible."

When Bhayatupa sighed, smoke poured from his nostrils. "I suppose you watched my encounter with Mala from the ziggurat. Did you and your horrid little witches take pleasure when the wretched creature managed to escape?"

"I did watch, a little, but I spent more energy veiling the whole affair from Invictus. Mala's survival makes things more difficult for me, too, you know. Without the Chain Man to lead my grandson's armies, it would have been easier for me to manipulate the necessary outcomes. With him still alive, I will have to be even more careful."

"Then why don't you just destroy Mala yourself?" Bhayatupa snarled.

"You know the answer to that as well as I. It's the same reason I've put up with your threats and insults for hundreds of centuries. I am only able to secrete a portion of my power into the Realm of Life, which is not enough to destroy Mala, especially considering how Invictus coddles him. The energy that surges within that damnable chain is the same energy that flows in my grandson's flesh. So don't feel like such a failure, dragon. Mala was closer to being your match than you realized."

Bhayatupa groaned. "I have learned that firsthand. So tell me, what now? I seem to have become another of your pawns. What is my *next* assignment, master?"

"Oh, don't be so droll. You're no more my pawn than I am yours. You've already agreed that we both will benefit from this arrangement. So stop whining, and listen instead."

"What else is there for me to do but listen?"

"I wish you would say *that* more often. But enough about Mala. There is another obstacle in the path of our success that is more immediate. The horrid Faerie is sticking her nose into things again. And if she isn't removed, she could cause even more problems than the Chain Man."

"I've never liked her, particularly," Bhayatupa said. "But she's always seemed rather harmless. Why has her 'removal' suddenly become so important to *our* cause?"

"Can't you trust me just once and not ask so many questions?"

"I will never trust you, Vedana. But in this instance, I appear to have little choice. All right then—tell me what you would have me do."

Later that day, he crept from his lair and sprang into the sky. He soared high over the Gap of Gamana, impressed by the number of Mogols, wolves, and other *Adho Sattas* he saw swarming along the open plain. He was tempted to fly low and wreak some havoc, just for amusement, but his business was too pressing. Vedana had given him two assignments: destroying Jord and her accompanying mountain eagles was one, but there was another of almost equal importance. According to the demon, the remaining eagles still alive in the world had gathered on Catu, the northernmost mountain in all of Triken. It was there that Bhayatupa headed first, skimming above the towering peaks that marched toward the end of the world.

When he approached, the eagles rose to meet his challenge, more than thirty in all. They fought as ferociously as dracools, but their anger over his abominable intrusion clouded their judgment. Rather than attack as an organized group, they flew at him as enraged individuals—and fell, one by one. As far as Bhayatupa could tell, none survived the battle. After devouring several of the fallen birds, he turned and headed back toward the City of Thieves, feeling more like his old self—*Mahaasupanno*, mightiest of all. In an irony of sorts, he felt grateful to Vedana for restoring his proper standing.

The birds of prey he found perched on the towering rock walls of Duccarita fared no better than those at Catu. But when the Faerie assumed the form of a dragon-sized eagle and rose to confront him, her ferocity amazed Bhayatupa. The green torrent that blazed from her beak scorched more than his scales; it slithered inside the smallest fragments of his being. He reacted with panic, blasting the Faerie with all his magical might. Thankfully, it had been enough. Her ruined carcass plunged to the ground beyond the wall in a flaming heap.

When Bhayatupa flew down along the rooftops of the city, his massive eyes glowed like cinders. He first sensed and then saw the Death-Knower. The magnitude of the wizard's essence impressed Bhayatupa. For something so small, *The Torgon* was formidable. He would have to be careful in his future dealings with Torg.

"*Abhisambodhi!* (High enlightenment!)" Bhayatupa howled. And as he sped away, he whispered: "Teach me the truth, Death-Knower. Release me from this madness."

Afterward, Bhayatupa lay in his lair and mused over his latest encounter with a supernatural foe. His failed attempt to destroy Mala had bruised his ego, but his successful defeat of the Faerie had bruised his soul. Her green radiance burned like no other. Even Invictus' golden energy had done less damage.

But not in a surface way. Rather, the Faerie's assault had hurt him underneath.

"*Bhayatupa amarattam tanhiiyati* (Bhayatupa craves eternal existence)," he said out loud within his hidden lair, unaware he had given voice to his thoughts. A pair of Mogol slaves fell to their knees and covered their faces. But Bhayatupa was too deep in concentration to pay them heed.

For several days after his battle with the Faerie, he lay as still as one of the bejeweled statues scattered among his vast treasure, accumulated over eighty millennia of existence. Bhayatupa's mind wandered back to his youth, when Triken had been a much different place. Once there were thousands of dragons roaming the skies. Though they often fought among themselves, the dragons were the undisputed rulers of the land. None could stand against them—and rather than try, the kings and queens of the mortal world became their willing servants, like pawns in a game of chess played from above.

There was a time, early on, when Bhayatupa was not supreme among his kind. Ulaara the Black was the greatest of the great, and his brother and sister named Sankhayo and Sankhaya—both of whom were almost as powerful as their leader—ceaselessly accompanied him. When Bhayatupa was twenty thousand years old, the first of the Dragon Wars began in earnest, and they continued for an additional thirty millennia, until fewer than one hundred great dragons remained active in the world.

Among the casualties was Sankhayo, who drowned in Lake Hadaya after suffering a terrible wound and tumbling from the sky. Bhayatupa found Sankhaya lying by the shore of the lake, mourning her brother's death, and he slipped down from above and pounced on her back, snapping her neck with his massive jaws. Now that Ulaara was unprotected, Bhayatupa issued an official challenge to a duel for supremacy, with the winner being accorded the coveted title of *Mahaasupanno*, mightiest of all.

But in one of history's great anti-climaxes, Ulaara refused to fight.

Instead, he fled to Nirodha and was never seen again, revealing himself as craven. At first Bhayatupa was enraged at being robbed of his opportunity to reign supreme, but as it turned out, Ulaara's cowardice worked to Bhayatupa's advantage. The remaining dragons were awed that the mere rumor of Bhayatupa would cause Ulaara to flee, and most bowed to Bhayatupa. He destroyed those who didn't. The few who remained realized that Bhayatupa would abide no others, and they began to disappear from the world. As Bhayatupa lay in his lair after his battle with the Faerie, only nine great dragons remained active in the world—though he could sense three times that many still survived, hidden here and there throughout Mahaggata, Kolankold, and even Okkanti. Perhaps one day, when Invictus was destroyed and the Death-Knower had taught him how to achieve eternal life, Bhayatupa would re-awaken the remainder of his kind and form a new ruling class, less mighty than before, but still far too powerful for the *Adho Satta* (Low Ones) to resist.

*How grand it all had been. So many wars. So many kingdoms. So much glory.*

But much to Bhayatupa's chagrin, nothing seemed to last forever. Over the last twenty millennia, he had begun to experience the first hints of mortality. His magic remained as strong as ever, but there was a subtle change in his metabolism, a strange sort of hollowness, that terrified him. The specter of death, ever secretive and mysterious, had begun to pay him shadowy visits. When it did, Bhayatupa shivered like a coward. He had lived for eighty thousand years, but he had somehow expected to live far longer than that.

*I am Bhayatupa the Great. How does Death dare threaten me?*

After destroying the Faerie and paying the Death-Knower a quick visit, Bhayatupa had been pleased with his accomplishments. The annoying demon had promised him full access to the wizard after Invictus was destroyed. And once *The Torgon* helped Bhayatupa achieve immortality, no one would be able to stand against him, including the meddlesome she-devil. He put up with her for now because he needed her help, but he would deal with her later—and that would be oh-so-amusing.

Bhayatupa's brief good mood began to sour. The hollowness and weariness returned with a vengeance. The Faerie's green energy was a substance he had never before encountered, and it made him feel strange and lonely, as if the bitter truth of all things had been revealed.

*There is no such thing as immortality*, voices whispered in his mind. *There is only impermanence.*

To Bhayatupa, the concept of impermanence was unacceptable.

*Eighty thousand years isn't long enough. Not nearly long enough. I crave . . . eternity.*

"Death-Knower," he said, his voice causing the very stone to tremble. "You *must* help me."

The frightened Mogols bowed again, though their terror paled in comparison to the fear that humbled Bhayatupa the Great.

# The Great Evil

# 6

NOT SINCE Sōbhana died in his arms had Torg felt such despair. The destruction of the mountain eagles left a wound that could not be healed. The others of their kind, of which there were only a few, would hear of this and most likely flee to the frozen heights. Even so, the loss of Jord hurt worse.

Given Invictus' ruined relationship with the dragon, Torg doubted that the sorcerer had ordered this abomination. But the killings served Invictus' purposes, nonetheless. Without the assistance of the white-haired woman, the forces of good were considerably weakened.

At first, Torg didn't feel the tugging on his arm. Finally he turned and saw Laylah standing beside him. Not until she wiped tears from his cheeks did he realize he had been crying.

*I wander from one lament to the next, weak as a baby. Rathburt's right. I'm nothing but a showoff.*

And then Laylah was saying, "Beloved, the innkeeper wants us to come back inside." She pointed toward the dormer. The Jivitan spy was leaning out the window, gesturing for them to depart the roof.

Torg looked eastward one last time. The gibbous moon lighted the sky, but other than the moon and stars, the firmament was empty. Even the charred remains of the slain eagles no longer glowed. A few wisps of smoke, that might have been clouds, drifted overhead. Otherwise, it was as if nothing unusual had occurred.

When Torg climbed back inside, he discovered Ugga and Bard kneeling on the floor in a tearful embrace. Torg wasn't sure how much of the aerial battle they had witnessed from the window, but it was clear that the crossbreed and his longtime companion knew what had happened to Jord. Elu was stroking Ugga's back, while Rathburt and the spy stood off to the side, looking uncomfortable. Laylah knelt beside Bard and hugged him from behind. Torg walked over and attempted to console his two dear friends.

"Do not despair," he said. "Jord is a spirit who exists beyond the bounds of physical incarnation. There is hope that her time among us has not yet ended."

Ugga looked up, his small eyes brimming with tears. "Jord isn't dead? The dragon didn't kill her?"

"She has fallen," Torg said. "But I believe she is capable of rising again."

This seemed to cheer up Ugga and Bard considerably.

Rakkhati stepped forward. "I also feel grief over what has occurred," the Jivitan spy said to Ugga and Bard in the common tongue. "I knew the white-haired woman well, though she was not known to me as Jord. Her name was Sakuna, and she could take the form of an eagle—or perhaps the other way around. Several days ago, she appeared at my window and told me to prepare for the arrival of the Death-Knower. But that is not the entire story. Sakuna said there would be *two* Death-Knowers."

"She lied to you," Rathburt sneered.

"Ignore him," Torg said to Rakkhati. "The slumped one is indeed a Death-Knower, but he prefers to deny it wherever and whenever he can."

"I see," said the innkeeper, who then bowed in Rathburt's direction. "Forgive me, Lord. I did not intend to offend you."

"I'm no lord," said Rathburt, crossing his arms and facing the other direction.

"If I may be so bold, I would suggest that you return to the second floor," Rakkhati said to Torg. "There is a parlor large enough for all of you to gather together and mend your grief. Please make yourselves comfortable in your rooms while your meal is prepared. Clean water and towels will be brought to you. I also have soap, though it is not of the quality deserved by this exquisite woman."

"Thank you, sir," Laylah said. "But soap of any quality is more than I deserve."

Rakkhati chuckled. "Humble as well as beautiful," the spy said to Torg. "You and she are well-matched, Desert King."

Rathburt turned around, his eyes bloodshot. "Your laughter is ill-timed, sir. Can't you see that my friends are in pain?" Then in a tone of distrust, he added, "How do you know so much about the 'Desert King'?"

"I am a soldier of Jivita," Rakkhati said. "Though I have lived apart from the White City for many years, I have not forgotten my upbringing. Children who are barely able to speak know of The Torgon and pretend to be him when they play. Is it not so everywhere?"

Hearing that was too much for Rathburt to tolerate. He whipped around and pounded down the stairs.

Torg sighed. "As my Vasi master used to say, 'There is more to him than meets the eye.' But he's right. Our grief is far too fresh for mirth. Let us join him below."

"Very good," Rakkhati said. "Once you have bathed in your rooms, I suggest you retire to the parlor, where I will bring you a hot meal and cold ale. In Duccarita, food tends to be an afterthought, but the ale will more than meet your approval."

Hearing the word ale caused Ugga and Bard to lift their heads.

"The Bitch wouldn't want us to be thirsty," the crossbreed said.

"Nor will you," Rakkhati said.

Ugga wiped the tears from his eyes and licked his lips. "Are there any Brounettos 'round here? A couple of them might help me feel better."

Bard chimed in. "Or Blondies?"

Despite the all-too-recent trauma, the others couldn't help but grin.

AS NATURALLY as brothers, Ugga and Bard entered the first of the four bedrooms. Rathburt and Elu, also longtime companions, chose the second. Now, two rooms remained to be divided among Lucius, Torg, and Laylah, who stood together in the narrow hallway, engulfed in awkward silence. To Laylah's surprise, the firstborn was the first to speak.

"You're both adults," he said, his expression bearing wounds of jealousy. Then Lucius opened the door to the third room and disappeared inside.

Torg and Laylah remained outside in the hall.

"I'll go with him, if you prefer," the wizard said.

"No," she said, a little too sharply. Then, softly: "*No.*"

Still holding Obhasa in her left hand, Laylah opened the door with her right. Then she led the wizard into the room and closed the door.

"I wasn't sure if you'd want to upset him," Torg said.

"*Quiet,*" she whispered, and then pressed her mouth against his, feeling his body tense and the muscles of his chest swell. The strength of his arms as they wrapped around her torso amazed her. Her tongue fought its way past his lips and into his mouth. He gasped and almost pulled away, then met her persistence with pressure of his own. Instantly their bodies began to glow, white energy mingling with blue and green. Finally the wizard did push her away . . . but gently.

Laylah stepped back, breathless.

A knock on the door interrupted the intensity of the moment. The wizard reluctantly answered. A woman entered bearing a heavy basin of steaming water. She was dressed similarly to Rakkhati, wearing a long waistcoat over knee breeches and stockings. A scarlet scarf was tied around her neck, matching the color of her hair, which was cut just below her ears.

"Bonny is my name," she said in the common tongue. "I am here to bring you niceties, courtesy of the inn. I hope you are all right after the terrible thing that happened."

She sat the basin down, raced out of the room, and came back with towels and a cake of gray soap. Then she disappeared before returning again with an armful of clothing.

"You need some new outfits," Bonny said, with a wild look in her dark eyes. "These will make you look real pretty."

She took her time leaving, staring at Torg with a mischievous smile. Finally Laylah scowled at her.

"All right, all right, I understand." Bonny rushed out of the room, slamming the door behind her.

Laylah turned to Torg. "Don't get any ideas."

His response caused the large muscles of her thighs to quiver. "For as long as I live, you are the only one for me."

Without taking her eyes from Torg's face, Laylah backed toward the door and slid down the latch. She leaned Obhasa against the wall and then slowly undid the shawl that covered her upper torso, exposing her breasts. The wizard's eyes widened, and the hair on his head began to dance. Blue and green motes appeared in the air, sparkling around his ears and eyes.

"Laylah . . ." he murmured.

She dropped the second shawl from around her waist and stood naked before him. The sparkles intensified, drifting about the room.

She sauntered over to the basin and held up the soap. "Will you bathe me, my love?"

At first Torg continued to stare, unable to move. But then he walked over and picked up Obhasa. Rather than wash her with soap and water, he used his ivory staff to bathe her with fire, as he had done in the cave. But that first time, she had been too ill to appreciate it. Now she arched her back and moaned. The silky energy was warm and sensual, causing her skin to tingle. And it cleansed her better than the purest water and finest soap.

*"Torgon,"* she murmured, her eyes closed. "Torgon . . . Torgon . . ."

He sighed deeply. "If I were able to choose from all the women who have ever been or ever will be, you would still be the one. I have never seen anyone—or anything—so beautiful. Every part of me desires you. Every shred of me loves you."

Laylah slowly opened her eyes. "May I bathe *you?*"

"Do you know how?"

Laylah giggled. "I meant in the traditional fashion."

"Ohhhhh."

Laylah unbelted his tunic and lifted it over his head. Upon seeing his chest, she gasped the way Torg had when he first saw her breasts. The wizard's body was muscled like none she had ever seen. In some ways it was almost inhuman, with as many bulges and ripples as the torso of a dracool. Though more than a thousand years old, his dark skin bore no blemishes or scars, which was even more amazing considering the horrors he had endured while trapped in the pit on Mount Asubha.

Laylah was tall for a woman, but Torg's nipples were even with her eyes. She touched the taut muscles of his chest with her fingertips, then reached for his breeches and began to slide them off his hips.

"Careful . . ." he said.

"I'm being *very* careful."

The breeches dropped to the floor. Torg's exposed member responded, almost embarrassingly. Laylah gasped again.

"*Torgon* . . ." she said.

Then she reached for it with her hand.

The wizard took a step back. "There are things about me you still don't know," he said nervously. "With all this running and hiding, we've never had the chance to talk about *personal* matters. Long ago, I accidentally killed a woman . . . an innocent Tugarian woman. When I have sex, I lose control of my powers and . . ."

As if she already knew the story, Laylah was undeterred. "Like you said, it was accidental," she purred, reaching for him again. "I don't believe *I'll* be harmed."

Torg took another step back. "*You* won't be harmed, perhaps, but half of Duccarita will end up in flames."

Tears welled in her eyes. "I've waited my entire life for this. How much longer must I be denied?"

The wizard smiled, but it was bittersweet. "When the time and place are right, we both will know it. Do not despair, my love. Our moment will come. And as my Vasi master used to say, 'It will be well worth the wait.'"


FOR THE FIRST time since he could remember, Lucius was entirely alone. He scanned the room distrustfully. There was one window with a wooden shutter, closed and tightly latched. Two small beds with straw-stuffed mattresses were pressed against the side walls. In the middle of the room stood a wobbly wooden table with a pair of crooked chairs. Another of the foul-smelling oil lamps provided the only light.

Lucius removed the Mogol war club from the belt at his waist and laid it and the *uttara* on one of the beds. He sat down on the other and buried his face in his hands. Though the sight of Jord being blown from the sky still tormented him, the thought of Torg and Laylah alone in the room next door tortured him even more. How could he stand it? How could he not?

Lucius sat there for what felt like a very long time. He was startled when his door swung open without a knock. He looked up, hoping beyond hope it was Laylah come to tell him that it was all a big mistake, and that he was the one she truly loved. But instead of his queen, a feisty woman with short red hair stomped into the room bearing a basin of steaming water that looked far too heavy to carry so easily.

"Don't look so disappointed. I'm not that ugly."

"Huh?" was all Lucius could manage.

"Ha! A man of few words. I *love* it. You and I might have a future together! Why waste time talking?"

"Huh?"

"Do you have all your wits? Ah, never mind." She sprinted merrily out of the room and returned with towels, soap, and a change of clothing.

"These ought to fit you real good," she said, her dark eyes sparkling. "You are a fine figure of a man. Don't let anyone tell you otherwise."

"Thank you," Lucius muttered.

She exploded with laughter. Then she leaned down, kissed him on the cheek, and sprang from the room, slamming the door behind her.

Lucius sat in stunned silence, trying to digest what had so frenetically occurred.

*You are a fine figure of a man . . .*

Lucius felt a tingling in his groin. The strange woman had somehow changed his mood from sour to sweet. He stood and removed his grimy clothes, then took a long time scrubbing himself with soap and drying himself with a towel. He put on black trousers and boots, a white shirt, and a red waistcoat. Everything fit surprisingly well.

*You are a fine figure of a man . . .*

Now it was almost midnight, but Lucius didn't feel like sleeping. He was starving and "thirsty," as dear ol' Ugga would put it. Lucius opened the door and peeked out. A ways down the hall, he could see a wavering light from a blazing hearth. Some of his companions already had found their way to the parlor, it appeared.

The door to Torg and Laylah's room remained closed. Lucius felt another stab of jealousy, but just then the woman reappeared and grabbed his hand.

"Come on, slow-poke! What are you waiting for?"

With a surprising display of strength, she dragged him down the hall toward the parlor. Ugga, Bard, Rathburt, and Elu were already there, each drinking from pewter mugs. Though all four had eyes that were red and swollen from their recent upset, they still managed to smile when he joined them, and it warmed his heart. Suddenly he realized that he loved them like brothers.

"Come sit by the fire, Master Loo-Shus, and have something to drink," Ugga said. "It will help ya to forget your trub-bulls. It's helping me, at least."

"Me too," Bard said.

To Lucius, that sounded like a good idea. He plopped down in one of the cushioned chairs near the hearth and stretched out his legs. Soon after, the flirty woman handed him a mug of ale, which he gulped enthusiastically. Then he studied the others, who were dressed in garb similar to his own. Ugga and Bard wore full-length velvet coats with gold tabs and brass buttons, though the crossbreed's coat was too small to close around his stomach. Rathburt looked thin and dashing in a waistcoat of green suede. Little Elu had been outfitted in a special suit probably designed for a boy: a blue jacket over a checkered shirt with canvas trousers. Lucius felt as if they were ready for a costume ball.

"I hate to admit it, but you gentlemen are a handsome lot," he said. "I'm proud to be a member of your party."

In unison, their jaws dropped. Though Lucius had been much better behaved in recent days, they must have considered this the nicest thing he had ever said to them.

"See, Bard," Ugga said. "I told ya Master Loo-Shus was a good guy."

"Ya were right all along," Bard agreed.

Lucius chuckled. "You kind of rub off on a person, Ugga. Even in times of sorrow, you manage to cheer everyone up. When you're around, it's hard not to be nice."

Elu leapt up from his chair and hugged one of Lucius' legs. "Elu likes you too. It's wonderful to have such great friends, who'll always take good care of each other."

"Speaking of taking care of each other . . . here comes lovely Bonny with more ale," Rathburt said. He turned to Lucius. "She may dress like a man, but she's every bit a woman underneath, I'd surmise."

"Why, Master Rathburt . . . I didn't know you were such a charmer," Bonny said. "But if you are trying to win my heart, it's too late. I am quite taken by the yellow-haired gentleman. What a looker!"

Rathburt feigned disappointment, but he obviously was amused. Ugga and Bard slapped their knees. Once again, Lucius was speechless; his face turned as red as Bonny's scarf.

"He doesn't talk much, does he?" she said.

"Not unless he's got something to complain about," Rathburt said ironically. They all laughed, including Lucius.

"I'm sorry, my lady," Lucius finally managed. "I've spent so much time as a soldier, I don't know how to act around women—especially one as fine as you."

"Good one, Loo-shus!" Ugga said. "Say something else nicey to her, and ya will be bedding her in no time."

For the first time, Bonny's face reddened, which Lucius assumed didn't happen often. "Oh, my . . ." was all she said, and then she trotted off—but not before glancing back at Lucius and winking.

After she left, the men guzzled more ale and congratulated Lucius on what appeared to be the start of a successful seduction. Even Rathburt got into the act, describing in intimate detail his secrets of how to pleasure a woman in bed. They all laughed, louder and louder. Elu ended up rolling around on the floor, hugging his legs against his chest.

How quickly his friends were able to rebound from tragedy amazed Lucius. The terrible occurrence between Jord and the dragon earlier that evening had failed to dampen their spirits. Perhaps it was the wizard's doing, for sounding so convincing that Jord would return.

In the midst of the mirth, two more approached—and their appearance stunned them all to silence. Laylah and Torg stood before them. The sorceress was dressed in a long-sleeved blouse of white silk with tight-fitting black trousers and knee-high boots. A crimson sash with gold embroidery and fringes was wrapped around her waist. The wizard wore a black coat with button pockets and cuffs and a pleated back. He also sported black trousers with high boots. A sky-blue scarf was wrapped around his head and tied in the back. The Silver Sword hung at his waist in the scabbard he had obtained in Kamupadana.

As a couple, they were so beautiful it amazed even Lucius. No one seemed able to speak. Finally it fell to Bonny, who was returning with another pitcher of ale, to break the silence.

"Lordy . . ."

Torg and Laylah sat down in the two remaining chairs that had been arranged around the hearth. Each picked up a mug of ale and took long sips, but they continued to gaze at each other with twinkling eyes, making Lucius uneasy. When Bonny refilled his mug and again kissed him on the cheek, Lucius felt a whole lot better. Would his life be so bad if he ended up with someone like her instead of Laylah?

The pirate woman left the room and returned with the innkeeper.

Rakkhati bore a wooden tray crowded with bowls of fragrant custard that he told them were made with chicken broth, rice, and goat's milk and garnished with seeds of anise, which were good for digestion. Bonny's tray held several loaves of dark bread along with chunks of salted mutton.

Rakkhati had said that the food in Duccarita would be less palatable than the ale, and he was right—but not by much. After having spent weeks in the wilderness, the simple meal enthralled them. They ate ravenously, and when they finished, not a spoonful of custard, a crumb of bread, or a shred of mutton remained. Afterward they drank more ale, while Rathburt smoked sweet-smelling tobacco from the pipe he had pilfered from the Mogol camp.

When the meal was cleared, Rakkhati and Bonny drew up two more chairs and joined them. Though the others were becoming drowsy, Lucius noticed that Torg was on full alert, as if something very important was about to occur. Not wanting to be outdone, Lucius sat up too. But the others, including Laylah, seemed too sleepy to pay much attention.

"Lord Torgon," Rakkhati said, addressing the wizard with a level of respect that Lucius found impressive, "am I free to speak in front of your companions, or should the three of us—"he nodded toward Bonny "—retire to a more secluded location?"

With these words, the rest began to pay attention. None of them, it seemed, wanted to be excluded from important matters.

"You may speak freely," Torg said.

Rakkhati nodded. "Very well. Allow me to tell you what I know. First, the streets are active. The battle in the skies has stirred the pirates."

Reminded of the tragedy, Ugga and Bard lowered their heads.

Rakkhati took notice of this and then continued. "Usually, even the bravest among us do not venture outside after dark, unless it's to sprint from one tavern to the next. After all, there are thieves, and there are thieves. Some only steal from those who reside outside the city's walls, while others make their living robbing the robbers. Still, that is not the worst of it.

"Many things roam the streets in the darkness, and some are not human. Creatures lurk in the crannies and alleyways, pouncing on their victims with murderous intent. It is not unusual to be awoken from sleep by screams, but most of us just check the latches on the shutters and press our pillows against our ears, hoping the horrors of the night don't find their way into our own bedchambers. Remember, Arupa-Loka is only ten leagues away, and its evils frequent the City of Thieves . . . to feed. There are vampires, demons, trolls, and ghouls among us—and they are always hungry.

"But the worst are the ruined Daasa, who have escaped the slave pits and live on the streets like wild dogs. These rogues remain permanently in their heinous state, and they are not pleasant to encounter. Even the monsters give them a wide berth, for they are more powerful and dangerous than mountain wolves. I am a strong man, well-trained with sword and bow, but even someone like me would be hard-pressed against such beasts."

"Rakkhati is right," Bonny said in a cold tone. "The streets *are* dangerous. I have wandered them myself." She lifted her waistcoat and undershirt, revealing a nasty scar on her abdomen. Then she turned to Lucius, and her playfulness returned. "The rest of me is still fine to look at."

"I don't doubt it," Lucius said, and then reflexively glanced at Laylah, who appeared amused by the tête-à-tête.

Torg gestured toward Rakkhati. "Continue . . ."

"Yes, lord," the innkeeper went on. "I was first sent here by my superiors almost twenty years ago, and since then I have spoken with many and seen much. I am trusted—at least as trusted as anyone can be in a place like this—and my establishment has earned the reputation as a haven of sorts. In other words, if you pass through my doors, the odds are less than usual that your throats will be slit in your sleep."

Bonny chuckled. "You can thank me for that."

Rakkhati nodded. "There is truth in her words. She is much stronger than she looks."

The more the innkeeper spoke, the more annoyed Lucius became. He had obeyed Torg's wishes and entered Duccarita willingly. But now the whole affair seemed like folly.

"All along, you've been saying that we must avoid Duccarita, and all along I've agreed with you," Lucius said, surprising the others with his vehemence. "But then this Jord creature appears out of nowhere and changes your mind. And now we're even worse off than before. With the eagles gone, how are we going to escape? Rakkhati says there are more than just thieves wandering the streets, but there are more than just monsters too.

"Golden soldiers and other servants of the sorcerer frequent Duccarita. And what if Invictus finds out we're here and pays a personal visit? If that were to happen, everything else that wanders the streets will seem like fuzzy little bunny rabbits. *So please enlighten me*: How do we get out of here?"

Rakkhati's eyes widened, Lucius' unexpected outburst obviously stunning him. "Would you have me silence him, lord?" he said to Torg.

Lucius tensed and started to stand, his face feeling flushed and swollen, but Torg reached over, quick as a snake, and placed his hand on Lucius' knee. Instantly, a surge of soothing energy slid up his thigh, and his body went temporarily limp.

"I would not have you silence him," Torg said to Rakkhati, while still looking at Lucius. "He does not yet know me well enough to be aware of who I am."

Torg removed his hand, but Lucius still found it difficult to move.

"Allow Rakkhati to finish, and then I will reveal my intentions."

Lucius nodded.

The innkeeper appeared puzzled. "These are indeed strange times when one such as he can be permitted to speak thusly to a king of kings."

"Strange doesn't begin to describe it," Rathburt added.

Rakkhati raised an eyebrow, then continued. "As I said before, I have become well-connected within the City of Thieves and have learned a great many things that others do not know. The importation of Daasa slaves from across the ocean has increased every year. It used to be that slaves were brought here from all over the north: fishermen from the coast of Akasa, settlers from the borders of Dhutanga, savages from Mahaggata—"at that, Elu scowled, "—and villagers from the banks of the Ogha. But more recently, the slave traders have become obsessed with the pink-skins. There are obvious reasons for this. Avici desires them by the tens of thousands and pays in gold. And the Porisādas also covet them, for their flesh is said to be tender and sweet. But these are not the only reasons. Have any of you ever heard rumors of the *Mahanta pEpa?*"

Lucius spoke again. "I once heard Mala say those words."

At the mention of the Chain Man, Rakkhati leapt to his feet and drew a dagger from his belt. Before he could attack, Torg sprang up and wrenched the weapon from his grasp. The dagger dropped to the floor and stuck point-down in the hard wood. Rakkhati stared at Lucius, his eyes wild and angry.

"Who *is* this man?" the innkeeper said to Torg.

"All you need know is that he is a trusted companion," the wizard said. "If you threaten him again, I will do more than squeeze your wrist." Torg released him and returned to his chair.

Lucius settled back in his seat, but his heart was pounding. Laylah seemed shaken. Rathburt looked like he wished he were somewhere else.

In an attempt to diffuse the tension, Rakkhati faced Lucius and bowed his head.

"I apologize for my behavior. It's just that I do not take the mention of Mala lightly. The Chain Man has visited Duccarita on several occasions, and he was terrible to behold. When you spoke of him in such a blithe manner, it . . . shocked me."

Lucius grunted. "Don't think that my previous association with Mala means I respect him. There are few, if any, on Triken who hate him more than I."

That seemed to satisfy Rakkhati. He drew the dagger from the floor and replaced it in his belt. Then he sat back down. "When you heard Mala speak those words, did he tell you their meaning?" the innkeeper asked.

"No. But it seemed to me that he said them with reverence, which is highly unusual for the Chain Man. About the only thing he respects is Invictus."

"I know the meaning of the words," Torg said. "But I have never associated them with Duccarita until Jord described the wickedness that holds sway over the Daasa. In the ancient tongue, *Mahanta pEpa* means Great Evil."

"In the City of Thieves, those words hold special meaning," the innkeeper said. "As Jord must have already told you, the *Mahanta pEpa* resides somewhere within our walls—and is rumored to have done so for decades. But I do not believe it was born here. Like the Daasa, the Great Evil came from across the ocean, and like Avici and the Mogols, it hungers for the flesh of the pink slaves."

Rathburt finally spoke, though his voice quivered. "Lucius is right. Weren't we already in enough trouble? We're being harried by an army of monsters, but instead of running away, we come to a place where an even more hideous creature holds sway. Do you really think we can destroy it?"

"I am not to be taken lightly," Torg said in a steely tone. "I have *chosen* to come here to destroy the Great Evil that resides within the City of Thieves. Have you forgotten Jord's words already? If the *Mahanta pEpa* is destroyed, the Daasa will be freed."

Then Torg turned to Lucius. "How will we escape Duccarita, you ask? On the heels of an army . . . *your* army."

# 7

TORG RECOGNIZED the amazement in Lucius' face. A lot had been sprung on the firstborn in a short time, but Torg knew no other way. The forces of good needed allies.

Elu was first to break the silence. "Tell us your plan, great one."

Torg looked down and smiled at the Svakaran. The tiny warrior had the spirit of a Tyger.

Rathburt interrupted his reverie. "If it means leaving us here while you go off gallivanting again, then it sounds good to me. We'll stay by the fire and drink the rest of the ale. Come and get us when you're finished."

"I is going with Master Hah-nah!" Ugga said. "There's no way Bard and I will let him go off by himself."

"No way," Bard agreed.

"They're right," Laylah said. "You had better include all of us, even Rathburt."

Torg chuckled wearily. "My friends . . . let me tell you my plan before you so readily decide to be a part of it. From the beginning, it depends on whether Rakkhati and Bonny will agree to it. Without them, we cannot succeed."

"Bonny and I are at your service," Rakkhati said.

"Very well," Torg said. Then he looked the innkeeper squarely in the eyes. "Can you lead me to the *Mahanta pEpa?* I want to destroy the creature—whatever it might be—before dawn."

"I can show you the way," Rakkhati said, though his voice trembled.

Lucius shook his fist in anger. "Why are you so *certain* that killing the *Mahanta pEpa* will free the Daasa? Just because Jord said so? And even if she was right, how can you know what will happen next? I'm not so convinced that the Daasa will instantly be at our beck and call. Rathburt's right when he says this is madness."

"In these dire times, I am certain of little," Torg said. "But I have quickly come to believe in the words and wisdom of Jord. The demise of the Great Evil *will* release the might of the Daasa. Whether or not we can control them is another matter. But I have faith in you, general. You were born to lead the Daasa."

"I'm glad you're so confident in me," Lucius said sarcastically. "But I have no idea how I could even *begin* to get them to follow me. As far as I knew, Invictus was the only person in Avici who could make any sense of their whistles and squeals." Then he turned and spoke to Rakkhati directly, as if to ward off another confrontation. "And believe me, I'm no Invictus."

"If Jord were still with us, our task would be simpler," Torg said. "She would be able to communicate with them in ways we cannot. But when the great fall, the lesser must take their place. Lucius, you will not stand alone. Bard, Ugga, and Elu will be at your side, as will Rathburt. As a group, you'll find a way, even without Jord to guide you."

"There is something else you must know," Rakkhati said to Lucius. "We cannot understand what the Daasa say, but they seem able to understand us. So maybe, yellow-hair, your task isn't quite so impossible."

"That's good to know," the firstborn said, with even more sarcasm. Then he swung back on Torg. "You left Laylah's name out of the mix. Does that mean you intend to take her with you to hunt down the *Mahanta pEpa*? How can you love her and still be willing to put her in such peril?"

Laylah started to protest, but Torg interrupted her.

"Until Invictus is destroyed, we are all in peril—and Laylah more than any of us," Torg said. "I would much prefer she be kept from danger of any kind, but the creature I intend to slay has powers that in some ways might be greater than mine. I will need Laylah with me. Her magic is also strong. Maybe she can find a way to defeat the Great Evil, if I cannot."

Laylah was torn between conflicting emotions. Torg's faith in her thrilled her, but Lucius' constant meddling enraged her. She owed the firstborn her life, but she no longer owed him fealty. She had never intended to cause the general pain, but her love for Torg had grown stronger than her guilt. It was time Lucius stepped aside.

"And what if it's more powerful than both of you?" she heard Lucius saying, rising from his chair. "How are you going to feel if . . . "

"*LUCIUS!*"

Laylah shouted his name, with supernatural fury. The force of it knocked the firstborn off his feet back into the chair. The fire also reacted to her emanation, blazing from the hearth and scattering cinders across the floor. A particularly large one fell into Bard's beard and began to sizzle.

"Somebody's always trying to burn me up," he said.

Laylah's show of strength amazed Rakkhati, and he bowed.

Bonny, however, was less impressed. "Unless you want everybody in Duccarita knocking on our door, you had better not do that again. You were almost as loud as the dragon."

Lucius stood, glared at Laylah, and then rushed down the hall to his room, slamming the door behind him.

There was an awkward silence. Laylah was the first to speak. "I'm sorry if I've endangered us. I had no idea my voice was going to be that loud. It even frightened me."

"There's no reason to say you're sorry, pretty lady," Elu said. "Lucius is nicer than he used to be, but he still complains almost as much as Rathburt. We're *all* tired of it."

"Hmmmph!" Rathburt said.

Bonny started to protest, but Torg stared her down. "Because we are friends as well as companions, I have permitted certain liberties. But even I have a temper, and none of you would like it if I turned my anger on you. Laylah is also dangerous. You can push either one of us only so far."

Bonny's face flushed and seemed to swell. Laylah felt guilty for creating such a fuss, but she knew Torg was right. Friendship was a wonderful thing, but a group facing this degree of peril needed leadership more than consensus.

"Sorceress, please forgive Bonny for her rash words," Rakkhati said. "She has the recklessness of a pirate."

"Enough of this," Laylah said. "There's nothing to forgive. I was wrong to overreact the way I did, but it's over and can't be undone."

She turned to Torg. "I need to speak to Lucius . . . alone. From what you've said about the Daasa, it sounds like we need his cooperation. He'll be no good to us in this mood."

Like a schoolgirl in class, Bonny raised her hand. "May I speak to him, Missus? No offense, but I doubt he's in the mood to talk to you, if you know what I mean. Let me be the one to cheer him up."

Laylah smiled. "That's a wonderful idea."

"But be quick about it," Torg said. "It's well past midnight. Time runs short."

Suddenly pleased, Bonny winked and then sprinted down the hall.

Rakkhati chuckled. "The yellow-hair is in good hands. He'll soon have a smile on his face wide enough to charm every Daasa in Duccarita."


LUCIUS SAT down on the bed with a thump. Part of him felt like crying, but the rest was too exasperated. In truth he was angrier at himself than at Laylah. He knew in his heart that it was time to let go. Why couldn't he find a way to turn off his emotions? He understood that things like this took time, but it felt like he was making little progress.

There was a tapping at his door. He looked up with delight, prepared to apologize profusely and promise he would never interfere again—if Laylah would just be his friend.

"Come in," he said, as cheerfully as he could muster.

But when the door swung slowly open, his expression soured. Instead of Laylah, it was Bonny who entered, and she bore a rascally smile on her face, her teeth crooked but glistening white.

The pirate must have recognized his chagrin. Her smile faded. "Sorry to disappoint you. I just came to see if you needed anything."

Lucius sighed. "I'm not good company right now."

Bonny, it seemed, was incapable of experiencing anger, hurt, or sadness for more than a moment. Her smile returned. "Why don't you let me be the judge of that," she said, sitting next to him on the bed. And then she grabbed his face in her hands and pressed her lips against his mouth. When she pulled away, her dark eyes were glassy. "You are *very* good company, sweety. Why don't you forget about the fancy bitch out there and give *me* a try? You and I were made for each other."

At first, Lucius could barely speak. His face felt hot and swollen, and his body tingled. He was almost eighty years old, but this was the first time he had been kissed with such passion. "Why . . . why do you like me so much?" was all he could manage.

She purred. "What's not to like? You are handsome, strong, and brave. And I have always been partial to blond men, if you must know."

Lucius attempted a smile. "If you knew more about me, you wouldn't feel so partial. What *do* you know about me?"

"When I meet a person, I judge them from that first moment. You haven't done anything bad to me, yet."

Now Lucius did smile. "I liked the way you kissed me."

"Then let me do it again."

# 8

TORG WAS surprised to see Lucius and Bonny coming down the hallway so soon after she had entered his room. Sure enough, the pirate had managed to cheer up the firstborn. It was as if the recent incident with Laylah had never occurred. Torg breathed a sigh of relief. Things had suddenly become less complicated.

"Your scarf is missing, madam," Rathburt said to Bonny.

"Huh? Oh! It must have fallen off somewhere."

"Yes, it must have," Rathburt said drolly.

Torg cleared his throat. "For Anna's sake. Everyone stop staring at them—and listen carefully. Rakkhati, Laylah, and I will search for the *Mahanta pEpa*. The rest of you will wait here for sixty slow breaths before leaving the inn and following Bonny to the slave pits where the Daasa are held prisoner. Once there, stay out of sight and wait. If by midmorning nothing unusual has occurred, you'll know that Laylah and I have failed. After that, you'll be on your own and may go where you will."

"Don't talk like that," Ugga said. "It's bad enough we've lost Jord. We won't be able to stand it if ya and Laylah don't come back to us."

"We shall see what we shall see."

Before they left, Torg heard Laylah say one last thing to Bonny. "Take good care of my friends . . . please."

"I will, Missus. Do not worry."

Torg was amazed when Laylah placed her hand on Bonny's muscular shoulder. "What you've done for him means a lot to me. From one woman to another, thank you."

Bonny gently removed Laylah's hand. And kissed it. "Believe me, Missus . . . it's *my* pleasure."

Torg, Laylah, and Rakkhati then started down the stairs to the first floor, entering a common room several times larger than the parlor. A dozen men sat near the hearth, drinking ale and smoking tobacco with long pipes. They appraised Torg and Laylah, their eyes full of mischief. Though their new outfits served as a partial disguise, Torg's size and Laylah's beauty were uncommon in the City of Thieves. Plus, Laylah carried Obhasa, which looked even more unusual—and valuable.

"What are ya staring at, ya scoundrels?" Rakkhati said in the northern tongue. "Mind your own bizz-nuss and stay outta ours."

They did just that, turning back to each other. Apparently the innkeeper was a man to be reckoned with, even among the riffraff.

The trio left the inn through a side door, entering an alley that was wide and well-lit, at least by Duccaritan standards. Torg drew the Silver Sword from its scabbard and held it at the ready, which was routine behavior in these streets at night. Laylah wielded Obhasa, which glowed in the scant moonlight. Rakkhati carried his long dagger.

"There are secret ways," Rakkhati whispered in the common tongue, "where you can avoid unwanted attention. But they are even more dangerous than the streets. If it weren't for you and the sorceress, I would not dare such a thing after sunset. The monsters are powerful and numerous, and they are far more active in the darkness. An ordinary man cannot stand against them.

If attacked, I will need your protection."

"If at all possible, Laylah and I will not fail you," Torg said. "Lead on. The night grows old, and there is much to do."

Rakkhati nodded and then turned to his right, racing down the alley. They came to a street poorly lit by sputtering torches on short iron poles driven into the ground. Rakkhati peeked out in both directions and then whispered again. "We'll be in the open for more than a mile before we reach the alley that leads to the dwelling place of the Great Evil. Few humans go near, even in daylight, but ogresses often are seen dragging chained Daasa slaves into the alleyways. The ogresses return, but the slaves are never seen again."

Rakkhati turned left and entered the street, but he stayed close to the ramshackle buildings, flitting from shadow to shadow beneath the eaves of a series of rickety porches. Torg and Laylah followed, alert for any disturbance. Light crept from crevices in the shuttered windows and weathered entryways, along with loud arguments and unpleasant laughter.

At one point, the door of a noisy tavern swung open just a few paces from where they stood, and a drunken man was thrown head over heels into the street. He lay in the dust and cursed at his assailants. Torg watched his expression slowly change; once the man got over his anger, fear took its place. He shuffled across the street toward another tavern, pounding on the door and begging for someone to open it.

Rakkhati pointed above the man's head to a dark shape creeping along the wall on all fours like a lizard. It got within a cubit of the man and started to reach out a long arm, but the door swung open just in time for him to leap inside, oblivious to how close he had come to being a vampire's late-night meal.

Torg felt Laylah shiver beside him, but she knew enough to remain silent. The vampire stayed above the door for a few moments before skittering off. Torg watched it creep into another alleyway and disappear. Laylah let out a long breath.

When Torg looked back at Rakkhati, he saw that the Jivitan's eyes were wide with horror.

*It must be frightening to be so near such monsters when you can't match their power.*

Torg was comforted that Ugga and Bard would be with the others when Bonny led them from the inn. Though they wielded no blatant magic, Torg believed that their bodies were imbued with supernatural strength. And they would need every bit of it. Torg doubted Rathburt would perform well under duress. The battle with the black mountain wolves had nearly done him in, and there were creatures in Duccarita more dangerous than wolves.

Torg, Laylah, and Rakkhati went on for more than a mile.

Each wooden building resembled the other. Torg couldn't tell an inn from a tavern, or a shop from a house. Occasionally, a warped plank would creak beneath their feet, betraying their whereabouts to anyone or anything nearby. But for whatever reason, they were never challenged and saw no other beings. Eventually the street narrowed, and torches no longer lighted it, but the gibbous moon shone brightly. The buildings now lining the street were more decrepit than the previous ones. Most of the doors and shutters were broken, and no lights came from inside.

Rakkhati seemed even more apprehensive than before.

Without warning, a dark shape lumbered out of an alley and headed right for them, snorting and slavering. Rakkhati flattened himself against the nearest wall and slid down to a seated position, though the creature had appeared not to see them.

Torg recognized it as an ogress, at least seven cubits tall. Ogresses, being distantly related to Kojins, were far larger than their male counterparts. They also were mean-spirited and dull-witted. Torg was more concerned about the noise it might make than any danger it presented to him.

All three knelt in the shadows, hoping it would pass without detecting them, but at the last moment it stopped, sniffed the air, and turned in their direction.

*It smells Rakkhati's fear,* Torg thought, before springing forward and beheading the beast with a single stroke of the Silver Sword. Blood as black as tar squirted from its neck, splashing down like a sudden burst of rain. The beast's bulbous head fell like a stone; the rest of its huge body followed. Torg picked up the head by its scraggly hair and tossed it inside one of the open doors. Then he dragged the heavy carcass into the shadows.

Rakkhati remained against the wall, still trembling. Torg knelt beside him and exhaled. Blue-green vapor oozed from his nose and crept into the Jivitan's nostrils. Soon after, Rakkhati was able to stand. Torg turned to Laylah to see how she was holding up. The sorceress looked alert but unafraid. His respect for her swelled another notch. She seemed to see it in his face and smiled.

They heard a shuffling sound on the roof of one of the porches. Rakkhati waved for them to follow and then darted away. Fifty paces later they stopped and spun around. From this distance they could see only a vague outline of the ogress' carcass, but they could make out several dark shapes swarming around it, accompanied by tearing and slurping sounds. The vampires had come to feed. Torg was disgusted, but at the same time relieved that their attention was elsewhere.

Just then, a deep-throated growl startled all three of them. Torg turned just in time to see a shape as large as a Buffelo thunder past on its way to the carcass. When it reached the ogress, it tore into its flesh with a hysterical rage. The others fled from its wrath. Torg's first encounter with a ruined Daasa would not be his last.

Leaving the carnage behind, the trio crept along for another half-mile before Rakkhati came to a halt.

"May I have more, lord?" he whispered.

"More?"

Rakkhati tapped the tip of his nose.

"Ahhh."

Torg blew another dose of the blue-green vapor into the Jivitan's nostrils, calming him enough to continue. Finally they approached an alley that was narrower than most of the others, its opening as black as the surface of a lake on the night of a new moon. Torg was reminded of his visit to the Realm of the Undead.

"Lord, I have never entered this place after dark," Rakkhati whispered. "In the daytime, you can see a little of what lies ahead—and even then, dozens of armed men carrying torches accompanied me. A slave trader hired our group to retrieve a prized ring lost by one of his assistants who had been attacked by a ruined Daasa and dragged inside. I have never been so terrified in my life, and we never located the ring. But we found parts of the assistant's body, strewn about here and there inside the alley."

"You are free to return from whence you came," Torg said, "but neither Laylah nor I will be able to escort you."

"I will not forsake you, Lord," Rakkhati said. "Nor you, my lady. The way is yet far and complicated. Without me as guide, you would be lost. I have been inside just once, but it is burned in my memory. I can recall every twist and turn as if it happened just a moment ago. I believe that Sakuna played some role in this. She came to me the night after I went inside and did something to my mind that enabled me to remember. I asked her how she knew to come, and she said only that it had been foretold."

Laylah held up Obhasa. "Do we dare to light our way?"

"Without light, even I will become lost," Rakkhati said.

Torg agreed. "You cannot wander in darkness among creatures of darkness. Though Obhasa will announce our presence, I see no other option. Laylah, it is up to you."


LAYLAH WAS startled. In a repeat of their encounter with the vines, Torg again was asking her to play a crucial role in a dangerous situation. But this time, her use of the staff would have to be more subtle, and she wasn't sure she had sufficiently mastered it.

"I think you should take the staff," Laylah said. "I can carry the sword."

"Obhasa has grown fond of you," Torg said. "It will obey your commands, whatever they may be."

"As you say, beloved."

"One of you will have to go first," Rakkhati said. "Only then will I have the courage to enter. Where we are going is not pleasant."

"We'll stay close together," Torg said. "I'll go first, then you, then Laylah. Obhasa will light the way from behind."

"I'll do my best," Laylah said.

Holding the sword in front of him, the wizard stepped into the darkness. Rakkhati shuffled behind. Laylah was the last to enter, and the sudden virulence took her aback, as if she had entered a crypt filled with decaying corpses. The air stank like rotting flesh, and the ground became squishy as a bog. She grasped Obhasa and willed it to life. For a moment it shined like a star, casting light far along the narrow alleyway and revealing walls covered with foul growths and wiggly worms.

Rakkhati yelped. "It's worse than before," the Jivitan said. "*Much* worse. And we have so far to go before we find the thing you seek. Lord, this cannot be done!"

"Retreat is not an option," Torg said. "Keep your wits about you. And Laylah, I said we need light, but not *that* much."

Laylah barely heard him. Like the Jivitan, she also felt hopeless, having never seen anything so disgusting, even in her nightmares. The alley had no ceiling, but its walls and floor squirmed like a living entity. And there were fibrous tendrils strewn between the walls that looked like spider webs—only thicker, wetter, and oilier.

Torg sliced at them with the sword as if clearing a way through a jungle choked with wispy vines. "My love, we need light, but not *that* much," the wizard repeated, attempting to gain her attention. "If you're not careful, you're going to burn down Duccarita and melt the glaciers of Nirodha along with it."

Despite the horror of their situation, Laylah giggled nervously. "Sorry . . . sorry."

Then she focused her attention on Obhasa, soon finding that she could control the intensity of light by adjusting the pressure of her hands on the shaft. She quickly willed it down to a magnitude that illuminated just a few paces ahead and behind.

"Excellent," Torg said.

The three of them delved deeper into the alleyway, going on for about fifty paces before it split in two directions. Torg looked at Rakkhati and shrugged. The Jivitan pointed to the right.

The wizard followed his instructions, moving slowly along the alley, which continued to narrow. With arms outstretched, Laylah could have touched both walls at once, though she had no intention of doing so. The sorceress had never smelled such stench. The surface of the walls writhed as if the light maddened it. Laylah felt nauseous and dizzy. Rakkhati fared even worse, stumbling along like an old man. If Torg was affected, he didn't show it.

Laylah began to feel increasingly anxious. Each step became more difficult, and it seemed as if they were being watched. Assailants could be lurking within ten paces, and she wouldn't have known it. Paranoia gripped her. In response, she squeezed the staff harder, causing blinding light to leap outward in all directions.

Suddenly, a bony but powerful hand grasped her shoulder from behind. She spun around and found herself face to face with several ghouls. Dozens of cold fingers reached for her, snatching at her hair and pawing at her breasts. She screamed and lashed out with Obhasa, pounding it downward like a stave. The ghouls were jammed so tightly together, several were struck by the same blow. When the staff touched their flesh, they burst asunder.

The survivors turned and fled, disappearing into the distant darkness. Laylah felt a sense of elation, but it was short-lived. She noticed too late that the walls were closing around her. Suddenly the noxious substance fell upon her, sticking to her face like glue and squirting into her nostrils and ears. She tried to scream but her mouth was flooded, causing her to choke. At that moment, she believed she would die. But then a warm pair of hands clasped hers where they held the staff, and there was a concussive blast. Her mouth, nostrils, and ears were miraculously cleared.

Torg stood beside her, still gripping her hands. He had somehow managed to reach her through the congestion, and their combined power—funneled through Obhasa—had incinerated the loathsome goo.

When Torg released her, she let go of the staff and hugged him, tears filling her eyes. She felt an odd combination of relief and shame—relief that they both lived, shame that she had failed him. The wizard snared Obhasa before it struck the ground. The staff continued to glow, providing enough light to see for about the length of an arm. Laylah looked down and saw two things at the edge of the gloom: the Silver Sword stuck point-down in the ground and Rakkhati sitting on his rump, hugging his legs.

She reached for the innkeeper, but when she touched his shoulder, he moaned.

"Rise!" she heard Torg saying to Rakkhati, his voice as hard as granite. To her amazement, the Jivitan spy complied. But his eyes were glassy and his expression confused.

"Secrecy is no longer an option," Torg said to both of them. "The *Mahanta pEpa* is aware of our presence. But if we move swiftly enough, we might yet succeed. We must find and destroy its brain before it regains its courage and strikes again."

"Lord . . . lord . . ." Rakkhati mumbled. "I cannot . . . go farther. Leave me. I am useless."

"You are our guide," Torg said. "You must lead, nothing more. Leave the fighting to Laylah and me. We are your only chance."

Rakkhati started to sob, but Laylah took him in her arms. When she did, magic emanated from her flesh, bathing him in alabaster. It seemed to temporarily strengthen him, and he stood upright and was able to breathe more calmly.

Finally he pointed down the alley. "This way."

After Torg drew the sword from the ground, they resumed their original positions in line. Laylah willed Obhasa to glow again. The writhing walls shied from the light, but she sensed a lurking malice.

Soon they came to another crossroads, this time with three offshoots instead of two. Rakkhati pointed toward the middle of the three, and Torg plunged in. This part of the alleyway was enclosed by a rooftop. The goo clung everywhere. Putrid drops of liquid spilled onto their heads, sizzling and stinging. The air became stuffy and suffocatingly warm.

"I cannot . . . cannot . . ." Rakkhati mumbled, and then collapsed on his face. The wizard crouched down and rolled the Jivitan onto his back.

"He's gone," Laylah heard Torg say. "He is no longer." But it was as if he were speaking to her from the other side of a wall. She could hear his voice but could not see him.

"Laylah? Are you all right? Can you hear me? Laylah . . . Lay . . . lah . . . laah . . . laaah . . . laaaaaaaaaaaah . . ."

"LAYLAH! LAYLAH!" Torg said, holding her face in his hands. Both Obhasa and the Silver Sword lay at their feet, alongside the corpse of Rakkhati. Everything was falling apart before Torg's eyes, and he couldn't seem to regain control. His beloved had fallen into a trance and wouldn't respond. The Great Evil's will was more powerful than a Kojin's, more pervasive than a druid queen's. If he didn't think of something immediately, he too would succumb, and all would be lost.

Torg started to reach for Obhasa, planning another burst of energy in an attempt to drive back his foe. But he changed his mind and instead grasped the sword and plunged it into the wall. The point sheared through the goo-coated wood all the way to its guard. Torg felt more than heard a high-pitched shriek that caused the walls and ceiling of the alley to shiver. Then he kicked at the wall, and it burst apart, revealing a wide room that in times past must have served as a meeting hall. Now it was empty, other than a wobbly table and some splintered chairs. He dragged Laylah inside and sat her down on the floor, kneeling in front of her, his deep-blue eyes glowing so brightly he could see their reflection on her skin.

"Laylah, come back to me. I need you. There is much to be done."

Torg set down the sword, picked up Obhasa, and laid the rounded head of the ivory staff on the bridge of her nose. Prickly blue-green beams crept down her cheeks. In response, the glaze left her eyes, and she looked at him with recognition.

"My beloved, you found me. I was wandering in darkness . . . lost . . ."

Torg smiled, but only briefly. "Other than Invictus, the *Mahanta pEpa* is stronger than any creature I have encountered. It appears able to enter our minds and control our thoughts. But I still believe we can kill it, if we can find its brain. Can you go on, my love?"

"I think I can, if you are with me. But without Rakkhati as our guide, do we have any hope? It was terrible the way he died. He was killed by his own fright."

"Even if Rakkhati were still with us, I don't think he would have been of much use from here on. This creature is too powerful for an ordinary mind to abide. I curse whoever brought it here from across the ocean. Rise, my love. We must plunge even deeper into the lair."

Laylah stood shakily.

Torg turned toward the tear in the wall, but then he froze. They had a visitor. Standing in the shattered opening was a beast out of a nightmare, as ugly as the hideous version of a Warlish witch. The ruined Daasa was the size of a boulder and resembled a bloated tick covered with bony spines. It crept into the room, ripping away more chunks of the wall as it entered. Holding both the sword and Obhasa, Torg placed himself between the beast and Laylah. But instead of approaching nearer, the Daasa stopped and stared.

Torg felt Laylah press against his back and peer over his shoulder.

"I don't think it intends to attack us," she whispered. "Can it sense that we mean it no harm?"

"It is probing my mind," Torg responded softly. "I can feel its intentions. There is decency within the rage."

The Daasa made a strange grunting sound, then turned and lumbered back into the alley, heading deeper into the labyrinth.

"It wants us to follow," Torg said. "It hates the *Mahanta pEpa* far worse than we. Are you ready?"

"Yes."

Neither one of them wanted to go anywhere near the goo, but there was no other choice. The ruined Daasa already had shuffled beyond their sight, and Torg—now holding Obhasa—willed enough light to illuminate the creature's tail-end. They followed for what seemed like half the night, turning this way and that, and at times even walking up or down creaking sets of stairs that somehow supported the beast's great weight. The goo became thicker and more grotesque, but the Daasa seemed not to notice, lumbering along at a surprisingly brisk pace. They saw no other monsters, including vampires and ghouls. At first Torg was relieved, but then he began to feel his own strength fading as he neared the center of the Great Evil's lair. What would happen when they found the brain? Torg could barely breathe, much less fight.

"We're inside of it," he heard Laylah say, but her voice sounded far away. Torg wished Jord was with them. She would know what to do. He wasn't so sure he did anymore—or if he even cared. Though he continued to keep the Daasa within sight, the desire to lie down and rest was overwhelming. How pleasant it would be to sleep.

Torg became so bewildered he almost bumped into the back of the beast, which had stopped and was staring down a set of stairs leading to a smoky basement.

The brain of the *Mahanta pEpa* was just a few steps away.

The Daasa pressed against the side of the wall, its bulbous body flattening just enough to allow Torg and Laylah to pass. But Torg seemed unable to will his body forward.

"We're almost there," he heard Laylah say from some distant place. "I am with you, beloved. The Daasa can go no farther. We're on our own."

"We're all on our own," Torg whispered, with no intention of taking another step. But he felt her hands push against his back. "All right, Laylah, I'll go . . . but you'll have to carry Obhasa. It's too heavy for me. It has always been too heavy."


AS THEY DESCENDED the stairs, Laylah gained a sense of what was happening. The will of the *Mahanta pEpa* was enormously strong, but apparently not powerful enough to subdue them both simultaneously. When it was focused on her, Torg remained lucid. Now it had turned its supernatural attention to the Death-Knower, which was a wise choice on its part, considering the wizard was the deadlier of the two. Without him, Laylah doubted she had the power to destroy such a monster.

The room they entered was far larger than any ordinary basement. Beneath the impossible tangle of decrepit wooden buildings, the *Mahanta pEpa* had constructed a lair huge enough to contain its ever-growing body. Because the creature was ignoring her and focusing on Torg, she was free to read its thoughts, which hung in the roasting air like steam.

Hunger drove the Great Evil. When it had first arrived in Duccarita—hidden in a sack of nuts collected by pirates in the forest across the ocean—it had been an infant, about the size of an ordinary rat. After a pirate cut open the sack, it had leapt out and scurried into the city, barely avoiding being crushed by stomping feet.

In its native environment, its kind often grew as large as trees, lurking in hidden places and feeding on anything that came within reach of its gooey flesh. The Daasa—in their gentle form—were its favorite food. But in this

new world, there was so much more to eat. Over the years, its body had
grown to outrageous proportions, as had its psychic domination of the
Daasa. The humans that brought it over the sea were easy to control, and
they willingly supplied it with as many Daasa as it could devour. In return, the
creature held the Daasa in check, preventing them from changing into the
form that would have made them impossible to manage. A few slipped
through the cracks of its domination, but there were not enough ruined
Daasa to cause major problems.

Laylah realized first with relief, and then with dismay, that Torg had
begun to move forward again. But this time he was walking too quickly,
heedless of whatever dangers lay ahead. With a surge of speed, he rushed
deep into the chamber.

"Torg! Wait . . . WAIT!" But he did not heed her calls. Suddenly
panicked, Laylah squeezed hard on Obhasa, forcing a burst of light to
illuminate the cavern. What she saw sickened her. The foul-smelling goo
coated the ceilings, walls, and floors. Scattered throughout were thousands of
bones, some unrecognizable, some disturbingly familiar. Laylah finally
identified the smell that had disgusted her from the moment she first entered
the alley. It was one she had come to despise while a prisoner of Invictus. The
goo smelled like vomit.

They were inside the creature's stomach.

Torg had been wrong. The *Mahanta pEpa* did not have a single point of
vulnerability. There was no brain to stab with the sword or blast with
Obhasa. The creature had evolved into a throbbing blob of ravenous flesh
that spread throughout the buildings and alleys for hundreds of cubits in all
directions, and its will was embedded in every shred of its titanic body.

Laylah experienced a wave of revulsion. A mist passed over her vision.
She imagined herself abandoning Torg. In return for the wizard's life, the
Great Evil would permit her to go free. She could rush up the stairs, past the
Daasa, past Rakkhati's corpse, and flee into the street. *Who could blame her?* She
would find the others, and they could go back to the inn and hide.

Laylah heard Torg sobbing.

The sound shattered her trance. The wizard stood in the middle of the
room, arms at his side, the Silver Sword at his feet. The goo was creeping
over the top of his high boots. But that wasn't right. Rather, her beloved was
sinking into it like quicksand. At that moment, Laylah realized she was their
only hope. For the first time in her life, there was no one else to depend
on—not her parents, or Takoda, or even Lucius. Her beloved's life hung in
the balance, and hers, as well, for when the wizard was destroyed, she would
be next.

She held Obhasa aloft, squeezed it with all her strength, and willed
whatever magic she contained into its ivory shaft. Blue energy laced with

white leapt upward in a concentrated beam, blasting through the ceiling of the chamber and several floors of wooden building before erupting into the sky. Such an expenditure of power felt exhilarating, but Laylah's rapture soon diminished. Other than a hole in its immense flesh, the *Mahanta pEpa* was unharmed. She lashed out again and again, but failed to do any serious damage. Meanwhile, Torg had sunk to his knees, his head bowed to his chest.

She ran to him, faced him—now taller than he—and shook him. Slapped him. Struck him. All to no avail. The creature held him in its psychic embrace and was slowly attempting to digest his body. As if resigned to his fate, Torg did not resist. Even the Silver Sword had disappeared from view.

Laylah couldn't let him go, not like this, not ever. She dropped Obhasa and wrapped her arms around him, hugging him, kissing him, begging him to awaken. She pressed herself against him, wrapped her legs around him, clawed at his back like an animal. Still he did not react . . .

. . . but, *she* reacted. A glowing warmth seemed to rise from her skin, and once again light flooded the room, only this time the illumination came from her own flesh, not from Obhasa's magical ivory. Like a spark fallen upon dry grass, Laylah's energy caused Torg to respond—involuntarily—to her release of power, and he too began to glow, his blue-green energy merging forcefully with her alabaster. Their magic fed off each other's, growing brighter and hotter and more dangerous, and Laylah realized that whatever was about to happen had grown beyond her control, not that she had any desire to stop it. Instead, the intensity of it filled her with bliss, as if the two of them were making love on a plane higher than a physical one.

Laylah remembered the words Torg had spoken in their room at the inn when she had attempted to seduce him.

"*You* won't be harmed, perhaps, but half of Duccarita will end up in flames."

*Could it be?*

By now, Torg had sunk halfway up his thighs. His head remained bowed, but his body had tensed, and his back had arched. Heat emanated from his flesh, along with a blue-green glow. The hair on his head stood straight up, his hands drew into fists, and his chest expanded and contracted in a series of rapid convulsions. Her own body performed similar histrionics. Her brow oozed sweat. Her heart raced. Her body became consumed in luscious warmth.

It built and built and built . . .

Suddenly, a cacophony of power erupted from both of them. Blue-green energy—laced with white—blared out in waves, radiating in all directions. Laylah cried out and was thrown back a hundred paces, and though her clothes were consumed, she was not injured. The wizard's chaotic magic speared through her like stones through water, piercing her but causing no harm. Obhasa and the Silver Sword also were undamaged.

But everything else within a thousand cubits, including the *Mahanta pEpa*, was incinerated.

When the smoke cleared, they strode toward each other through the rubble. Even as they embraced, the sun rose above the eastern wall of Duccarita, casting an explosion of yellow light upon the smoldering remains of the destruction.

# 9

WHEN BONNY told them it was time to go, Lucius jumped up quickly. But Ugga remained in his chair, his eyes closed and body frozen.

"Get up, ya booger!" Bard said impatiently. "Didn't ya hear Missus Bonny?"

Ugga opened his eyes. "But I has only counted fifty breaths," the crossbreed said, clearly puzzled. "Master Hah-nah said to count to sixty."

"For Anna's sake!" Rathburt said. "Would you jump off a cliff if he told you to?"

Ugga considered that for a moment. "Master Hah-nah would have a good reason, I supposes."

"Arrrggghhh!"

Lucius went to his room to get his *uttara* and war club. When he returned to the parlor, the others were waiting: Ugga with his axe, Bard his bow and arrows and a pair of daggers, Rathburt his staff, and Elu his Tugarian dagger. Bonny, looking as luscious as ever, returned with a steel cutlass in a leather scabbard at her waist and a dagger strapped to each muscular calf.

"The more dangerous you look, the more you will fit in," Bonny said. "While it's still dark, we'll need to move quick and quiet. The monsters are active until dawn. But they'll think twice before attacking our bunch, especially with him around."

She motioned toward Ugga, who smiled proudly.

"He does make ya feel safe," Bard agreed.

"Elu loves Ugga too."

"Let's get moving," Lucius said. "We might as well get this over with."

"Yes, sir!" Bonny said, saluting. "I will do whatever you say, whenever you say it."

With Lucius blushing, the pirate woman led them down the stairs into the common room. Half a dozen men remained by the hearth. A pair of them had fallen asleep, snoring in their chairs. The others huddled around a small table, smoking and drinking and playing a game of cards. They looked up with curiosity—their eyes opening especially wide when they saw Ugga—but quickly lowered their heads when Bonny gave them a threatening stare.

"I knows every one of ya, so ya'd better mind your manners while I is gone," she said in the northern dialect to the ones who remained awake. "If there's any trub-bull, I is going to get angry. And ya know what happens when I gets angry."

"Yes, missus," the largest of them mumbled.

Bonny led them through a side door into a wide alley and gathered her companions around her. "We have a long way to go," she whispered, returning to the common tongue. "You need to do what I do, run when I run, hide when I hide." Then she focused her attention on Lucius. "By the time we get to the slave pens, the sun will have risen. There will be lots of people around, so we'll have to be careful." She looked at the rest of them. "Are you ready?"

They nodded vigorously, except for Rathburt, who bore the expression of someone suffering from stomach cramps. "I can run and hide with the best of them," he mumbled.

Elu snorted.

After that, Bonny turned to the left and hurried down the alleyway in a crouch, staying close to the wall. Soon she came to a wide street, lighted sporadically by torches. There was a tavern across the street that was larger and more active than Rakkhati's establishment. Several dozen men stood outside the main door, unafraid because they were pressed together and heavily armed.

*Strength in numbers*, Lucius thought. *Monsters rarely attack large groups, if they can help it. They prefer to sneak up on isolated prey.*

"We need to get by these guys, somehow," Bonny said. "If they see us, they'll want to know our business—and it'll end up in a fight. I'm not saying we'd lose, but it'd cause too much of a ruckus."

"We need a diversion," Lucius said.

Bonny smiled. "Do you have any ideas?"

"Now that you mention it, I do." What he whispered in her ear caused her to giggle.

A few moments later Bonny ran into the street, screaming like a banshee. Her blouse was unbuttoned, exposing her small breasts. Lucius thundered after her, grabbed her from behind and groped her in full view of the pirates.

"Where ya going, ya bitch!" he shouted. "I isn't done with ya yet!" He flung her over his shoulder and trudged down the street while the men hooted and hollered approvingly. A hundred paces later, Lucius and Bonny ducked into a dark alley, joining their companions.

"Did you enjoy yourself?" Bonny said after Lucius put her down. "Where I come from, they call that a freebie."

"I had to make it look real."

Rathburt rolled his eyes. "When you lovebirds are finished chatting, can we get on with it?"

Bonny gave Lucius a quick kiss on the lips before starting down the poorly lit street, which quickly grew darker and spookier. They passed row upon row of shabbily constructed wooden buildings. There appeared to be activity inside their walls, but no one dared to venture outside.

Lucius' thoughts strayed to Laylah. He wondered where she was and how she was faring—and if he would ever see her again. Bonny must have sensed his distraction, because she grasped his arm and gave it a hard squeeze. Then she pointed down the road toward a particularly thick patch of darkness. At first Lucius saw nothing, but then he began to make out shapes lumbering toward them.

"Ghouls," Bonny hissed. "We must not be seen. Follow me."

Several large barrels, empty and splintered but large enough to provide cover, fronted one of the buildings. They crouched behind them and did their best to stay out of sight. The ghouls, at least twenty in all, marched down the middle of the street like a grotesque parade, their stench preceding them by a good distance.

As the ghouls passed their hiding place, Lucius saw that several of them were lugging a large, round body that appeared to be dead or unconscious. Lucius felt Bonny tense, and for a moment he feared she might leap up and attack. But the ghouls suddenly veered to the left and stumbled into an alleyway, carrying the body with them. Soon they were gone.

"*Bhümadeha!* (Dreadful flesh!)," Bonny whispered. "How dare you murder the Daasa? I spit on all your kind."

"It was a Daasa?" Lucius said. "Are you sure?"

"Of course I'm sure," Bonny said with irritation. "It was probably given to the ghouls as a gift by the slavers in return for performing some terrible deed. I'm glad you have come to Duccarita. It's time we put an end to this, once and for all."

"Is that what we're going to do?" Rathburt said. "And here I thought we were just going out for a pleasant stroll through the scenic part of town."

"Those ghoulies smell bad, but they don't look so dangerous to me," Ugga said, slapping the shaft of his axe against the palm of his hand. "Why are we hiding from them, Missus Bonny? They should be hiding from us."

"The ghouls are more dangerous than they look," Bonny said. "Even so, the less noise we make, the better. If we attract a crowd, that won't be good."

She continued down the roadway, finally stopping near the entrance of another alley. Lucius peered inside but could not see beyond its pitch-black maw.

"If we go this way, we'll save lots of time," Bonny said. "If we keep to the streets, we'll have to go a long way around, and we might not make it before midmorning."

"But . . . ?" Lucius said.

"But . . . the alleys are dangerous at night. We're almost sure to run into more ghouls. And vampires too. Sometimes there are even Mogols. If we're real quiet—and real lucky—we might make it without a fight. But I wouldn't bet on it."

"If we take the long way, the odds are still high we'll run into trouble?"

"I'm afraid so."

Lucius turned to the others. "I don't pretend to be your commander, but I vote we go through the alley. It sounds like any way we choose will be difficult, so the quicker the better, as far as I'm concerned."

"That would be my choice too," Bonny said.

The rest agreed, though Rathburt, as usual, added a snide remark. "My choice would be to return to the inn and sleep in our chairs by the fire. But no one ever listens to me."

Bonny chuckled and then looked down at Elu. Her expression grew serious. "You look plenty strong to me, and I'm sure you can take care of yourself, but to the monsters, you will look like the easiest prey."

"Elu understands. He will stay close to mighty Ugga."

After that, they were forced to backtrack several dozen paces to find a torch that still had some life. Then they returned and entered the alley with Bonny in the lead. Lucius, Rathburt, Bard, Elu, and Ugga followed. Lucius held the war club in his left hand and *uttara* in his right. The club felt hot, as if just pulled from a fire. When he entered the corridor, it began to glow.

"You carry two great weapons," Bonny whispered. "The club must have belonged to a Mogol chieftain. There is magic in it that is responding to something nearby. I'm not sure what, but it makes me nervous."

"We're all nervous," Lucius said.

Even though it had no roof, the alley was claustrophobically narrow. Rusty nails and warped planks reached out like claws. The air stank of garbage, urine, and feces. Bonny held the torch and led them slowly forward. Instantly Lucius felt paranoid that something was going to pounce on his head from above, and he found himself looking up compulsively.

There were occasional tears in the walls—some at eye level or above, some low to the ground. From one of the low holes, a pale hand emerged and grasped Elu's ankle, attempting to yank him inside. But the Svakaran was too quick, whipping the Tugarian dagger downward and cutting the arm in two near the wrist. After a snarling yelp, the bloodied stub withdrew, leaving the severed hand behind, its fingers still wriggling.

"Good going, little guy," Ugga said, squashing the hand with a large booted foot. "They'll think twice before grabbing for ya again."

Lucius was impressed too. The Tugarian dagger had cut through the bone of the arm like a scythe through grass. It appeared they all carried formidable weapons.

They came to a crossroads where several alleys intersected. Without hesitation, Bonny turned right. This alley opened onto another road, but here there were no torches, and the buildings that lined the street appeared deserted.

"This is a bad part of town," she said.

"And everywhere else is so *nice*," Rathburt said.

They continued down the street. Bonny led them into another alley, this time on the right. Again they were submerged in darkness, their sputtering torch providing scant relief. After they had walked about a hundred paces, Bonny halted and raised the torch.

"Do you hear something?"

"I don't hear a thing," Rathburt said. But then, without warning, he let out a yelp, and blue flame burst from his staff, spurting upward and illuminating the corridor.

Lucius turned and saw Ugga staring up at an enormous cave troll that had somehow managed to squeeze into the alley by scooting along sideways. Tendrils of drool hung from its bulbous lips, and its eyes were wild and angry. The troll swung a boulder-sized fist at the crossbreed's head, but Ugga blocked the downward blow with his axe. The huge hand struck the edge of the blade and tore away from the wrist, flopping past Elu and knocking Rathburt off his feet. Black blood sprayed the walls. Ugga had little room to maneuver, but he managed to drive the upper point of the axe blade into the screaming creature's chest, forcing the troll backward. Quick as a fox, Elu leapt forward and stabbed the troll in the knee with his dagger, piercing the thick sinew. The troll trumpeted like an elephant and fell onto its side.

"Run!" Bonny said.

Off they went, but not before Elu stabbed the beast again in the sole of its foot, prompting another howl.

Bonny led them to a second crossroads, turning left and then right. Rathburt was limping and complaining, and whatever magic he had temporarily wielded seemed to have once again gone dormant. The light from the torch barely extended beyond Ugga, but it became obvious they were being pursued. A strange cacophony hounded them, growing louder and more frightening.

Lucius heard Bonny scream. Only it sounded more like a high-pitched squeal.

In the dim torchlight, he could see large figures slipping toward them—from both directions.

"We're trapped!" the pirate woman said. "We'll have to fight our way out."

Though his face felt hot and his vision blurry, Lucius managed to squeeze past her, holding the war club above his head and the *uttara* at waist level. The first of their assailants entered the torchlight: a Porisāda almost as large as Bard. The Mogol cannibal also wielded a war club, which glowed in response to the one Lucius held. Apparently the weapons were magically entwined.

There were more Porisādas behind the leader, and they too crept forward into the light. Lucius braced himself for attack, but he knew he was no match for these warriors. He found himself wishing Torg were with them.

*Goodbye, Laylah,* he thought to himself.

That's when he heard Ugga growl.

THOUGH UGGA'S vision was no better than that of his companions, his sense of smell was superior. He knew Bard's scent better than anyone's, but he had grown familiar with his other friends, as well. When the ghoulies had passed by them on the street, the stench had been overwhelming, assaulting his senses like a blast of foul wind. Even after they passed, the reek had lingered, making him want to vomit.

When the cave troll approached, Ugga smelled it before he saw it, turning just in time to counter the blow. Then Elu had come to the rescue, stabbing the beast with the dagger Master Hah-nah had given him.

*What a brave little guy!*

After that, they ran like fools, stumbling down the dark alley as quick as they could. But even as they fled, Ugga could smell the approach of more pursuers, including ghoulies and vam-pie-ers. But there was something worse, a scent unfamiliar to the crossbreed. And it was growing in intensity. Even the ghoulies and vam-pie-ers fled from it, crawling up the walls and disappearing onto rooftops.

The crossbreed felt hairs on the back of his neck start to rise. Aggressive instincts from his former existence took over, and he started to growl.

BARD HEARD Ugga's growl, but he had no time to turn and help his companion. The leader of the Porisādas pounded his war club against Lucius', knocking the weapon out of the firstborn's hand and driving him to the ground. Despite the cramped alleyway, Bard nocked an arrow, drew the feathers to his ear, and loosed it. The arrow zipped over Radburt's left shoulder, passed within a hair of Bonny's nose, and pierced the Porisāda chieftain in his heart.

With surprising agility, Missus Bonny met the next attacker, ducking under his club and stabbing him in the stomach with the point of her cutlass. But there was another behind the one she had just got—and many more beyond. In rapid succession, Bard loosed three more arrows, striking a different warrior each time. But for each fallen body, another immediately replaced it.

Bard cast down his bow and drew his daggers, which were carved from the talons of a mountain eagle—a present from Jord long ago. He squeezed past Rathburt, leaped over the fallen Lucius, and shoved Missus Bonny aside just in time to deflect a deadly blow. A poisoned dart struck the wall near his neck and another stuck in the sleeve of his coat, just missing his bicep. In a fit of anger Bard surged forward, wielding the daggers like claws. He was stronger than the wicked Mogols, and the close quarters worked to his advantage. At first the Porisādas were driven back, but then a dart found its mark, piercing Bard in the cheek. Instantly his vision clouded, and his legs went all wobbly.

As he collapsed, he heard Elu shouting in his high-pitched voice: "A Daasa comes. A Daasa!"

WHEN THE BEAR-man growled, Elu ran to his side, ready to confront whatever approached. But what he saw next caused even his brave heart to quail. The oddly shaped creature that came forward was as thick as a boulder, the walls of the alley breaking apart as it passed. Three pairs of snapping fangs sprang from its round, brown head.

A part of Elu wanted to run. He saw a hole at the bottom of the wall just large enough for his body, and he imagined himself crawling inside and escaping. Afterward he would find Torg and Laylah. *Who could blame him?* One of them had to survive to tell the story of the others. It was the smart thing to do.

But Elu had a warrior's courage, and his concern for his friends overwhelmed his desire to flee. He raised the Tugarian dagger and waved it in front of him. Blue fire leapt from the blade. The ruined Daasa halted for a moment, then came forward again. Elu braced himself, knowing he would prick the beast at least once before he was squished.

Instead of lunging, the Daasa stopped a pace away from Ugga, leaned back on its powerful haunches, and then hurdled Elu's companions, crushing down on the Porisādas. The Daasa continued forward, fast as a Buffalo, driving the rest of the warriors back and clearing the way for the others.

Bonny tossed the torch to Rathburt and then helped Lucius to his feet. The firstborn still held his *uttara*, but his war club lay on the ground. Rathburt knelt over Bard and plucked the dart from his cheek. The trapper remained pale and lifeless.

"We have to run," Bonny shouted. "Follow the Daasa!"

Ugga reached down, picked up Bard, and slung him over his shoulder. Rathburt grabbed Lucius' war club, and Elu scooped up Bard's bow. As a group, they chased after Bonny. Lucius' right shoulder seemed to Elu to be off-kilter, and his arm dangled limply, but he kept up the quick pace. The Daasa turned left, then right, then left again, and suddenly they were charging out of the alley. Before them was a vast open area teeming with Mogols, monsters, and pirates. Elu stopped and sighed. Surely they were doomed.


RATHBURT STOOD in the street and stared at the tumult, his eyes adjusting slowly to the morning light. Bard was hurt, maybe dying; Lucius also was injured. But even worse, the six of them—seven if you counted the ruined Daasa—had come face to face with an army of Mogols, pirates, and monsters. For one of the few times in his life, Rathburt found himself wishing Torg was with them. Showoff or not, he at least would be able to conjure enough magic to put up a respectable fight.

Still, Rathburt was not afraid. An eerie calm had come over him, sweeping away his cowardice. He held his staff in his right hand and Lucius' war club in his left and prepared to meet his doom.

*I'm no warrior*, he thought, *but I'll get at least one of you boogers.*

Even as his enemies closed around him, Rathburt felt a sudden surge of energy rush over his body—like a blast of wind filled with fire—causing him to cry out. The next moment, an enormous explosion shook Duccarita, and a great pillar of flame rose from an inner portion of the city. Shards of fiery wood, thrown high into the air, tumbled upon them like meteors, stunning the Mogols and pirates. Some of them ran, and others covered their faces, but the bravest raised their weapons and shouted words of defiance.

At that moment, the sun peeked over the eastern wall of Duccarita. The blinding light reflected off swords, daggers, and helms. In addition to all their other problems, Rathburt saw that there were golden soldiers in attendance. Could it get any worse? He shielded his eyes and stared.

Suddenly, as if leaping from the bedrock itself, a Daasa, transformed from timid to monstrous, sprang from a hole in the stone. Dozens, then hundreds, then thousands followed, emerging from the slave pits in a rush of rage. As if in a feeding frenzy, the horrid-looking beasts tore into their captors. Now even the bravest fled. But it was no use. The Daasa were too many and too fierce. The City of Thieves would soon be overrun.

An angry Daasa approached within a single pace. Rathburt had no desire to harm the creature. Even if he managed to kill it, he couldn't kill the rest. He lowered the war club and his staff, exposing his neck to the beast's clapping fangs.

But the Daasa did not attack. Instead, it raced off in search of other prey. *They mean us no harm. We are protected.*

At that moment Torg and Laylah appeared, walking toward them hand-in-hand, both as naked as the day they were born. The wizard held the Silver Sword in his free hand; the sorceress carried Obhasa. The Daasa avoided them as well, but killed everyone and everything else. The streets began to clear. The City of Thieves was being cleansed of its sinful keepers.

"Modesty is not your finest quality, *Torgon*," Rathburt whispered to himself. "Do you never tire of showing off?"

# 10

TORG WAS growing weary of being naked so much. Often when he wielded his magic, he could preserve his clothing with a protective sheath of blue energy. But when Laylah had released his chaotic power, his pirate outfit had been incinerated, as had hers. Silly as they were, he'd become fond of his colorful new clothes. At least they were warm. He wished he had Jord's ability to conjure magical clothing, but that highly convenient art surpassed him.

When a pair of terrified pirates tried to run past him, he reached out and banged their heads together, cracking their skulls. Then he removed their knee-length jackets and gave one to the sorceress.

"Here is my first present to you, my love," Torg said. "I made it myself."

Laylah laughed. "Why, thank you. I'll treasure it always, even if it does stink like cigars."

The carnage continued all around them, but Torg paid it little heed. His concerns over how Lucius initially would manage the Daasa no longer worried him. It was obvious the creatures were grateful for being rescued and knew whom to credit for it. But would that be enough for them to follow Lucius into battle against deadly enemies? That remained to be seen.

Amid the confusion, Torg noticed Ugga leaning over Bard, who was lying motionless on the street. He and Laylah raced over and knelt beside the handsome trapper. When Ugga saw Torg, his broad face brightened.

"Master Hah-nah, ya must help me Bard. A nasty dart stuck him in the face, and he is dying, I swears."

Torg saw a tiny prick of blood on Bard's cheek, just above his beard. A purple ring had expanded around it. He took Obhasa from Laylah.

"This must be done quickly," he said to the others. "Form a circle around us and be certain nothing disturbs me. I need to concentrate."

Torg lowered the rounded head of Obhasa and held it a finger-length above Bard's cheek. A tendril of blue-green flame, thin as a human hair, sprang from the staff and leapt into the wound, vaporizing the poison that lingered near the surface. Then Torg touched the wound with his sensitive fingertips, sensing that some of the poison already was working its way into Bard's brain. Torg willed more healing energy into the wound, until the trapper's entire face became encased in magical fire. Suddenly Bard's back arched and body convulsed. Without hesitation, Torg pressed his mouth against Bard's, exhaling healing essence into his companion's lungs. Bard's body went limp, but the color slowly returned to his face.

Ugga sobbed. "Have ya healed him, Master Hah-nah? Have ya saved me Bard with a kiss?"

"The Mogols use terrible poisons that usually kill within moments, but Bard is stronger than most," Torg responded. "He'll sleep a little bit, but I believe he'll be fine when he wakes. It was close. A while longer, and it might have been too late."

Bonny tugged on the sleeve of Torg's new coat.

"Lucius is hurt too," the pirate woman said, motioning to the firstborn, who tottered nearby.

"I'll be all right," Lucius said with a grimace, but his right shoulder drooped, and his arm was swollen throughout its length.

"He saved me from a Porisāda," Bonny said, her eyes full of adoration. "Can you heal him like you healed Bard?"

Torg walked over to Lucius. "I can heal you. But it might be a while before you regain full strength in the arm."

"Do I have any choice? I won't be much good at leading my new army the way I am now."

Torg smiled. "From the looks of your arm, a bone has been broken. And your shoulder needs to be forced back into place. That might hurt the worst."

Lucius nodded and gritted his teeth. When it was over, the firstborn's arm and shoulder were healed, and his posture returned to normal. This relieved Bonny, but she finally noticed that Rakkhati was not among them, giving Torg a quizzical look.

"Rakkhati did not survive the horror of the *Mahanta pEpa*," Torg said to her.

Bonny's dark eyes filled with tears. "I will miss him so much. He rescued me from the streets and introduced me to the glory of *Ekadeva*, the *One God*. I was a terrible person before I repented."

The pirate woman then took Lucius' left hand in hers. "I'm a good woman now," she said to the firstborn. "With Rakkhati gone, I have nowhere to go. Can I come along with you? I promise not to cause trouble. And I can fight better than you might think."

Lucius smiled at her. "My lady, it would be an honor if you joined me. As for your past, it can't be any worse than mine. But I can't swear to you that I'll ever believe in *Ekadeva, Uppādetar* or any other. In fact, right now I'm sick and tired of gods of any kind."

"The *One God* will change you, but I promise not to bother you about it. We'll win our war first and talk about God later."

Lucius said, "Fair enough."

Torg agreed. *Fair enough.*

WHEN BONNY came to him and offered her services in battle, Lucius was stunned again. Why she cared so much about him was baffling, but he wasn't about to complain. In a short time he had grown quite fond of the red-haired pirate. Any time he thought of her, his emotional pain over losing Laylah became far more tolerable to bear.

However, something entirely new distracted Lucius even more than his injuries or feelings for Bonny. A source he could not identify assaulted a portion of his mind, as if someone or something was trying to communicate with him in a language he could not comprehend.

Bonny noticed his strange expression and patted his back. "Are you all right, sweety? Is the pain still bugging you? Maybe you should sit down and rest."

Lucius heard her voice, but it sounded far away.

"Firstborn, what disturbs you?" said the wizard, who also noticed his distraction.

"I'm not sure," Lucius muttered. "There's a weird sort of buzzing in my head. Could one of those darts have hit me? Wait . . . listen . . . can't you hear it?"

Laylah moved beside Torg. "The Daasa are making all kinds of noise," the sorceress said to Lucius. "It sounds as if they're tearing down half the city. Is that what you mean?"

But Lucius could not understand her. The noise inside his head continued to intensify. Lucius' vision began to blur, and his legs went out from under him again. This time Bonny caught him and lowered him gently to the ground. Now he was barely lucid, his mind spiraling out of control.

In a series of frenetic memories, the firstborn found himself reliving his life—backward.

He was in Avici, helping Laylah escape.

He was humiliated by Mala in the training grounds east of Uccheda.

He was reporting nervously to Invictus.

He was riding in a wagon from Kilesa to Avici.

He was being taught to read and write in the learning academies deep in the catacombs of Kilesa.

He was rising, twisting, tearing out of a pod of clingy goo, taking his first gasps of air. Invictus was there with his scientists and magicians, watching his birth with fascination. Lucius could see the shredded remains of the body that had borne him. It was swollen, pink, and splattered.

It once had been a Daasa.

In sudden comprehension, Lucius realized with horror that Invictus was using the living bodies of the pink-skinned creatures to magically breed his army of newborns. No wonder the sorcerer had been resistant to Mala's requests to tame Duccarita. Invictus needed the *Mahanta pEpa* to prevent the Daasa from shape-shifting, not so that he could torture them, but so that he could use their bodies as birthing chambers.

Lucius had been the first to be born this way.

The Daasa, in effect, were his kin. They shared the same flesh.

And the same oneness of mind.

Lucius sat up and let out a shout, nearly giving Bonny a heart attack.

"You bastaaaarrrrd!" he screamed with all his might.

"What's wrong with Master Loo-shus?" he heard Ugga saying. Somehow the crossbreed's gentle voice brought Lucius back to full awareness. The others stood in front of him, their expressions a mixture of confusion and concern.

"For Anna's sake," Rathburt whined. "Not even *The Torgon* ever scared me that bad. Are you trying to end all our lives?"

But Lucius wasn't listening. "Jord must have known. That's why she brought us here. She must have *known*. But how is that possible? Did she *see*?"

"See what?" Ugga and Rathburt said in perplexed unison.

"What Invictus has done. Of all his cruel acts, this is the worst."

Though the others remained baffled, Torg seemed to intuit what Lucius was trying to say. The wizard turned and faced the slave pits, raising Obhasa aloft. A burst of blue flame, laced with tendrils of green, scorched the air like dragon fire. "Behold!" he shouted in a voice so loud even Lucius was startled. "The army of the *Pathamaja* (Firstborn) has won its first battle. And now it returns to its general!"

Only what returned was not ten thousand monsters with clapping fangs and swollen bodies. Instead, the Daasa had reverted to their gentler form. One by one, they wandered up, their pink faces beaming like children without a care in the world.

"Aaaaah . . ." Bonny said.

Lucius felt the same kind of affection. And when he stepped forward, the first of the returning Daasa gathered around him. Some even lay on their backs, like submissive dogs wanting their tummies scratched.

# Faerie and Ghost Child

# 11

JORD WAS NOT helpless, but her powers to maim were limited. In an aerial battle pitting flame against flame, she was not Bhayatupa's match. Her charred carcass had fallen from the sky, smiting the outside of one of the walls and tumbling downward before finally coming to rest on a patch of bare ground tucked within a jumble of boulders. There her remains sizzled like an old bonfire. Later that night, it rained hard for a brief time, extinguishing the cinders and leaving a scorched bundle of flesh, feathers, and hollow bones.

After the rainstorm, the night air became clear and warm. Invisible to the naked eye, millions of mushroom spores floated in the breeze. A few hundred came to rest in the damp dirt near the corpse, forming a circle around it as if planted by an unseen gardener.

On the same morning that the Daasa bowed to Lucius, the mushrooms began to sprout. At first their miniature caps and stalks were barely recognizable, appearing as tiny buttons on the surface of the soil. But they quickly grew to maturity, the stalks rising upward and the caps enlarging and then unfolding like a series of pale umbrellas, forming what the native people of Mahaggata would have called a *fairy circle*. According to legend, tiny winged sprites danced within these circles until exhaustion overtook their playfulness. The sprites then used the mushrooms as seats on which to rest.

As the thin gills beneath the caps spread wide, the mushrooms released more spores. But instead of floating off in search of new habitats, the spores were drawn within the circle, where they began to spin faster and faster, eventually forming a miniature whirlwind that glowed like green phosphorus and crackled like lightning. As the sun rose round and hot above the horizon, the whirlwind collapsed upon itself, consuming Sakuna's remains as it imploded.

The giant eagle was gone, replaced by something else. A woman lay quivering on the ground. Not until noon did she manage to struggle to her knees.

Her skin was pale, her eyes green, her hair long and white.
Jord had returned to the Realm of Life.

# 12

IN THE BLACK, barren depths of the demon world, the baby had cried.
Once again she had been abandoned in the darkness, hungry and afraid.
Thousands of *efrits* gathered around her, her wails attracting them like moths
lured to light. Demons wandered by and listened, but they knew better than
to get too close. If the baby were harmed, the mother's wrath would shower
upon them. In the Realm of the Undead, Vedana reigned supreme.

The baby looked like nothing that existed in the Realm of Life. The
closest comparison would be a black worm constantly changing size and
shape, though at one end there was something that resembled a face with a
mouth and tongue.

Within the wriggling worm, a consciousness had begun to emerge. Like
that of any infant, it was buried deep in a foggy haze of hunger and desire. But
it was there, gaining focus.

Every moment it grew stronger. Every moment its awareness increased.

At a crucial juncture of development, when Mother was away, the baby
had reached out and spoken to Father as he wandered through the wilderness
with his companions.

*I'm alive,* she had told him.

"*Dhiite! Dhiitaake!*" he had cried in response. (Daughter! Little daughter!)

But the wizard had recognized her as more than just his offspring.

Though born of a demon, the karma now thriving within his first and
only child had been familiar. After all, it had once been known as . . .

. . . Peta.

# March of the Asēkhas

# 13

SINCE THE TUGARS' encounter with Mala at Dibbu-Loka several months before, Chieftain-Kusala, leader of the Asēkhas, had learned once and for all that it was better to obey Torg without asking too many questions, even if his lord's mood had seemed fey. Kusala understood—as did the Tugars—that the Death-Knower was their only real hope against Invictus.

Since that time, Kusala and the Asēkhas had been reunited with Torg at Kamupadana, the Whore City, and had escorted him and his companions into the wilderness, where they were pursued and finally chased down by Mala and his army. Rather than permitting Kusala to remain with Torg, Kusala's king had issued yet another baffling command.

"Kusala, deter Mala for as long as you can. But *do not die*. When you are overmatched . . . *flee!*"

Kusala had been loathe to abandon his king. But from the sound of it, the enemy approached too quickly for further argument. Kusala had bowed and then raced up the path, followed by eighteen other Asēkha warriors. When they emerged from the thicket of vines, the leading edge of Mala's army greeted them. More than one hundred black wolves surged toward them, each bearing a Porisāda warrior loosing arrows and launching poisoned darts from the wolves' backs.

Podhana, Churikā, and seven others released a spray of missiles from their slings. The small iron beads pierced flesh and bone, and soon more than twenty Porisādas, and at least that many wolves, were slain. Meanwhile, Kusala, Rati, Tāseti, and the seven remaining warriors charged forward, wielding *uttaras* in one hand and Tugarian daggers in the other. Though the wolves stood as tall as horses and weighed close to half a ton apiece, the Asēkhas were not intimidated.

Kusala somersaulted forward, hacking off the front legs of the wolf on his right with his *uttara* and simultaneously stabbing another between the ribs with his dagger, twisting the blade with deadly force. As the beasts tumbled to the ground, their riders were thrown. Rati decapitated both before they could stand.

Tāseti leapt high over the head of a wolf and landed on its back above the rear limbs, then drove a lightning-quick backstroke into the rider's neck, killing him instantly. She severed the wolf's spine with another stroke before pouncing onto a second wolf to record more kills.

In a short time, more than one hundred wolves and riders had fallen. Now the Asēkhas stood in a spread formation, awaiting the next wave of assailants. Not one of the desert warriors had suffered an injury. However, when the main strength of the enemy thundered into view, the Asēkhas found themselves outnumbered fifty to one. To make matters worse, several cave trolls and a dozen druids joined the melee. The trolls wielded iron hammers that weighed as much as small trees. A straight-on blow from one of these weapons could injure even an Asēkha. The druids also were terrifically strong, and they spat acidic liquid from their mouths.

Kusala and his warriors fought with increased intensity, hacking six of the druids to pieces and butchering two trolls. During this skirmish, Rati suffered a glancing blow to the back of the head from a Porisāda war club, which he most likely found more embarrassing than painful, knowing him.

Next to emerge from the woods was Mala. Because of the heavy chain he bore, the monster could no longer run as fast as an ordinary snow giant, though he still seemed able to move quickly when the mood struck him. But when Mala appeared, he was in no particular hurry, seeming content to allow his minions to do the brunt of the fighting. A Kojin shadowed Mala, and the arrival of these two giants inspired the rest of the army. Not even the Asēkhas were capable of withstanding that much might for any significant length of time.

Kusala shouted a Tugarian command.

"*Paharati ca Evati!*" In the ancient tongue, this meant *kill and flee*. Kusala knew all too well that his warriors despised retreat, so he was at least giving them permission to wreak as much havoc as possible during their flight. Then Kusala let out a high-pitched shriek that only Tugars were capable of hearing. The sound carried for more than a league. For better or worse, Torg now knew that Kusala and the rest of the Asēkhas were withdrawing.

"Take care, my lord," Kusala whispered. "We hope to meet you again in better times, whether in this life or the next."

Then he blended into the forest and was gone.

AT DAWN THE following morning—the same day that Torg and his companions, now separated from the Asēkhas, entered the valley of the Hornbeam—Kusala sat cross-legged on a gray sheet of shale that overhung a bubbling stream. The northern foothills of the Gap of Gamana were as quiet as a soft breath. A flock of birds flew playfully among the trees, unaware of Kusala's presence. His eyes were closed, his face peaceful, his body motionless. A starling with a yellow beak flew down and perched on the thick muscles at the base of his neck, probably mistaking him for an odd-shaped boulder.

Soon Tāseti and the others joined Kusala. They sat together by the stream and watched their inhalations and exhalations with extreme concentration, emptying their minds of thought. It was possible to pass within a few paces of the warriors and not see a single one, so naturally did they merge with their surroundings. Tugars believed invisibility was a state of mind: Silence the mind, and the body became difficult to see.

Eventually Kusala spoke, his voice blending harmonically with the ripples of the stream. Only then did the starling take flight.

"We will cross the gap, skirt the eastern foothills, and proceed to Nissaya."

Another period of silence greeted these words. As expected, Tāseti was the next to speak. "Chieftain, should we not circle around the *Badaalataa* and search for *Lord Torgon?*"

Kusala took a deep breath and released it slowly. "You saw what he did to me at Dibbu-Loka when I pressed him. I will not do so again. He wants me to return to Anna with the noble ones—and for the rest of you to join the defense of Nissaya. Torg will attempt to reach the White City without our help. Call it madness, if you like, but it is our duty to obey him. And it is not like he is defenseless."

"*Lord Torgon* is *Maranavidu* (a Knower of Death). He is beyond us," Churikā whispered. "Naught else need be said."

Kusala's eyes flared in response to the young Asēkha's bold words. Churikā was Sōbhana's replacement, the most recent of their order, and she was similar to her predecessor in manner and appearance, though a finger-length taller.

"Sometimes the young—even those who are brash—perceive things more clearly than their elders," Kusala said. "Churikā speaks the truth. Torg *is* beyond us. We are merely his soldiers."

"There is no shame in that," Podhana said. "I would rather be Lord Torgon's pawn than a king among kings."

"*Satthar . . . Satthar . . . Satthar . . .* (Master . . . Master . . . Master . . .)" several others chanted in response.

"It is well we are reminded of whom we serve and why," Kusala added. "In the words of the great and wise Churikā, 'naught else need be said.' So let us begin our journey southward. Nissaya is more than one hundred and twenty leagues from this place. I intend to reach the fortress in fewer than ten days."

"The land is rugged, and it is likely we will encounter resistance," Tāseti said. "If we have to stop and fight, ten days will be unattainable."

"*Fewer* than ten days," Kusala reminded.


WHEN THE NEED is dire, Asēkhas can journey amazing distances in relatively short periods of time. On the blazing sands of Tējo, Kusala once traveled more than thirty leagues in a single day on the back of a camel, and it was not unheard of to walk a hundred leagues in five days. But despite their adaptability, Asēkhas still were creatures of the desert. The mountains and foothills of Mahaggata were not their preferred terrain.

The most difficult part of their journey would be near its beginning, when they would be forced to cross the Gap of Gamana. Kusala had no idea how they would accomplish this without skirmishes, but he hoped he and his warriors would clash with relatively small groups, dispatching and moving on. If they could reach the foothills south of the gap, there would be plenty of cover and less enemy activity. From there, he believed they could proceed to Nissaya with relative ease.

After their meeting at the stream, it took the Asēkhas a full day and night to march between a pair of mountains and reach the northern border of the gap. At dawn, they crouched beneath a rock shelter and chewed on Cirāya, the green cactus that provided liquid and nutrition. If rationed carefully, the cactus fiber would last the entire journey, but Kusala didn't believe they would have to go to that extreme. South of the gap, game and wild vegetables would be plentiful, and there were villages and farms near the western shore of Lake Ti-ratana. The enemy might occupy some of these, but the Tugars had friends in many places.

This forest lined the northern border of the gap, followed by a league or so of tall grasses that also provided concealment. But after that came at least five leagues of open plain. The Asēkhas would have to wait until dark before attempting to cross.

"Let's eat, then get some sleep," Kusala said. "It's been a while since we've had a good rest. At night, our chances of proceeding unseen will be improved, though the black wolves can see better in the dark than day."

"We could split apart and regroup," Podhana suggested.

"I prefer we remain together," Kusala said. "If . . . *when* we have to fight, we'll be more effective as a single unit. Besides, I'm in the mood for killing. Let them come."

They broke camp at dusk and moved through the forest into the tall grass. A broad layer of clouds swept across the sky, glowing in the moonlight. Even ordinary eyes could see for hundreds of paces.

"Karma is not on our side," Kusala said. "But I will wait no longer to cross. Too much is at stake to linger."

They left the security of the tall grass and entered the plain. Their black outfits and hair provided camouflage in the darkness, but they still felt exposed. The Asēkhas moved silently at a steady jog in a single line, soon encountering their first signs of trouble, a large enemy camp stretching for more than a league in both directions. At least five thousand soldiers, Mogols and wolves were strewn across the field, gathering around at least a hundred bonfires. Kusala marveled at the effort it had taken just to drag this much deadwood into the plain.

"We might as well have crossed this morning," he whispered to Tāseti. "Do you have suggestions?"

"We have no choice but to take the long way around," the second in command said. "Not even the Asēkhas can fight this many. We must withdraw now. But do we flee to the east or west?"

"If we go east, we'll eventually reach the shores of Ti-ratana," Kusala said. "Forest borders most of the lake, so we would again have cover. But the farther east we travel, the closer we'll come to the specter of Avici."

A scuffling sound interrupted their debate. Churikā came forward bearing a struggling captive, her hand clasped over his mouth. The golden soldier, minus his armor, had a terrified look in his eyes. His padded breeches were down at his knees.

"I found this one relieving himself away from the others," the warrior said. "Perhaps he can enlighten us."

Kusala glared at the captive. "When she removes her hand, make no sound," he said. "If you do as you're told, I will allow you to live."

The wild-eyed soldier nodded, his face so red it appeared swollen. Churikā slowly released her grip.

"Whisper . . . remember to whisper," Kusala warned. "Now, tell me: Is there any place we can cross where the land is free of eyes?"

"The gap is full," the soldier said in a voice so low even Kusala strained to hear. "The bosses are claiming that a wizard is about, and the King wants him dead. But I don't care about no wizards, and I don't want no troubles with you. I just had to pee, is all. I was about to go to *bed!*"

"If that's all he's worth, we might as well end his life now," Tāseti said.

The soldier started to yelp, but Churikā clasped her hand over his mouth once again. Kusala waggled his finger.

"No . . . no . . . no."

The soldier nodded. Again Churikā released him.

"There is something that could work . . . maybe," the soldier whispered hopefully.

"Name," Kusala said.

"Name?"

"What is your name?"

"Ohhh, uh, Fabius . . . sir."

"You were saying, Fabius?"

"I was saying? Ohhh . . . yes. It's just a thought, mind you, but I *might* know a way you could sneak across. I heard some of the bosses talking earlier about a big bunch of wagons coming from Avici to help with the war. They were to be brought around north of Ti-ratana and stocked with supplies as they moved through the farmlands—and then taken to Nissaya to help feed our army when it arrives there. When the wagons cross the gap, they'll be lightly guarded—you know, because they're empty right now. You might be able to steal a ride. Could you sneak into the beds without being seen? Or maybe you're strong enough to hang on underneath?" Kusala said nothing, intensifying the soldier's discomfort. "Does that help at all?" More silent staring. "Are you going to kill me, anyway?"

Kusala's face grew soft, as if he had been sincerely mollified. "Your idea has merit. We'll consider it. But I have another question: What should we do with *you?*"

The soldier's eyes brightened. "If you let me go, I promise I won't say anything to anybody. I'll wrap myself in my bedroll and go right to sleep."

"You expect us to believe that? Do you take the Asēkhas for fools?"

"The *Asēkhas?* I . . . I . . . no, of course not. I meant no offense, SIR!"

"Shhhhhh . . . *lower* your voice."

"Yes . . . *sir.*"

Kusala rested his hand on Fabius' shoulder. "Do you doubt the honor of the Asēkhas?" he said sternly.

"Doubt it? Of course not. No one doubts it."

"You wouldn't lie to me, would you?"

"No . . . sir."

"Do you remember my vow?"

"You said you wouldn't kill me if I behaved. Which I *did.* I'm not lying about the wagons, neither."

"An honorable man can sense honor in another. I want to believe you, Fabius, but it behooves me to be *cautious.*"

"Cautious? Does that mean you're going to kill me?"

"No. A vow is a vow. This is what I'm going to do, for the sake of *caution.* While the rest of us go to find the wagons, Churikā will remain here with you . . . just to ensure we get a good head start. At midnight she'll let you go, but she'll stay here and watch you enter the camp, just in case. If you betray us, she will hunt you down and kill you in the most painful manner she can devise, regardless of who tries to stop her. Do you doubt it?"

"No, sir. And I'll stay quiet as a mouse, I promise. I *am* an honorable man, just like you."

"Very well, Fabius. We'll be going now. If you're not 'quiet as a mouse,'

Churikā will cut off your head. Do you think you can stop her?"

"I know I can't," the soldier whispered. "But she won't have to. I'll behave myself, I promise."

"From one honorable man to another, I hope you do."

A LITTLE BEFORE midnight, the cloud cover thickened, and cool rain began to fall. The soldier shivered miserably in his underclothes. Churikā took mercy and motioned for Fabius to return to his camp.

"I'll be watching from the darkness," she said. "If you betray us, the first thing I'll do is fillet your little cock with my dagger. Then I'll jam my sword into the hole between your buttocks—and twist the blade."

Fabius went pale. "Yes, sir . . . er, ma'am . . . er, mistress. I won't say a word to nobody. All I want to do is curl up in my blanket. No one will ever know this happened."

"Go, then."

"Now?"

"Yes. Now!"

"Thank you, mistress."

Then he stumbled toward the nearest fire. Soon after, Churikā sprinted off—but not in the direction of Ti-ratana.

The moment Fabius entered the camp, he lost his honor and began to scream at anyone and everyone. "The Asēkas are here . . . and the Tugars—a whole *army* of them. Someone save me. She's going to cut off my cock!"

Meanwhile, the rain began to fall harder, causing the bonfires to hiss and crackle. Soon, it became a downpour. Internally the bonfires remained blazing hot, but externally they were temporarily extinguished, causing them to exude enormous amounts of smoke. Wolves bearing Mogol warriors were sent east to hunt down the invaders, along with several hundred hastily gathered soldiers. A dozen more wolves and riders went off in the direction that the Asēkha assassin was said to be lurking. But Kusala and the other Asēkhas, who had paid little heed to Fabius' earlier suggestion, had moved half a league to the west and were watching the delirium while lying on their chests in the short grass.

The Asēkhas watched and waited—for just the right moment. When the downpour intensified yet another notch, Kusala leapt up and ran toward the western flank of the camp.

"*Paharati ca Evati* (Kill and flee!)" he shouted. The Asēkhas raced forward like a herd of snarling beasts armed with razor-sharp claws. Golden soldiers fell, along with Mogols, wolves, vampires, and ghouls. Kusala and the Asēkhas entered *frenzy*, and they were not to be denied.

By the time the storm ended, several hundred of the enemy lay dead or maimed.

The Asēkhas, meanwhile, had accomplished their goal. They had crossed the gap.

THOUGH KUSALA had never had any intention of following the soldier's *suggestion*, it did plant a seed in his methodical mind. If indeed there were a line of wagons headed southward along Ti-ratana's shore, it would be wise to disrupt it. Kusala believed Torg would have agreed, if he were with them. His king rarely passed up an opportunity to befuddle the enemy.

"But you said you wanted to reach Nissaya in *fewer* than ten days," Tāseti argued after being told of Kusala's plan. "Now you want to add more to our duties?"

"We're very close to Ti-ratana already, a couple of leagues at most," Kusala countered. "I simply want to go to the shore and see what we see. If there are no signs of wagons, we'll continue southward. But if they do exist, and we can disrupt their passage, we'll reduce Mala's supply line. It's a temptation I can't resist."

Churikā, whose youthful boldness seemed to have no bounds, spoke next. "It appears our ruse fooled the enemy. But it could end up working against us. Many of them had already marched off—in the direction of Ti-ratana—before we assailed what remained of their camp. If they reach the wagons before we do, they will no longer be lightly guarded."

*She reminds me so much of Sōbhana.* "If that's the case, we won't reveal ourselves," Kusala said. "Torg made it clear that he wanted all of the Asēkhas to stay alive. That is my intention, as well. But I'll allow no further discussion on this matter. Let us make our way to the lake. Dawn approaches, and I would prefer to arrive while a little darkness yet remains."

Kusala and the Asēkhas trotted into the lightly forested area between the eastern foothills of the Mahaggatas and the western coast of Ti-ratana. Eventually they passed into the open field of a lakeside farm that its human inhabitants appeared to have abandoned. Spinach, carrots, and corn had already been planted, and even this early in the spring, some of the spinach was ready to harvest. In the distance they could hear the bleating of goats and the yapping of cattle dogs. Something stirred these creatures, but the desert warriors were too far away to determine what it might be.

As they neared the lake, the field dipped sharply downward, revealing Ti-ratana's glittering surface. A pair of fifty-oared galleys was anchored offshore, and several kabangs roped to a half-dozen dinghies had been dragged onto the sandy bank. Just a few paces from the water's edge, an angry interrogation was taking place in the light of a blazing fire. The Asēkhas crouched in the darkness, gauging the situation. Soon after, they moved in close enough to hear what was happening.

A tiny man—entirely naked—was being harshly questioned by what appeared to be a high-ranking golden soldier and a ship captain probably in the soldier's employ. A dozen other tiny people, two of whom were cradling whimpering infants, were roped at their ankles, Mogol-style, off to the side. They looked nervous, but not cowed.

"Where did she say she was going?" the soldier shouted at the prisoner.

"I tell you before," the little man responded, "she say nothing to Moken. She and man who look like you fly away on *baby dragon*. Moken and his people see them no more."

The Mogol reached down and slapped Moken hard on the face.

"If you don't tell me the truth, I'll kill all of you," the soldier said. "But the children will die first—and it won't be quick or quiet. I'll ask you one last time, where did she say she was . . ."

". . . goiiiiing" came out of his mouth as his head separated from his shoulders and tumbled into the fire, still wearing an expression of disbelief. The Mogol was the next to lose his head, and the thirty or so other captors died, silently, within the next few moments. After being freed of their bindings, the boat people bowed at the feet of the Asēkhas.

"Rise, there is no need for deference," Kusala said. "Your enemies are our enemies." Then he pointed at the galleys anchored offshore. "Do you know how many of our enemy remain aboard?"

"At least thirty on each boat, and one hundred other big people who are their slaves. They somehow find us in darkness. Moken surprised."

"What did the soldier want to know?"

"Golden-haired lady and golden-haired man were with us. The bad man wanted to know where they go. But Moken does not know."

"Very well. Rest assured that those who remain on the ships will soon be removed from their posts. Where you go from here is your business. We'll take one of the galleys. You may have the other."

"Moken grateful, but big oars too heavy," the little man said. "My people just want to return to our kabangs and be left alone."

As the first sliver of sun peeked over the lake's horizon, a team of Asēkhas boarded each galley. Most of the crew surrendered without a fight, knowing the futility of facing the most supreme of desert warriors in battle. The few who did resist were quickly dispatched, taken ashore, and thrown into the fire. The air stank of burning flesh.

The slaves onboard were composed mostly of men and women kidnapped from villages along the shores of Ti-ratana and the banks of the Ogha, but there also were several Mahaggatan natives, including a female Bhasuran who had been forced to serve as a cook.

Kusala and Tāseti interrogated the captain of the second vessel. After surrendering faster than anyone else, he claimed to have found Moken and his people more by luck than design, though he and the others had been searching for almost two weeks.

"The day after the sun went funny, we were sent out," he said, obviously trying to please Kusala any way he could. "It was big stuff straight from the tower. Somehow the dracools figured out that the boat people knew things about the king's sister, though how the little lake rats would know anything about her is beyond me. But when it comes to the tower, you do what you're told and don't ask questions."

"If you call my friends 'little lake rats' again, I will hack off both your legs just beneath your scrawny butt," Kusala said. "After that, you'll get to feel what it's like to be little."

The captain flushed and made a series of hysterical squeals.

Kusala slapped his face. "Be quiet! I have more questions. The value of your answers will determine whether I allow you to live."

"I'll do my best, I promise."

"Shut up and pay attention. When will Invictus' army march on Nissaya?"

The captain answered quickly, his voice quivering. "When I left Avici, the army was almost ready. But General Mala was gone in search of the king's sister, and I don't know what's happened since."

Kusala sighed. "What *do* you know?"

Sweat erupted on the captain's brow, but he did not respond.

"Here's another question," Kusala said. "What can you tell me about supply wagons supposedly moving this way?"

The captain's face brightened. "This I *do* know," he said with hopeful eyes. "Yesterday eve, we anchored in a harbor to restock, and there I saw wagons moving along the northern shore—at least a hundred of the big eight-wheelers."

The captain grinned as if he had just made a friend, but Kusala remained stern.

"How well were the wagons guarded?"

"Guarded? There were a few dozen armored horsemen sniffing about. And . . . and . . . come to think of it, a woman drove each of the wagons, or at least it looked that way to me from where I was standing."

Then the captain scratched his head, as if trying to comprehend why the Asēkha chieftain would care about a few wagons. "If you're thinking of a raid, there's no reason. Those wagons were *empty*, except for some old wooden barrels. They're not carrying anything of value, unless you've got an urge to raise oxen." He laughed nervously.

Kusala's eyes grew darker. "My reasons are my own. Do you presume to tell me what to do?"

"No . . . *no!*" the captain said, still trying to sound accommodating, though spittle oozed from the corners of his trembling lips. "Whatever you want is fine with me."

Kusala spat at the captain's feet. "I'm through with you. Tell your men to sit still and behave themselves. Anyone who tries to flee will be slain."

"Yes . . . *yes,*" the captain said, and then he stormed about and yelled at his men in a pathetic attempt to sound brave.

Meanwhile, Kusala pulled Tāseti aside. "What do you make of it?"

"I'm not sure what to think . . . because I have no idea what *you're* thinking. You've gone from being in a rush to reach Nissaya to wanting to trot all over Triken. I admit that gaining control of these ships was a bold move that will hasten our journey, but only if we leave now. The captain is a fool, but he's right about one thing: The wagons are a waste of our time."

"As my Vasi master used to say, I've had a gut feeling about those wagons from the beginning," Kusala said. "If they are truly meant to bring supplies to Mala's army, wouldn't they need a sizeable force to secure and load the supplies? Something doesn't feel right. Either Invictus wants to make it seem as if the wagons are worthless, or the women guarding them are more formidable than they appeared to our brave captain."

Kusala then told Tāseti more details about his conversation with Torg on the ledge above the rock shelter, including the wizard's description of the *undines*, creatures of the demon world who infect human bodies and turn them into zombies.

"And you think these barrels might contain these hideous things?" Tāseti asked.

"The captain said that women drove most of the wagons. Could they be witches and hags in disguise? Torg was worried that the *undines* would be released into the Ogha north of Senasana—but why not Ti-ratana, as well? Tens of thousands of innocents live along its western shores and drink from its cold waters. Invictus and the witches could be scheming to create an army of zombies that could march on the fortress, while infecting everyone in its path. We might be in a position to stop something before it starts."

"All right, chieftain. I suppose we should investigate. But if you want me to stop whining, then you'll have to do one more thing."

"Yes, Tāseti?"

"Allow us *eleven* days to reach Nissaya."

They both laughed.

# 14

THE BOAT PEOPLE made it clear that they wanted nothing to do with the war between the big peoples, but Moken agreed, out of respect for the Asēkhas, to take charge of the captain and his crew. The Asēkhas bound their wrists and ankles and crowded them into the dinghies, which were secured by long ropes to Moken's fleet of kabangs.

"Take them to the middle of Ti-ratana and set them adrift," Kusala said. "No matter how much they plead or beg, show them no mercy—for they would have shown none to you. If karma allows, they will be found before they starve or drown."

"But we surely will die," the captain whined. "The lake is as vast as the Great Desert."

"You know nothing," Kusala said. "Tējo would swallow Ti-ratana in a single gulp."

When the boat people departed with their captives in tow, it was nearly noon on a clear, warm day.

More than warm. Hot.

But to the desert warriors, the heat was blessed.

Afterward, Kusala met with the slaves. "You are free to go where you wish. But we will not be able to accompany you to your homes. If you proceed alone, the dangers will be great. If you stay with us and man the oars, you will remain under our protection. There are strong men and women among you. The boldest will be armed and invited to fight at our sides. I plan to strike the enemy where it least expects. After that, we will travel in haste to Nissaya—and I will see to it that you will be allowed to pass within the safety of the fortress' walls. What say you?"

The Bhasuran woman was the first to step forward. "I will seek my own people," she said in the common tongue. "There is no place for me in halls of stone. But I will return with warriors and aid you, if I can."

Kusala bowed and bade her farewell. A dozen others also departed, but almost ninety remained. Within the ship's hold, the Asēkhas found enough swords and daggers to arm twenty of the strongest, including three women, one of whom was a Senasanan countess well-trained in the art of swordsmanship.

"I prefer the rapier," she said, gripping the hilt of a heavy longsword with disdain. "But this will do. I have long wanted to test myself against an Asēkha, but fighting next to one will be almost as fulfilling."

"Fighting an Asēkha with a rapier would be like fighting a slab of stone with the stem of a water willow," Churikā said in characteristic brashness. "You are welcome to fight alongside us, but do not insult us."

The woman started to protest, but the look in Churikā's eyes stopped her cold. Instead, she lowered her head and hurried away.

"Remind me never to assign you the role of diplomat," Kusala said to the newest Asēkha.

"Do you wish me to apologize?"

Kusala chuckled. "Just go easy on the others. None of them are Tugars, Churikā. But for now they'll have to do."

It was late afternoon before they finally launched the galleys and proceeded northward along the coast of Ti-ratana. Kusala and eight Asēkhas rode in one of the long crafts, while Tāseti and eight others occupied the other. Earlier that day, Kusala had sent away Rati, the nineteenth warrior.

"I do not wish to split us apart, but the need is dire," Kusala had said to Rati. "You must journey with great haste to Senasana. Once there, patrol the river north of the city and watch for anything suspicious. Torg feared the witches would try to release *undines* into the Ogha to infect the citizenry. Do whatever is necessary to prevent this from happening."

Rati had nodded and then trotted off. Kusala hated to waste a fine warrior on such a vague assignment, but he believed Torg would have issued a similar command.

As fate would have it, the wind had grown annoyingly still. But the galleys—smaller and sleeker than their ocean-going cousins—were equipped with only a single square sail and depended more on oarsmen than on wind. All but half a dozen of the oars on each boat were manned, so the galleys soon glided along at almost ten knots.

Kusala purposely kept them about a mile offshore, just close enough for a decent view of the shoreline. Occasionally they witnessed activity near the water's edge: a skirmish between villagers and several Mogols mounted on black wolves; a flock of vultures feasting on the remains of an unidentifiable carcass. But no wagons. As dusk approached, even Kusala began to lose enthusiasm for the mission.

"I had hoped karma would intervene and reveal the whereabouts of the enemy," he said. "But it appears that fate is against us."

"Our oarsmen appear able to row great distances without rest," Tāseti said with admiration. "If we turn about now, we can still reach Ti-ratana's southern shore in a day. From there, if we press hard, we can make it to Nissaya in nine days or less. What say you, chieftain?"

"We'll continue north until dusk," Kusala said. "If we've found nothing by then, I'll be ready to give up."

This seemed to satisfy the second in command. "Perhaps karma *will* intervene. For the two centuries you and I have been comrades, karma has always flowed smoothly alongside you."

"Your words honor me," Kusala said.

But as darkness crept across the lake, he finally raised his arms in defeat, ordering the ships to be brought about. Just then, however, Podhana let out a shout. "Chieftain, wagons approach!"

The first of them rolled into view along the shoreline—and they kept coming, stretching for half a mile. As the cowardly captain had described, each wagon bore just one driver. In addition, fifty armored horsemen accompanied the caravan.

"What now, chieftain?" Tāseti said.

"I doubt they've seen us," Kusala said. "Regardless, they would not recognize us as enemies. Once they pass, we will bring the ships in and attack from the rear."

When the last of the wagons were out of sight, the Asēkhas and twenty of the freed slaves climbed off the galleys and waded the short distance to shore. Once there, Kusala gathered them together to discuss his plan.

Soon after, Tāseti, Churikā, and Kusala crept up on the rear-most wagons, while the rest of the Asēkhas and their armed companions crouched in the gloom. Churikā was the first to strike, hopping noiselessly onto the seat next to the driver, clamping one hand over mouth and nostrils and jamming her dagger between the upper ribs and into a lung. From his vantage point, Kusala saw a good deal of blood but heard little sound, though he noted that Churikā struggled mightily to keep the flailing body from making too much noise.

*Only a hag would have that kind of strength,* he thought to himself, and then looked at Tāseti, who nodded in recognition. The second in command went next, performing basically the same set of moves, with similar success. But when Kusala took his turn and slashed with his dagger, crimson flames and putrid smoke burst from his victim's throat. Howling freakishly, the Warlish witch grasped her neck and tumbled backward into the bed of the wagon, her legs and arms flailing.

The commotion alerted the other drivers, and they snapped their whips and drove their oxen forward, depending on the armored horsemen to confront the enemy. As planned, the remaining Asēkhas came out of hiding and met the charging cavalry head on. Without pikes or other protection, it appeared the desert warriors would be trampled. But Kusala knew better. He watched as the Asēkhas leapt high into the air and landed on the backs of the destriers, swinging their elbows and knocking more than a dozen riders to the ground. Then they leapt off the horses and slew the fallen.

The other horsemen regrouped, but during the second charge the mounted riders fared even worse. All but two were thrown to the ground and easily dispatched, and the remaining pair fled into the darkness.

Meanwhile, Kusala, Tāseti, and Churikā went about the business of destroying the barrels in each of their wagons. Clear water spilled into the beds, and small worm-like creatures flopped and wriggled on the gnarled wood. Kusala snarled in disgust. Then he leapt from his wagon and began to chase down the rear of the fleeing caravan. But he didn't have to run far. Half the wagons already had halted, and their drivers—some astoundingly beautiful, others hideously ugly—were running *toward* him. The hags had been unleashed.

Their speed and numbers caught Kusala by surprise, and he was swept off his feet. Fangs clamped on his neck, and claws tore at his stomach, thighs and groin. Kusala's flesh was impervious to their attacks, but their combined weight overwhelmed him. Unable to wield his weapons or regain his feet, he had no choice but to tuck into a ball and await rescue.

When his Asēkhas arrived, the rescue occurred quickly. Every hag was slain without a single desert warrior suffering a serious injury.

Kusala finally stood and dusted himself off. "What took you so long?" was all he could manage.

The Asēkhas burst into laughter.

A few moments later, the freed slaves joined them. Only fourteen remained of the twenty, but none of the armored horsemen—other than the two that had fled—still lived. The Senasanan woman was bleeding from a cut above her right ear, but her expression was fierce.

"I slew a rider," she said proudly.

Churikā bowed. "I apologize for my harsh words earlier. Your courage is admirable."

"Speaking of courage," Kusala said, "we are about to need a good deal more of it. See for yourselves."

From the direction of the wagons, more than forty witches approached, almost a fourth of all the known witches left in the world. Each bore a tall wooden staff, and they came forward almost casually—some beautiful, some ugly, some transforming between incarnations. Red fire spat from their eyes, and black smoke oozed from their ears. In eerie unison, they sang a horrid song, its lyrics unrecognizable, though a demon would have known them well, Kusala surmised. And that was not the worst of it. From the west, another threat arrived. Several hundred black wolves bearing Mogol riders as well as a battalion of golden soldiers—ten score at least—appeared at the crest of a hill. It appeared the cowardly soldier Fabius would have his revenge after all.

Kusala turned to the former slaves. "Flee to the galleys!"

"We will not abandon you," the Senasanan woman shouted.

"We all must flee," Tāseti said. "Even the Asēkhas are outmatched."

"But the barrels," Kusala said. "We have destroyed so few."

As they argued, the witches came nearer. The stink of their malice caused the freed slaves to panic, and they scrambled toward the lake—all except the Senasanan countess, who held her ground despite her terror. The wolves and Mogol riders came forward in a slow jog to join the fray. But just when it appeared the Asēkhas would be overrun, a hundred shadowy figures on horseback emerged on the crest of the hill behind the advancing enemy. At first Kusala could not identify them, but upon their charge he recognized their battle cry. They were Bhasuran warriors, fewer in number than their foes but a welcome sight, nonetheless.

The Bhasurans loosed flint-tipped arrows into the wolves' hindquarters and pounded stone war clubs onto the golden soldiers' helms. But when the main strength of the enemy turned to face them, they were forced to retreat, only to regroup and attack from another direction. In a short time, more than a third of the Bhasurans had fallen; the wolves were faster than horses, and the Mogol warriors were stronger than their Bhasuran counterparts.

Still, the unexpected assistance inspired the Asēkhas, who let out their own high-pitched battle cry and sprinted toward the hill, slaying anyone or anything that dared come near. The desert warriors punched into a thick formation of armored soldiers, cutting through them like a dagger through flesh. Some of the soldiers panicked, threw down their weapons, and fled. For a moment Kusala thought that the bulk of them might scatter. But then the Warlish witches joined the battle, and the courageous Bhasurans were routed. Eventually only the Asēkhas remained, and they were surrounded by golden soldiers, wolves, Mogols, and the coven of witches.

The desert warriors formed a defensive circle. The night had deepened, and it was difficult to see more than a dozen paces, accentuating the fiery glow of the witches' eyes. Their leader came forward, approaching within five paces of Kusala. She held a wooden staff almost twice her height, and when she pounded its heel against the ground, the head spewed crimson flames. The other witches did the same, illuminating a wide area. In response, the Asēkhas' blades glowed blue.

A sudden silence ensued. All eyes focused on the witch and the chieftain.

"Have you come to plaaaay?" the witch said. She was as beautiful as any woman Kusala had ever seen. "Did you really think you could succeed in destroying our little babiessss?"

Kusala's face was grim. "Whatever else happens here tonight, *you* will perish."

This enraged the witch. Her long auburn hair danced, and her nostrils gushed putrid smoke. Kusala watched as she transformed into a creature of obscene ugliness. But this did not dismay him.

"If you flee from us and leave the wagons behind, we will not pursue," Kusala continued. "But if you stay, we will kill all of you. What do you choose? Answer quickly! My patience withers, much like your face."

Kusala knew his threats carried little weight. The Asēkhas were outnumbered fifteen to one. But he didn't care. He and his desert warriors might die this night, but they would not be the only ones.

Suddenly, a commotion in the nearby darkness distracted Kusala. A pair of Mogols entered the firelight, dragging a struggling woman. The Senasanan countess fought against her captors, but they were too strong. Kusala saw that she had been stripped of her clothing and whipped. The Mogols heaved her roughly to the ground within a few paces of Kusala.

"Put down your weaponsssss," the witch said, "and we will let her live."

"Don't listen to her!" the woman screamed, rising to her knees.

A Mogol warrior clubbed her between the shoulder blades, knocking her face-down in the dirt.

Kusala looked at the Mogol and repeated his earlier statement. "Whatever else happens here tonight, *you* will perish."

"We shall ssssee!" the witch said, pressing the fiery head of her staff against the Mogol's chest. The other witches joined their leader, launching crimson flame from their own staffs. The torrents blended together to envelope the Mogol warrior, swirling around his muscled torso. The Mogol cried out and collapsed to his knees, but a moment later he was able to stand, his body now engorged with supernatural might. He glowed like a ghost.

"Our champion against yourssss," the witch said. "Winner takes all."

"Contesting this devilry is beneath you, Kusala," Tāseti shouted. "Let us attack now and be done with this."

But Kusala did not seem to hear. His blazing blue eyes met the witch's challenge. "Winner takes all," he growled, and then he strode to confront his magically enhanced foe.

# 15

WIELDING HIS *uttara*, Chieftain-Kusala closed on the Mogol. The savage's face, chest, and arms were slathered with grotesque tattoos depicting various forms of sadistic violence, and he wore only a loincloth stained the color of blood.

Under ordinary circumstances, a dozen Mogols would have been no match for Kusala. But the power of the witches had changed this one into something superhuman, every shred of his flesh shimmering like phosphorescence. Even his war club glowed. It too had absorbed the evil magic.

In Tugarian fashion, Kusala faced his opponent and bowed. The Mogol sneered and then lunged, swinging his club at Kusala's head. Kusala ducked out of the way and stabbed his *uttara* at his enemy's heart with enough force to punch through bone. But where the point of the blade met flesh, a crackling burst of crimson energy erupted, blasting Kusala backward onto the hard ground. The Mogol howled with delight, and the witches joined in, shouting the foulest imaginable obscenities.

The savage leapt forward and swung the club at Kusala again. He rolled away, avoiding the blow with little effort, but this time he stood more warily. The Mogol's powers were similar to a Kojin's. The witches had given him a magical shield that not even a *uttara* seemed able to penetrate.

Too quick for the eye to follow, Kusala lunged at the Mogol, spun on his right foot, and whipped the *uttara* at his opponent's throat, a blow powerful enough to behead a cave troll with a single swipe. But where the blade met flesh another explosion occurred, once again knocking Kusala to the ground and momentarily stunning him. The Mogol might have had him then, but the force of his blow also sent the savage tumbling, and he fell into the arms of a soldier. When the Mogol's shimmering flesh pressed against the soldier's armor, the golden metal glowed red-hot. In response, the body within the armor swelled to an immense size, and for a moment it appeared that the golden soldier had become some kind of horrid monster. But then he burst asunder.

The Mogol wiped gore from his face and managed to stand. By this time, Kusala also had regained his feet.

"The chieftain of the Asēkhas has met his match, it would sssseem," the leader of the witches snarled, still choosing to appear in her hideous state. "If you surrender now, Kusala, I will let you live. You can return to Kamupadana as my personal slave, a position you would not find unpleasssant."

"Whatever else happens here tonight, *you* will perish," Kusala repeated.

His brashness enraged the witch further, intensifying her repulsiveness. "End his life . . . now," she shouted at the Mogol.

When the mountain warrior charged at the desert warrior, Kusala surprised everyone by sheathing his sword. The Mogol swung a deathblow, the club rushing at Kusala's head in a shimmering blur. But with strength second only to *The Torgon*, Kusala caught his enemy's wrist in mid-swing and wrenched the club from his hand. The witches gasped, and the rest of the gathering fell into silence.

Now wielding the war club, Kusala reared back and struck his enemy with the force of a trebuchet heaving a boulder. The magic in the Mogol's flesh yielded to the magic of the weapon, and he was slain.

Before anyone could react, Kusala picked up the still-glowing war club, took three long strides, and thudded the leader of the coven on her hideous head. The fulmination of flesh and bone was followed by a gruesome eruption of red fire and rancid smoke. For a moment, everyone froze in place.

But Warlish witches are not cowards, and they love each other like sisters. After recovering from the initial shock, the rest of them charged at the Asēkhas in a snarling fit of fury. The Mogols, wolves, and golden soldiers also attacked. Without Torg to offset the coven's powerful magic, the desert warriors were outmatched. Despite their prowess, it was only a matter of time before they succumbed.

UNNOTICED IN the melee, the naked Senasanan woman crept away on hands and knees, barely avoiding being trampled. Once she was free of the fighting, she stood and scrambled toward the galleys, which remained poised just offshore. Then she unexpectedly came to a standstill, sensing the approach of a mysterious power. Off to her left was a small hill, barely taller than a berm. A horse appeared upon its summit—but surely no horse could be so large. And then something even more amazing rose into view: a giant, twice as tall as the horse, with a fell look in his eyes.

FOR THE FIRST time in his long life, Yama-Utu—brother of Yama-Deva, now known as Mala—shed the blood of another . . . and another and another . . . using his enormous fists to bludgeon everything he confronted. Though the witches and their minions had been filled with the desire to kill, their rage was minuscule in comparison to his. None could withstand his madness. He made sure of it.

First the soldiers fled.

Then the Mogols and wolves.

The witches stood their ground, but even they were no match. Utu crushed them as easily as the rest, their strength pale in comparison to his. All but a few perished, and those few fled to places beyond Utu's range of vision.

In the end, he had followed Jord to this place and then destroyed these followers of Invictus and Mala.

But at what cost?

In Utu's scattered mind, that was yet to be determined.

WHEN THE BATTLE was over, Kusala found the snow giant sitting cross-legged by the edge of the lake, his face buried in hands still stained with blood. The beast wept, a pathetic sound coming from something so huge and powerful.

Kusala approached cautiously, though not necessarily out of fear. During the deadly rampage, the creature clearly had avoided harming the Asēkhas, and at times he and the desert warriors had fought side by side like allies. Kusala had never been to Okkanti, but he had listened many times to Torg's recountal. It was obvious this creature was a snow giant, and since there were so few—less than a dozen in the world—it was likely the Death-Knower had once been in his presence.

Seemingly out of nowhere, a female voice startled Kusala. He drew his *uttara* and crouched in a defensive position, turning to his left to confront the surprise intruder. A woman with long white hair stood before him, her white robes aglow. Once again, Kusala recognized a stranger. Torg had described her briefly during their talk on the ledge above the rock shelter.

"His name is Yama-Utu," the woman said to Kusala, gesturing to the giant, who continued to weep.

"And you are Jord," Kusala said. "The Torgon has spoken of you."

"Kind words, I hope?"

"Nothing you would not have been pleased to hear."

Jord smiled.

"Did Torg send you to help us?" Kusala said.

"I haven't seen your king for several months. The last time was early winter. But our paths will cross again. After I leave here, I will go in search of him. I have things to show him."

"How did you come to be here?"

"I've been many places—mostly to observe, but sometimes to extend aid, if I am told to do so. The times are dire, as you well know. You needed me. And so I came."

"If that is so, why did you bring the giant? Could you not have defeated the witches yourself?"

"My powers are limited . . ."

Seemingly oblivious to their conversation, the giant suddenly stood and strode into the lake. Then he sat down, splashed his face, and cried some more.

"Yama-Utu has never killed before," the Faerie said. "His kind claim to be incapable of violence, but apparently that is not the case. Since the rise of Invictus, this snow giant's pacifism has been sorely tested. His beloved brother was once known as Yama-Deva. But he is now known as Mala."

Kusala could not tell if Utu had heard Jord's words, but the giant seemed to react, standing up and stomping through the water toward the chieftain. Tāseti and several other Asēkhas came forward to protect their leader, but

Kusala waved them off. Cleansed of his victims' blood, Utu stood a few paces away in knee-deep water, and though the giant had the wizened face of an ancient being, he now bore an almost childish expression.

"Have you seen Yama-Deva?" Utu said to Kusala. "My brother went away and never came back."

"Does he not know?" Kusala said to Jord, amazement in his voice.

"His awareness comes and goes," Jord said. "I journeyed with him from Okkanti all the way here, and though we traveled many leagues in not much more than a day, we still managed to have several conversations, some more wearisome than others. At times, he knows what we know and is thoroughly preoccupied with killing Mala, thereby ending his brother's suffering. Other times, he seems to have has no knowledge of Mala or Invictus. Either way, I believe he is an ally."

"I *miss* him," the giant said. "Have you seen my brother?"

Kusala was impressed. Without further comment, he laid his sword and dagger in the dirt and then stepped, fully clothed, into Ti-ratana. There was a commotion behind him, but he paid no heed. As he approached the giant, the water came up to his waist. He looked up at Utu and smiled.

"I owe you my life, dear sir," Kusala said, bowing until his nose almost touched the lake's black surface. "Will you journey southward with me and my friends? Perhaps we will encounter your brother somewhere along the way."

"I would be honored to join you," Utu said.

Kusala believed that he meant it.

When Kusala emerged from the water, the Faerie was gone.

"Where did Jord go?" he said to Tāseti.

"Jord? I do not know that name."

"She was standing right beside you—the woman with long, white hair. I was just speaking to her. Surely you heard our words."

"We heard *you*, chieftain, but it was as if you were talking to air," Churikā said. "There was no white-haired woman. But until just a moment ago, a jade mare stood among us, her mane as white as the great giant's. When you entered the water to speak to him, the horse galloped off toward the mountains. Did you not hear the thunder of her hooves?"

"I heard something," Kusala admitted. "What it was, I cannot say."

Kusala sighed. The giant came beside him and sighed too. Then without warning, his childish expression changed, replaced by a snarl.

"My name is Yama-Utu," he said to the Asēkhas in a rumbling voice, "and I have chosen to join you. Take me where you will . . . but when we encounter Mala, leave him to me. Such evil cannot be permitted to thrive inside my brother's doomed body."

By now, all the Asēkhas had gathered around, and they bowed in unison.

"We will not thwart you, Yama-Utu," Kusala said. "In fact, we will gladly risk our lives for you and your quest. Consider us your friends."

"My *friends* cower in Okkanti, obsessed with chants, prayers, and words of wisdom," Utu said. "But I no longer care what they think of me or my desires. Mala will die . . . at my hands. Do not doubt it."

Before continuing their journey southward, the Asēkhas went to each wagon and destroyed all the barrels. Utu joined in, smashing them as easily as watermelons. Kusala warned the giant to not let any of the infected water splash into his mouth.

"The Asēkhas and I cannot be harmed by the *undines*," he said to Utu. "But of you, I am not certain."

"I too am beyond such things," the giant said, matter-of-factly.

After that deed was done, Kusala ordered the rest of the freed slaves to come ashore and help with the cleanup. The wagons were pushed together and set aflame, along with the remnants of the barrels. The corpses of the witches were also thrown into the fire, in case they were somehow capable of magically reviving their bodies. The dead wolves, Mogols, and golden soldiers were left to rot, though the freed slaves took as many weapons as they could carry.

By the time they were finished, it was the middle of the night, and Kusala was worried that more of the enemy—attracted by the fire—would soon arrive. As quickly as possible they returned to the galleys, including Utu, who continued to transform randomly between his naive and angry personas. His naive personality claimed never to have been on a boat, but he seemed to enjoy the feel of it and enthusiastically offered to wield an oar. But he pulled with too much power, making it difficult to keep the narrow-hulled ship from going in circles. The oarsmen on the port side eventually complained, and Kusala finally asked Utu to stop. The giant's naive personality took offense. But when the chieftain explained the reason, Utu smiled apologetically.

"I'm sorry. I haven't spent much time around little people, and I didn't know how weak they were."

"Compared to you, a desert elephant is weak," Tāseti said.

Utu seemed pleased. "I am strong, but Deva was the strongest of all—and the bravest. That's why it's so strange to me that he is lost. How could that be?"

Just then, Podhana appeared on deck.

"There is enough food to last several days," the Asēkha warrior reported to Kusala. "We're preparing a vat of vegetable soup. We also found a few crates of salt pork."

Kusala nodded. "That's good to hear. All this fighting has made me hungry. How about you, Utu? Do you eat soup?"

"The vegetable soup sounds tasty," Utu said. "But snow giants do not eat 'salt pork' or any other kinds of flesh."

"You would get along well with the noble ones of Dibbu-Loka," Tāseti said. "They eat only vegetables—not even fish."

"Fish? I love to watch them swim in the crystal waters of a mountain lake, but I would never tear one apart and chew on its flesh. Do you really *eat* them? Poor little fish."

"We 'little people' do a lot of things you might not understand," Tāseti said. "That doesn't make it right. It's just the way it is."

"Poor little fish," Utu repeated.

But when Podhana and his kitchen crew—which included the Senasanan countess—served the meal, Utu strode forward, grabbed enough salt pork to feed a dozen people, and devoured it in several angry bites. Grease dripped from the points of his fangs and the corners of his mouth.

"You're right," he said. "Fighting makes you hungry."

Kusala shuddered.

During the journey down the western shore of Lake Ti-ratana, the galleys encountered no opposition. The next morning dawned clear and warm, and they soon passed close to another community of kabangs. The boat people remained hidden from view. The sudden appearance of the larger crafts had frightened them. To everyone's surprise, Kusala removed his black jacket and boots, dove into the water, and swam over to the kabangs. He returned with several boat people, who greeted the Asēkhas and freed slaves enthusiastically, giggling like over-excited children. When they saw Utu, they dropped to their hands and knees at his feet, as if in the presence of a god.

"Don't bow to me," said Utu, his angry personality taking over. "I'm a killer, like the rest of you. Get away from me."

The boat people were terrified and leapt into the water, disappearing into Ti-ratana's dark depths.

"That was a little harsh, even for you," Churikā said to the snow giant.

"Do you challenge me?" said Utu, eyes aglow.

This time it was Kusala's turn to become angry. "If we are to become your enemies, let it be known now. You are great, but we are not helpless. Do you challenge *us?*"

In response, the naive Utu returned, the change of tone and facial expression becoming apparent to all. "I would never hurt you or your friends. I am a peaceful creature. You have nothing to fear from me."

"Tell that to them," Churikā said, motioning toward the kabangs.

"Of course," Utu said cheerfully, and then he dove into the lake, rocking the galley. The Asēkhas peered over the bulwark distrustfully, some even preparing their slings. A long moment passed without any sign of the snow giant, then he burst from the water like a breaching whale, tossing a pair of boat people more than twenty cubits into the air. They somersaulted gleefully and screamed in delight before gracefully piercing the surface. Soon more than a dozen—each about the size of one of Utu's hands—were clambering onto his shoulders, begging to be thrown. It was delightful to watch.

When Utu climbed back on board, he walked directly to Churikā. "You see, these tiny creatures are beyond me. That is all I meant. I am not worthy of their adoration."

Then Utu cast himself onto a pile of netting on the deck and fell fast asleep. But not before Kusala noted, for the first time, that the giant's conflicting personalities were not entirely unaware of each other.

Kusala shuddered again.

# 16

EARLY THE NEXT evening, the galleys reached the southwestern tip of Lake Ti-ratana. Kusala ordered the others to abandon the crafts and come ashore, bearing as many weapons and as much food as eighteen Asēkhas, eighty-two freed slaves, and one snow giant could manage.

Once on land, Kusala gathered everyone for a brief council.

"As we know, Mala will soon begin his march on Nissaya, if he has not already. But his army is huge and will move slowly, so we have little to fear from it here. However, we are closer to Avici than any of us would prefer, and it's possible we'll encounter wolves, Mogols, or other enemies. If they dare to assault us, even in large numbers, they will be hard-pressed, but there are those among us who are not fighters. My warriors will do their best to protect you, but you must do as you're told *when* you're told. Above all else, do not panic and attempt to flee. If danger approaches, huddle together and allow us to encircle you. Does anyone have questions?"

"How far is Nissaya?" the Senasanan countess said.

"More than sixty leagues, but I hope to make it to the fortress in nine days or less," Kusala said. "I know that must sound disheartening, considering what you've already been through, but I will demand it of those who accompany me, nonetheless. Are there other questions? Be quick."

No one else spoke.

"Very well," Kusala said. "We are weary and must recoup our strength. Though I'm anxious to continue, we'll rest here until midnight before beginning our march. The massacre of the witches is sure to attract attention. The farther south we advance, the safer we'll be."

Before lying down to rest, they ate bread, cheese, and freshwater sardines. Utu, in his angry persona, devoured far more than his share of the fish. Then he walked a hundred paces from the main group, cast his huge body onto the ground, and fell into a deep sleep. Kusala was grateful that the snow giant didn't snore.

Everyone was exhausted. Churikā took the first of a series of brief watches. After counting ninety slow breaths, she tapped Podhana on the shoulder. He woke instantly and began his count. A moment later, Churikā was asleep.

When they broke camp, the gibbous moon was well past its midpoint in the sky. Utu had assumed his naive persona, acting puzzled as to where he was and why he was there. Kusala could sense that the others were becoming more and more uncomfortable with the snow giant's presence. Would Utu's unpredictability eventually cause him to turn against them? If so, everyone's life would be at risk. Even the Asēkhas might not be able to subdue him. Kusala wished that Torg still was with him. Or even Jord. Either would know better how to manage Utu's moods.

Early on, the terrain was level, much like most of the Gray Plains. They were near the far western border of the vast prairie, which covered hundreds of thousands of hectares, extending as far north as the foothills of Mount Asubha, as far south as Dibbu-Loka, and as far east as the Salt Sea.

Kusala took them in a southwesterly direction toward the foothills of the mountains, where they would be sure to discover hiding places among the trees, caves, and tumbled boulders. Even in the dark, he felt too exposed out in the open. They would need shelter, both from their enemies and the elements, though this night was clear and warm—almost uncomfortably warm.

Kusala sent out eight Asēkha scouts. When they returned, they had little to report. The plains were empty for leagues. There was no sign of the enemy or of the Nissayans, though Kusala doubted the black knights would patrol this far north with war so close at hand. Still, he dared to hope they would stumble upon a Nissayan company, making the rest of the journey easier and safer.

By morning they had traveled six leagues from their original camp. The eastern foothills of Mahaggata were within sight, but still a good distance away. They came to an abandoned farm. Near the main house was a well with potable water. Tāseti, Churikā, and Podhana entered the house to look around—and quickly emerged.

"The exodus to Nissaya has extended well beyond its borders," Tāseti said. "It appears the farmers gathered what valuables they could carry and left in a hurry. It's possible they were still here as recently as yesterday eve."

"I saw no signs of Mogols or other evils having desecrated this place,"

Churikā added. "They would have ransacked the house and befouled the well had they been here before us."

"The sorcerer's forces gather at Avici for the great march to Nissaya—and most of the Mogols and wolves have joined him," Kusala said. "Will this continue to work to our advantage? I hope so. I do not desire any more fighting until *after* we reach Nissaya."

Utu placed his huge hand on Kusala's shoulder, startling him.

"Are you certain Mala will march on Nissaya?" the snow giant said.

Kusala looked up at his broad face. "I am certain of few things. But of that, there is no doubt."

"I will be ready," said Utu, his voice as dark as obsidian.

After several hours of rest, followed by a meal of carrot and cabbage soup prepared in the farmhouse kitchen, they continued toward the foothills of Mahaggata. Now it was early afternoon and as hot as a summer day, though it still was early spring. This wouldn't have been unusual in Tējo, or even Dibbu-Loka, but it was strange this far north.

"Is the heat some devilry of Invictus?" Tāseti said. "Has he grown so great he can control the weather?"

"Nothing would surprise me," Kusala said. "But I don't understand how or why it would benefit his army any more than ours."

"How can you stand such heat?" the naïve Utu said, his face almost frantic. "It burns the skin like fire."

"Heat is our friend," Churikā said. "It warms the heart."

Utu smiled broadly, exposing glistening fangs. His angry-self returned. "My heart will be forever cold."

"That has become obvious to all," said Churikā, before sprinting off to the front of the group.

They reached the foothills before dusk and rested inside a cavernous rock shelter with a ceiling so high even Utu could stand upright without bumping his head. Drawings on the stone wall seemed to fascinate the snow giant, and he studied them ceaselessly while most of the others slept. Sensing a moment of clarity in Utu's troubled mind, Kusala joined him.

"What do you see?" he whispered.

At first Utu appeared not to notice Kusala's presence, but when he looked down, Kusala gasped. The expression on the snow giant's face was unlike any he had seen before. Kusala believed he was seeing the Yama-Utu who had existed before despair had invaded his mind.

"To you, these drawings must seem very old," Utu replied softly. "But I have lived for a long time, almost as long as the great dragons, and even longer than the dracools. And what I see here is not ancient to me."

Utu pointed to drawings high on the wall that had remained relatively intact, despite the passing of millennia.

"Whoever made these once visited Okkanti," the snow giant said. "Do you see over here? These are *my* mountains. And to the right are two figures. The largest is Yama-Deva, and I stand next to him. The little people bow at our feet. But Deva's arms are upraised, encouraging them to rise. Despite his greatness, Deva was humble. And he loved to talk to the little people who came in search of us with their countless questions. Still, our answers seemed to baffle them. What snow giants have to say isn't what others desire to hear."

A single tear slid slowly down his broad cheek. "Why would anyone want to harm Yama-Deva? What possible gain could there be in such a blasphemy?"

Kusala was surprised to find himself repeating the teachings of Sister Tathagata. "A wise woman once told me that suffering exists for all living creatures. It is caused by desire and ignorance. Desire for love, pleasure, and wealth, all of which are impermanent. Ignorance of the true nature of things, which only those with fully developed minds can comprehend. What happened to Yama-Deva was his karma. And what drove Invictus to harm your brother was the sorcerer's karma. Of the two, who will suffer the most? That is hard to say. But it is plain that both will suffer, as will you and I, as will all living creatures, until we are able to attain the end of suffering through enlightenment."

At first Kusala's words seemed to move the snow giant, but then his face twisted into a rage so vile it caused Kusala to back away.

"I also have spoken with Tathagata, you fool!" Utu shouted, startling everyone in the shelter. "She *loves* the sound of her own voice. But she never *does* anything. I have no more use for talk. Words are as worthless as air." Then he picked up a rock the size of his own skull and pulverized it with his bare hands. "Give me Mala! I will gladly end *his* suffering."

In a storm of rage and despair, Yama-Utu thundered out of the shelter.


AT MIDNIGHT, they resumed their march, but Utu was nowhere to be seen. The freed slaves, and even the Asēkhas, seemed relieved. The giant's unsettling presence had disturbed everyone. Though they owed him their lives, they felt much safer now that he was gone. Still, they were not completely relaxed, looking this way and that—fearful not of the enemy, but of someone who was supposed to be a friend.

Through the night and the next day, they walked without encountering Utu or anyone else who might threaten them. Asēkha scouts came and went, always returning with the same report. It was as if the surrounding lands had become barren. And there continued to be no sign of the snow giant. They began to hope that he had left them for good.

The next night the moon was almost full, glowing silver in a clear sky. The Asēkhas and freed slaves traveled faster than Kusala had expected, and they now were only a dozen leagues from the northwestern border of Java. Every few miles they came upon abandoned farms, most of which still contained crops and livestock. This unexpected boon enabled them to discard their own supplies, lightening their loads and making the march easier on everyone.

The next morning they camped in a sheltered hollow near the northern fringes of Java. The Dark Forest had a sinister reputation, but the travelers had grown so used to not being threatened that even the evil trees felt benign. However, Kusala and the Asēkhas knew better. All had spent harrowing moments near or within Java. Kojins were not the only danger. Ghouls, goblins, and vampires wandered its borders—as did the mysterious homeless people known as the Pabbajja. Kusala decided to put everyone on alert. After they had eaten breakfast, he called them together.

"We have marched more than thirty leagues in three days, and everything has gone our way thus far."

After some back-slapping and applause, someone shouted, "And the giant is gone too." A spate of nervous laughter followed.

Kusala held up his hands, as if to quiet them. "Nissaya is little more than thirty leagues from where we stand. If we are not harassed en route, we might be able to arrive at the fortress in three days, though your legs will be sore and your feet blistered. We are near those who can protect us, but the potential for danger still exists—especially from the forest. Until an escort of black knights comes to greet us, we will remain vulnerable. We have accomplished much, but our journey is far from finished."

They rested until noon and then continued on, despite grumblings from some of the freed slaves. At least a dozen were limping, and their overall pace slowed considerably. To make matters worse, the terrain became lumpy and difficult. By the time dusk neared, they had managed only five leagues. The grumbling increased with every step.

Kusala called a halt and met with Tāseti.

"We have driven them too hard," the second in command said. "They need a full night's sleep more than anything else. We are far ahead of your schedule, chieftain. Let us make a more permanent camp and rest through the night. It will work wonders for morale."

Kusala sighed. "I suppose you're right, though I despise every moment that keeps me from Nissaya."

"Then go on ahead with Churikā or Podhana," Tāseti said. "As our Vasi masters like to say, the rest of us can take care of ourselves."

"I have considered this," Kusala said. "But if the giant reappears, I want to be with you. I feel responsible for Yama-Utu. If not for my decision to pursue the wagons, we never would have required his services."

"If you wish to stay, then stay," Tāseti said. "But relax a bit. Time is of the essence, I know, but one extra day won't make the difference between success and failure."

Kusala chuckled ruefully. "My senses tell me otherwise. Something peculiar is in the air. And I don't like the feel of it."

To their west was a series of foothills laced with quick, shallow streams. To the east was the border of Java, its trees resembling an army of crooked monsters in the deepening gloom. While the freed slaves searched for places to spread their blankets on the hard ground, Kusala sent six Asēkhas to scout the interior of the forest. It was here that their company would face the greatest danger. By this time tomorrow night, they would be at the southern borders of the forest and within a two-day march of the fortress along a well-maintained road.

Still, Kusala was restless. During his long life he had always been able to detect the presence of evil before it showed itself. To some extent every Tugar had this ability, but Kusala's senses were superior to all but Torg's. And now he found himself drawing his *uttara* and taking a defensive stance.

"What is it?" Tāseti said, Kusala's sudden movement puzzling her. "What do you see?"

"It's not what I see, but what I feel. Order the Asēkhas to encircle the company and prepare for the worst."

The second in command had learned through experience to trust Kusala's instincts. She sprinted off and gathered the remaining Asēkhas around the freed slaves, who huddled together, looking frightened. The twenty bravest, led by the countess, also took up swords and rose to the company's defense.

As the full moon rose above the canopy of Java, they heard shouts from within the forest. A moment later, the Asēkha scouts scrambled out of the woods.

"*Paccosakkaahi!* (Retreat!)" the warriors shouted. "A Kojin comes!"

But it was too late to flee. There was nothing to do but turn and face the enemy.

To make matters worse, the Kojin was not alone.

# 17

WHEN YAMA-Utu fled the rock shelter, he had no idea where he was going. He only knew that he had to get as far away as possible. Though his thirst for murder and mayhem grew by the moment, he had no desire to harm his new companions. It was Mala he was after—or more accurately, the blasphemy that Yama-Deva had become.

The thought of his brother's ruination filled Utu with a rage that roared through his mind like wildfire. When the fire grew too hot, it temporarily burned away his lunacy . . . and his mind wandered in the bliss that had existed before his brother's destruction. Eventually his exultation faded, giving way to a return of misery. His beloved brother, the pride of the snow giants, had been taken and tormented by Invictus.

However, this alone had not caused Utu to abandon the *Santapadam* (Path of Peace), which his kind had embraced for countless millennia. What finally had broken Utu was this simple fact: During the ten years that Invictus had tortured Yama-Deva, the snow giants had done nothing. Though they were too few to storm Avici and defeat Invictus' army by force, the realization that they had made no attempt whatsoever to rescue Deva ate at Utu's sanity like a cancer. They should have tried.

*He* should have tried.

Of course, the other snow giants didn't view this as cowardice. The only way to rescue Yama-Deva was through the use of violence, which was not in their nature.

"My dear husband," Bhari had said over and over. "Nothing can result from violence but more violence. The day Yama-Deva was captured, he was lost to us forever. We spoke to the birds, remember? They told us that your brother did not even attempt to flee, much less put up a fight. How could we dishonor such greatness by leaving our home and attacking the aggressors?"

Now Yama-Utu wandered alone in the darkness of the Gray Plains, the unseasonable warmth feeling like flames on his flesh. Even during midsummer, it was below freezing in the peaks of Okkanti. The snow giant was not used to such oppressiveness, nor was he used to the madness of murder.

He thought back to the battle near Ti-ratana. For the first time in his existence, he had purposely killed. The first to die was a golden soldier who had stumbled while frantically attempting to get out of the snow giant's way. Utu had stomped the soldier with the sole of his foot, squishing his body within the metal armor like a turtle inside its carapace.

Next to fall was a Mogol warrior who had somehow found the courage to charge Utu and heave a spear. One sweep of a massive arm broke the warrior into pieces. The first witch did not die so easily. Utu wrapped the creature in his arms and squeezed, but when her bones shattered, a foul crimson flame had burst from her eyes, burning like acid. Utu had howled, but blended with the pain was wicked pleasure. The intense physical anguish overrode the mental agony of Deva's loss. The brief moment had felt like paradise.

After yelling at the Asēkha chieftain and then fleeing the rock shelter, Utu had alternated between running, walking, and crawling. Sometimes he was lucid, and during those moments he would consider returning to his companions, only to feel the rage rise up again. Other times he was utterly lost, like an infant who had fallen noiselessly off the back of a wagon and been unknowingly abandoned in the wilderness. When morning came, the daylight further disoriented him, blinding his eyes and searing his skin. Where was he? Why was he here? He couldn't remember—or perhaps, didn't dare.

Finally he lay down beneath the blessed shade of some strange-looking trees and sobbed. That is where the Pabbajja found him. The homeless people seemed to rise from the ground, as if hitherto they had been part of the gray grass. Soon hundreds of them surrounded Utu, staring with wriggly eyes that protruded half a finger-length from their sockets.

Utu leaped up and towered over the Pabbajja, but when he made a pair of fists and prepared to fight, their manner seduced him and caused his arms to fall limply to his sides. Then he sat down, drew his knees to his chest, and permitted the homeless people to press against him.

They touched him in groups of three with small, gnarled fingers that resembled the branches of trees. Each contact sent a dizzying jolt of energy into his sinews. Yama-Utu collapsed onto his back, spreading out his arms and legs in the shape of a giant X. This way many of them could touch him at once, but they always came in divisions of three: a dozen, eighteen, thirty.

The intense flow of psychic energy drew his awareness back to a time long past, when Java was many times its current size, and hundreds of Kojins roamed the Dark Forest. The hideous female ogresses and their smaller male companions were not Java's only inhabitants. A race of humanlike creatures—each less than three cubits tall—also roamed the dense woods, foraging for nuts, roots, and berries in the dreary darkness of the inner forest. They were highly intelligent, relying on wiliness, rather than strength, to outwit a myriad of predators, including vampires, ghouls, and wolves. They communicated with each other telepathically, sometimes over distances of a league or more. Despite a daily dose of danger, their community thrived. At their height, they had numbered more than one hundred thousand.

But then the *Supanna-Sangaamaani* (Dragon Wars) began, and the land surrounding Java was turned into a fiery battleground, pitting all manner of man and monster against one another, while the ruling dragons roamed the skies, enjoying the destruction from above.

Though the ogresses and ogres fought hard to protect their precious homeland from the devastating effects of battle, the Dragon Wars took their toll. Trees fell. Fires raged. Java was reduced in size and scope. For the Pabbajja, this was particularly troublesome. With their territory diminished, fewer places remained for them to scavenge and to hide. Their numbers decreased.

In order to survive, the Pabbajja were forced to flee the inner forest and live on its borders. But they paid one final price. Their bodies, unable to tolerate direct sunlight, transformed in terrible ways. Their heads bloated, their eyes protruded from their skulls, and their fingers and toes became bent and twisted. In a genetic attempt to ward off the sun's damaging rays, they grew thick mats of hair over most of their bodies. The Pabbajja were changed.

However, their minds were unaltered. No madness came upon them, other than an all-encompassing desire to return to the inner forest and resume their previous lives. Over the millennia they waited, biding their time.

That time was now. Invictus had changed the course of the world. The homeless people could not stand against the Sun God, but perhaps they could aid those who might. They even sent thousands of their kind to join the sorcerer's army, feigning allegiance. But when the opportunity arose to strike a blow against him, they would be ready.

The Pabbajja did not have the strength to fully heal Yama-Utu's troubled mind, but he now knew that they were not without considerable power. When they revealed to him their plight, Utu regained a portion of his sanity. His desire to destroy Mala—and anyone who stood in his path—remained intact. But his lack of control over the emotions that raged within his mind was temporarily remedied. He sat upright and smiled, exposing long, white fangs.

In response, the Pabbajja sang . . . within his mind. The song was sweet.


THE SUDDEN appearance of the Kojin and the ogres filled Kusala with despair. The gigantic ogress alone was a nearly impossible test for the Asēkhas. As far as he knew, desert warriors had never managed to kill a Kojin in battle. Only a Death-Knower of Torg's caliber had that kind of strength.

To make matters worse, there were at least ten score ogres, many armed with axes. By themselves, the ogres were no match for the Asēkhas, but while the desert warriors were fending off the Kojin, her smaller male counterparts would be in position to slaughter the freed slaves. It was a difficult situation, to say the least. But Kusala steadied himself and prepared to fight. There was no other choice.

The Kojin signaled the attack with a high-pitched screech and then thundered forward, along with her snarling brood. Several freed slaves panicked and broke from the ranks. They quickly were chased down and hacked to pieces. Kusala, Tāseti, and Churikā encircled the ogress and slashed at her from all sides, their *uttaras* blazing and sparking with blurring rapidity but causing no noticeable injuries. Each of her six muscled arms was as thick as a tree, yet she somehow was fast and limber.

Churikā was knocked off her feet and momentarily stunned. Podhana took her place, but it was clear they were in trouble. Few creatures that walked the land could kill a Kojin.

Meanwhile, the other Asēkhas met the ogres' assault. Each desert warrior slew at least five of the enemy within the first moments of their clash, but even that was not enough. The monsters broke past them and attacked the huddled slaves, killing at will. The Asēkhas went into *frenzy* and drove them back, but by then the Kojin had forced its way past Kusala and was closing in on the others. Soon it would be a slaughter. The Asēkhas would have to flee or perish. And it was not in them to flee, unless their king ordered them to do so.

More ogres sprang from the trees. Gray forest wolves and ghouls also joined the fray. In desperation, Kusala fought past a sea of monsters and leapt onto the Kojin's shoulders, reaching around and running his dagger along its bulbous neck beneath the jaw line. Where the dagger met flesh, there was a purple explosion that splintered the blade. Though the Kojin was not seriously harmed, Kusala was cast to the ground with such force that he lost his grip on both the ruined dagger and his *uttara*.

An ogre picked up the precious sword and howled, waving it skyward as if claiming the ultimate booty. Kusala lifted his head and saw the Kojin scoop up Tāseti and hurl her a dozen paces into a mob of ghouls. Then the ogress pounded her fists against her chest and stomped toward the huddled slaves.

Kusala started toward the Kojin again, but a pair of incredibly strong hands held him back. He turned and looked up at Yama-Utu's face.

"Leave her to me," the snow giant said. "It will be good practice . . . for later."

Utu stomped forward, growling menacingly. The Kojin obviously sensed his approach and screeched again. In response, the other fighting halted, all eyes turning to witness the clash of titans. The Kojin was big, but the snow giant was even taller and broader. He struck her with a huge fist. She staggered and fell, smiting the ground.

Quick as a Tyger, Utu pounced upon her and wrapped his fingers around her throat. Purple energy raced up Utu's arms and exploded in his face, hurling him backward. Temporarily released from his grip, the Kojin tried to stand. But the snow giant was faster than the ogress. He rolled to the side, slipped behind her, and wrapped his arms around her neck in a stranglehold powerful enough to pulverize granite. Her protective purple energy enveloped Utu's entire body, but despite the obvious agony, he squeezed ever tighter.

While the others watched in stunned silence, the Kojin struggled, quivered, and then breathed her last.

Emboldened by the demise of the ogress, the Asēkhas and freed slaves charged at their assailants, killing recklessly. But they still were many times outnumbered. The death of the Kojin had bought them time, but not victory.

The enemy regrouped and went after them again, snarling and slavering. The Asēkhas did everything possible to protect the freed slaves, but it was difficult against so many. Kusala had broken the back of the ogre who had dared to desecrate his *uttara*, regaining his sword and then killing fifty of the monsters. But for every one slain, two more seemed to emerge from the forest. Utu ran here and there, butchering dozens at a time, but they fled from his wrath and were difficult for him to corral. It was only a matter of time before the freed slaves were overwhelmed.

Kusala felt further despair when several thousand Pabbajja emerged from the darkness, their three-tined spears aglow. But to his amazement, the homeless people joined the fray as allies, not enemies. With their magical tridents enhanced by psychic power, the Pabbajja were a formidable force. Finally, the enemy was outmatched. When the Asēkhas re-joined the fray, the monsters were routed, fleeing back into the forest with the homeless people in pursuit.

For the first time since the battle had begun, Kusala was able to stop and catch his breath.

Tāseti, a little sore but otherwise uninjured, came up to him and patted him on the back. "We have new friends?" she said.

"It appears that way . . . though I am yet to comprehend their motives."

Churikā joined them. "Chieftain, the heavens have noted our victory. Do you see the moon?"

Kusala looked up—and gasped. The golden orb was partially shrouded in darkness. A full eclipse of the moon was underway. Kusala found himself wondering about Torg and his companions. Where were they, and how did they fare? Then Kusala heard a thump and turned to see Utu beside him.

"I rather like Sister Tathagata, to be honest," the snow giant said. "But after what I've done the past few days, she and her kind seem beyond my comprehension."

Kusala had to chuckle. "I have been known to utter similar words." Then he reached up and placed the palm of his hand on Utu's massive abdomen.

"Twice now you have saved us."

The snow giant nodded.

"But I have a question for you," Kusala said.

"Yes?"

"Next time, can you come to our aid a little sooner?"

THOUGH NONE of the Asēkhas were seriously harmed, fewer than thirty freed slaves survived the attack—and many of those were injured, including the countess, who bore a deep gash on her right forearm. If not for the arrival of the Pabbajja, all the slaves would have been slain. The Asēkhas carried the human corpses, some butchered almost beyond recognition, a few hundred paces from where the worst of the battle had occurred. They then built a pyre to burn the dead.

"*Tumhe marittha bahuumaanena ca vikkamena. N'atthi uttara pasamsaa* (You died with honor and bravery. There is no higher praise)," Kusala said in the ancient tongue, before striking his dagger against a flake of flint and setting the pyre aflame.

Meanwhile, the Pabbajja returned from the forest, their tridents glowing mightily in the darkness made even deeper by the eclipse. One came forward to greet Kusala and Utu. Though his appearance was bizarre, he spoke with eloquence.

"Allow me to introduce myself. I am Bruugash, overlord of this cabal. We have destroyed all remnants of the enemy. Tonight, you are under the protection of the Pabbajja and are in no further danger."

"I am Kusala, chieftain of the Asēkhas," he said, bowing. "On behalf of us all, I thank you for your help. But I admit that I'm confused. The Tugars believed you to be allies of Avici."

"To serve our own purposes, we have feigned an alliance," said Bruugash, his eyes wriggling as he spoke. "In reality, we will join with anyone who would help us to rid *Kala-Vana* (Dark Forest) of our enemies. When the time comes, my people will aid you again, though the *Kalakhattiyas* (black knights) do not love us and often hunt us for sport."

"The knights of Nissaya are stern and haughty, but they are not evil," Kusala said. "When we reach the fortress, I will report what I have witnessed to the king. After that, the hunting will stop, as long as you remain true."

Now it was Bruugash's turn to bow, bending stiffly at the waist. Then he waddled away and shouted orders to his cabal. Soon several thousand Pabbajja encircled the Asēkhas and surviving freed slaves. Even so, they did not sleep well that night, though it was not fear that disturbed them as much as grief over the fallen.

Kusala spoke long with Utu, listening to the tale of his encounter with the Pabbajja. Afterward, he went off by himself and sat cross-legged, watching the final moments of the eclipse. His mind kept drifting to Torg and his companions. *Where are you now, my king? Will you ever return to us?* Finally Kusala slept.

The next morning was even hotter than the preceding day. The company, now greatly reduced, began yet another torturous march, its pace frustratingly slow. The Asēkhas took turns supporting the wounded, several of whom had to be carried. Kusala now feared it would take three or even four more days to reach the fortress, unless mounted knights were to find them and provide aid.

The Pabbajja stayed with them, resembling a herd of two-legged sheep. They charmed and amused the freed slaves, who thoroughly enjoyed their companionship. There was something comforting about the homeless people, a radiating calmness that touched even the Asēkhas.

Utu seemed the most affected. Suddenly the snow giant was charming and gregarious, stomping from person to person while shouting encouragement. He also took turns carrying the injured, often taking one on each broad shoulder.

Even so, by nightfall they had managed just six leagues and still were almost twenty leagues from Nissaya. But Iddhi-Pada, the great road that led from Avici to Jivita, was within easy reach. Once there, they were almost certain to encounter assistance. On the west side of the forest, the road still would be safe—though in half a month, Kusala guessed, the army of Invictus would pass this way during its inevitable approach to the fortress.

They rested until midnight before continuing their march. The moon was nearly full, but there was no sign of anything peculiar in its appearance. They stumbled three more leagues, skirting the western border of the forest. The Pabbajja followed tirelessly, their tridents providing as much light as torches. If anyone saw them pass, they dared not reveal themselves.

Kusala felt safe, but frustrated. He needed to meet with King Henepola as soon as possible. Afterward, he would travel by himself to Anna, stopping first at the haven to gather the noble ones, as Torg had ordered, though it galled Kusala to remove himself from the place he would be needed most.

A short time before dawn, while they ate and rested again, Bruugash approached Kusala.

"We must leave you," the Pabbajja overlord said. "The road is near, and we are not welcome. I know you would attempt to protect us, but the *Kalakhattiyas* are quick to anger, and I fear some of us might be harmed before you could convince them of our intentions."

Kusala placed his hand on top of Bruugash's furry head. "If this war is won and I survive it, I will return to Java myself and help your people regain their homeland. If I do not survive, a chieftain will come in my place. This I pledge to you."

Bruugash reached up and put his gnarled hand on Kusala's chest. "If you do such a thing, you will not regret it."

Then he turned and led the Pabbajja into the woods, where they vanished like ghosts.

# 18

THE COMPANY reached Iddhi-Pada a short time before noon. Kusala and his companions were still near enough to Java to see where the road dove eastward into the Dark Forest and disappeared into darkness. Westward, the road shined like a beacon of hope in the late-morning light.

If the Pabbajja still watched, they were well-concealed. Just in case, Kusala and the others waved farewell, hoping they would one day meet their new friends again.

Kusala turned and trudged along the road. Though thoroughly exhausted, the company began to make better time. More than fifty paces wide in most places, Iddhi-Pada was a raised, five-cubit-thick layer of sand, packed dirt, and stone blocks that was durable and easy to traverse, whether by foot, wagon, horse, camel, or even elephant.

Initially, they saw no sign of activity, which was not typical even this far east of the fortress. Merchants from Senasana made a fine living trading goods with Nissaya, and they usually were numerous on the road, as were farmers from as far north as Lake Ti-ratana. Even in times of peace, the black knights patrolled this area frequently, making sure that whatever evils dwelled within the forest remained there. But now it was clear that the fortress had called in its forces. Nissaya's only hope against the army of Mala was to slam shut its great doors and prepare for siege. Outside their walls, the outnumbered black knights, despite their renowned prowess in battle, stood little chance against the Chain Man's minions.

Once again, Kusala sent forth Asēkha scouts. The newly effusive Utu volunteered to go with them, but Kusala beseeched him to remain with the company, telling the snow giant that he would be needed if they were attacked. Secretly, Kusala desired to be present when the time finally came to introduce the giant to emissaries from the fortress. In times of war, the black knights could be distrustful and quick tempered—and Kusala was certain that none of them had seen a snow giant, except in drawings stored in Nissaya's vast library. Kusala wasn't sure how they would react to Yama-Utu, but he didn't want them mistaking him for a Kojin—or even worse, Mala himself.

Churikā was the first to return, a flush of red on her darkly tanned cheeks. "Chieftain, large portions of the road have been razed less than a league from where you stand. The stone blocks have been torn from the ground and piled into jagged walls extending a dozen paces or more beyond the sides of the road. Half a mile beyond the first wall is a second one—and a third after that."

"King Henepola has been keeping his vassals busy, it would seem," Kusala said. "I saw none of this during my last visit to the fortress less than a month ago. This will buy Nissaya time, though not much more than a few days. The cave trolls and Stone-Eaters will quickly reopen a way."

"At least this explains why we haven't encountered anyone," Tāseti said. "We might have to march a ways yet before finding aid."

Kusala sighed. "I was hoping help would come sooner. Time is short."

"I could carry you to Nissaya," Yama-Utu said. "I can run faster than any horse, and I do not tire. These walls of broken stone will not deter me."

"Consider the snow giant's offer, for all our sakes," Tāseti said. "You no longer need to protect us. It's unlikely we'll encounter dangers other than our own sore feet and stiff backs."

Kusala relented, partly out of frustration, and partly because he knew that it meant Yama-Utu would be with him when they first encountered the knights of Nissaya.

"If you would carry me, I would be most grateful," he said. "But when the black knights approach, let me do the talking . . . please. They can be rude to strangers, especially ones as large as you."

"Rudeness seems common among the little people," Utu responded, but he was smiling as he said it.

DURING HIS LONG life, Kusala had ridden on the backs of camels, horses, elephants, mountain eagles, and emus, to name a few creatures common to the world—but never on a giant. Utu had not exaggerated when he said he could run faster than a horse. Each of his strides covered twenty cubits or more, and when they came to the first wall, the giant leapt over it with ridiculous ease. The wind blasting in Kusala's face caused his eyes to water. In what seemed like a very short time, they reached the first of the three remaining Asēkhas.

"Return to the company," Kusala shouted as they blazed past the amazed scout. He gave the same order to the others. After that, he and Utu were alone on the road. Now it was midafternoon, and they were within ten leagues of the fortress. At this rate, Kusala guessed they would reach Nissaya before dark.

Iddhi-Pada dipped and swelled, but for the most part it gradually ascended from east to west. Because of this, the fortress, when approached from the Gray Plains, was not visible from a distance, while from the west it could be seen many leagues away. Kusala and Utu came upon a stretch of road that had been demolished, its stones disgorged and cast recklessly about, forming a spiny surface nearly impossible for a large army to traverse. More than just muscle had performed this work. Nissaya's conjurers had played a role in the destruction. This amazed Kusala. And also dismayed him. Why go to so much effort, when it would do little more than slow Mala down?

Regardless, the giant bounded over the rubble with ease, pouncing from broken boulder to jagged rock with the grace of a mountain goat. Once past the wreckage, they continued at an astounding pace, witnessing no further damage to the road. Either Nissaya wanted to keep the last few leagues clear, or it had run out of time. Kusala also noticed that the fertile fields bordering the road had been razed, and that nearby villages had been burned to the ground. The keepers of Nissaya were determined to leave as little as possible for the invading army in terms of food, supplies, and building materials—a devastating but necessary expenditure.

Approximately five leagues from the fortress, Kusala and Utu finally encountered a mounted squadron of black knights. When the Nissayans saw the giant and its rider, they rushed forward and encircled the unusual pair, their black destriers stomping rhythmically on the stone. The knights were lightly armored, each wearing a coat of plates over a mail hauberk—both of which were black, matching their ebony skin and short-cropped hair. All the knights were at least a span shorter than Kusala, but they were thick in the chest, arm, and leg—and armed with powerful crossbows.

Kusala climbed slowly off the snow giant's back, being careful not to reach for his sword. He was relieved to see amusement in Utu's expression. He had been afraid what might happen if the giant were to do anything threatening, though Kusala worried more for the welfare of the knights than for his companion.

Kusala placed his palms together and bowed low to the ground, then stood upright and folded his arms across his chest. He knew he would be recognized, but out of respect, he formally introduced himself.

"I am Chieftain-Kusala, leader of the Asēkhas and longtime servant of Nissaya. My companion is Yama-Utu, a snow giant from Okkanti, who comes to offer assistance in the war against Mala. It would be wise for you to accept. I have seen few his equal."

One warhorse was urged forward, bearing a proud knight with keen black eyes. The knight dismounted and came face to face with the chieftain, pausing briefly before dropping to one knee and lowering his head. When he looked up, he was smiling.

"Chieftain-Kusala, it is with honor that I greet you. May I rise?"

"Of course, sir."

The knight stood and clasped Kusala's forearm, in Tugarian fashion. "I am Palak, a senior commander of the *Kalakhattiyas*. We are pleased that you have returned, though we hoped Lord Torgon would be with you. You set out from the fortress several weeks ago to find him. Were you not successful?"

Kusala sighed. "I mean no offense, Commander Palak, but time is short, and I do not wish to repeat the same story several times. Please take me to your king, and you can hear all that I have to say at that time. As for Yama-Utu, do you bid him welcome?"

The commander stared with wonder at the snow giant's broad face. "Any friend of Kusala is welcome in Nissaya." He bowed again.

Utu also bowed. "You will not regret your decision. When Mala assails your walls, I will be there to greet him."

"What little hope we have of victory has grown more on this day," Palak responded.

Before they continued toward the fortress, Kusala told the commander about the freed slaves and asked him to send help as quickly as possible.

"There are enough horses among you to carry them to safety, if you were to ride in pairs, though your own barriers will make the journey more difficult. What you have done to Iddhi-Pada would be quite impressive, if it were not so depressing."

"Everything about this war is depressing," Palak said. "How can we be expected to prevail against such evil? Nonetheless, we will meet Mala in battle. As for you and the snow giant, you will enter the gates as my guests, and from there I will take you to the king.

"As for your other companions, do not fear. The rest of my squadron will ride to them and carry them to safety—and once within our walls, they will be provided with food and shelter. I would also say warmth, but there is precious little of that nowadays. The chill of doom consumes our hearts. As always, Nissaya will bear the first and mightiest strike. And as always, few will comprehend how hard we toil in the name of freedom, both for ourselves and others."

"You receive more credit than you know," Kusala said. "But you are not the only ones who sacrifice in the name of freedom. You will not stand alone. The Tugars will be with you."

"Some of you, but not all," Palak said. And then he urged his horse forward.

Despite carrying Kusala, Utu had to slow his pace considerably in order for Palak's destrier to keep up. As dusk approached, the trio came to the peak of a great swell in the road—and for the first time, their view of Nissaya was no longer obstructed. They still were a league from the main gate, but even at this distance the fortress was an awe-inspiring sight. The snow giant slammed to a halt and stared, his green eyes aglow.

"I have heard tales of Nissaya," Utu said, "but they pale in comparison to what stands before us. Surely, not even Mala and his army can hope to assail such a thing. They might as well attempt to defeat a mountain."

"The grandeur of Nissaya moves any who view it for the first time," Palak said. "There is no greater stronghold in the known world, nor has there been since our ancestors first occupied it more than twenty millennia ago. In all that time, the black fortress has never fallen. But neither has it faced an enemy of such rumored might."

"The might is rumored no longer," Kusala said. "Lord Torgon looked upon Mala's host and spoke to me of its immensity."

As they continued their approach, a host of knights galloped out to greet them, cheering the arrival of the Asēkha chieftain and the snow giant as if an army had come to join them. The land surrounding the fortress swarmed with knights, squires, and vassals. Kusala also recognized Tugars scattered among them, their gracefulness obvious even from a distance. But compared to the immensity of the fortress, they all seemed as tiny as ants.

Indeed, Kusala knew that Nissaya was as close to impenetrable as any fortress that had ever existed on Triken. It was situated on a rounded body of black granite that rose from the ground like an inverted bowl, its surface gently ascending more than six hundred cubits above the surrounding terrain. Much like the stone walls of Duccarita, the bulwarks and some of the buildings of Nissaya were mainly the work of nature, but the knights and their ancestors had spent thousands of years hammering, chiseling, and sculpting the igneous rock into the most majestic walls and towers in the world.

The base of the mammoth outcrop, which guarded the Gap of Gati's eastern maw, extended deep into the ground, its bedrock interlaced with a spider web of caverns and passageways, a few of which extended outward more than a dozen leagues—north to hidden places in Mahaggata or south to Kolankold. The secret entrances and exits were known only to the knights, and if an enemy ever did breach the walls, at least some of the defenders of Nissaya still would be able to escape to the mountains without the likelihood of pursuit. Any who tried to follow their flight without knowing the way would become lost within the intricate catacombs.

Iddhi-Pada swept past the fortress, continuing westward through the gap until encountering Lake Hadaya, but a hundred paces north of the portion of the road upon which they now stood, the black granite of Nissaya began its slow rise from the otherwise level terrain. At first, the stone floor was only a cubit above the plain. But even then, grass and vegetation ceased to exist, except for a voracious form of lichen that gnawed at the stone, creating depressions that gathered soil and dust, which in turn became home to gnarled bushes and miniature trees. Some of the depressions filled with rain water, forming pools within which edible shrimp lived and bred. And in the summer, a strange species of grasshopper abounded, becoming a noisy nuisance to the human inhabitants of Nissaya. Voles, snakes, and songbirds inhabited crannies in the stone year-round, serving as prey for thousands of black-feathered hawks that circled the skies above the fortress like a ring of storm clouds.

The black granite was too smooth and slippery for the passage of wagons and horses, especially when wet. So the Nissayans had constructed a broad avenue of pebbles and sand that led from Iddhi-Pada to the only visible entrance to the fortress. As dusk took firm hold, the unusual trio made its way toward the first gate. The toughened soles of the snow giant's feet crunched on the crumbled surface. Thousands of black knights cheered their arrival, both from the ground and the towering battlements. Kusala also could hear the high-pitched screeches of Tugars.

Three concentric walls of black granite encircled the fortress. Each had been given a name from the ancient tongue: the exterior wall Balak, the middle wall Ott, the inner wall Hakam. Each was a natural bastion of stone that human hands had sculpted only on the battlements, inner stairways, and tunneled entrances.

Balak was the shortest and longest of the three: fifty cubits tall, thirty thick, and more than four leagues in circumference, surrounding all of Nissaya. Its crenellated battlement was fitted with thick wooden shutters that could be held open with iron props or removed entirely, depending on the course of the battle, and it also contained numerous loopholes for archers. Fifty trebuchets on the wall walk could be rolled into different positions, depending on the placement of the enemy far below. On its interior side, several hundred sets of stone stairs led up from the narrow walkway at its base to accommodate its guardians.

Balak contained just a single entrance, thirty cubits wide and tall, that was guarded by a stone door as thick as a man was tall. The door, which was said to weigh seventy thousand stones, took more than half a day to be mechanically raised or lowered. Behind the door were five iron portcullises flanked by "murder holes" in the ceiling of the entryway from which defenders could unload an avalanche of debris onto any that might have performed the seemingly impossible task of crashing down the door.

Balak and Ott stood one hundred cubits apart and were separated by a moat filled with black water, concealing thousands of razor-sharp spikes. Anyone or anything that fell into the moat was unlikely to survive.

Four wooden drawbridges spanned the moat. The largest was directly behind the gate, and it was wide and strong enough to hold four wagons abreast. During peace time, this bridge remained lowered except for repairs; but during a siege, it was raised to prevent the enemy from crossing the moat. The defenders of the wall used the other three drawbridges to cross the moat back and forth.

Ott was identical in design to Balak, except twice its size with twice the number of trebuchets. A stone walk five cubits wide encircled the outside of its base, allowing just enough room for the movement of troops around the moat. Ott also contained just one door, though it was twice as large as Balak's with ten portcullises protecting the tunneled entryway.

No moat or other obstruction lay between the second and third walls. None was needed. Just twenty cubits of open space separated the walls. Any enemy who somehow managed to breach the second wall would then be caught between Ott and Hakam, where it would be bombarded with arrows, stones, boiling water, acidic liquids, quicklime, and burning oil—an untenable situation, to say the least, that was made even more difficult by the immensity of Hakam, which dwarfed all other bulwarks on Triken.

Hakam was two hundred cubits tall and one hundred and twenty thick. Due to its great height, its battlement contained just a single low wall with no crenellations or trebuchets. Only a bowman of extraordinary strength and ability could hope to strike effectively at someone so high above.

Hakam's only weakness was its single door, if you could call such a masterwork a weakness. The door was twelve cubits thick and weighed three hundred thousand stones. Twenty portcullises stood behind the door within the tunneled entryway, and there were chambers above the iron grates that contained enough rubble to clog the passage if the main door were somehow defeated.

Within the third bulwark stood the inhabited portion of the fortress, a titanic labyrinth of roads, alleys, courtyards and buildings. Some of the buildings were made of ordinary brick and wood; others were natural stone towers with hollow interiors. At this point, the labyrinth ascended so steeply that the buildings toward the center stood even higher above the floor of the gap than Hakam.

In some ways Nissaya was as much a city as a fortress, and it could house—on a temporary basis—more than one hundred thousand, in addition to its army and populace. There were hundreds of markets, mills, taverns, and shops, and the large business district hosted armorers, goldsmiths, shoemakers, oil merchants, wine sellers, and numerous craftsmen and makers of wares. Throughout the interior there were courtyards large enough to sleep thousands.

At the center of the fortress, the great keep of Nissaya rose like a titanic spire into the sky. Nagara it was called, which meant *citadel* in the ancient tongue, and it was second in size only to the tower of Invictus. The keep was a natural formation of black granite as huge as the arm of a god, its interior laced with passageways and chambers, most of which had formed naturally over the passage of time long before humans existed on Triken. But some of the chambers had been chiseled and molded over the millennia to better accommodate its most-recent inhabitants.

On its exterior, Nagara was pockmarked with hundreds of natural windows, causing it to resemble a mountainous termite mound. At ground level, it had four massive wooden doors, each protected by a portcullis. Behind these doors were boulders that could be rolled and chained into place, plugging the openings as securely as cave-ins. And even then, there remained a final method of escape. A passageway descended into the bedrock, winding for many leagues in damp darkness and leading to chambers where large quantities of food were stored and deep pools of potable water existed, even during times of drought.

Over the millennia, the knights had explored the tunnels, mapping every rise and fall, twist and turn. They could walk in the dark like the cleverest of blind men, navigating their surroundings without the use of sight, even though some of the caverns were thousands of cubits tall and wide with precipitous cliffs offering certain death to anyone wandering the pathways without foreknowledge of their meanderings.

The Nissayans had delved deep—too deep, some said—and had uncovered many mysteries in the hidden bowels of the world. Dangerous creatures still resided in the farthest depths, but the knights—who reigned supreme over the fortress, both above and below—had destroyed or chased away most of the monsters.

The conjurers of Nissaya had wandered with the black knights and brought back great wealth, including all manner of precious metals and jewels. They found pockets of black iron to forge their weapons and armor, and black crystal, resembling obsidian in color and feel, which glowed brightly when brushed by magic or flame. The knights and conjurers named the crystal *Maōi* and prized it above all else.

Among the people of Triken, it was said that the knights of Nissaya had not always been black-skinned. Some believed they were descendants of the pale-skinned Jivitans whose prolonged exposure to the ebony stone had stained their skin and hair. Others believed the knights had not even begun their existence as humans; rather, they were black bears or panthers that had evolved over the millennia, taking on human form in order to better defend their beloved fortress. Still others believed the knights were spirits of the stone in the guise of men and women.

The Nissayans believed none of these things. They were intricate recorders of history, especially in terms of their purebred ancestry, and their vast libraries contained the names and descriptions of every man and woman who was ever born of uncorrupted Nissayan blood. Like the Tugars and Jivitans, the Nissayans preferred the company of their own kind, and it was considered uncouth to breed outside their race. The purity of their physical appearance—including the marvelous color of their skin—was sacred to their order. The few who dared to produce children with outsiders faced banishment.

The religious aspects of the Nissayan culture also were highly prized. They disdained the beliefs of others—not so much out of disrespect but out of an all-encompassing conviction that their way of thinking was indisputable. Their neighbors, the Jivitans, believed in the *One God*, whom they saw as an omniscient being that had created humans in his own image. The Tugars believed in karma, in which all behaviors resulted in consequences and in which living beings existed in an endless cycle of birth, death, and rebirth. The savages of Mahaggata believed that gods existed in nature, and they worshipped the stars and the entities of the world in equal measure. The followers of Invictus venerated only the sorcerer, who proclaimed himself God.

The Nissayans, of course, knew the truth. There was a single God, but he/she/it was not a male deity resembling humans in appearance. *Uppādetar,* the Creator, was the loving energy that existed in all things, whether living or inert. God was beyond nature and beyond the stars, paying no interest to the petty machinations of mortals. Instead, God drove all goodness, and for that reason was to be worshipped and revered. Who could possibly believe otherwise, when there was so much proof in existence itself?

The Jivitans and Tugars shared many of Nissaya's views on morality, so the black knights tolerated them. The Mogols of Mahaggata did not, so the black knights despised them. And Invictus was the ultimate evil, so they were determined to resist him at any cost. But the Nissayans saw themselves as the true champions of good and were incensed that their allies did not gather enthusiastically behind their banner to counter the sorcerer's first—and greatest—strike.

Chieftain-Kusala knew all these things in immense detail. He had visited the fortress many times during his centuries-long life, and he was well aware of its strengths and weaknesses, both literally and figuratively. The Nissayan kings seemed close-minded to anything other than the welfare of the fortress, and King Henepola X was no exception. In fact, he was the most prideful of the Nissayan sovereigns that Kusala had encountered. Even Torg had said so—several times to Henepola's face. But what the king lacked in diplomacy, he made up for in power. Henepola was the first of his bloodline to be born with the innate magic of a conjurer. As far as Kusala was concerned, if anyone other than Torg could stand against Invictus, it was Henepola.

As Kusala, Utu, and Palak approached the first gate, the darkness deepened. But the road was lined with torches, providing plentiful light. Thousands cheered their arrival, including the Tugars among them, who bowed before Kusala as if he were a king.

Despite the raucous welcome, Kusala was unable to enjoy the moment, mainly because of the presence of Yama-Utu. The snow giant still seemed in awe of his surroundings, but it was one thing to be well-received among the masses, and another to be respectfully greeted by the king. Since his encounter with the Pabbajja, the snow giant seemed more in control of his emotions, but Kusala still didn't trust his combustibility. If Henepola were insulting, would Utu lose his temper? If so, would there be bloodshed in the hall of Nagara? Kusala feared the worst.

Commander Palak rode a few paces ahead, his black destrier clopping along proudly. The enthusiastic greeting seemed to thrill the Nissayan commander, and Kusala could see that—"senior" commander or not—Palak was not used to being treated with such reverence. Though Nissaya now boasted more than thirty thousand knights and another twenty thousand sergeants and squires, its high court was disproportionately small and—in Kusala's opinion—heavily weighted by those who agreed with everything the king said. Henepola was not one for open discourse.

"Behold the glory of Nissaya!" Palak shouted at Kusala and Utu.

Just then a company of knights emerged from the first gate, flanked by men bearing Nissayan banners: black flags with white lightning bolts outlined in gray, the bolts symbolizing the puissance of *Uppādetar*, the gray his minions, the black his dominion.

At the head of the company rode a woman and a man, both clad in glistening black armor. The woman's hair was as black as the surrounding stone, much like a Tugar's, but it hung past her waist, shiny as silk. The man's ebony skin mirrored those around him, but his hair—almost as long as the woman's—was the same color as the snow giant's mane: a stunning alabaster. Of course, Kusala recognized them: Henepola's only daughter, Princess Madiraa; and a powerful conjurer named Indajaala. All true conjurers of Nissaya had white hair.

Kusala had always admired Madiraa, who was almost as strong in body and mind as a Tugarian female. Indajaala was another story.

The company halted just outside the gates and remained atop their mounts, awaiting the trio's approach. Palak urged his destrier forward, riding toward Princess Madiraa with the confidence of a man bearing excellent news.

Kusala and Utu followed the commander on foot.

The daughter of the king spoke first. "Welcome, Commander Palak. I see that you bring guests to Nissaya. Have they come to strengthen our arms or brighten our halls?"

Palak also remained mounted, but he bowed slightly while still in his high saddle. "My lady, my guests shall do both," he said with laughter. "Chieftain-Kusala, of course, requires no introduction. But his companion has traveled far to join us. Allow me to present Yama-Utu, a snow giant from Okkanti and mighty among his kind. He offers his assistance in the war against Mala. His arrival is indeed a boon for our people."

At these words, the conjurer rose in his saddle. He held a glowing spike of *Maōi* in his thick black hand.

"Only our king can determine whether this beast's presence is boon or calamity," Indajaala snapped. "Or have you become so proud, Commander Palak, that you believe *you* speak for Nissaya?"

Palak lowered his head in obeisance.

Utu growled just loud enough for Kusala to hear. Kusala sensed trouble, but it was Madiraa who regained control of a potentially volatile situation.

"Nonsense," the princess said to the conjurer. "Palak does not need our king's permission to be pleased by the arrival of a snow giant. A being of such greatness should not be treated with scorn."

Madiraa then cast her gaze upon Utu. "You are most welcome in Nissaya. Though I must admit I'm surprised you have come. I've never heard of a snow giant leaving Okkanti—willingly."

Utu's lips curled, exposing the full length of his fangs. "I am here for one reason—to destroy Mala, who was once my brother. He is a bane that must be eliminated."

Indajaala spoke again, as if to prove that he was not easily cowed, either by a princess or a giant. "And who is to say that you are not a bane, as well? Who is to say you are not like your brother? If rumors are to be believed, your kind succumbs easily to the guiles of the sorcerer."

Kusala stepped between Utu and Indajaala, convinced the snow giant would pounce upon the conjurer and tear him to pieces. Instead, Utu lowered his head and sighed. "Easily?" the snow giant said softly. "Yet succumb he did. Will I? That is yet to be seen."

Madiraa whirled toward Indajaala and spat at the ground beneath his destrier. "Enough!" she said, drawing a heavy black sword from her scabbard and whipping it above her head in an impressive display of strength. "If you say one more foul word to our guest, I will strike you down."

For a moment, the conjurer smiled wickedly, but then his defiance wavered. Indajaala turned his horse and spurred it through the first gate, galloping wildly in the direction of the keep. Several of the company followed, but most stayed with the princess. She sheathed her sword and dismounted, walking over to Kusala. Though she was three spans shorter than the chieftain and barely a third the giant's height, she did not appear small. Her pride enlarged her presence.

"I apologize for such uncouth behavior," she said to Utu, and then she placed her hand on Kusala's shoulder and looked earnestly into his deep-blue eyes. Her eyes were black. "Since you were here just a few weeks ago, the mood of the fortress has changed—for the worse. I have never seen my father so . . . *bitter*. It's as if he would rather go to war against our allies than our enemies. And Indajaala is not helping matters.

"Your arrival, Kusala, could not have come at a better time. You are one of the few who dares speak openly to the king. But I had hoped The Torgon would be with you. The Death-Knower is the only person my father regards as an equal . . . other than Invictus himself."

"I, too, wish that Torg was here," Kusala said. "But my lord takes no directions from me. Will you escort me to Henepola? I must speak to him, for my journey does not end here."

"You will not stay and fight by our side?" Palak said from his mount. "Those are cruel words. Perhaps the king is right, after all. It seems none but his own people will stand by Nissaya."

"Tāseti will stay, along with the other Asēkhas," Kusala said. "Two thousand Tugars are already here, and five thousand more are within a three-day march. Do not say again that none will stand at Nissaya's side. The *Kantaara Yodhas* (desert warriors) do not cower."

"If only the white horsemen of Jivita could say the same," Madiraa said. "But enough debate. We linger too long outside the gates and bandy words in the absence of the king. Indajaala will soon report my insolence to Father. Let us go to him before his impatience turns to rage."

"I fear no man's rage," Kusala said.

"I fear no man at all," Utu said.

# 19

THE HALL OF Nagara was as magnificent as any chamber in the world—almost as broad as the entire keep, with ceilings higher than a strong knight could hurl a stone. Boulder-sized chunks of *Maōi*, as beautiful as the finest chandeliers, protruded from the ceiling like glowing eyeballs. Circular windows of glazed glass lined the upper third of the walls while palls of black silk framed the windows and extended all the way to the sunken floor, which was covered with rugs of strewn herbs and flowers. A long table constructed of black oak dominated the center of the chamber, with enough chairs to seat five hundred. At the far end of the hall, a granite platform rose ten cubits above the floor, and on it rested a black throne studded with rubies and fist-sized balls of *Maōi*.

Upon the throne sat King Henepola X, his long white hair cast about his shoulders, displaying to all that he was a conjurer as well as a king, a rare and formidable combination. Minus only his helm, Henepola wore full armor, black as kohl, except for silver spikes on the knuckles of his gauntlets and the toes of his sollerets. At his side stood Indajaala, a sneer on his dark face. The conjurer had changed quickly into a black robe speckled with pin-sized chips of *Maōi*, a garment worth a fortune anywhere on Triken.

At the base of the platform, fifteen steps beneath the throne, Madiraa and Palak were on their knees. Several paces farther back stood Kusala and Utu. Kusala wore the black outfit of an Asēkha, though it was stained gray from dust and grime. Utu wore only a loincloth, and his white mane was knotted and filthy. Compared to the king and the conjurer, they looked like peasants—though particularly large ones. Kusala was at least a span taller than any of the knights, and Utu was two and a half times their height and many times their girth.

When Henepola stood, all others in the room—save Kusala and Utu—mimicked Madiraa and Palak and dropped to their knees. The king held a long staff, ornately chiseled from *Maōi* and worth far more than Indajaala's robe.

"So, Madiraa, you have finally deigned to alert me that Kusala has returned to Nissaya. You certainly took your time doing so. Do you deem me so trivial—a doddering old man incapable of greeting guests of high esteem?"

Madiraa raised her head, her expression grim. "Those are *his* words, not mine," she said, nodding toward Indajaala.

The conjurer hissed. "She has always needed a mother to teach her the meaning of respect. See how she speaks to you."

For a moment, Henepola glared at the conjurer. Then his face softened. "When her mother died, I vowed never to remarry, so deep was my love. It is I who raised my daughter. If she is insolent, I am to blame."

To the amazement of all, Kusala stepped forward, without introduction. "And no sons have you, as well," he said to the king, "so when you pass, it is Madiraa who will rule Nissaya." Then Kusala glared at Indajaala. "Perhaps you would be wise to speak with pleasantry while in her presence."

The conjurer hissed again. The chamber became as silent as a tomb.

But Henepola laughed. "Ahhh, Kusala, it is refreshing to be in the presence of one so bold. You have always spoken your mind, even to your *own* king. Come, my friend, let us retire to less opulent surroundings, where we can converse in private."

Then he turned to Madiraa. "My daughter," he said, with a touch of playfulness in his voice, "I will forgive you, if you personally see to it that the snow giant is fed and well-cared for. After all, Kusala has vouched for him."

Madiraa smiled, her expression relieved. "It will be as you say, Father."

Kusala looked up at Utu. "Would you mind if we separated?"

The snow giant shrugged disinterestedly.

"I will seek you out in the morning and tell you all that I know," Kusala promised. "I would recommend your taking pleasure in the luxuries of Nagara while you can. There will be few opportunities for rest and relaxation in the coming days."

"I desire neither," Utu said.

WHILE HENEPOLA'S squires removed the king's armor in his personal quarters, Kusala waited in a nearby antechamber on the top story of the keep. At the approach of midnight, Henepola, now wearing flowing white robes, joined Kusala at a stone table set adjacent to a northward-facing window that provided a panoramic view of the Mahaggata Mountains. The moon, waning gibbous, glowed like a malformed boulder of *Maōi* in the cloudless sky, illuminating the mountains, fortress, and surrounding terrain.

A servant arrived with goblets of wine, crusty brown bread, white cheese, and several dozen skewers of tiny pink shrimp bathed in butter and herbs. Finally realizing the extent of his hunger, Kusala devoured the shrimp, which were one of his favorite reasons for visiting the fortress.

"You see, my friend," the king said, "I do not forget . . . only the best for Chieftain-Kusala."

Kusala wiped grease from his mouth with the side of his hand. "As always, your hospitality is much appreciated. If you would ever visit Anna, we would return the favor. There are delicacies in the desert, as well."

Henepola grimaced. "I will never leave the fortress again. I have grown too old and weary for journeying. Besides, have you not noticed? There is a war to wage."

"Have I not noticed? I am here, as are two thousand Tugars. And the rest of the Asēkhas will soon join us. Or have *you* not noticed?"

The king rested his elbows on the table and leaned way forward so that his glowing eyes were just a span away. "The Asēkhas are a boon, I cannot deny. But two thousand Tugars, you say? The last I heard, there were *ten* thousand *Kantaara Yodhas.* Have the rest become lost on their way from Tējo?"

Kusala leaned forward until the tips of their noses nearly touched. "Will you have us abandon Jivita?"

"*We* stand between Avici and Jivita."

"Have you forgotten Dhutanga?"

"Dhutanga? Do the white horsemen fear a few miserable druids? The army of Invictus is two hundred thousand strong."

"Two thousand Tugars are at Jivita, but five thousand remain near Hadaya, ready to march to the aid of whichever side needs it most. Only one thousand remain in Anna, by the way. Have you missed the subtlety of that?"

Henepola grunted. "Leave two thousand at Jivita. I care naught. But call the five thousand to Nissaya . . . now. It is what your king would do, were he here. And speaking of The Torgon, where has he gone? When you and I last spoke, you were on a quest to find him. Did you fail, chieftain?"

Kusala leaned back in his chair. "Torg is alive. But where he is, and how he fares, is beyond my present knowledge."

Henepola grunted again. "And yet *you* managed to return to Nissaya, so it must not have been such an impossible undertaking. The fate of Triken hangs on victory or defeat . . . *here.* And yet it seems no one deems Nissaya of much import. The Torgon is needed *here,* not gallivanting in the wilderness like a love-struck boy. Do you know, chieftain, that the great army of Invictus began its march this very day? I say again, the Tugars and Jivitans should be *here.*" The king lowered his head. "And yet, there are only two thousand Tugars, eighteen Asēkhas, and one snow giant," he whispered. "Too few have the courage to stand with us."

Kusala felt a chill run up his spine. "I am confused, sire. How could you know the exact size of Invictus' army and when it began its march? How could you know there will be only *eighteen* Asēkhas at Nissaya? And why do you use the words 'love struck' when you speak of Torg?"

Henepola's black face crinkled.

"Let me show you," the king of Nissaya said.

"Show me what?" Chieftain-Kusala said to King Henepola X.

"Follow me," Henepola said. "There is an object within my private quarters that you will find interesting."

The look in the king's eyes and his eerie tone disturbed Kusala, but he was not one to shy from any form of danger, so he stood and followed Henepola. The chamberlain and several other servants trailed behind.

The king waved them off. "Leave us . . . and allow *no one* to disturb us."

Henepola closed and barred the heavy door, which hung on iron hinges driven into the stone. Though Kusala had visited Nissaya hundreds of times, he had never been inside the king's personal bedchambers. It was smaller than the massive royal bedrooms of Jivita's opulent castles, but impressive, nonetheless. The bed was large enough for six and bore a white damask quilt trimmed with black lace. Four round windows had been chiseled out of the wall, each bearing curtains that matched the quilt. The other furnishings included tables, chairs, and a looking-glass as tall as a man. There also were several closets and a private latrine.

Henepola strode past all this with disregard, his white robes flowing behind him like wings. Kusala followed him into a narrow hallway that led to a door made of solid obsidian. Though Henepola remained a powerful man, he had to rest his staff against the wall and use both hands to push this door open.

The room was small, round and windowless. It also was dark and filled with a fetid mist that caused the skin on Kusala's face to tingle. The king slammed the door shut. The room became utterly dark.

Henepola sensed his discomfort. "Is the great Kusala, Chieftain of the Asēkhas, frightened? I would not have believed it possible."

"Neither you nor I have time for games. What have you to show me?"

The king laughed. "Patience has never been one of your virtues, Chieftain. Your lord has far more of it than you. Will you never learn from him?"

"As you have so *delicately* pointed out, my lord is not present."

This time, Henepola didn't laugh. Kusala heard shuffling, then murmuring. Suddenly the king's *Maōi* staff filled the room with light. He placed its tail in a hole in the floor, balancing the staff like a lamp post. A U-shaped curtain hid something against the far wall. The king drew black silk aside, revealing the mysterious contents that lay beyond.

A wide basin of transparent crystal rested on a pedestal chiseled from obsidian. Kusala leaned over the basin and saw that it contained a silvery liquid within which he could see his own reflection. Its raggedness startled him. He hadn't properly groomed since before meeting Torg in Kamupadana. Filth was encrusted in the lines on his face.

"Do you know what this is, Chieftain?"

"An expensive mirror?"

Henepola smacked him playfully on the back, though far harder than was necessary. The blow would have injured an ordinary man, but Kusala simply grunted in annoyance.

"Expensive? Most definitely. A mirror? In a manner of speaking. But it is far more than that. Allow me to demonstrate."

The king waved his hand over the basin. Milky tendrils oozed from his fingertips, and the silver surface burst into color.

Kusala gasped.

An image of Torg and the woman named Laylah appeared. They were walking down a dark mountain path. He also recognized their other companions: Ugga, Bard, Elu, Lucius, and Rathburt.

"You asked earlier why I used the words 'love-struck,'" Henepola said. "I have been watching your lord for several days now."

"But how? What is this thing?"

"As a warrior, you have few rivals, but this level of magic is beyond your comprehension. Suffice it to say that it is not beyond *mine*. I made this myself . . . and with it, I can see far. Would you care to view more?"

"You have shown me that my king still lives. But that I already knew, for my heart told me so. What can you show me that I don't know?"

Henepola laughed again, but this time it sounded more like cackling.

"Behold, Chieftain!" And then the image changed to a darkness illuminated by tens of thousands of flickering torches. The huge army of Invictus had begun its march.

The enormity of it caused Kusala to groan.

"It moves slowly," Kusala said in a low voice, "but still, you will be besieged within a month."

"The army marching toward Nissaya is the most powerful that has ever existed," Henepola said. "Even during the Dragon Wars of ancient times, no ground force was greater. And yet, this army—led by Mala himself—is the lesser of our concerns. Compared to Invictus himself, it is but a trifle. Here, Chieftain, come closer. Have you ever seen the sorcerer in person? I can show you his face."

Sweat burst from Kusala's brow, plopping like raindrops in the basin. He tried to pull away, but a will stronger than his own forced him to look even closer. A face appeared, boyish and handsome—and it smiled. The whites of the man's eyes were disturbingly flawless. Kusala saw strength in those eyes, strength beyond Nissaya, beyond the Tugars, beyond even The Torgon. Then the man's skin began to glow. Golden light exploded from the basin. Kusala cried out and fell backward. Henepola managed to keep his feet, but even he was staggered.

Afterward, the basin went cold. Kusala rose unsteadily. When he dared to look again, the liquid had returned to flat silver.

"Now do you comprehend our plight?" the king said.

"If your goal was to shock me, then you have succeeded," Kusala said. "Tomorrow morning, I will call the Tugars from Hadaya. All told, there will be seven thousand desert warriors within your walls before Mala's army reaches your doorstep. And I have made another decision. I will defy my king's own command and send Tāseti to Anna in my place."

If Henepola was impressed, he did not show it. Instead, he shoved open the obsidian door and pointed down the hallway. "Go now," he said wearily. "Bathe and sleep. It is obvious you are in need of both."

"And what will you do?" Kusala said, eyeing the basin distrustfully.

"What I do is my business," Henepola said. "After all, I *am* a king."

# 20

ONE OF THE squires who had been guarding the king's chambers escorted Kusala down several flights of clammy stairs, eventually leading him to a small guest room with a single round window. Kusala had stayed in this room before and knew it well. A basin of steaming water, a wooden comb, a pair of crude metal scissors, a cake of soap, and a wool towel had been placed on the table next to the bed. There also was a flagon of wine and a pewter cup. Before settling in, Kusala availed himself of the garderobe a few paces down the curving hall. After emptying the chamber pot, he returned to his room and spent a long time bathing and grooming. Then he changed into gray robes his host had provided.

Kusala had not been permitted to bring his weapons to the king's quarters, so he had left his *uttara*, short sword, and dagger with a servant, giving strict orders to deliver the weapons to the nearest Tugar. Now he saw that they had been returned, but not before being cleaned and polished. All three were encased in new Tugarian scabbards, which were made of flexible cactus skin wound with black cloth. He also found a black jacket, breeches, belt, and boots. Kusala bowed, silently thanking the nameless Tugar for his or her efforts.

Kusala leaned out the window and inhaled the night air.

The inside of his room—and much of the keep, for that matter—tended to be damp and chilly, but the outside air was warm. Kusala leaned way out, so that half his body protruded from the window, and stared at the fortress from his perch two-thirds of the way up the keep. Though it now was the middle of the night, the wall walks of the three concentric ramparts swarmed with defenders, torchlight revealing much of their movements. Kusala recognized Tugars scattered among the black knights, squires, and bowmen of Nissaya. The desert warriors were larger than the others, yet moved more gracefully. He was unendingly proud to be considered the greatest of them, next to Torg himself. It was an honor bestowed to a very few, and he had held it now for almost three hundred years, having attained the rank of chieftain when he was one hundred and ten.

About fifty cubits beneath him, a barely visible figure crept slowly up the wall of Nagara like a human-sized lizard. Kusala watched its approach with fascination. Not even a Tugar had the skill to scale the keep's slippery surface, which contained few handholds. Yet the climber made steady progress, coming ever closer to Kusala's window. When it was just a few spans away, he leaned down and hauled the figure into the room.

Indajaala, the highest ranked of Henepola's conjurers, stood before Kusala, wearing a snug-fitting black doublet with matching breeches and leather slippers. He breathed heavily, his ebony skin slathered with sweat.

"I'll never understand how you're able to do that," Kusala said softly. "Wouldn't it be easier just to cast some kind of spell in the hallway and then knock on the door?"

Though he still was out of breath, Indajaala managed a smile. Then he grasped Kusala's forearm in Tugarian fashion. "Good to see you again, old friend," he whispered.

"I feel the same," Kusala said. "I'm glad to see you're still in one piece. I haven't yet opened the flagon. Would you care to share some wine with me?"

"I wish that I could, but I must speak quickly and then depart. The moon will soon reach a point in the sky where it will reflect off the keep and reveal my presence. That must not occur."

"I knew that would be your answer. You have always been careful. So, tell me then, what have you learned since we last spoke?"

"My worst fears—*our* worst fears—have been realized," Indajaala said, his voice barely audible. "Henepola has grown more and more unstable. Other than eat and sleep, the only thing he wants to do is gaze into his crystal basin. Did he show it to you?"

Kusala nodded. "Yes . . . and I did not find it the least bit pleasant."

Indajaala grimaced. "I have spent many tedious moments with him in that miserable room, watching this person and that, including the wanderings of our Lord Torgon. Our eyes were present when the wizard ordered you to separate from him and return to the fortress. The king became very angry over The Torgon's decision to head for Jivita instead of Nissaya. He has become difficult to comprehend . . . and control."

"Does Henepola still trust you?"

"I believe so, but only because I pretend to be as disdainful of others as he has become. He sees me as one of his few true allies. He even distrusts his own daughter, whom until recently he loved like no other."

Kusala shook his head slowly. "Henepola's reputation as a warrior and conjurer is admired throughout Triken, but he has always been prideful and headstrong. Still, I have never known him to be disdainful of Madiraa. What has caused this change? Is it *all* the fault of the magical basin?"

"You tell me. What happened while you were with him? Did you see anything disturbing?"

"To me, it was all disturbing. But one thing was worse than the rest. Henepola showed me the face of Invictus, and then the room became filled with blinding light. Afterward, Henepola ordered me to leave . . . but he remained."

A look of dismay swept across the conjurer's face. "That is the worst news I could have heard. Henepola has never revealed Invictus to me. He must have known that I would recognize how dangerous it would be to lock wills with the Sun God. How much damage has already occurred? And when Mala's army assaults our walls, what then? I fear that the fortress will lack leadership at the time it is needed most."

"I fear that as well," Kusala said.

"If only The Torgon were here," Indajaala moaned.

Kusala placed his hand on the conjurer's shoulder. "For many long years, you have been one of Torg's most faithful servants, and he still remembers fondly the time you spent at Anna as his apprentice. But Lord Torgon is not here, and when the great are not present, the lesser must lead. For that reason I have decided to remain at Nissaya and send Tāseti to Anna in my place. Torg would be angry with me, if he knew. But when the heavy hand of Invictus falls upon the fortress, I want to be here—especially since it appears that Henepola might no longer be dependable. What of Madiraa? Can she still be trusted?"

"The king's daughter is stern to her core," Indajaala said. "In some ways she reminds me of a Tugarian woman. Yes, she can be trusted—above all others who dwell here, though because of my charades, she loves me not."

THE NEXT MORNING, Kusala went down to the banquet hall at the base of Nagara. At breakfast time, the room was usually filled with high-ranking knights listening to Henepola preside over the gathering at the head of the long table. But on this day, only Madiraa was present, leaning over her tray and seeming to eat without pleasure. Though it was barely past dawn, the princess was adorned in full armor, minus only her helm and gauntlets. Kusala was amazed she could sit comfortably, much less eat. When he came over beside her and cleared his throat, she was startled—more so than the occasion deserved.

"I'm sorry, Chieftain," she said, her eyes red and watery. "I've been jumpy lately. The specter of Mala wears on us all, it seems."

"Where are the others?" Kusala said, sweeping his hand about the empty room. "And your father? If memory serves, breakfast was always his favorite meal."

Madiraa sighed. "Father has not supped in this room—any meal at all—for more than a week. He prefers to eat alone in his chambers, no longer desiring my company or the company of the *Kalakhattiyas* (black knights). Only Indajaala pleases him, and even he for short stretches."

Kusala sat next to her and ran his fingers one time through her long, black hair, which hung over her backplate.

"Well, that means there's more food for you and me," he said, trying to sound cheerful. "I have been long in the wilderness and have grown thin from starvation. May I join you, my lady?"

"It would be my most sincere pleasure," she said, returning his smile. Even as a child, she had been good-natured and easy to succor.

A servitor came forward and offered Kusala a tray of stirred eggs, sliced sausages, and toasted bread. Kusala ate greedily with his spoon, washing the large meal down with black tea.

Madiraa watched him with amusement. "I do not have your appetite, Chieftain. Would you like the rest of mine?"

Rather than chuckle at her jest, Kusala took her tray.

Her eyes grew wide, and then she laughed heartily. "Aaaaah, Chieftain, you lighten my heart," she said, her black eyes suddenly sparkling. "As you always have."

*Gods, but she's beautiful. Damn near as beautiful as a Tugarian woman. But she's too young for you, old man. Of course, outside of a very few, who isn't?*

"What are your duties today?" he said.

"My duties?" She grunted. "I have none. I do what I can to keep things organized, but no one commands me, if that's what you mean."

"In that case, will you walk with me? I *do* have duties to perform, and it would please me if you were at my side."

"I would like nothing better."

"Excellent." Kusala smiled. "The first thing I must do is find the snow giant."

"Then you've chosen the right companion. I know where he is and can lead you to him as soon as you've finished stuffing food into your mouth."

A few minutes later, Madiraa led him from the banquet hall to the outer door of the keep. Crunchy layers of pebbles and sand covered the streets. Black knights marched here and there, in units or individually, appearing slightly disorganized. Kusala started to question Madiraa about this, but he was interrupted when a tall, dark-haired woman ran over to him and bowed low.

"Rise, Dalhapa," Kusala said.

The Tugarian warrior straightened to her full height, just a finger-length shorter than Kusala. "Your arrival has been noted," Dalhapa said. "It was I who honored your weapons. I hope my performance met with your approval. The Tugars who now dwell in the fortress await your orders."

"You have done well, as always." Kusala knew, as did all Tugars, that Dalhapa was next in line to ascend to Asēkha, once one of the *Viisati* (The Twenty) was to fall or retire. "Tell the Tugars to gather in the field outside Balak's door a short time before noon. In the meantime, I need you to call the others back from Hadaya."

"It will be done," said Dalhapa, obviously pleased by Kusala's praise. "And those at Jivita?"

"They are to remain at the White City."

Dalhapa bowed and then sprinted off, disappearing around a street corner in a matter of moments.

Madiraa was impressed. "She is *big*, but is she as strong as she looks?"

"No black knight, save Henepola himself, could stand against her," Kusala said, without a hint of boast.

"Lack of confidence is not a weakness of the Tugars."

"We speak plainly."

Madiraa laughed. "*We speak plainly*. Kusala, you're funny even when you're not trying to be."

Kusala shrugged.

"See?" she said, giggling and then grabbing his muscular arm.

They continued down the wide street. A dense assortment of buildings lined both its sides. Most were constructed of stone and wood with exterior walls faced with dark ashlars, but a few of the larger edifices were natural extensions of the stone mountain on which they stood, resembling black stalagmites with hollow interiors. The black granite was virtually impervious to hammers or chisels, except over extended periods of workmanship. To chip out a single window could take a mason the better part of a month. In this tedious manner, the inner workings of Nissaya had been molded over the millennia, flake by flake.

Even this early in the day, the interior of the fortress swarmed with people. Most resided year-round in Nissaya: black knights, sergeants, squires, and bowmen, all of whom were black-skinned Nissayans; and armorers, merchants, and craftsmen, some of whom were outsiders who had won a permanent place in the city through long years of labor. But the farmers, villagers, and fishermen who had recently fled there from as far west as Hadaya and east as the Ogha had more than doubled the usual population of the fortress. All seemed in a nervous rush to go from one place to another. "There are so many to feed," Madiraa said in a loud voice, attempting to make herself heard over the din. "Our stores are impressive, but they are not limitless. If Mala chooses to camp outside our walls and wait for us to starve, we will be forced to flee the secret ways to the mountains."

"That is the least of your concerns, my lady," Kusala said. "Mala is many things, but patient is not one of them. It is the only thing he and I have in common. When his army arrives, he will give it time to settle. But after that, I believe he will attack with all his power."

"Let him, then. If there were but a few hundred defenders on each wall, Mala could not prevail. And yet, our numbers have never been greater. From the battlements, our bowmen alone could destroy an army. How does he hope to defeat us?"

"If Mala were an ordinary man, and his army made up of ordinary men and women, he would stand little chance. But among his host are monsters more terrible than any seen on Triken, save the dragons themselves. Who knows what these monsters are capable of? But one thing is certain. If any place in the world can withstand Mala, it is Nissaya. And if his army somehow prevails, it will not do so without loss."

"Which will please the white horsemen, I'm sure," Madiraa said bitterly. "In this regard, at least, I agree with my father. The Jivitans should be here, where the hammer will fall the hardest, not cowering a hundred leagues away. They speak so highly of their *One God*. Are they not ashamed to behave so meekly in his presence?"

"I have never known the *Assarohaa* (white horsemen) to cower," Kusala said. "Do not believe such talk. Their motives may be selfish, but they are not cowardly. On horseback, they fear nothing. Do not forget the threat of Dhutanga. The druids are dangerous, as well. And their hatred is older and deeper."

"All of what you say may be true. But what good does it do my people?"

For that, Kusala had no answer.

They continued down the street, turned into an alley, and emerged onto a narrow roadway. Finally they came to the foot of a zigzagging stair that led to the top of the third bulwark, which towered some two hundred cubits above them.

"Why have we come here?" Kusala said. "I need to find the snow giant."

"So you shall."

The stairway was built of ordinary stone, though cleverly constructed and well-maintained. However, it was not made for anyone suffering from a fear of heights. The stairs themselves were four cubits broad, but there was no rail. A false step meant certain death. But neither Madiraa nor Kusala was cowed. The princess had played on these walls since she was a toddler, and Kusala had faced things far more frightening than falling.

The stairway rose at a left angle for fifty cubits before the first landing, then turned right, left, and right again. They finally reached the wall walk of Hakam, where black knights and bowmen greeted them ceremoniously. Several Tugars also approached, bowing low and then clasping Kusala's forearm.

The view was magnificent. Kusala could see for leagues in all directions. Mahaggata loomed to the northwest, Kolankold to the southwest.

"This day will be beautiful," Madiraa said. "But it is already so warm. It feels more like a summer morning than early spring."

"I find it odd too," Kusala said. "If this were Dibbu-Loka, it would not be so unusual. But this far north . . ."

From the head of the stairs, Kusala caught sight of Yama-Utu. The snow giant stood on top of the low wall of the battlement, his bare toes clinging to the stone like roots. As was typical of his kind, he wore only a loincloth. When Kusala and the princess approached, he paid them no heed.

"Good morning to you, Yama-Utu," Kusala said. "I trust you slept well. Or did you sleep at all? And were you properly fed?"

At first the snow giant didn't answer, but then his head slowly turned, and he looked down somberly. "Sleep and sustenance are not my concern," he said, his white mane swirling in the heavy breeze that swept through the air at such a height.

Kusala tried to sound friendly. "But won't you grow weak? Nissaya will be in need of all your strength in the coming days."

"*Eso aham himamahaakaayo* (I am a snow giant)," he said, as if no other answer were required.

Madiraa was clearly uncomfortable, but she also tried to sound cheerful. "It must feel awfully hot to you, being so far from Okkanti. Can I at least have someone bring you something to drink?"

Utu hopped off the wall and faced them. Except for a few of the Tugars, Kusala was the tallest man on the battlement, yet the snow giant was more than twice the height of the Asēkha chieftain.

"How long before Mala arrives?" Utu said. "I grow weary of waiting."

"I left you in a much better mood last night than I found you in today," Kusala said. "You remind me of the Utu I met before the Pabbajja succored him."

"How *long?*" said Utu, his voice like a growl.

"Three weeks," Kusala said.

"Three . . . weeks," Utu repeated.

Then without warning, he scooped both Kusala and Madiraa into his arms, stepped onto the low wall—and jumped off Hakam.

# 21

KUSALA'S ARMS were pinned against his sides by strength more crushing than he had ever encountered. Even if he had tried, he could not have drawn his *uttara* from the scabbard on his back. But he was too amazed to entertain the thought. Air rushed against his face and exploded in his ears—and above the roar, he could hear Madiraa screaming next to him.

Utu landed feet-first on the battlement of Ott—just thirty cubits away from Hakam but one hundred cubits farther down—and then pounced again, flying through the air across the spiked moat before landing on Balak with equal aplomb. Then he leaped one last time, with much greater force than before, and finally came to rest on the grassy field that surrounded the granite base of the fortress, several hundred paces from the first gate.

The snow giant put Kusala and Madiraa down and backed away.

Instantly Kusala drew his *uttara* and the princess her longsword. A dozen others, who had witnessed the spectacle from the ground, raced to their aid, including several angry-looking Tugars.

Utu was encircled. The snow giant seemed more amused than threatened.

"Do you doubt my strength *now?*" he said.

At first, this stunned Kusala into silence. He was angry, frightened, and exhilarated at the same time. Never before had he been bested in such a manner, and so easily.

"Shall we slay the beast, chieftain?" said a female Tugarian warrior poised nearby. "We await your command."

Utu grunted but did not speak.

"We were not injured," Madiraa said.

Her words surprised Kusala, who said, "Nonetheless, our *friend* has again become unpredictable. What say you, snow giant? Is there a reason to trust you further?"

Utu grunted again. "Snow giants love to jump. We leap from peak to peak just for fun. I meant no harm."

Even as they spoke, a thundering squadron of mounted black knights charged out of the fortress—with Henepola in the lead, his staff of *Maôi* burning like fire.

"It appears you have accomplished something that the rest of us cannot. You have awakened the king," Kusala said. "Your fate is no longer in my hands."

"Nor his," Utu said. "Nor any mortal's."

Suddenly the snow giant let out a piercing cry, so loud that even Kusala had to hold his ears. And then he sprinted northward far faster than any horse could gallop, save Bhojja herself. The Tugars started to follow, but Kusala ordered them to halt. Several Nissayan bowmen loosed arrows at the fleeing beast, but none met their mark. In a matter of moments, Utu had vanished.

Henepola and the Nissayan squadron veered to the left and gave chase, but it was clear they could not catch him. For better or worse, the snow giant was gone again.

"When my father returns, he will be angrier than ever," Madiraa said.

"But the giant sealed his own fate. It was as if he *wanted* to be banished. Do you think he will return to Okkanti?"

"No, he will not return to his home," Kusala said. "At least, not yet. His desire to confront Mala is too great. Amid his madness and anger, a fierce intelligence still burns. Sometime before the Chain Man strikes, his brother will show himself. And we all must keep in mind that as dangerous as Utu may seem, Mala is far deadlier. I will feel more comfortable with a snow giant on our side, even if he is unpredictable."

"After what just occurred, my father will not permit it," Madiraa said.

"Then it will be up to you and me to change his mind."

A short time later, a thousand more mounted Nissayans rode off after their king. To say the least, it was not a good time to exhaust knights and their mounts, especially in pursuit of a single foe that might not even be a foe.

KUSALA WAS LEFT standing, in the words of a Vasi master, with his hands in his pockets. So he left the field and went to meet with the Tugars already encamped at Nissaya. The desert warriors packed around their chieftain, encircling him so tightly that no others could hear his words, save Madiraa. But first they bowed low.

"Rise," Kusala said. "You all know that I am not one for ceremony." This was met with scattered hooting and applause. "Let it be known," he continued in a more serious tone, "that The Torgon lives!"

This elicited cheers and clinking of swords, though Kusala knew that his warriors already were aware of this news. If Torg had fallen, they would have sensed it internally, so in tune were they to their king.

"I have ordered the Tugars camped near Lake Hadaya to come to the fortress. Soon we will be seven thousand strong." Cheers and whistles. "Also, the Asēkhas will arrive in a short time, and with them a score of freed slaves who fought bravely by our sides during a perilous journey. They will be weary. See personally to their comfort."

And then, unrelated to Kusala's speech, there were more loud cheers and then a hearty chant. "The Asēkhas come! Just as you say!"

Kusala was relieved. "We are together again," he whispered to himself. "If only Torg were here to complete us."

NOT OVERLY FOND of socializing outside their own people, the Tugars had set up camp in a field west of Nissaya, pitching tents made from camel hide woven with sagebrush leaves and waterproofed with resin extracted from piñon pines. Kusala, Madiraa, and Tāseti sat cross-legged on the ground in the center of an open pavilion, the female Asēkha supping from a bowl of goat-stomach stew and drinking Tugarian wine from a tubular skin.

"I'm not trying to get rid of you," Kusala said to the princess, "but shouldn't you go back to the fortress and await your father's return?"

"This is the first place he'll come," Madiraa said. "He has always preferred to deal with men over women. Regardless, I want to be here when he confronts you."

"Your father will never catch the snow giant," Tāseti said. "When the black knights found us, we shared their mounts and rode all through the night and morning at a brisk pace, and yet the snow giant managed to cover the same distance—with the chieftain on his back—in a third of the time or less. The beast can run as fast as a dragon flies."

"My father is stubborn, but not stupid," Madiraa said. "Once he realizes the cause is lost, he will return. But he will be enraged."

When Tāseti finished her meal, she prepared to rise so that she could bathe and then rest. She had not slept for several days. But Kusala bade her to remain seated. "I have an assignment for you. You will not like it, but you must obey me."

"Chieftain?"

"The Torgon and I spoke for a brief time before I left him," Kusala said, "and our king made it clear that he feared for the safety of Anna. He ordered me to return there as soon as possible."

"You've already told me this."

"Yes. But since arriving at Nissaya, I have learned some things that concern me greatly, and I have made a decision to remain at the fortress."

"That is excellent news," Tāseti said. "Nissaya will need you in the battle to come. Anna can take care of herself—especially with Dvipa in control. Besides, no invading army could pass through the Simōōn and survive."

Kusala lowered his gaze. "You do not understand. Yes, Dvipa is capable, as are all Asēkhas, but our lord was not comfortable with only his presence. He greatly feared the wiles of the sorcerer and wanted me to retrieve the noble ones from the haven and return with them to Anna. Since I now cannot go, I must send you in my stead."

Tāseti's facial expression remained calm, but Kusala knew her too well. She was furious. An uncomfortable period of silence followed Kusala's words, prompting Madiraa to excuse herself and leave the pavilion.

When the princess was gone, Tāseti finally spoke. "I am a warrior, not a *babysitter!*" she said, her lips quivering. "I have trained my entire life for this moment. Not a day has passed in more than two centuries that I have not striven to better myself. And now, with battle at hand, you order me to leave? Send someone else. Send Podhana or even Churikā. Please, Chieftain, *anyone* but me."

Kusala sighed deeply. "If Lord Torgon were here with us and made the same request of you, how would you respond?"

It was Tāseti's turn to sigh, long and deep. Kusala could see the defeat in her eyes. "Very well, Chieftain . . . when do you wish me to depart?"

"Rest today and leave tomorrow morning . . . and Tāseti?"

"Yes?"

"When I pass, you will take my place as head of our order. In no way will this have any effect on your position."

"To be honest, I have no desire for you to 'pass.' I don't like you very much right now. But I will always love you."

And then she rushed out of the pavilion. Though he could not explain it, Kusala somehow knew that he would never see her again.


FOR A LONG time afterward, Kusala sat by himself, battling conflicting emotions: guilt over what he had done to Tāseti; dread over his soon-to-occur confrontation with Henepola; apprehension over the fate of the snow giant; sorrow over what was about to happen at Nissaya and then the rest of the world. To diffuse his growing agitation, he chose to meditate, watching the beginning, middle, and ending of each slow breath. When thoughts inevitably arose, he observed them too—and let them pass, returning to the breath . . . peaceful but alert.

Henepola found him this way, sitting cross-legged, eyes closed, and body still. The king pounded the base of his black staff into the ground just an arm's-length from where Kusala sat. The *Maōi* flared and crackled, causing the stakes of the pavilion to tremble. At first Kusala did not react, but then he opened his eyes and looked up at the conjurer king, noting that Indajaala and two dozen black knights flanked him.

Behind them stood five times that many Tugars, *uttaras* drawn.

"Who is your enemy? Mala or me?" Kusala said slowly. "Do you wish to begin the battle now, between two peoples who hitherto have fought side by side for centuries? The sorcerer would find that amusing, I'm sure."

Though he appeared weary, Henepola's eyes smoldered. Wisps of smoke oozed from his nostrils and ears. The *Maōi* glowed like a log long in the fire. "I would ask you the same questions, desert warrior," the king said, his voice low and sinister. "Under the guise of friendship, you willfully brought a monster into our midst, and it nearly cost my only child her life. What say you to that?"

There was a commotion off to the side—and then Madiraa came forward, shoving her way past Indajaala. "Father, don't do this. It is unnecessary."

"This is no longer your affair," the king said angrily. "Leave this to me."

"I will not! Just because I'm a woman doesn't mean I'm some feeble creature, too delicate for important matters. Do not our women wear armor and fight alongside the men? And are we not best with the bow? I will speak on my own behalf."

Indajaala gasped but said nothing.

Henepola glared at her. "Very well, *daughter . . .* speak."

"The snow giant meant us no harm," she said quickly. "If he had wanted to kill us, we would be dead. We challenged his . . . strength . . . and he met the challenge. To be honest, the jumps were exhilarating. You know how much I love the heights. If he were here now, I would ask him to do it again."

Kusala sensed the tension begin to diffuse, if only slightly. He rose to his feet and snapped his fingers. In long-practiced unison the Tugars sheathed their swords. It was a symbolic gesture only—they could re-draw faster than the eye could follow—but one Kusala hoped would be viewed as concession.

"Yama-Utu was . . . is . . . not under my sway, I admit," Kusala said. "But if we could have somehow kept him in control until Mala arrived, I believe he would have proven to be our most valuable ally. What happened to Madiraa and me was unplanned and unfortunate, but in the end no harm was done." Then he stepped closer to Henepola and stared hard into his eyes. "Regardless of how you feel about the snow giant, you cannot believe that I brought him here with the purpose of murdering the princess or anyone else. As you know better than all others, these are perilous times. Where strength can be found, we must seek it."

Indajaala's expression grew sly. "Perhaps you should ask the Tugars to leave. Do we really need the desert warriors? Send them all to Jivita and let them cower with the white horsemen."

Henepola tilted his head toward the conjurer and then smiled ruefully. "Your loyalty means much. But your counsel is oft foolish. With Mala thirsting for my blood, would I banish the Tugars? I love my people too much for that." Then he turned back to Kusala. "And if the snow giant returns?"

"His fate will be yours to decide," Kusala said.

"You are assuming I have the strength to enforce his fate," Henepola said.

"If you do not, then the snow giant is greater than all who stand among us."

"Flattery, Chieftain?"

"You have always been susceptible to it."

"How dare you speak to the king with such insolence!" Indajaala said.

But Henepola chuckled. "Relax, my friend." He patted the conjurer on the shoulder. "Kusala is *almost* a king himself, and he and I have known each other since your grandmother was a child. I will not live as long as an Asēkha, but I have lived long, nonetheless. Too many years, it feels to me now."

Then he strode out of the pavilion with Indajaala attending him closely. When they were gone, Madiraa glanced at Kusala. "I'd better go after him and try to make peace. He despises it when I talk back to him, especially in front of *men*."

"Remember one thing," Kusala said.

"What's that?"

"You are the equal of any man I know."

"Flattery, Chieftain?"

Kusala smiled. "And remember something else."

"What else could there be?"

"Everything you said to your father was the truth."

"Sort of." Then she laughed her lovely laugh.


AFTER HIS confrontation with Henepola, Kusala spent the rest of the day mingling with the Tugars in an attempt to improve morale. The desert warriors did what they were told when they were told, but they were not particularly comfortable spending long stretches of time away from Tējo. They worried about their families and friends and missed the desert's blazing sands. In comparison, Nissaya felt barren.

The next morning, Kusala went in search of Tāseti to say his farewells, but found she had departed without seeking him out, another obvious sign that she was angry. Part of him regretted his decision to send her in his place. After all, Torg had ordered Kusala to return to Anna, not the second in command. But he knew that he was the best suited among them to deal with Henepola's increasingly disturbing behavior. Tāseti was a powerful warrior and would make an excellent chieftain when he died or retired, but she tended to lead more by example than by words. Among her people, this was an effective tool, but it was not the best way to deal with the current king of Nissaya. Besides, Kusala had known Henepola since the king was a boy. In fact, Kusala had been a guest of Nissaya, along with The Torgon, at the royal birth. The baby's father, Henepola IX, had been so proud.

"His hair is white," the king had said to both of them. "He will be the first Conjurer King of my family's line. How strong he will become. God's lifeblood surges through his veins."

Now it was noon, more than two hundred years later, and Kusala stood at the first gate, watching the black knights and an occasional Tugar bustling along Balak's battlement far above. The Conjurer King had indeed grown strong, but the stability of his mind had never equaled his other faculties. This worried Kusala, to say the least. If Henepola X collapsed, the fortress would need a steady—and vocal—leader to replace him. Kusala was no Torg, but he was the next best thing.

Madiraa startled him by touching his shoulder. He turned and smiled at the king's daughter, and his mind drifted again, this time to the day Madiraa had been born thirty years ago. That day's joy had been overshadowed by sadness. The queen had died while bringing Madiraa into the world.

*I remember it as if it were yesterday.*

The princess gave him a puzzled look. "No words for me, Chieftain?"

Kusala chuckled. "As my Vasi master liked to say, 'The Tyger got my tongue.'"

"You looked almost pale. Are you a Jivitan in disguise?"

"Neither Jivitan nor Nissayan, my lady. For better or worse, I am a Tugar."

"We both know it's much for the better. At the least, your people are less judgmental than the rest of us. Will you join me for dinner in the great hall?"

"It's such a long walk to Nagara," Kusala said. "Come instead to my pavilion. Churikā slew an elk early this morning. Our cooks are making a stew with strips of Cirāya added to enhance the flavor."

"I could think of nothing better," she said.

Then they walked together beneath a hot sun.

"Today is warmer than yesterday, and yesterday was warmer than the day before," Madiraa said. "If this continues, Nissaya will be an oven by the time the battle begins. Is Invictus somehow to blame for this?"

"Nothing that the sorcerer accomplishes would surprise me. But right now, I'm more concerned about your father. You were going to try to make amends. How did it go?"

The luscious corners of Madiraa's mouth curved downward. "It was worse than I expected. Not so much because he shouted at me, but because he didn't. When I caught up with him, it was as if he barely recognized me. Indajaala, of all people, treated me with more courtesy. The conjurer and I followed him all the way to his quarters in the keep, but Father slammed the door in our faces. His eyes looked strange, Kusala. He reminded me of a man addicted to the milk of poppies. That *thing* consumes him. He has not emerged since yesterday afternoon. What can I do? What *should* I do?"

"How well do you trust me, my lady?" Kusala said.

"You are like a second father to me. I trust you with my life."

"And you are wise to do so. I will say this: Your father has a strong will. He won't change—for good or ill—just because we tell him to. But when Mala arrives, someone must lead Nissaya. Do not be surprised if the rule falls to you and me."

"If he heard you say these words, he would imprison you in the caverns beneath Nagara. Indajaala would chuckle all the while."

"Indajaala is not as he appears," Kusala said, causing Madiraa to cock an eyebrow. "Do not be overly quick to discount him. As for your father, we shall see what we shall see."

While they ate, Madiraa pleased Kusala by telling him that the freed slaves who had accompanied the Asēkhas to the fortress had been provided food, clothing, and accommodations inside one of the lesser keeps within the third wall.

She also said that there still had been no sign of the snow giant. None knew where he had gone.

Messenger pigeons—the few that still dared to fly—had returned with reports from Nissayan scouts that Mala's army had moved fewer than fifteen leagues in three days. At this rate, it indeed would take three weeks before the entire army reached the fortress, especially considering the difficulties it would encounter on the sabotaged road west of the forest. By then it would be the middle of spring.

"The only good news is that Nissaya has never been stronger," Madiraa said, reiterating words oft-spoken by many. "Of knights, bowmen, sergeants, and squires, we number more than fifty thousand. And we have one hundred conjurers, which is unprecedented. Never in our proud history have we been so well-armed. Entire storage chambers are stacked with armor and weapons, all excellent in make and condition. Even our stable of horses—though no rival to Jivita's—has never been so well-stocked, being five thousand strong.

"Indeed, if the Chain Man's army were made of ordinary men and women, it would stand no chance of breaching our walls were it ten times our number."

"The sorcerer would not unleash this army if he did not believe it would succeed . . . and not just in defeating Nissaya, but Jivita, as well."

"Believe me, I am anything but overconfident," Madiraa said. "But if I were Mala, I would not attack immediately. A prolonged siege would make more sense. By the end of the summer, the refugees alone would deplete our provisions. More than one hundred thousand swarm within our walls."

"I agree that a prolonged siege would be the wisest course for the enemy, but Mala's pride will not permit it. He will give his army time to arrive and dig in, but once that occurs, it will be all or nothing. Starvation is not our concern. Victory or defeat will come before that."

When they finished eating the stew, Madiraa took her leave, telling Kusala that she again would attempt to meet with her father.

"If he doesn't come out of his room soon," she said, "I might have to order the guards to bash down the door."

"If it comes to that," Kusala said, "leave it to me. I might have more success with your father, if you are not there to watch. And here is something else that I should have already told you. The Pabbajja are not your enemies. Inform the black knights that Kusala knows this as fact. It appears there are traitors within Mala's army. This could work to our advantage in the coming days."

"If anyone else uttered such words, I would only laugh," Madiraa said.

"The Pabbajja have always been a nuisance. I will tell as many as I can, though not all will believe it. Such are the times."

And then she strode away, her long black hair flowing freely down her back. Unlike her father, she was no conjurer. But she was strong, nonetheless. If she outlived Henepola and became queen, Nissaya would be better off.

FOUR DAYS AFTER Kusala's angry encounter with Henepola in the pavilion, five thousand Tugars arrived from Lake Hadaya. Kusala, the Asēkhas, and the desert warriors already at Nissaya greeted their comrades in the open field west of the fortress. Madiraa was also there with a vanguard of black knights also numbering five thousand, including five hundred mounted, each carrying a Nissayan banner. Trumpeters filled the air with sweet music, accompanied by the rhythmic pounding of a *Bheri*, a Tugarian drum as thick as a snow giant. Shouting and clamor arose from the walls a mile distant. The coming of the Tugars was a major event. An army ten times their size would not have been more welcomed. Despite all this, King Henepola X was not in attendance.

The arrival of the Tugars provided a lift for the entire fortress. Given the multitude now residing within the walls, it wasn't practical for everyone to make merry, but the Tugars arranged a feast outside the walls for themselves that lasted long into the night. They built a mammoth bonfire and consumed great quantities of beer and wine. Afterward there was lovemaking in almost every tent, but between Tugars only. A few Nissayans and refugees attempted to join in but were summarily escorted from the camp.

Even Kusala became caught up in the revelry, and he ended up making love to Churikā. The next morning he awoke sore and exhausted, though she seemed as sprightly as ever.

*I am getting old. It's more than possible this war will mark the end of my reign. That is, if I—or any of us—survive it.*

THE DAY AFTER the Tugar's arrival, King Henepola X leaned motionless over his crystal basin, his hands resting on the transparent rim. His long white hair, normally silky and clean, was knotted and greasy, its ends dipping into the silvery liquid. His face looked ancient compared to the last time he had been seen, as if he had aged another half century. Strange-colored lights reflected off his vacant eyes, which were laced with spidery veins. What he witnessed during his long bouts of scrying would have broken almost anyone else. Few could have endured it for more than a few moments, much less day upon day.

Invictus screamed at him. Laughed. Sneered. Forced him to watch drawn-out scenes of sexual torment. Replayed the ruination of Yama-Deva, the torture of the Daasa, the taming of Bhayatupa. With the immense strength of his will, the sorcerer engulfed Henepola with every conceivable depravity. Finally Henepola found it impossible to turn away. And now, his will was nearly ruined. All he could do was watch.

For obscene stretches of time, he did not even blink.

When you stare into the sun, you go blind. When you stare into the mind of a god, you go mad.

AT MIDAFTERNOON of that same day, Kusala, Podhana, and Churikā entered the main entrance of Nagara and began the long walk up the winding stairs to the top of the keep. At first they were saluted amicably, but when they approached the royal quarters, the king's squires became suspicious. By the time the Asēkhas entered the hall that led to the king's bedroom, they were practically dragging a dozen guards with them. Indajaala stood by the door, alongside six heavily armed sentries. The white-haired conjurer made a big show of it, on their behalf.

"How dare you approach unannounced," Indajaala said. "The king is working tirelessly in preparation for battle. He needs his rest and has ordered that no one come near."

"If the king rests any more, he will never wake up," Kusala said, shoving his way toward the door. "It is time he comes out and *prepares* in full view of his people."

The sentries were confused. They, too, did not understand Henepola's behavior, but they were trained, above all else, to do what they were told. With their king not present, they looked to Indajaala for orders. To their surprise, the conjurer stepped aside.

"Let him enter, then," Indajaala sneered. "Henepola will deal with this mongrel himself." When the conjurer spoke, milky vapor streamed from his mouth and filled the hall like smoke. The sentries and guards sagged, then collapsed. Kusala and the other Asēkhas were unaffected.

"You must hurry," the conjurer said. "More guards may already have been alerted."

"Come with me, Indajaala," Kusala said. "Podhana and Churikā will hold the narrow way."

Kusala tested the thick wooden door, which was made of a special black oak he knew was found only in Java. As expected, it was barred. He leaned against the far wall and flung himself forward, battering the door with his right shoulder. It blew apart as if a tumbling boulder had smitten it.

Kusala and the conjurer rushed through the royal quarters and down the hallway that led to the scrying chamber. If its obsidian door were barred, Kusala would be unable to break it. Torg himself might not have had the strength. But when Kusala came to the end of the hall, he saw with relief that it was ajar.

The peculiar mist oozed from the crack. Kusala grabbed the door, shoved it open, and entered the small room, which was dark except for bright yellow lights leaping from the crystal basin like flashes of lightning at midnight. Henepola had collapsed face-first in the basin, his face submerged in the strange liquid. Kusala grabbed him by the hair and yanked him away, then lifted the king in his arms as easily as an ordinary man would pick up a boy.

"Take him to the balcony," Indajaala said. "He needs fresh air and sunlight. I will bring his staff."

A large portal opened onto a ledge with a low wall. Kusala swept aside the thick curtains and carried the king into the light, laying him on his back on the stone. Henepola did not appear to be breathing.

"I have no magic to save him," he said to Indajaala. "What can be done?"

"I, too, have no such strength," the conjurer said. "Maōi has many uses, but it cannot heal such wretchedness. I fear the king is lost to us."

Just then, there was commotion outside the bedroom door, followed by a clashing of swords. Madiraa's pleading voice could be heard about the tumult.

"Allow her to enter!" Kusala said. A moment later, the king's daughter burst through the curtains onto the ledge.

"Father?" Then she stared at Kusala. "In the name of God, what has he done?" She knelt and took Henepola in her arms, tears bursting from her eyes. "Is he dead?"

Indajaala tenderly placed his hand on her shoulder. "Child . . ." the conjurer whispered.

That is when Kusala felt a thud that caused the balcony to quiver.

YAMA-UTU RAN. He was not afraid of Kusala. Or the princess. Or the king and his knights. He feared only his own tattered mind. His desire to destroy Mala and end his brother's torment raged as strongly as ever, but he did not want to harm innocents in the process. A few days before, the Pabbajja had given him temporary relief from his torment, but the strange black stone of the fortress—so unlike the pale bones of Okkanti—had unnerved him again. Making matters worse, the heat had intensified his pain. Even in the middle of the night, it was hot.

Faster than any land animal save Bhojja, he ran toward Mahaggata. These mountains were unlike Okkanti in age and appearance, but their grandeur impressed Utu nonetheless. He climbed ten thousand cubits to where the air was thin and blessedly cold. Then he stood on the mountaintop, his feet buried in snow. A brisk wind blew against his brow, causing his eyes to water. It felt like paradise.

From the peak he could see Nissaya, a black stain in a sea of gray. He stood in silence for several days, taking no sustenance, his mind fighting an internal battle. Part of him wanted to return to Okkanti, where his own kind would succor him. But his own healing would not end his brother's suffering. Once again, his desire for vengeance took precedence.

Finally he broke his silence, laughing, crying, and stomping about like a lunatic, then casting boulders the size of houses down the mountainside. With frozen tears on his cheeks, he curled up in a ball and slept. When he woke, it was morning.

He started back toward Nissaya.

Something drew him to the keep. He managed to scale the black walls on thick rope ladders that hung from their sides, evading the eyes of the busy soldiers. Then he climbed up the side of Nagara and scrambled onto the huge keep's flat roof.

Soon after, he heard the princess screaming below him.

Utu leapt onto the balcony. The woman sat there, embracing the king. Utu could sense that the white-haired man still lived, but an ill magic had stolen his consciousness. Still, it could be cured if the healing began soon. He pushed past Kusala and knelt beside the woman.

"Will you allow me to lay my hands upon him?" Utu said.

"Yes" was her response, without hesitation.

# Warrior, Army, and Witch

# 22

ON THE SAME night that Kusala, the Asēkhas, and Yama-Utu did battle with the Kojin and her monsters, Asēkha-Rati sat cross-legged on a boulder and stared at the full moon, watching the slow development of the eclipse with single-minded attention. He had managed to travel more than one hundred leagues in an astonishing four and a half days, though large portions of that distance had been spent on the backs of several different horses.

With rumors of war reaching a fever pitch, most of the villages that lined both sides of the Ogha were deserted, the frightened fishermen and farmers fleeing west to Nissaya or east into the vastness of the Gray Plains. A few brave souls remained in their homes, most of those more than willing to aid an Asēkha, either out of respect, fright, or hope of protection.

Only once since leaving Kusala and his fellow Asēkhas had Rati been forced to fight. By accident, he had encountered a rogue band of Mogols—eleven in all—terrorizing the remaining inhabitants of a once-thriving fish camp.

When Rati came upon them, the men and boys had already been cruelly bound, and their wives and daughters stripped of their clothing. It seemed the Mogols were in the mood for entertainment, but they would not find it on this day. Eleven strokes, one apiece, killed them all.

Rati had always taken pride in his ability to use a minimum of movement to slay his enemies. Kusala often teased him about this, calling it "Rati's Obsession," but he had ignored the frequent chides. Besides, he was still humiliated that a Mogol had managed to hit him with a war club during the skirmish with Mala's army. He actually bore a tiny welt on the back of his head. It was the first time in more than a century that an enemy had struck him solidly.

The villagers thanked him profusely, offering food, shelter, and even the use of some of their women if he would remain with them. Rati politely declined, but he did trade the horse he was on for their finest stallion, along with a sack of dried sardines and a round loaf of bread. As he was leaving, many cast themselves on the ground and wept.

From his perch on the boulder, Rati now was little more than a league north of Senasana. Without regard for the eclipse, the Ogha River roared beneath him, its frothy rapids more powerful than an avalanche. Rati, however, did not share the river's disdain, staring with fascination as a shadow consumed the moon.

He had arrived in late afternoon, set the stallion free, and then scouted the riverbanks as far as the northern outskirts of the city before turning back and returning to this spot. He had seen nothing unusual, and he could not deny that he was annoyed. Rati, above all others save Tāseti, loved to fight, and yet it appeared he had been sent to a place where fighting was unlikely.

Podhana should have gone in his place; he was more of a loner and would have enjoyed wandering about in such peaceful darkness. Besides, it wasn't as if Rati or any single person could patrol enough of the river to prevent someone from dumping something into it. All twenty Asēkhas combined could easily fail in such a task.

This part of the river narrowed considerably, forcing its angry waters past a slew of gray-green rocks, some stabbing above the water's surface like accusing fingers, others partially obscured by the froth. Directly beneath Rati was a chute that flowed between two immense boulders. Just beyond the chute was a whirlpool. And several hundred paces beyond the whirlpool was an eddy, one of the few places of safety in the broiling uproar.

Even while in a state of contemplation, the senses of an Asēkha were unrivaled. Above the droning of the rapids, few would have heard the subtle creak of the wagon wheel. But Rati instantly fell into a crouch and slid off the boulder, working his way up the western bank like a shadow cast from a gliding bird. About a quarter-mile north, he came upon the wagons, five in all, stopped a dozen paces from the opposite bank. The wagons had been driven to the water's edge through a small gap between rocks and trees: a perfect place to dump something into the river, if that was your goal.

Rati scolded himself for not discovering it before.

At this point, the river was wider—perhaps fifty cubits—and slightly calmer than some of the more dangerous areas, but it still would be difficult, even for him, to traverse the wicked currents. He needed to find an easier place to cross, but first he crouched in a pool of shadows and observed the enemy. Though the wagons were shrouded in darkness, he identified at least twenty Mogol warriors and five Warlish witches, each flanked by a hag servant. And to make matters worse, objects in the beds of the wagons resembled barrels.

Rati knew five witches could outmatch even an Asēkha, but it was his assignment to try—and try he would. He scampered a hundred paces farther

upriver until he came upon another chute about thirty cubits broad. In the
center of the chute, a single spear-shaped stone, just a span in diameter,
protruded above the surface. Without hesitation, he scrambled onto the top
of a boulder and flung himself over the river. He landed on the stone with
one foot and propelled himself to the far bank. Just as quickly, he raced back
to the wagons, hoping he wasn't too late.

When he arrived, a pair of Mogols already was lugging a barrel toward
the water's edge. The witches stood ankle deep in the tumult, holding tall
staffs and singing in their eerie fashion. Almost too quick for the eye to
follow, Rati cracked the barrel into pieces with a single stroke of his *uttara*.
With two more strokes, he beheaded both of the Mogols.

His sudden intrusion stunned the witches, whose slow reaction bought
Rati enough time to wreak more havoc. He raced past the Mogols, pounced
into the bed of the nearest wagon, and destroyed five barrels with two
strokes. Inwardly, this efficiency pleased him, but he allowed himself only a
fraction of a second to enjoy it. There was more work to be done.

An arrow struck him between his shoulder blades and bounced off his
dense flesh, the shaft snapping and falling away. Ignoring the brief flare of
pain, Rati leapt into the second wagon, this time using three strokes to
destroy six barrels.

Though only a few moments had passed since his arrival, the Mogols
were now gathering around the remaining three wagons, their war clubs
ready. Rati was not overly concerned about the savages' ability to thwart him.
The witches, however, were another matter. They faced him, full of fiery
rage, and concentrated their energies. Tendrils of crimson flame danced on
the head of each staff, rising into the air and coalescing into a single beam as
powerful as a bolt of lightning and pounding Rati squarely in the chest,
throwing him a dozen paces backward.

The hag servants fell upon him.


# 23


TWO DAYS AFTER Rati's battle with the witches, the greatest ground army
ever assembled began its ponderous march from the Golden City to Nissaya,
announced by drums as large and clamorous as Tugarian *Bheris*. Hundreds of
thousands of civilians cheered from the streets of Avici, but only Invictus and
a few servants were permitted outside the southern gates.

Invictus stood on a golden platform erected on the steep eastern shore of the Ogha River while the army marched beneath the bridge on the opposite shore along a cobbled road that eventually led to Iddhi-Pada.

Mala, of course, was at the head of the procession. Thanks to Invictus, the ruined snow giant was fully healed from his encounter with Bhayatupa, and he now rode on the back of a massive elephant. The beast, which wore a thick iron collar at the base of its neck to protect its flesh from the searing heat of Mala's chain, stood fifteen cubits at the shoulders and weighed more than fifteen hundred stones. Still, the Chain Man looked overly large for the elephant to carry a long distance. In fact, this ride was only for show. In a league or so, the general would dismount, feed his elephant to the Kojins, and walk the rest of the way.

"My liege," shouted Mala, his booming voice heard for more than a league. "I beg your permission to lead your army into battle."

"It is *your* army, General Mala," Invictus said, his voice equally pervasive. "Lead it where you will."

"We march on Nissaya, my liege. And after we topple the fortress, Jivita will follow."

"Go forth and make me proud. But wait one moment. I have a gift for you."

Invictus stepped off the platform and floated slowly to the ground, his golden robes flowing like wings. A dozen newborn servants rushed to him, carrying a special weapon made by Invictus' own hands: a golden trident three times as long as he was tall and weighing twenty stones. Despite its size, Invictus lifted the trident with ease and strolled to the river's edge, halting just a step from its hungry currents.

"When I was a young boy, I nearly drowned at this very spot. At least, that is what I have been told, for I remember it not. The concept of my dying seems rather absurd now."

Then he strode forward, as if to complete the act he had barely avoided a century before. But instead of being swallowed by the uproar, he stepped lightly onto the surface of the water and walked across unharmed. If Mala was amazed, he didn't show it. Invictus came to the foot of the elephant and handed his general the magical trident.

"I have named it Vikubbati. You know what it is for," Invictus said, before returning to his platform on the far bank.

On cue, a cave troll thundered toward Mala, bearing a massive war horn made from the hollow leg bone of a long-dead dragon. The ruined snow giant took the horn, put it to his lips, and blew a single blast that was heard as far north as Kamupadana and as far south as the borders of Java. In response, the elephant sprang forward on its columnar legs. The drums began anew, and the army of Avici started its slow march.

Behind Mala came representatives from the various races, each carrying the banner of Avici: a yellow sun outlined in red on a white field. The human-sized creatures were mounted on golden destriers. These included a newborn soldier named Augustus, who had replaced the traitor Lucius as Mala's second in command; a pirate from Duccarita named Maynard Tew who had provided Kilesa with a steady supply of Daasa slaves; a Warlish witch named Wyvern-Abhinno who represented her kind in the stead of Queen Jākita; a Stone-Eater named Bunjako who was the eldest son of Gulah; a vampire named Broosha who was a daughter of Urbana; a Pabbajja named Gruugash who was the chief overlord of the homeless people; a Porisādan chieftain named Tohono who rode a black mountain wolf; a demon named Uraga who chose to be incarnated as a man with the head of a boar; a wild man named Wooser who had come from the foothills of Kolankold; a ghoul named Angont who was large for his kind and especially odiferous; and an ogre named Hrolma who had successfully begged forgiveness for the rude behavior of the now-deceased Olog.

Several other beasts, too large to ride a horse, strode alongside the mounted creatures: a cave troll named Orkney who could tolerate sunlight because of the magic of Invictus; a Kojin named Harīti who was rumored to be infatuated with Mala; a druid named Druggen-Boggle who was one of the few of his kind possessing a will of its own; and a dracool named Arula who had been a longtime rival of the traitor Izumo.

Five thousand golden soldiers were next to appear, the first of thirty-two legions. The newborns marched ten abreast in cohorts of one thousand each, their golden helms and rectangular shields glistening in the morning light. Included in each legion were two hundred horsemen. Drummers and trumpeters announced their approach.

Invictus waved at them and smiled. He was so proud. Each one of the newborns had been magically bred from a single drop of his own blood—with the help of the Daasa, of course. And Invictus knew exactly what role they would play in the siege of Nissaya. How *interesting*.

After that came one hundred cave trolls hauling supply wagons as large as houses. Five thousand Mogols mounted on black wolves followed. Among all of Invictus' allies, none had been more loyal than the savages from Mahaggata. Invictus loved them and waved enthusiastically.

Five more legions of infantry came after the Mogols, along with more supply wagons hauled by oxen and asses. After that came ten thousand druids, five thousand wild men, and five thousand Pabbajja. From then on, the rest of the golden soldiers—one hundred and sixty thousand strong—were interspersed with several hundred pirates from Duccarita, one hundred Stone-Eaters, one hundred Warlish witches accompanied by one thousand hags, and one thousand each of demons, ghouls, ogres, and vampires. Three more Kojins also joined them, along with a variety of nameless monsters, some of which had to be kept in cages to prevent them from attacking the lesser among them.

All told, two hundred thousand marched toward Nissaya, stretching five leagues from front to back. Though Mala had left Avici long before noon, it was almost midnight before the tail of the great army exited the southern gates. The last in line was a pair of three-headed giants, each thirty cubits tall and bearing iron hammers as heavy as trees. By then, Invictus wasn't there to witness their passing, having long since retired to his chambers in the bowels of Uccheda. But he knew they would be there, because he had planned the entire thing.

Fewer than ten thousand of Mala's army remained to protect Avici, but Invictus wasn't concerned. If anyone dared attack his city while the Chain Man was elsewhere, it wouldn't matter. After all, the army was just a plaything. He didn't really need it to accomplish his purposes. But it made things more fun—and kept Mala entertained, as well.

A lot was happening that held his interest. He so enjoyed not being bored.

# 24

TWO DAYS AFTER Mala's army departed Avici, Jākita-Abhinno landed on the pinnacle of Uccheda aboard a dracool. Jākita, queen of the Warlish witches, was surprised to find the rooftop of the tower unguarded, as if the sorcerer feared nothing.

"Would a grown man wielding a longsword fear children armed with goose feathers?" the dracool asked her.

Jākita felt unnerved in the bright sunlight, wondering if she had made a mistake in daring to approach the king. "What do weeee do now?"

"Wait," the dracool responded coolly.

Eventually, a small portal hissed open, and Invictus strode onto the rooftop, wearing yellow robes that matched the color of his shoulder-length hair. His eyes were brown spheres floating in a sea of disturbingly flawless white. Though he made no threatening gestures, Jākita found herself backing away from the sorcerer and unexpectedly transforming into her hideous state.

"Do not fear," the sorcerer said, in a tone that sounded boyish and amused. "I have not come to harm you, Jākita-Abhinno. But I *am* curious as to your motives. Come with me to my bedchambers, and we will discuss them."

When she entered his room near the top of the tower, Jākita willed herself to change back to her beautiful persona. Instantly her scent filled the room with intoxicating perfumes. She assumed the sorcerer would want to have sex with her, and she started to disrobe, but Invictus only smirked.

"Do not flatter yourself," he said, licking his lips with his thick red tongue. "Warlish whores have never been my type. But it might be that we both can profit from a partnership. At least, I am willing to listen. What have you to offer, other than your body?"

"I have the ability to deliver your ssssister to you . . . unharmed."

"Why should I believe that you possess this *ability*, when others, far greater than you, do not?"

"Of all your loyal sssservants, only I have been with Vedana when she spied on Laylah and The Torgon. Only I know where they have been and where they are going. Even youuuu, my king, have been blinded. Your grandmother told me herself that she has cast a veil over your eyessss to discourage you from following their movements."

Jākita could not gauge the sorcerer's reaction. He stared at her with a blank expression for what seemed like a very long time. When he finally responded, the room grew wickedly warm, causing the witch's sweet-smelling armpits to become drenched with sweat.

"It is true that I have had difficulty in locating her. And I am unaccustomed to difficulty."

"My liege, pleasssse do not punish me for my bold words. I meant no offense. I come to you for one reason only. The wizard is the sworn enemy of my coven, and it is my utmost desire to destroy him. I need but one thing from youuuu: protection from Vedana. If she finds out that I plan to betray her, she will vanquish me. Only you have the power to prevent her. Will you shield me from the vengeance of the demon?"

Invictus laughed loudly—and then seemed to converse with himself.

"Grandmother, grandmother . . . do you inspire so much fear? Aaaah . . . but you are a treasure. I must admit that I miss your company . . ." Then he gazed into Jākita's eyes. "I can accommodate your request. But first, tell me your plan."

As she spoke, the sorcerer's smile widened.

After the witch departed, Invictus remained in his upper bedchamber near the top of the tower, sealing the door with a demonic spell that was simple in design but invincible because of the strength of his magic. Mala himself could not have pounded his way inside.

Invictus sauntered to the far side of the room, approaching a folding screen with an obsidian frame and golden silk panels that was carefully arranged to conceal one of his prized possessions. He stepped behind the screen and approached his toy: a basin of yellow glass balanced on a pedestal of white crystal.

He leaned over the basin, which was filled with a thick liquid that captured his reflection like polished silver. He smiled at himself, unendingly proud of his boyish handsomeness and yellow hair.

*All people should look like me. And one day, all people will.*

Waving his hand over the basin, his fingertips exuded a yellow glow that caused the liquid to erupt with color. His experimentations with scrying were relatively new—at least when compared to Vedana's. His first attempts occurred when he was a teenager searching for Laylah after the death of their parents. By then his relationship with his grandmother had—how would you describe it?—soured. Invictus had come to discover, in ever more frustrating fashion, that scrying was one of the few dark arts he could not easily master, requiring a delicacy that eluded him. If he used sheer power to force the liquid to reveal its visions, it steamed up and evaporated. But when he tried to be gentler, the visions often became too hazy to decipher.

Over the decades his proficiency had improved, at least enough to make it useful. He could see to the far corners of the land, peeking into bedrooms and spying on private affairs, from kings to peasants, saints to monsters. All brought him a perverted sort of pleasure. But all eventually bored him.

Almost *everything* became boring—even the approach of the war that so tantalized Mala, though Invictus found it amusing that the Tugars, Nissayans, and Jivitans believed they had any real chance of defeating him. Mala's army was greater than they realized, containing hidden surprises that not even the quick-witted Death-Knower had foreseen. But even if they somehow conquered the army, what did it matter? Invictus was a thousand times more powerful than all of them combined. He could destroy everyone with a sweep of his hand. For these reasons, he preferred to remain in Uccheda and work behind the scenes. It would be too easy—too *boring*—to force himself on his enemies, unless it reached a point where he would have no other choice.

In reality, boredom was his greatest foe. Not even acts of torture and sexual perversion, which he performed on an almost daily basis to keep his mind alert, would interest him forever. He was a god, after all. And gods are easily distracted.

Blessedly, a few things still engrossed him—his obsession with Laylah being one. Everything about his sister amazed him. Her beauty and vitality were unrivaled. Her magic was far more powerful than she realized. And then there was the matter of the *efrit* that Vedana had so cleverly planted in her belly. How exquisite! An obstacle he couldn't overcome? Marvelous! But, he had to admit, also frustrating. It had prevented him from achieving the one goal that inspired him beyond all others: an heir . . . a son. Someone so much like him that no one would be able to tell them apart.

Invictus had to admit that the Death-Knower also enticed him. There was something about the wizard's smugness. The Torgon had dared to call Invictus a "spoiled and wicked child." *Was it true?* Invictus wasn't sure—and not being sure was *interesting.*

Now the Death-Knower wandered in the wilderness with Laylah, wreaking all kinds of havoc. It must have been the wizard and his sister who'd killed the *Mahanta pEpa.* Few other beings, besides him, wielded that kind of power.

Invictus had sensed the Great Evil's demise, but it would have been obvious to him anyway. The Daasa he himself had imprisoned in Avici had also been released from the *Mahanta pEpa's* sway, and they had gone on a rampage that had taken several days to quell. Invictus could only imagine what must have happened to the slave traders in Duccarita. The dracools he had sent to investigate still hadn't returned. And for reasons he did not comprehend, his attempts to magically peer within the walls also had met with failure. Was Vedana so strong that she could veil an entire city?

To make matters even more annoying, Invictus had surmised that Vedana's special *efrit* wasn't designed to harm Laylah if she actually enjoyed it—which meant, of course, that his sister and the Death-Knower were destined to become lovers during the course of their adventures. The pesky wizard would be just her type: a moralistic do-gooder . . . ha! The absurdity of it tantalized Invictus.

Regardless, he was intent on recapturing Laylah. It wasn't that he really loved her or even cared about her. But he was concerned that she might get herself killed, which would seriously hinder his quest for an heir. The wilds contained many dangers, not all of which were under his immediate sway. None were any threat to *him*, of course, but Laylah remained vulnerable.

During the days that followed her second—and far more recent—escape from Avici, Invictus had attempted to locate Laylah with the art of scrying. He was convinced he had come close several times, but when he tried to focus on a specific location, the vision blurred and vanished. One time he seized on the image of a waterfall, and behind it, a small cavern containing several shadowy shapes. But that, too, fizzled away.

Still, the Warlish witch had supplied him with valuable information, making him aware that his grandmother was playing a role in his inability to pinpoint Laylah's whereabouts. But why? Was it simply Vedana's unquenchable thirst for revenge? Surely she knew that harming him, in any permanent manner, was beyond her—or anyone.

He was forced to acknowledge, though, that his failure to perfect the art of scrying proved one thing: He actually had weaknesses. Unlike his grandmother, who existed more in the world of the ethereal than the physical, he could not travel great distances without the help of a Sampati or dracool, his spirit remaining trapped within his flesh. In time, he would find ways to overcome this, but it would take longer than a mere century. He was, after all, still very young.

Also, there was that nagging incident involving the eclipse. In his entire life, even as a toddler, Invictus had never felt so vulnerable. Immediately, his scientists had gone to work on the problem, and they promised the sorcerer that another eclipse of the sun wouldn't occur in the skies of Avici for several hundred years. During that time, there would be frequent lunar eclipses, but these would have little effect on him.

It was a good thing that none of his enemies had known about the solar eclipse. Otherwise, they could have killed him then and there. If not for Mala, he might have died, anyway. Dear Mala. The ruined snow giant was the most loyal of all his servants, even more so than the Mogols.

Invictus' thoughts returned to Jākita and her plan.

"It just might work," he said out loud, causing the magic liquid to ripple. "Pisaaca is an especially nice touch. I will make sure that grandmother is unaware of Pisaaca's role."

Providing the Warlish whore with protection from Vedana had been simple. Now he would sit back and wait for the witch to deliver. He looked into the basin, saw Jākita soaring over the Gap of Gamana on the back of a dracool, saw Urbana flying alongside her—queen of the witches and queen of the vampires, together. How *interesting!*

Then the liquid momentarily clouded, and when its clarity returned, a new vision appeared. Invictus stared into the wrinkled face of King Henepola X. The old man was searching for him again, believing himself strong enough to spy on a Sun God. This was too easy. If Invictus weren't such a "spoiled and wicked child," he might have felt sorry for the fool.

# Wicked Deception

# 25

ON THE SAME day that Jākita and Invictus met on the rooftop of Uccheda, Lucius and his companions fled the City of Thieves. Now the general of a newly formed army of Daasa, Lucius was both pleased and disturbed by the effectiveness of his soldiers: their ability to change rapidly into "meanies," as Ugga had begun to call it, pleased Lucius, while their bloodthirstiness once they transformed disturbed him. With the destruction of the *Mahanta pEpa,* the Daasa had been freed from their psychic imprisonment. But it had been a grievous experience to watch gentle creatures become ruthless monsters.

Lucius and the others had gathered their weapons, packed what clothing and supplies they could find, and departed Duccarita through a crevice in the western wall with Bonny in the lead. Torg and Elu had gone ahead to scout, leaving Lucius and the others with ten thousand odd, but charming, companions.

Each of the Daasa had two purple eyes, a squat nose, and a wide mouth, which gave their facial features a human-like appearance. Their bodies, however, resembled pigs more than people, and they walked on four legs. Their spongy pink skin looked as tender as a baby's bottom. Imagining such wondrous animals being maimed, tortured, cooked, and eaten was a blow to Lucius' heart.

Endlessly curious and easily distracted, the Daasa took from noon until late afternoon just to get through the crevice and into the rugged terrain on the far side of the towering wall. About a dozen ruined Daasa, those unable to transform back to their original selves, remained in the city, watching with tormented eyes as their brothers and sisters left them behind. Apparently, they were unwelcome among the main group, destined to roam the deserted streets of Duccarita until their deaths.

"Why won't they come with us?" Ugga said to Lucius.

"The other Daasa would kill them if they tried to follow," Bonny said. "They do not like the path the few have taken."

"How do you know this?" Lucius said.

"I know a lot about them," the pirate woman said. Then she added, "I lived in Duccarita a long time."

They walked until dusk. Then Lucius gathered his "troops," planning to attempt a short speech to test their understanding and compliance. He stood on top of a hillock, his recently healed arm still throbbing, and cleared his throat.

The Daasa packed in as close as possible, seemingly fascinated by anything Lucius might do.

He started to say, "My good friends . . ." But a blast of blue-green fire flared into the sky a short distance away and interrupted him.

A moment later, Torg and Elu came running out of a stand of trees, with a large band of Mogols and black mountain wolves in pursuit. Ugga snarled and started down the hillock. Bard would have followed, but he was still too weak from the effects of the dart. Lucius turned back to the Daasa, fearing a slaughter, but instead of seeing ten thousand frightened pink faces, he found himself looking into the eyes of a slavering host of monsters.

The Daasa had transformed instantly, their fangs clapping in unison, and they stampeded past Lucius like a herd of nightmarish Buffelo, their ferocity permitting neither pity nor remorse. In a short time the Mogols and wolves were reduced to a pile of shredded flesh and fur.

Tears streamed down Laylah's cheeks. Rathburt bent over and vomited. Lucius could tell that the extent of the violence dismayed even Torg. But when the Daasa returned to the hillock, they transformed just as quickly to their original selves, except for the blood still dripping from their whiskers. Otherwise, they seemed as if nothing unusual had occurred.

"The meanies killed them all," Ugga said with a kind of awe.

A pink Daasa came up and rubbed tenderly against the crossbreed's leg.

Lucius watched Rathburt vomit again.

HE KNEW WHAT they were thinking: *Cowardly ol' Rathburt, afraid of everything, can't even stop from vomiting when there's a little bloodshed.* But they didn't know what *he* was thinking.

Rathburt could sense it in every shred of his being. When the Daasa transformed into monsters, pain consumed them—not ordinary pain, but an agony that transcended any Rathburt had previously experienced. They were not like the Warlish witches, who seemed equally comfortable in beauty or hideousness. At their core, the Daasa truly were good-natured beings, as gentle and benign as snow giants, but their violent conversions came with a price. Somewhere in their distant past, the Daasa had chosen to pay this price rather than perish as a species. In the forest beyond the ocean, evil also existed, and the Daasa had no other way to combat it but to change.

The pain fueled their anger.

Their strength.

Their guiltlessness.

But when they returned to their true selves, their memories of the agony were blessedly erased. Only in their ruined state did they remember. Only in their ruined state did they scream.

Why was he alone in knowing this? Lucius was their master; it should have been clear to him as well. Torg seemed to know everything . . . why now was he ignorant?

They were asking the Daasa to do more than just fight. They were asking them to endure unimaginable suffering by becoming something contrary to their nature.

*Why am I the only one who can see it?*

When Torg touched him, Rathburt almost swooned.


TORG APPROACHED Rathburt cautiously, sensing discomfort in his demeanor that went beyond ordinary disgust. It seemed obvious to him that his fellow Death-Knower was experiencing something the others were not. Torg placed his hand on Rathburt's shoulder and willed a surge of healing energy into the gristle at the base of his neck.

Rather than take comfort, though, Rathburt cried out and spun away.

"What is it?" Torg said. "What do you see?"

Rathburt's eyes were wide with fright, but he did not respond. Elu ran over and hugged his leg. At the same time, Bonny approached and patted Rathburt on the back.

"I feel like puking myself, after what I just saw," she said. "There's nothing to be ashamed of."

Rathburt grunted. "It's just me being me. I feel better now. There are more important things to worry about than my occasional bouts of nausea. Shouldn't we be moving on? Surely there are more of them"—he nodded toward the shredded remains of the enemy—"nearby. We made enough of a ruckus to attract attention all the way to Avici."

Torg eyed Rathburt quizzically for a moment, then turned to Lucius. "He's right. We should get as far from here as we can. But now that the Daasa are with us, we have less need for stealth than before."

"Can we rest just a little whiles, Master Hah-nah?" Ugga said. "Me dear Bard is still weak from the poisons. I could carry him, but I'm tired, too."

"I'm feeling better," Bard said in a tone that betrayed his words. "Anyways, it's easier to walk than fight."

"Let's go," Rathburt said. "The Daasa move slow enough, as is. For all we know, they might decide to wander off. What's to keep them with us, now that the Great Evil has been slain?"

"I know I'm going to sound like Torg when I say this," Lucius said, grinning at Rathburt, "but something inside me believes they will stay with us until I release them. They are grateful and loyal—and will fight to the death to defend us. They've proven that already, wouldn't you say?"

"I agree," Bonny said.

AS IT TURNED OUT, Bonny knew the foothills near Duccarita as well as Elu knew those near Kamupadana. After a long march, the pirate woman guided their large company into a hollow guarded by massive stacks of stone laced with natural shelters. The pink-skinned Daasa crawled into a myriad of crevices and huddled together, falling fast asleep. Apparently, even they needed rest. As for sustenance, Laylah had no idea how they would manage to feed so many, but they would have to face that problem in the morning.

From Laylah's perspective, Bonny had turned out to be an invaluable addition to their company. But it wasn't her skill in the wilds that was most attractive. Instead, it was the pirate's obsession with Lucius that pleased Laylah. Bonny rarely left the firstborn's side, constantly touching him and whispering in his ear; Lucius seemed to enjoy the attention, which drew his jealousy away from Laylah, much to her relief.

When Laylah went to fill her goatskin over a bubbling springhead near the center of the hollow, Bonny came and knelt beside her, pretending to fill her own skin. After a period of uncomfortable silence, the pirate finally said, "Can I ask you a question, woman to woman?"

"Is it about Lucius?"

Bonny blushed, then smiled, revealing crooked teeth that somehow made her round face look even prettier. "Is it that easy to see, missus?"

Laylah giggled. "To be honest . . . *yes*. But first things first. Please call me Laylah. And may I call you Bonny?"

"Of course, missus. Er . . . Laylah, I mean." She sighed and took a deep breath to calm herself. "Well, my question is, does Lucius have any *ties* to you? It's easy to see the great wizard favors you, but what about Lucius? Am I intruding?"

Unexpectedly, Laylah's eyes welled with tears.

Bonny drew back, startled. "Missus . . . Laylah . . . I'm sorry if I upset you. If you want me to stay away from him . . ."

Amid her tears, Laylah began to giggle again. Then she gave Bonny a hug. "No . . . *no*. Please, don't misunderstand. I'm not crying out of hurt or jealousy. It's just that in the short time you've been with us, Lucius seems happier than I've ever seen him. I care about Lucius, but not in *that* way. I consider him a dear friend and want only the best for him. From what I can tell, you are exactly what he needs. It's almost as if the two of you were born to be together."

In reaction to Laylah's words, the pirate woman stepped back and smiled. "Do you believe in love at first sight?" Bonny said, a little too loudly.

"Oh, yes," Laylah said. "I most certainly do."

TORG HAD NO time for sleep, so he found a high vantage point, sat cross-legged on a ledge, and meditated. From centuries of practice, he quickly was able to focus his awareness on the rim of his nostrils and slow the rate of his breathing to nearly indiscernible levels. *Assaasa-passaaso rasso. Assaasa-passaaso majjhim. Assaasa-passaaso diggho.* (Short breath. Medium breath. Long breath.) He watched them all with utmost concentration, engorging his body with placidity. A short period of meditation revitalized him almost as much as a full night's sleep.

A vision of a blue sky with drifting clouds entered his awareness. Like his worries and concerns, the clouds came and went, as impermanent as existence. As the meditation progressed, Torg came to realize that he again was capable of attempting *Sammaasamaadhi,* the supreme concentration of mind that resulted in temporary suicide. He noted this thought—and then returned to the breath.

*Inhale . . .*
*Exhale . . .*
*Inhale . . .*
*Exhale . . .*

Torg detected her presence before acknowledging it. Her slow climb up the rock face had been just one more point of concentration for him. Though Laylah had approached with a graceful silence rivaling that of a Tugar, he could sense her standing a few paces behind him. His love and lust for her swelled. He noted these emotions—and then returned to the breath.

When she sat down beside him, he still didn't move, but her sweet scent entered his awareness. He had known her for such a short time, but already it felt like forever. *Kittakaani jiivitaani samosaritva puna samaagachaama?* (How many lifetimes have we spent together?) This was only the latest incarnation of their love. Torg noted these thoughts—and then returned to the breath.

After another moment of silence, she spoke. "Will you teach me?"

His eyes opened immediately. Meditation was not like sleep, which most often required a period of awakening. The meditator remained supremely alert.

"I will, if you desire."

She slowly lowered her head until it rested against his bicep. "Where do we go from here?" she said.

"The sooner we reach Jivita, the better."

"Will I be safe there?"

"Safe?"

"Will you be able to protect me from him?"

"I will try."

She began to cry, softly at first, but then more violently, until she seemed to convulse. He let her sob, just holding her, loving her.

"And if you fail?" she finally said.

"We shall see what we shall see."

She took his face in her hands and kissed him seductively on the mouth. He felt her tears against his own cheeks. Obhasa, which lay by Torg's side, began to glow. But the Silver Sword remained cold.

"If you fail . . . and if he *takes* me again . . . I'll need . . . a memory of you. Do you understand what I'm saying, beloved?"

Torg held her and then returned her kiss. Finally he stood and grasped her hand.

"Come with me."

She did not resist.

# 26

LAYLAH WATCHED Torg ascend farther up the rock wall, holding Obhasa in one hand while the Silver Sword dangled in its scabbard. The stacked stone contained numerous knobs and protrusions, making it easy to climb. Laylah followed, scaling the wall as deftly as the wizard. She and Takoda, her adoptive father, had spent many pleasurable moments during her childhood exploring the mountains near their home in the hidden Mahaggatan valley. She had little fear of heights.

Finally, the wizard came upon a crevice barely wider than his chest. Just beyond the narrow opening was a small chamber. Once they both had squeezed through and were inside the chamber, the glow from Obhasa cast as much light as a torch, as if the ivory staff sensed what she hoped was about to occur.

When they had fled Duccarita, the small company had found clothes in an abandoned shop that had escaped major damage during the carnage. Laylah now wore a full-length super-tunic with a tasseled belt fastened at the waist. Torg stood before her, slowly untied the knot, and removed the belt. Laylah looked surprised.

"Torg, the cave seems to go on for quite a ways. Wouldn't it be more private if we moved farther inside?"

"These are our only clothes," he said, chuckling, "and we'll have use of them yet."

"Ahhh," Laylah said.

When their outfits were removed, the wizard placed them on the stone floor and covered them with several large shavings of rock.

"When magic is involved, I sometimes can shield my clothes," Torg explained, "but in this case, my abilities cannot be trusted."

Laylah raised an eyebrow. "Let's hope we don't start an avalanche and bury everyone."

Beyond the chamber, a tunnel extended much deeper into the wall. It was barely large enough for Torg and Laylah to enter. The wizard didn't want to leave Obhasa or the sword behind, so he took one in each hand and crawled naked into the passageway.

Eventually the tunnel opened into a chamber much larger than the first, perhaps ten cubits tall and just as broad. The glow from Obhasa illuminated the room. A fine layer of sand covered the floor. Numerous boulders, resembling crude furniture on a white carpet, lay strewn about. Torg leaned Obhasa and the sword against the wall.

"I have seen this place in my dreams," Laylah said, looking around. "How did you know to come here?"

"I have seen it in my dreams, as well," he said.

The wizard approached a spear-shaped slab of rock that appeared to weigh at least forty stones. Yet he wrapped his arms around it and lifted it with ease. Then he shoved it into the maw of the tunnel, plugging the opening.

"This is the best I can do, my love," he said. "I would have preferred to have taken you to the top of a dune and lain with you on a blanket beneath the stars of Tējo. But I cannot bear to wait any longer."

"This will be fine. Wonderful, in fact. The time and place mean little," Laylah said. "You are all that matters, Torgon. You are all that ever mattered."

BETWEEN THE ages of eighteen and sixty-eight, when Torg was in training to become a warrior, he had made love to many Tugarian women. Though almost all purebred desert warriors were beautiful, the son of Jhana was considered exceptionally attractive even among his own kind, and there was no shortage of partners at his disposal. Many of them were older, more experienced, and very eager. Between sixty-eight and eighty-two, Torg was a full-fledged warrior and then an Asēkha, and his sexual promiscuity increased. But the night after he had achieved *Sammaasamaadhi* for the first time, he had made love to a Tugar and killed her with the unexpected fury of his orgasm.

After that terrible occurrence, Torg was forced to live in celibacy, going more than nine hundred years without sex—except for masturbation, and even that was limited, because of his explosive propensities. He had to be far away from everyone just to do that.

To say that Torg was *ready* for Laylah was a gargantuan understatement. And that was only part of it. Even greater in importance was the depth of his love for her. He desired not just the sorceress' body, but her mind, her voice, her scent, her spirit. To complete matters, Laylah was capable of withstanding his orgasm.

For the first time in close to a millennium, Torg was in a position to release his pent-up frustration with a woman he had loved over a series of lifetimes, extending further back in time than even he could conceive.

Now, as he stood naked in front of her in the rock chamber, he fought back tears of joy, despite an internal conflict. He had been taught that all things were impermanent. That all things had a beginning, middle, and end. You could no more grasp desire than you could flee from aversion; doing either eventually caused suffering. Sister Tathagata believed that sexual passion was just one of countless hindrances to the attainment of enlightenment, a state that eliminated suffering forever. Torg had learned all these things. But when he took Laylah in his arms, these teachings seemed to lose their meaning. Was enlightenment superior to this? It didn't seem possible.

Torg cupped the back of her head and looked down at her beautiful face, her wide eyes, her flushed cheeks. When he pressed his lips against hers, he felt like a man who hadn't eaten in weeks suddenly seated at a table laden with a feast.

He lifted her marvelous body in his arms and laid her on the blanket of sand, kissing her lips, her neck, her nipples. He placed one of his hands between her legs, her wetness tantalizing him. Using the tip of his index finger, he applied pressure. He knew what to do. It was just that—over the centuries—he had been denied the chance to do it. Laylah cried out.

She reached for him and guided him toward her opening. When he entered her, all other sensations were overwhelmed. He began to howl like an animal; she did the same.

They climaxed together.

Blue-green energy erupted from every pore of his body. Her white fire met it with equal force. The room superheated, causing the rocks to glow and the sand to melt into glass. Obhasa fell to the ground and flopped about like a fish stranded on a beach. The Silver Sword remained in its original position against the wall, unaffected.

Torg screamed. Laylah screamed. The sounds merged into one. For a few mindless moments, all forms of suffering ceased.

WHILE TORG and Laylah made love, the *efrit* that nestled in the sorceress' abdomen did not stir. Vedana had trained the creature to react only to sexual abhorrence, and nothing that resembled loathing was occurring, so it continued to sleep blissfully in its warm chamber, oblivious to what was about to happen.

When they climaxed together, the *efrit* was incinerated.


# 27


A SHORT TIME before dawn, Lucius fell asleep in a seated position on the floor of the hollow, the last of the company to succumb to weariness. Like ants returning to the mound, the Daasa had long since crept into caves and crevices. Bonny slept beside him, her face seemingly content.

A sound similar to rain falling on dry leaves woke Lucius. At first unable to overcome his exhaustion, he struggled to open his eyes. But then something small and hard struck him on the forehead, startling him awake. When he tried to stand, pain swept through his recently healed arm, making him so dizzy he sagged against a boulder. Soon after, a salvo of pebbles showered down from above, clattering like pea-sized hail.

"Avalanche," Lucius shouted, grabbing Bonny's hand and yanking her to her feet. "Get under cover!"

Still in a daze, the pirate woman grunted something nonsensical and then yelped when Lucius dragged her toward the rock wall, where they stumbled beneath a ledge and rolled smack into a dozen Daasa, still slumbering peacefully despite the disturbance.

Now Bonny was awake, and it was the first time Lucius had seen her angry with him. "Lucius, what in the world are you doing? You nearly pulled my arm out of the socket. It's just a few pebbles falling off the wall. Maybe there's a goat up there or something . . ."

But even as Bonny stated her case, a tremor shook the hollow, causing the pirate woman to clasp her hand over her mouth. Even the Daasa were awakened, their purple eyes bleary and confused. The tremor lasted only a few moments before all went silent, except for a tinkling of stones that continued to fall from high above. Lucius and Bonny remained crouched by the Daasa, waiting to see what else might occur. Finally a familiar voice broke the silence.

"Master Loo-shus? Miss Bonny? Where are ya? Are ya hurted?"

Then Lucius saw Ugga's grinning face peering under the ledge. The crossbreed's small eyes met the firstborn's. "Ya are all right," he said happily. "I is glad to see ya. Was there some kind of earthquake or something?"

Despite the pain in his arm, Lucius couldn't help but smile. He crawled out and looked around. If there had been an earthquake, the damage was minimal.

Soon Bard and Elu joined them. A whining Rathburt followed, claiming that rocks the size of watermelons had hit him in the head several times. Somehow Lucius found the complaints almost comforting. The Daasa also emerged, still sleepy but not overly distressed.

As the hollow filled with light from the morning sun, Rathburt looked around, perplexed. "Has anyone seen Torg and Laylah?"

Everyone became concerned.

"Elu will find them," the Svakaran said. Then he sprinted along a stone trail that angled up the steep wall.

"Wait, you little booger!" Rathburt shouted. "We didn't say you could go trotting off . . ."

But Elu paid no attention, clambering up the side of the wall with impressive ease. As they looked farther upward, they saw Torg and Laylah climbing down. Elu met them halfway and gave them both hugs. Then all three followed the trail back to the floor of the hollow. When the wizard and sorceress approached, Lucius could have sworn they were blushing.

"Where have you been, Torgon?" Rathburt snapped. "Have you been drinking or something?"

Ugga's ears perked up.

"Do ya have some beer?" he said hopefully.

Torg and Laylah chuckled.

"No beer, my friend," the wizard said. "It might be a while before we have any more beer. But I'll treasure the moment when I can share some with you again."

"You still haven't answered my question," Rathburt said. "Where have you been? Didn't you feel the earthquake?"

"I felt it," Laylah said, barely suppressing a giggle.

Now Lucius was certain: Torg *was* blushing. For a moment, Lucius experienced a torrent of jealousy, but it fizzled away as soon as Bonny wrapped her arm around his waist.

"The good news is, nobody is hurt," she said. "But now that it's daylight, we'd best get going."

"Can't we at least have something to eat?" Ugga said, pounding the head of his axe on the ground for emphasis. "I is starving."

"We brought enough from Duccarita to last a few light meals," Lucius said. "But I have no idea how we're going to feed the Daasa. I don't even know what they eat."

Even as the firstborn was saying those words, he noticed that the Daasa already had begun to file out of the hollow.

"I'm starting to think the Daasa can take care of themselves," Bonny said. "The rest of us should eat something quick and then get moving."

THEY FOUND THE Daasa climbing in a thick stand of trees, chittering raucously as they feasted on unripe acorns and pine nuts. Their dexterity amazed Laylah. She watched them scramble along the thicker branches as deftly as squirrels.

Torg had kissed her on the cheek, whispered some pleasant words in her ear, and then trotted off with Elu to do more scouting. Their company was still less than a league from Duccarita, which was dangerous territory. Though the Daasa had routed most of the golden soldiers in the area during their cleansing of the city, there was an ever-present threat from Mogols, wolves, ghouls, and other less-numerous monsters.

Despite their dire circumstances, Laylah couldn't help but feel wonderful even in the direct sunlight. The aftermath of their lovemaking still glowed inside her, and her stomach felt light. In fact, everyone seemed in a good mood. The Daasa were cheerful, Lucius and Bonny were inseparable, and even Bard was looking stronger. On top of everything else, it had become unseasonably warm for so early in spring. Laylah could almost imagine that the bad times were behind them.

When Torg returned with Elu, Laylah's heart skipped a beat. Just seeing his face again almost caused her to swoon. She rushed over and hugged him, causing the Daasa to chitter even louder. For a moment Torg smiled and hugged her, but then his face grew serious.

"A great force marches from the east, no more than five leagues distant," the wizard said. "I didn't believe that such numbers were amassed this far from Avici, especially after the demise of Duccarita. I cannot determine the makeup of this army, but I would guess that our numbers are evenly matched. Our choice then is to meet them in battle on the open plain or attempt to outrun them."

Torg turned to Lucius. It amazed Laylah how much taller he was than the firstborn. She had always thought of Lucius as a large man.

"What are your thoughts, General?" the wizard asked. "Do you have any idea who and what we're facing?"

"Everything I know about our . . . I mean . . . *Invictus'* forces in the gap is several weeks outdated," Lucius said. "Before I fled Avici, Invictus patrolled Gamana with just a few thousand—and of those, most were Mogols and wolves. After Laylah and I escaped, we all know that he sent Mala's army after us. But with the onset of war so close at hand, I can't imagine he will send too many more into the gap, unless his obsession with Laylah is so immense that he no longer cares about the siege of Nissaya.

"As for the makeup of the approaching foe, most of the deadly monsters of Mahaggata are in Avici. The mountains themselves have probably never been safer."

Bard walked over to Torg, the color in his cheeks returned. "Why can't we just sic the Daasa on them and be done with it?" he said. "They killed five times their number in Duccarita. And ya said this army is only about our same size."

"Thus far, the Daasa have shown us two things," Torg said. "They like to kill pirates and Mogols—and we all know the reasons for that. And they will protect us if we are threatened. But we don't yet know if we can send them into battle without provocation."

"Nor should we," Rathburt blurted, far louder than needed, it seemed to Laylah. Then he lowered his head and said no more.

Torg raised an eyebrow and started to speak, but Lucius interrupted.

"Though the enemy is closer than we'd like, we still have a good head start. I say we continue toward Dhutanga and see if we can outrun them. If they gain on us, then we'll make a stand."

"Let's go then, as fast as we can," Torg said, "and see if the Daasa will follow."

# 28

TORG HAD NOT told them the full extent of his confusion. Even from great distances, he usually could surmise the makeup of an army. But the force that approached from the east produced signs unlike he had ever encountered, kicking up a cloud of dust even thicker than a division of armored infantry. Despite their size, mountain wolves treaded lightly, barely leaving tracks of any kind—as did Mogols. This didn't mean that a few wolves and savages might not be among this new enemy, but there had to be other things, as well—large, clumsy, or both. Torg could think of only three possibilities: trolls, elephants, or giants. None of these options were good.

To make matters worse, other evils besides the druids lurked to the west within Dhutanga, meaning they were sandwiched between dangers. Vampires, ghouls, goblins, and—worst of all—great apes almost as large as snow giants hunted along the forest's perimeter.

Torg took the lead, trotting out of the trees into the gap's open plains and establishing a strong pace—not fast by Tugarian standards, but faster than the approaching army was proceeding—and then turned to see how well everyone was doing. The Daasa kept up easily, chasing after him on all fours. Laylah, Elu, Ugga, and Bonny also stayed close. Even Bard seemed able, though he still was weaker than normal. But Lucius was not a man built to run, and Rathburt... well... was Rathburt. The slump-shouldered Death-Knower immediately started whining about his sore legs and bad back.

Torg slowed their pace to a fast walk. Lucius did fine after that, though his Mogol war club was weighing him down. But Rathburt continued to struggle. Still, as far as Torg could tell, the mysterious army was not gaining on them.

A voice like, and yet not like, his own whispered inside Torg's mind. *Shouldn't you see for yourself what follows you?* As he mused over this, it began to make sense. It *would* be safer—for all of them—if they went back and had a look. *Not they. YOU. Go by yourself. That way no one will slow you down.*

"Do you know this land?" Torg said to Elu in an odd-sounding voice, startling the Svakaran.

"Elu has been here once or twice, but it was long ago. He remembers little."

"And I've never been farther west than Duccarita," Lucius said.

"I has been there, but I was different then, and I doesn't remember," Ugga said.

"I was just a boy when I was last there, and it was even longer ago than when Elu was here," Bard said.

Even Bonny's mastery of the terrain extended only a few leagues outside of the City of Thieves.

Then, as a group they turned to Rathburt, who instantly became defensive.

"All right, all right, I've been this way before, a couple of centuries ago. But who cares, Torgon? You're our guide, not me. I'm sure you've entered Dhutanga a million times . . . a *billion*. You were probably there before there were *trees*."

Torg ignored Rathburt's sarcasm. "For a brief time, I cannot be your guide," he said in a sober tone. "I've decided to back-track and find out what it is that follows us."

"Torg, what are you saying?" Laylah cried out. "It's far too dangerous."

"From here on out, everything will be dangerous, but this is not about my taking unnecessary risks. If I go alone, it will be easier, and safer."

Elu made an angry face.

"As good as you are, there are times I prefer to act alone," Torg said to the Svakaran. "Rathburt, I need you to lead everyone into Dhutanga. At first, the trees will be sparse and the ground beneath them easy to traverse.

Proceed no farther than a league into the forest, and then veer to the south. When the sun is overhead, stop just long enough to eat. If all goes well, I will have returned to you by then."

Despite the exertion of walking, Laylah's face had gone pale. But she didn't protest, seeming to recognize that Torg's mind was made up.

Of course, Rathburt was as riled as ever. "Torgon, this is not the time for your shenanigans. I'm no leader, and you know it. We need you here with us, not off gallivanting in the wrong direction. What happens if we're attacked while you're gone?"

"Lead them to Dhutanga, Rathburt," Torg said, with more anger than was necessary.

Carrying the Silver Sword in a scabbard strapped to his back, Torg then swung about and started toward the enemy. He could feel Laylah's eyes for a long time. Somehow the Daasa knew not to follow.

# Witch, Vampire, and Druid Queen

## 29

ON THE SAME day that Torg and his companions left the City of Thieves, three dracools circled lazily above the open area of the forest, searching for a place to land. Tens of thousands of druids clogged the mile-wide clearing, which was anchored in its center by a single tree taller than any other on Triken—four hundred and fifty cubits it stood, and absurdly wide at its base. The druids seemed drawn to its magnificence like shamans to a prayer pole.

Finally the dracools landed on branches near the top of the enormous tree.

"We are not overly fond of the wood-eaters," one of the dracools said to Jākita-Abhinno, now in her beautiful state. "They are as stupid as sheep. But they are also dangerous, especially when there are so many. You and the vampire can deal with them, if you feel so bold."

Urbana was incensed. "This is not acceptable, dracool! How do you expect us to get down from here? Neither of us are monkeys . . . and neither of us can fly. Stop being such cowards and take us to the ground."

But the dracools only shrugged their wings. "We were told to take you here—and bring you and the sorceress back when the time came—but nothing more," said the second dracool, in a raspy voice. "We are not your slaves. Only the sorcerer has the strength to command us. But out of courtesy, the three of us will remain nearby. When you are ready, call us . . . and we'll find you. As for getting down, that will be less of a problem than you think. Behold, the druids come."

And then the *baby dragons* sprang into the air and soared toward a place they deemed more hospitable.

As soon as the dracools departed, Jākita and Urbana looked down at the druids, who were pressing against the base of the tree in enormous numbers. Their bodies and limbs seemed too long, angular and inflexible for them to be effective climbers, but their methods were successful, nonetheless. Hundreds and then thousands began to stack onto each other's backs and shoulders, forming a living ladder that quickly grew in height. As the druids came nearer, the peculiar humming sound intensified, causing the tree to shiver. In a matter of moments, the druids had reached the witch and the vampire.

Jākita and Urbana were lifted off the branch and carried to the ground, handed from druid to druid with surprising gracefulness. As Jākita expected, the druids had no desire to harm this pair. Their leader anxiously awaited their arrival.

At the base of the tree, a dozen druids half again as large as any of the rest, guarded a cavernous opening. When Jākita and the vampire stepped forward, the guards spread apart, beckoning them to enter the hollow trunk.

"She is here?" Urbana said. "It seems too obvious a place for her to hide."

"She doesn't care about obvious," Jākita responded. "She caressss only about revenge—as do I. Her strength has grown beyond the need to hiiiide. Soon you will see for yourself."

# 30

LESS THAN A league from the clearing, the dracools lighted on the upper branches of a black tree and immediately began to scan their surroundings for food. Dracools are as quick and athletic as mountain eagles, and individuals are capable of killing prey as large as an elephant, though they prefer smaller quarry such as Buffelo, deer, and the occasional human. Only a limited variety of animals thrived in the bowels of Dhutanga, but there were enough to provide three dracools with a tasty meal. After their long flight from Avici, they were hungry.

Ravens were barely a mouthful for a hungry dracool, and they were too quick and wily to make the chase worthwhile. So the *baby dragons* ignored the one that landed nearby, though even if they had attacked or tried to flee, it would have made no difference.

"*Namuci!*"

Already dead, the dracools fell from the tree, crashed through the canopy, and smote the ground with their ruin.

# 31

THE INSIDE OF the hollow tree was as immense as a banquet hall, though not nearly as lavish. The shadowy air reeked of sewage-like mist. But rather than be repulsed, Jākita felt comfortable in this foul place. When she turned to look at Urbana, she saw that the vampire also seemed pleased. The presence that resided inside the tree was worthy of their worship.

They bowed before the queen of the druids, who was the daughter of the previous queen that The Torgon had slain more than eight centuries before. Though she was young and her reign short in comparison to her predecessor's, the new queen had surpassed her mother in size, scope, and power. An all-consuming hatred of the one called *Maranavidu* (Death-Knower) had fueled her rapid ascendancy.

Several days after her mother's gruesome murder, the daughter had emerged from the hidden birthing chambers to take control of her kind. By then, most of the druids had wandered into the depths of the forest and died. Only a few hundred survived, just enough to nurture her until she became strong enough to lay eggs of her own. And lay them she did, without rest—one at a time, day after day, month after month, year after year.

Her name was *Kattham Bhunjaka*, though no druid could pronounce it in words. The rise of Invictus had further emboldened her, and now the druids were stronger than they had ever been in their long history. One hundred thousand worshipped her, more than twice the number that had last dared to attack Jivita, home of the horrid white horsemen.

After bowing to *Kattham*, Jākita advanced within an arm's-length of the pale, throbbing blob, which was broader than a dragon's torso. Jākita could sense the queen's immense telepathic power and was relieved it was not directed against her. She knew she could not survive such an assault. Few beings on Triken had that level of strength. But rather than attack her, *Kattham* bathed her with erotic energy, causing Jākita to gasp with pleasure.

"Thank you, *Kattham*, for your warrrrm welcome," Jākita said. "My companion and I are honored to be in your pressssence."

Urbana nodded, her bloodshot eyes glazed. "I am at your command," the vampire said blankly.

Jākita chuckled. "Your greatness overcomes her."

The druid queen could not vocalize, but her mind more than made up for it. She pummeled Jākita with a series of queries, causing her knees to tremble. When *Kattham* was finished, Jākita did her best to answer, wanting more than anything to please this wondrous being.

"Your ssssenses do not fail you, *Kattham*. The hated *Maranavidu* (Death-Knower) is indeed near Dhutanga, no more than fifty leagues from where you laaaay. He hopes to avoid the forest on his way to Jivita, where he will join the white horsemen and take ssssick delight in the murder of your precioussss offspring.

"But like you, I too despise The Torgon. My wounds are fresher than yourssss, but no less painful. I have come to you to beseech your aid, so that together we might destroy the Death-Knower, once and for all."

"I am at your command," the vampire repeated blankly.

Jākita nudged her with her elbow. "Urbana, you're *embarrassssing* me."

But the vampire was too enraptured to listen.

Jākita turned back to the druid queen, responding to further questions. "Yes, *Kattham*, I understand and respect your desire to witnessss the Death-Knower's demise. That would pleasure me, as well. If youuuu will lend me a portion of your druids for just a little while, I will set the stage for The Torgon's arrival. I only beg that you allow me to participate in his destruction. You can paralyze him while I perform the slowest and cruelest of tortures. That way, both of ussss will taste the sweetness of revenge. But first I need you to twisssst his mind, from afar. The Daasa's, too. And I'll tell you how."

Jākita endured another blast of psychic power. "Yes, *Kattham*, I understand that the druidssss will soon march on Jivita. Why do I need so many of your brave warriors? I only wish to *ensure* our success. And if my plan succeeds, very few will be harmed. Besides, isssn't The Torgon's demise more important than anything else?"

At that moment, the druids guarding the opening began to hum loudly, sounding an alarm. Something else had entered the chamber—unwelcomed. A raven settled on the floor and began to writhe and smoke. In its place, a gray-haired woman appeared, her robes and flesh eerily translucent.

"Jākita, slimiest of sluts," Vedana screamed. "Have I not warned you many times about the perils of disobedience? How dare you attempt this betrayal! Do you mistake me for a doddering old fool?"

"I am at your command," Urbana said.

Jākita ignored the vampire. "You have not lisssstened to me, Mother!" she shouted back. "The Torgon entered the ziggurat and killed many of my precioussss sisters. I will not allow it to go unpunished."

"*You* will not allow it? You are nothing but a witless whore I created for my amusement. It seems the Warlish witches are about to lose another queen. My patience with you has run out."

As the demon strode forward, Jākita backed up and pressed against the druid queen's slimy hide.

"Do you think *she* can protect you?" Vedana said. "You underestimate me if you think this worm is my match. Her mind has no power over me."

In reaction to the demon's words, the druids sprang to life, rushing into the chamber in large numbers to protect the queen.

Vedana paid them no heed. "The Death-Knower belongs to me. I will not allow him to be harmed until the time is right. You should have listened to me, Jākita."

The demon raised her gnarled hands above her head. Crimson lightning burst from her fingertips, blasting at Jākita face. In response, Jākita's flesh glowed like molten gold, absorbing the demon fire with unexpected ease.

Instantly Jākita launched a counter-attack, casting a pair of golden spheres from the palms of her hands that struck Vedana squarely between her breasts, knocking her physical incarnation against the inner wall of the tree.

Amazed, the demon struggled to her feet, her heart pounding visibly within her chest.

Jākita laughed wickedly. "Invictussss protects me, Mother. You cannot harm me. But I can harm *youuuu*!"

Jākita raised her arms to deliver another blow against her creator, but Vedana was too fast. A black hole opened in the wood, and the old woman leapt into it, howling as she disappeared. When the hole closed, the demon was gone.

Jākita turned back to the druid queen, her expression triumphant. "She will trouble ussss no longer, *Kattham*. My powers are beyond her. Shall we retuuuurn to our business?"

# Escape from Dhutanga

# 32

AFTER TORG disappeared from sight and raced eastward away from the forest and toward the gap, Lucius turned back to Rathburt. "You heard him. Which way to Dhutanga? Or is it as simple as turning right?"

Rathburt ignored the question. "Isn't that just like Mr. Showoff to run away when we need him most? What has gotten into that loon?"

Suddenly, Laylah stormed toward Rathburt and pounded the base of Obhasa at his feet, causing a portion of the ground to split. The Death-Knower cried out, dropped his own staff, and fell backward onto his rump. Lucius cringed, out of sympathy for Rathburt's clumsiness, but also fearful that Laylah might be angry enough to hurt him.

The sorceress loomed over Rathburt, spittle flying from her mouth. "Torg puts up with your insults," she snarled, "but I will *not*! He would never run away from anyone or anything. Do not say such a thing in my presence again."

Tears welled in Rathburt's eyes. It broke Lucius' heart to see it. After all, he had been bullied by superior powers himself many times when he was in Avici and still under Mala's sway.

Laylah continued to glare at Rathburt, refusing to move.

Finally Elu came over and tapped her lightly on the thigh. "He doesn't really mean it, pretty lady. Elu has heard him say things like that a thousand times. But deep down, he's a nice guy. And he respects the great wizard as much as you do, to tell the truth."

Still visibly shaking with anger, Laylah backed off. "Then he needs to grow up," she said. Rathburt remained on the ground, not moving. "Get up," Laylah said. Her voice was softer, much to Lucius' relief. "I'm not going to do anything more," she continued. "But time is short. Answer Lucius' question. Which way to Dhutanga? The quicker the better."

Rathburt struggled to his feet and leaned against his staff, his face gaunt. He pointed weakly toward the southwest. "It's been a . . . long time. But if my memory is correct, the quickest way to the forest is that way."

Still amazed by Laylah's outburst, Lucius started off in the direction Rathburt had suggested, hoping that if he got them moving, the incident might be forgotten.

The Daasa followed, seemingly pleased to be on the move. It was obvious they were less comfortable in the open than in the trees, and Lucius wondered if they could sense the nearby forest. He looked back several times for signs of Torg, but all Lucius could see were flat plains leading to the northern mountains. He also did a quick check of Laylah and Rathburt, who now seemed to be doing their best to ignore each other. Good.

As Torg had predicted earlier, they came upon the perimeter of the forest before noon. Early on, the trees were widely spaced—a mixture of pines, oaks, poplars, and occasional black walnuts, many of which already had sprouted their spring blooms. But Lucius quickly noticed something unusual: most of their branches stretched eastward, away from the forest, as if these ordinary trees wished they could somehow sprout legs and walk away from what loomed to the west.

The Daasa seemed enthralled. They poured into the forest at full gallop, foraging in beds of fallen leaves and crunching noisily on acorns that Lucius imagined must have been lying there for months. It was amazing the Daasa still found them to be edible.

Following Torg's earlier directions, Lucius continued forward until the forest began to thicken. At noon, they came to a wide stream. The Daasa rushed toward it and drank like fiends, lining the watercourse for almost a mile. Lucius called the others to a halt, and they sat and ate from what they had hastily gathered before leaving Duccarita.

"We only have enough food left for one or two more light meals," he said. "After that, we'll be on our own."

"Elu believes there is plenty to eat here, but it takes time to catch it and cook it," the Svakaran said. "You can live for days on wild berries, if you don't mind the grumbling of your stomach."

"I hopes not to live on berries for days," Ugga said glumly. "I is already so very hungry."

"We're all hungry," Laylah said. "But I'd rather be hungry and free than a prisoner with a full belly."

Even as they spoke, Lucius noticed Rathburt looking around nervously, his slump more pronounced than ever. "I wish the Daasa didn't make so much noise," the Death-Knower whispered.

Just then, Lucius heard a commotion in the trees.

Something approached from the west.


ON THE OPEN plains of Gamana, there were few places to hide, though the land sometimes changed elevation slightly, providing occasional concealment. Torg ran as fast as a trotting horse, covering several leagues in a surprisingly short time. The farther he ran, the larger and more visible the approaching cloud of dust became. He came upon a hillock rising about thirty cubits above the plain, and there he cast himself onto his stomach on the iron-colored grass . . . and waited. For better or worse, he soon would discover what pursued them. The desire to do so consumed him.

First to appear were black mountain wolves ridden by Mogols. It relieved Torg to see that they were ordinary warriors, not Porisādas. But they still were dangerous. The riders were having difficulties holding back the wolves, which yearned to rush forward and attack their quarry. But whatever commanded them from behind was strong enough to contain them. Torg was glad he had obeyed his inner voice and come to this place by himself. It was the wise thing to do.

As the dust cloud intensified, more mounted wolves, the vanguard of a larger force, came into view. But they passed by without noticing his presence; such was his ability to remain unseen. From his prone position, Torg could feel the rumblings of an approaching army, and he began to fear that he had underestimated their numbers. The vibrations were peculiar, unlike anything he had encountered before—chaotic instead of rhythmic.

Finally he could make out the leading edge of the mysterious army, which seemed to be gathered around a lone wagon, huge as a house and drawn by a pair of mountain trolls. Torg wanted to work his way around the side to get a better look, but there were too many Mogols and wolves. Instead, he was forced to wait until the army passed directly in front of him. Nearer and nearer it came, slowly but steadily—and yet Torg remained confused. He had never witnessed such disorder. The soldiers seemed to be bobbing this way and that, almost as if they were dancing.

Whatever stood at the front of the wagon emanated a cloud of noxious gas. The creature who led this army was a demon, incarnated into the physical world. Was it Vedana? No, her scent was different.

And then he recognized his adversary. The demon's name was Pisaaca, second in rank and power only to Vedana among their undead kind. She appeared in the Realm of Life as a grotesque beast with the head and body of a woman, but with bat-like wings protruding from her back. Though Torg knew her to be human-sized, she now chose to be twenty cubits tall, twice the height of a snow giant, and she held a magical whip as long as a dragon, slinging it this way and that so fast that the very air crackled.

The trolls dragged the enormous wagon forward with great effort, but it was not only the demon's weight that caused their exertion. The bed contained something else, but Pisaaca's bulky frame blocked Torg's view.

The sun loomed directly overhead, intensifying the unseasonable heat.

A mounted wolf trotted past Torg only a few paces away, but paid him no heed. Though the Duccaritan clothes he wore did not blend well with his surroundings, his stillness of mind made him virtually invisible.

Engulfed in a haze of dust, the soldiers who trailed behind the wagon continued to act crazily, jumping, waving their arms, knocking into each other, even fighting among themselves. And they seemed to be wearing no armor or uniforms of any kind. It was as if the sorcerer had called a mishmash of drunken villagers to duty. And still they came.

Finally Torg could see the side of the wagon. Its bed was jammed with at least fifty people, well-dressed but otherwise normal in appearance—equal numbers of men, women, and children chained together at the ankles, some screaming, some sobbing, some silent and pale.

Torg gasped.

The people in the wagon were bait.

Or an even better description: food.

And the army that followed was an abomination. Ordinary villagers had been infected with *undines*, creatures of the demon world that entered living flesh and multiplied until the mind and body were ruined. Torg saw at least ten thousand of the cannibalistic fiends. Obviously his efforts to destroy the *undines* in the ziggurat had been in vain. The witches had succeeded in summoning more, either from Kamupadana or elsewhere. And now these mindless monsters were on the prowl, stumbling behind the wagon in a state of bloodthirstiness.

But the fiends were frenetic and disorganized, moving too slowly to overtake the wagon. Instead, they remained a few paces behind, growling, slavering, howling. It was horrifying to watch, and he could only imagine the terror the chained prisoners were experiencing. Who were they, he wondered? Elite citizens of Avici who had somehow fallen into disfavor? And how long had they been forced to endure this level of torment? Surely not all the way from the Golden City. Torg could think of no way to rescue them. If he were to set them free, either the fiends or Mogols would kill them.

How and where this army had been assembled was a mystery, but not the why. Invictus had sent it to hunt down Laylah and kill all of those with her. Pisaaca must have been included to make sure Laylah wasn't harmed in the melee.

But something still didn't make sense. It would be relatively easy for Torg, Laylah, and their companions to outrun the fiends—all the way to Jivita. Surely Invictus—or whoever had planned this attack—knew this.

Torg was missing something.

The next instant, he was up and running, killing several wolves and Mogols who strayed too near. Otherwise, the enemy did not see him. He sprinted as fast as he ever had in his life, breath blasting from his lungs.

Rathburt had been right, after all. This was no time for gallivanting. What had he been thinking? Or what thoughts had been forced upon him?

Laylah and his friends were in danger.

And it was his fault.

# 33

LAYLAH GRASPED Obhasa in both hands and waited. Countless foes, seemingly driven by an immense will, surged out of the deep woods. She heard Rathburt moaning, Ugga growling, Lucius shouting commands, but those sounds were secondary to the intensity of the humming.

The druids came in droves, clattering forward like walking trees, their long fingers snapping, their eyes red with rage. There were more than Laylah could count, and it appeared obvious that she and the Daasa were outnumbered. But she was not afraid. She cried out in anger and then strode to meet them.

Instantly the Daasa reacted to her call, transforming into monstrous killing machines. They attacked the druid surge head-on, tearing into them with their own kind of rage.

Without hesitation, Ugga rumbled forward heedlessly, swinging his axe like a scythe. Bard cast his spear into the fray, then loosed every arrow in his quiver. Lucius stabbed a druid with his *uttara* and then battered another to pieces with his war club. Though less than a third their height, Elu wounded several with his Tugarian dagger. Even Rathburt got into the act, spewing blue fire from his staff with surprising effectiveness.

But to Laylah's dismay, she soon discovered that the druids were not alone. The enemy separated, creating a path for a Warlish witch, who appeared in her attractive persona. She was more beautiful than any witch Laylah had ever seen, even the legendary Chal. Her flesh glowed like gold, causing the dead leaves at her feet to crinkle and burst into tiny flames. And a woman Laylah recognized as her longtime nemesis, the vampire Urbana, followed.

As the witch approached, the druids froze.

The Daasa also halted, but not for the same reason. Their noses raised upward, as if sniffing something in the air. Without explanation, they shifted their bloated bodies and stampeded eastward. Lucius shouted for them to stop, but for the first time they paid him no heed. Laylah believed they were abandoning her and the others out of fear of the druids, but then she heard the ferocity of their growls and realized they weren't fleeing at all. Instead, they were hunting something that enraged them even more than the druids, leaving Laylah, Lucius, and the others to face a Warlish witch, a vampire, and an army of druids alone.

The witch strolled within a pace of Laylah. She wore golden robes that matched her skin. "I am Jākita-Abhinno, queen of the Warlish witches, and I have come to take you prisoner, ssssister of the king."

Lucius and the others, including Rathburt, gathered around the sorceress to protect her, but Laylah waved them off. "We cannot prevail by fighting. Not now," she said to her loyal companions. Then she turned to the witch. "I imagine you have come for me and care little for these others?"

"Sssso true," said Jākita, her smile remarkably lovely. "If you return with ussss without resistance, I will allow your friendssss to live."

Urbana interrupted in characteristically obnoxious fashion. "Why should we do that? Now that the Daasa are gone, we have no need to bargain. Let's kill them all—especially the traitorous firstborn—and *then* take her back with us, screaming and kicking. That would be so much more fun."

"We *might* die," Lucius said to the vampire, waving the *uttara* menacingly. "But you most certainly would."

Urbana hissed, but Jākita only laughed. Then she raised her hand, and a yellow glob of molten fire leapt from her palm and incinerated the *uttara*'s blade.

Lucius staggered back and dropped the blackened handle at his feet.

"For now, these otherssss are not our concern," Jākita said matter-of-factly, as if her display of power was beyond question. "Death will come to them all, whether now or later. All who oppose King Invictus will eventually perish or become his slavessss." She smiled at Laylah. "What say you, ssssister of the king? Your life for theirs? Or would you prefer I turn Urbana and the druidssss loose? As you have heard, they would relish an opportunity for slaughter."

"How can I know you'll be true to your word?"

"If you fight ussss, *you* might be hurt or killed," the witch said, her long auburn hair swirling, as if electrified. "That would not please your brother."

Lucius stepped between the sorceress and the witch, his hand still shaking from the blow of Jākita's power. "None of us will abandon you to these monsters, as long as we're able to stand."

The others nodded vigorously, but Jākita threw back her head and laughed. "Let me ssssee: a newborn freak, a pirate whore, a failed wizard, a dimwit crossssbreed, an overgrown boy, and an under-grown man against thirty thousand druidssss."

"We will die, but ya and the ug-gly beastie woman will die too," said Ugga, in a tone of voice that caused even Laylah to shiver.

Jākita, however, was not impressed. "None of youuuu, save the sorceress herself, is capable of harming me. But enough talk. What say you, Laaaaylah? Your cooperation will buy your friendssss their lives."

Laylah turned to her companions, her face resigned. "We are outmatched," she said, prompting all six of them to protest. "Listen to me . . . we are *outmatched*. And all of you know it. I must accept her offer. It is your only chance—*my* only chance. The rest of you must follow the Daasa and see if you can win them back."

To her surprise, Rathburt was the next to speak. "Do not fear, my lady. Though the battle appears lost, you will not be forsaken."

"Aaaah, Rathburt. I'm so sorry now for my harsh words."

"If you all don't stop it, I'm going to bawl like a baby," Urbana said. Then she turned to the witch. "Enough talk, Jākita. Let's take her and be done with it. I'm sick of this rabble."

Laylah looked into her friends' eyes, one at a time. "Do as I say . . . please. Do not fight. Leave now. Run." She started to hand Obhasa to Rathburt, but Urbana leapt up and yanked the staff from her hands.

"Give me that, you horrid little bitch. Do you mistake us for fools?"

Even as she wrapped her ugly fingers around the shaft, Obhasa crackled with explosive blue-green power. The vampire screamed and cast the staff to the ground, the palm of her hand charred and smoking.

Jākita laughed again. "Leave it," she said to the vampire. "Like its massssster, it cannot be tamed. Come, Laaaaylah. Honor your bargain, and I will honor mine."

The druids rushed forward, encircling the three women. Lucius and the others were shoved back and knocked to the ground. For several moments, the druids hovered over them, glaring with fiery eyes. Then they retreated, like a wave receding from shore. When the forest again was empty, Laylah was gone.

# 34

TORG'S VASI master used to say, "History repeats itself."

As Torg ran across the plain, he saw the truth in those words. For the second time in his long life, a druid queen's diversion had fooled him. The first time was during a war long ago with the Stone-Eater Slag. This, the second time, might cost him Laylah and everything else that mattered.

Eight centuries before, Bhojja the great mare had aided him, carrying him to the lair of the druid queen. Now he again heard the thundering of hooves. When he stopped and turned, she was there beside him, her jade coat glistening.

"I know you, in all your forms," Torg said, "and I dared to believe you still lived."

The mare pranced forward, her green eyes full of adoration. She flung her huge head from side to side, whinnying excitedly, and then bent down her neck, inviting him to mount.

Torg leapt aboard.

Without further encouragement, Bhojja galloped as fast as the wind, her hooves sparking on the grass.

Soon, they came upon the Daasa. All ten thousand were stampeding eastward, making a sound that resembled thunder. Bhojja stopped and allowed them to surge past her, some passing within a finger-length of her muscular barrel. At first Torg was confused, but then he understood. They were things of rage drawn by rage. And the druids, or whoever led them, knew they could bend the Daasa's will in this direction.

Torg urged Bhojja forward, but she resisted. Then to his surprise, she veered around and followed the Daasa.

"Wait! Wait!" Torg shouted. "I care naught for these beasts. Take me to Laylah. Only she matters. Only *she*."

Bhojja would not stop.

When Torg tried to leap off, a strange gravity pinned him to her back. For a moment he grew wild with frustration, drawing the Silver Sword from its scabbard as if to pierce her. But then he heard growls and screams and looked up to see the Daasa crashing into the fiends, tearing and rending in a rage unlike any he had ever witnessed. At first it appeared the Daasa would destroy the enemy with ease, but then the demon joined the fray, cracking her whip in a series of blurring snaps, each one striking a single Daasa and blowing it to pieces.

In the brief moment it took Bhojja to reach the demon, Pisaaca had killed more than a hundred. It was possible the demon could kill them all, if given enough time. But Torg saw Bhojja's mind and realized he still had a duty to perform before he could attempt to rescue Laylah.

All around the wagon, fighting and bedlam reigned. The Daasa battled both the fiends and the mounted wolves, winning with relative ease. But they were no match for Pisaaca, who rained death upon them as she wailed.

The winged demon was so preoccupied with killing, she seemed not to notice when Torg stood on Bhojja's back and leapt onto the seat of the wagon. This incarnation of Pisaaca was more than four times his height, the top of his head barely reaching her knee, but her immense size was more illusion than grandeur. If the demon had known who stood beneath her and what weapon he wielded, she would have fled back to the Realm of Undeath. But now it was too late to escape.

Torg drove the Silver Sword into the meat of Pisaaca's thigh, twisting it and tearing it out sideways with such force that he almost severed the leg.

The demon screamed—loud enough to be heard leagues away—and then collapsed on her wounded leg and tumbled off the wagon.

Torg leapt after her, landing feet-first on her chest and slashing at her throat—once, twice, three times, until her head fell away. Crimson flames and a putrid cloud of fumes burst from the base of the demon's neck, and she ceased to exist, both in this realm and her own.

Fleeing the deadly smoke, the trolls dropped the wagon tongues, but they managed only a few strides before the Daasa engulfed and mangled them.

With the threat of the demon removed, the Daasa had their way with the enemy. Like Torg, they were immune to the *undines*. The fiends were mindlessly vicious, but they lacked the Daasa's size and strength. Recognizing they were outmatched, the wolves and Mogols fled, riding northward toward the nearest ridge of mountains.

Bhojja came up and urged Torg to mount, but there was still one last thing for him to do. He climbed back into the wagon and freed the captives, hacking apart their metal chains. Afterward, they stared at him with pleading eyes.

"I know naught who you are or where you are from, but I cannot remain with you," Torg said. "You must find your own way. There are no safe places left in the world. If I were you, I would go south and search for haven in the mountains."

One elderly woman dared to challenge him. "You would leave us here with these monsters?" she said, pointing a wrinkled finger at the Daasa. "It would be more merciful if you slew us with your sword."

"They have no interest in you and will not harm you," Torg said. "As for mercy, it has become too precious a commodity these days. I cannot afford it."

Then he leapt onto Bhojja's back and headed west in a rush.


JĀKITA AND URBANA each grabbed one of Laylah's arms and dragged her toward the trees. The druids closed around them, forming an impenetrable wall, and then moved off with surprising speed. Whether her companions were spared or harmed, Laylah could not tell. The druids were almost twice her height, blocking her vision of everything but the ground at her feet and the uppermost portions of the trees. The volume of their humming dazed her senses.

They marched for more than a league before the trees thickened considerably. Though it still was early afternoon on a sunny day, it became as dark as dusk in the forest, its canopy closing above them like a thatched roof. Laylah did not recognize these trees, though it seemed obvious they were some form of evergreen because of their straight trunks and sharp scent. They reminded her of pines or spruce, but they were many times taller and broader than any she had seen before, and their skin-like bark was as dark as kohl. A spongy layer of fallen needles covered the ground, choking off plant life other than a few odd-looking ferns and some clumps of moss that glowed as if phosphorescent. Brown deer mice scampered near her feet, their pointed noses twitching. Nutcrackers and crossbills flew in startled bursts just overhead. Black-furred squirrels leapt from branch to branch.

Somehow the massive army of druids managed to pass by without damaging the surroundings. As ugly and evil as they were, Laylah sensed that they treasured this forest and anointed themselves its keepers.

One time she stumbled over a fallen branch and nearly fell.

"Keep your feet, your horrid little bitch," Urbana said, digging clawed fingers into the flesh of Laylah's arm. "There's a long way to go. If you don't keep up, I'll kick your curvy ass all the way there."

"I musssst say, Urbana, you have a way with words," Jākita said. "Don't you agree, ssssister of the king?"

"Except for my brother and his servant Mala, she is the most hideous creature in the world," Laylah said, glaring at Urbana. "No matter what else occurs, you will not survive this."

The ancient vampire hissed, but the Warlish witch remained amused.

"You have spirit, Laaaaylah," she said. "Perhaps, when all is said and done, you and I will become friendssss."

Laylah permitted herself a brief smile. If the witch believed that Laylah was becoming compliant, it might work to her advantage later—when Torg came for her, as she knew he would.

Then they all heard the far-off wail of the demon.

"The Torgon has destroyed Pisaaca . . . as planned," Jākita said, just loud enough for Laylah to hear. "Come to me, *Maranavidu* . . . and we'll plaaaay together, you and I. It will be sssso much fun."


WHEN THE DRUIDS had swarmed around Laylah, Lucius tried to force his way toward her, but one of the monsters had grabbed his shoulders and heaved him away. His friends had also been shoved aside. Ugga had put up the biggest fight, but eventually even he'd succumbed.

Then as quickly as they had come, the druids withdrew. In a matter of moments the forest was empty, including the bodies of the druids slain in the initial battle.

Now, only the carcasses of several Daasa remained, lying motionless beneath the trees. Mysteriously, they had reverted to their "nicey" selves, which made their deaths all the more difficult to bear. Elu went to each one and bowed.

When he returned, he was shaking his head, his eyes glazed. "They gave their lives for the pretty lady."

"We've got to follow her," Bard said, as he retrieved arrows from the ground near the sundered shaft of his spear.

Lucius noticed that the handsome trapper was moving more slowly and with less grace than he had when he had first met him at Kamupadana.

"Without Torg at our side, pursuit is meaningless," Lucius said, his face flushed and swollen. Even his fingers felt thick. "The result would be the same. The wizard is her only chance now."

"Maybe just Bard and I should go. We are the strongest," Ugga said. "We don't want the pretty lady to get herself killed."

Rathburt strode forward and stood in the center of their small group. "I remember Dhutanga as a strange and dangerous place, full of darkness and evil. If any of you tried to follow, you would eventually become lost and would never find your way out. The forest would not allow it. So you should not follow. Laylah was right. The rest of you belong with the Daasa. Your fates are tied to theirs. Besides Torg, there is only one among us who should go after Laylah . . . me."

Rathburt's brashness seemed to stun the others.

"If ya know the way, then show us," Bard said. "We've wasted too much time already."

"Master Rathburt is right," Bonny said to Bard. "Our place is with the Daasa. It'll take magic to free Laylah, the kind only Rathburt and Torg possess."

Lucius tried to protest, but Rathburt interrupted. "Go! And take the rest with you. Find Torg and tell him what happened. Find the Daasa and lead them to Jivita. The White City needs you."

Then Rathburt strode into the thicker trees, leaving the others behind—all except Elu, who refused to abandon his friend and sneaked up behind him.

Lucius waved his good arm in frustration. "Doesn't anyone listen to *me?* I thought I was in command."

"I listen to you, sweety," Bonny said. "But sometimes even the leader has to pay attention when wise words are spoken. Come, Lucius. Our fate lies elsewhere."

She jogged off, followed by Ugga and Bard.

Lucius was the last of the foursome to leave the forest, though several times he glanced back, seeing nothing now but the trees.

RATHBURT HAD amazed himself with his uncharacteristic bravado. Usually, he would have been the first to argue that Laylah was doomed, and it would be foolish to follow her. But when she'd yelled at him earlier, something inside him had come to life. The truth of her words had stung his pride—and awakened his courage; at least, what little he harbored.

Plus, he knew things his companions did not. The forest of Dhutanga was like no other, which included Java and much of the woodlands surrounding the Mahaggatas. In Java you were more likely to encounter an evil monster or beast, but in Dhutanga, the trees themselves were evil, as if they had minds of their own. They were similar to the Hornbeam, feeding off ruin and despair in nearly the same way that normal trees fed off sunlight and soil.

The *Badaalataa* had shied from Rathburt's power. Would the trees of Dhutanga do the same as the deadly vines? For his entire life people had bullied him, but for whatever reason, plants respected and even feared him. That's why he had told Lucius to flee. Rathburt was the only one who could bear this dreadful place, except of course for The Torgon, who could bear anything, always.

So when Elu appeared at his side, Rathburt was stunned.

"What do you think you're doing, you rascal? Didn't I tell you and the others not to follow? Have you gone deaf as well as dumb?"

"Elu did not want you to go alone. If there is fighting, he can help you." He drew the Tugarian dagger from his boot and held it aloft. In the murky darkness its blade shone like a torch.

"Put that away!" Rathburt hissed. "Don't let the trees see that weapon. Not even I will be able to control them if they believe you might use it on them."

"The *trees?*" Elu said, obviously confused.

Rathburt knelt and whispered in his companion's ear. "These trees are like the Hornbeam, only stronger and many times more numerous. Do *not* anger them."

Elu looked around, his eyes fearful. "As you say."

Rathburt knew from years of experience that Elu would be too stubborn to turn away. It was no use arguing with him. It would only delay him further. So he sighed deeply, turned and continued westward, with Elu in tow. The trees became even taller and denser, making it difficult to see and breathe. The few animals they encountered were small and timid: a peculiar menagerie of squirrels, mice, and birds. But eventually they saw larger things with glowing eyes and shiny white fangs that loomed in the shadows. Rathburt finally was forced to call on his staff to guide them—and when he willed it, blue streams of sparkly energy obediently rained from its head, lighting the forest and fending off the beasts that lurked nearby.

Elu stayed close, causing Rathburt to chuckle ruefully. He had never seen the little warrior so cowed. *I wasn't joking, Elu, this forest is dangerous. I wish you hadn't followed me. Then again, I'm glad you did, my dear friend.*

# 35

BHOJJA GALLOPED along the plain as fast as a gust of wind. But Torg's heart beat even faster. What lay ahead?

About a mile from the edge of the forest, he came upon Lucius, Bonny, Ugga, and Bard. Torg leapt off the great mare's back and rushed to the firstborn. "Where is she?" he shouted, causing the air to crackle.

Lucius stepped back, his legs wobbly. "They . . . they took her. The druids. And the witch. And the vampire."

"And you *allowed* it?" Torg drew the Silver Sword and thrust a sharp edge near Lucius' throat. "Kusala was right . . . you are *worthless*! I should have let the chieftain kill you."

Bard gasped. Ugga started to blubber.

Bonny, however, slithered between Lucius and Torg and positioned her own neck between the firstborn and the blade. "If you wants to kill him, then you will have to kill me first. But it might be better if you listened to our story before you act like such a bully. Besides, it's more your fault than ours. You are the one who wandered off and left her to the monsters."

Torg saw the truth in her words, and his rage faded. "Tell me what happened—quickly." He lowered the sword. "I must follow before their lead becomes too great."

Meanwhile, Ugga and Bard, always quick to recover, moved up next to Bhojja, admiring her with adoring eyes. "Where did ya find such a bew-tee-ful horsey?" Ugga asked.

"I don't have time to explain. But it appears you're holding something that belongs to me. Or do you plan to keep it for yourself?"

Ugga's cheeks reddened above his beard, and he handed over Obhasa. "It burned the vam-pie-er's hand real bad, but when *I* picked it up, it was cool," the crossbreed said. "So I brought it with us to give to ya."

"I'll have need of it soon, I'm sure." Then Torg turned and climbed onto Bhojja's back. "Corral the Daasa and head for Jivita, all of you. Hopefully we will meet again there." He left them behind without telling them what had happened with the fiends and demons. He could see that Lucius and Bonny were furious with him. But he was in no mood for apologies.

The great mare knew her way far better than her rider, and she seemed able to follow a scent as well as a mountain wolf. By midafternoon, they had plunged several leagues into the darkening forest, with Bhojja dodging branches and clumps of trees as if she knew every cubit of the terrain.

"I'm coming, my love," Torg whispered over and over.

He knew this was yet another trap. But that made little difference. He wielded Obhasa and the Silver Sword. Nothing short of Invictus could withstand him.


LUCIUS HAD never felt so humiliated, which was saying something considering how many times he had been tormented in Avici. Yet how was he supposed to have stopped the druids from taking Laylah, especially when the Daasa had inexplicably abandoned him? Not to mention that Laylah herself had ordered him not to resist the Warlish witch. If the wizard had stayed with them, things might have turned out differently. It was the Death-Knower's fault that Laylah had been captured.

Then again, a part of Lucius believed everything Torg had said. Lucius *was* worthless. It *would* have been better if Kusala had killed him. What good was he to anyone? He was as powerless as a child.

He also didn't feel very well. He was hot and flushed, and when he pressed his hand against his face, his cheeks were bloated and numb. He looked at his forearm, and it too appeared thicker—with rougher and darker skin. And since when had he grown so much hair on the back of his hand?

"Are you feeling all right, Lucius?" Bonny said. "You don't look so good. Sit down, sweety, and take a rest. Have a sip of water."

"I . . . I . . . don't know what's wrong," Lucius muttered. "I'm dizzy."

Ugga and Bard took his arms and lowered him gently to the grass. He drank some water and soon began to feel better. When he stood up he was almost normal again, other than being extremely hungry.

"I'm all right. Whatever it was has passed. I think I was just mad at Torg. I can see why Rathburt gets so aggravated with him."

Lucius tried to laugh it off, but Bonny seemed unconvinced, as if she knew something he did not.

"Have you ever felt this way before?" she said.

"A few times, I guess, when I get really mad. The blood must rush to my head."

"Ya was looking kind of scary to me," Ugga said. "Your face was da color of a beet!"

This time, Lucius did laugh. "Ugga, you have a way with words."

Just then the first of the Daasa came into view, appearing at the top of a rise and trotting excitedly toward Lucius. Soon he was engulfed.

"Look, they've gone all nicey again," Ugga said.

"They are cute, like their master," Bonny agreed.

Bard walked over to one, reached down, and wiped its muzzle with his hand. When he held up his palm, it was bathed in sticky blood. "They might look cute, but they've gotten into some sort of trub-bull. Must have had a nasty tangle with something. But it doesn't seem like many of them got killed, at least. We can be happy for that."

"They are so many, it's hard to tell," Lucius said. "And I'm not about to back-track and find out what it was they butchered. We have decisions to make, the four of us. Do we obey Torg's order and march to Jivita?"

"What other choice do we have?" Bonny said. "By now, it's too late to follow Laylah or Torg. Like Rathburt said, we'd probably get lost in the forest."

"True enough," Lucius said. "But I have another concern. Suppose we go to Jivita. What happens when we get there? Without Torg as our ambassador, who's to say the white horsemen won't mistake us for enemies?"

Bonny smiled and reached into her jacket, pulling out a small scroll wrapped in a sheath of soft leather. "Rakkhati gave me this before he left with Torg and Laylah. Will this help?"

After reading it, Lucius handed it back to her. "Keep it safe, Bonny." Then he turned to the others. "It's settled, then. We will march to Jivita."

In response, the Daasa chittered loudly. They seemed anxious to move on.

Lucius was quick to accommodate them.


THE WITCH AND vampire kept Laylah moving at a near trot. As she struggled to keep up, a druid pressed against her and thrust a dried root into her hand.

"Chewwww on it," Jākita said. "It will give you strength."

Laylah curled her nose and started to cast it away, but Urbana snapped at her. "Do as she says, you horrid little bitch. Do you think we're trying to poison you? If we wanted you dead, you'd be dead. If you don't eat it, one of the druids will have to haul you the rest of the way."

The thought of being carried was even more disgusting than the root, so Laylah broke off a small piece and tasted it. It was surprisingly sweet, causing her mouth to flood with saliva. Soon after, she felt strength surge through her body. She saved the rest of the root in a pocket in her tunic.

The trees became as dense as blades of grass, and it was almost too dark to see. Though a part of her enjoyed the relief from direct sunlight, Laylah now found it difficult to breathe. Jākita walked directly in front of her, weaving this way and that. Laylah was forced to follow in the witch's footsteps to avoid walking head-on into one of the dark trunks, some of

which were forty spans thick. At times she had to turn sideways to slip
between the trees, though the druids—who were twice her height and many
times her weight—were able to flatten their pliable torsos and squeeze
through the crevices without difficulty. Laylah could see thousands and
thousands of glowing eyes, bobbing about like fireflies. Occasionally, Urbana
shoved her from behind, all the while muttering obscenities that never failed
to make Jākita giggle.

Laylah was tempted to turn on the vampire and kill her then and there,
but it would have accomplished little. She knew she needed to bide her time.
Until Torg arrived, she stood little chance of escape or retribution.

Laylah wasn't sure how long they had been walking—she guessed five
leagues, at least—when she noticed the ground had begun to ascend, slowly
at first, but ever more steeply. To keep up her strength, she ate more of the
root. Even so, her thighs burned, and her breath came in heavy gasps, making
her feel light-headed and hallucinatory.

Somewhere in the distance, she heard, or thought she heard, a low roar,
but all she could see was the witch's glowing flesh—and beyond that, the
fireflies. Everywhere, fireflies.

Then, without warning, Laylah stepped out of the trees and into light so
bright it caused her to grimace. The roaring sound had not been her
imagination. She looked down and almost swooned. They stood at the edge
of a precipice that towered hundreds of cubits above a frothy river winding
between sheer rock walls. Swarms of druids loomed ahead of her, striding
across a slab of stone that had been cast across the gap. "Don't even think
about jumping," Urbana said, "unless you never want to see your precious
wizard again. Boulders are hidden just beneath the surface of the river, and
some of them are razor-sharp. Even if you somehow survived the fall, you'd
be battered to pieces in the currents. Not that I would care."

Laylah was not afraid of heights, but still it terrified her to step onto the
bridge, which was disturbingly narrow and slippery. The druids' thorny toes
gripped the mist-covered rock like roots, so they had no problems crossing.
But Jākita slowed her pace and positioned herself in the center of the
pathway. Again Laylah followed in the witch's footsteps. Part of her *did* want
to leap off the bridge and dare the perils of the river. That kind of death was
preferable to Invictus capturing her again. But she first had to give Torg a
chance to rescue her. Besides, she desired to see his face one last time.


BY THE TIME Rathburt and Elu made it to the river, it was near dusk.
Rathburt leaned heavily on his staff, and even the Svakaran seemed weary.
Several times during their hurried march they had come upon fresh water, so
thirst was not a problem. Hunger and exhaustion, though, more than made
up for it. They were out of food and had found none along the way. The sight

of the river so far below gave them both a start.

"That's a long way down," Rathburt said. "The last time I was here, I didn't dare go this far into the forest. The great river, Cariya, amazes me. It's every bit as nasty as the worst portions of the Ogha."

"Elu doesn't like this river. It has a mean feel."

"Everything about Dhutanga has a mean feel," Rathburt agreed.

"What are we going to do when we catch up to them? Do you have a plan?"

"I guess you could call it a plan. I'm going to do my best to tame the druids, sort of the way I tamed the vines. I'm hoping there's enough of the forest in their blood to make them susceptible to me."

Elu made a strange face.

"You think I'm crazy?" Rathburt said.

"No . . . Elu doesn't think you're crazy. He thinks you're brave. Elu is proud of you."

Rathburt smiled and patted the Svakaran on the head. "I know I've been tough on you all these years. But I've never really meant it. I've loved you like a son. No, that's not right. More like a brother."

The Svakaran hugged Rathburt's leg. "Elu knows that. You can't fool him. He will always be grateful."

Rathburt's smile broadened. "Well, now that we're finished saying 'nicey' things to each other, we'd better get back to business. You asked if I had a plan. Here's the first part of it. We cross this damnable bridge, find a place to hide, and wait for Torg to catch up. We can't do anything without him, anyway. And my guess is he'll be along shortly."

Elu took the lead, stepping cautiously onto the front portion of the bridge. "It's very slippery. But if you watch where Elu steps, you won't fall."

"Don't even say that word."

Soon after they started across the bridge, Rathburt heard unusual noises coming from the woods in front of where they stood. At first he thought it was just a swirl of wind rustling the trees, but the sound grew louder. Halfway across, Elu froze.

"Something *big* is coming," the Svakaran said, so softly Rathburt could barely hear him above the tumult. "Elu has never heard such a commotion. Could it be a druid?"

"I'm not sure what it is, but I'm not about to find out. Let's retreat and hide till it passes."

Even as Rathburt spoke, a dark beast burst from the trees, rumbling forward on its hind legs. His first thought was that the creature was every bit as large as the Kojin that had attacked them near the longhouse, but this beast seemed even quicker. Its short fur was dark brown and its head broad, with a flat nose and wide mouth. Compared to the length of its body, its legs were short and stocky. Its arms hung almost to the ground, and they were thicker than a man's torso, especially between the wrist and elbow.

In his haste to scramble backward off the bridge, Rathburt slipped and would have fallen had a powerful hand not grasped his arm and hoisted him to his feet. Rathburt turned in a panic, expecting to see another great ape; instead, he looked into the deep-blue eyes of The Torgon. He had never been so happy to see him.

Then he caught a glimpse of the mare standing a few paces farther back.

"Bhojja!" he said out loud. "I've heard so much about you, but now I've finally met you. As Vasi masters like to say, 'Will wonders never cease?'"

TORG STRODE forward, coming up behind Elu. The Svakaran had pulled out his dagger and was waving it at the ape, as if daring it to approach. The beast eyed Elu with a mixture of anger and perplexity.

"Your courage is beyond dispute," Torg said to Elu, "but this beast is overly large, even for you. Please allow me to confront it in your stead."

The Svakaran let Torg pass and then scrambled off the bridge. Torg crossed over to the far side. The ape raised its great arms and pounded its chest, making the same kind of drumming sound as a Kojin, only with four fewer arms. Torg left the Silver Sword in the scabbard on his back and instead held Obhasa aloft, carefully watching the beast's every move.

"Mighty One, I have no wish to fight you," said Torg, his voice steady and calm. "My quarrel is with the druids, whom you love less than I. Allow us to pass, and we will trouble you no more."

Torg's words seemed to soothe the ape, and it lowered its arms to its sides. Torg walked slowly forward, staring into its small but intelligent eyes. He approached within two paces and stood beneath the beast, dwarfed both in height and girth. Torg waved Obhasa hypnotically back and forth, and then he muttered words from the ancient tongue.

"*Niddaayahi, Balavant. Niddaayahi!* (Sleep, Mighty One. Sleep!)" A bluish smoke burst from his staff and swirled into the ape's face and flared nostrils. In an instant it was lying on its side, and soon it began to snore.

As Torg gestured for the others to cross, Bhojja knelt before Rathburt and Elu, urging them to mount. Then the mare traversed the bridge with both on her back. At the other end, Torg leapt upon her, and she sprang forward. Now with three riders, she left behind the great ape, which Torg believed would not wake until the following morning, confused but refreshed.

# 36

ONE OF THE druids finally did carry Laylah. Jākita had grown restless over the sluggishness of their march, and she ordered herself and Urbana carried too. The creature cradled Laylah in its angular arms, jamming her face against its bark-like skin, which was warm to the touch and smelled like pine needles. The druids moved awkwardly, but far faster than she could have managed in such dense trees. For the rest of the night they ran without stopping, covering league upon league in the suffocating darkness of the forest. If anything witnessed their approach, it dared not show itself. The wood-eaters were too great.

Laylah was amazed to find that she was dozing. She took another bite of the root to rouse herself and awoke just in time to be greeted by blazing sunlight every bit as startling as when she had come upon the river the previous afternoon. They entered a wide clearing filled with druids, humming insanely. She had to clasp her hands over her ears to keep from going deaf.

Laylah was cast down and again forced to walk. She stumbled behind Jākita, enduring occasional shoves in the back from Urbana. They approached the center of the clearing, where an enormous tree towered like a sentinel of despair. Druids several spans taller than the others guarded a large opening in its trunk. Laylah had no desire to enter that opening. But the choice wasn't hers.

She took out the root and chewed what remained of it, needing whatever strength she could find to face something enormously powerful, which she sensed waited for her inside the tree.

Urbana gave Laylah another hard shove, causing her to stumble through the breach. The immensity of the chamber inside the hollow tree stunned her. The circular room was as wide as a banquet hall, and if there was a ceiling, darkness obscured it. A foul-smelling mist swirled in the air, reminding her of rotten fruit. As she gagged, the vampire kicked her in the rump. She started to fall, but Jākita grabbed her arm. Something awaited them in the semi-darkness, and it was growing impatient. When Laylah finally came close enough to see it, she suppressed a scream.

"Princess Laylah, ssssister of the king, allow me to introduce you to *Kattham Bhunjaka*, queen of the druids," Jākita said.

Laylah recoiled.

But the queen's psychic power swept over her, blasting through her resistance with the power of an avalanche.

BHOJJA CARRIED Torg, Elu, and Rathburt through the forest for the rest of the night with amazing speed, but even she often had to slow to a canter to avoid crashing into the trees. The mare traveled south along the bank of the river, then abruptly turned west, ducking under branches and leaping over roots. Torg held Obhasa tucked under his right arm and pointed the staff forward like a lance, its glowing head lighting the way.

Although he lost track of time and distance, he guessed they had traveled at least twenty leagues since crossing the river. Rathburt and Elu had long since fallen asleep, and Torg dozed on and off before succumbing completely. Magic prevented them from falling off Bhojja's back.

Some time later, a gentle but persistent touch awakened him. He found that he was lying on a soft bed of needles. Jord knelt beside him, stroking his forehead. She was naked and pale, but her long white hair covered her breasts and genitals. Torg sat up. He saw Rathburt and Elu close by, still sleeping soundly.

Torg looked at Jord, puzzled. "Why have we stopped?"

"I've carried you as far as I dare," Jord said. "Just beyond is the clearing you and I observed from the sky. Laylah is held prisoner inside the great tree. It's up to you and your companions to rescue her. I am called elsewhere."

Jord stood and began to walk back toward the east, but just before vanishing, she turned and said one last thing. "Do not linger. Laylah is in danger. And so are the three of you. The trees bend their will upon you, which causes your sleepiness. They *wish* you to be helpless. Even you, Torgon, cannot withstand them forever. And beyond the trees, a trap has been prepared. Beware."

Then she turned and disappeared.

Torg leaned against Obhasa and used it to stand. Then he nudged Rathburt and Elu with the staff several times before they opened their eyes.

Elu stretched his arms and yawned.

Rathburt sat up, his voice raspy. "Why are you disturbing me, Torgon? I was having the most unusual dream, and now you've gone and ruined it."

"Get up, both of you," Torg demanded. Then he handed each of them a piece of jerky, the last of the food he had carried in a pack taken from Jivita. "There is much to be done. Laylah's freedom is at stake."

"Where are we?" Elu mumbled as he chewed. "Is it time for Rathburt to try his plan?"

"Hush, Elu. The Torgon doesn't have time to listen to your foolishness."

"What's he saying, Rathburt? What plan? Speak quickly. Is there some way you can help?"

"It was just an idea I had earlier. Now that we're here, it seems rather foolish."

"*Tell* me!"

"For Anna's sake, Torgon, you don't have to shout. I just thought that, well, my magic doesn't work very well on people, animals, and monsters, but it seems to have an effect on plants. And I was thinking . . . *hoping* . . . that the druids have enough 'plant' in them to make them susceptible to me. I know I'm being silly, but . . ."

Torg seized Rathburt's shoulders. "It might work." Then he started for the trees.

"Wait, Torgon! What if my magic fails?"

Torg shook his fist. "Then we won't be any worse off than we already are. Come with me or go your own way. But choose."

"Elu is coming! Wait for me, great one."

Rathburt sighed. "Very well, I'm coming. Someone among us has to have a little sense."

# 37

TO LAYLAH, THE druid queen's psychic force felt like a wave of heat beating upon her brow. While a portion of her mind cried out in disgust, Laylah found herself clambering onto the pale queen's rubbery back. Once there, folds of fetid flesh closed around her, leaving only her head and neck exposed. Jākita and Urbana cackled with delight.

"Are you nice and warm?" the vampire said from far below. "You look so comfy, Princess Laylah. Or I suppose, I should again call you *Queen* Laylah."

"Be careful how much you taaaaunt her," the witch said. "There'll come a time when she *will* be your queen again—and mother of the prince. When she finally surrenders and makes niiiice with Invictus, you could be in peril."

Urbana hissed, but then grew quiet. Despite her bizarre predicament, Laylah took pleasure in the vampire's discomfort. It would almost be worth "making nice" with her brother, if it put her in a position to be able to destroy Urbana.

Jākita spread her arms and spoke in a voice that echoed throughout the chamber.

"Prepare yourselves, everyone, for a magnificent spectacle," the witch proclaimed. "The Torgon will soon arrive, and what he finds here will not pleasssse him. All the better. I want him to ssssuffer as much as possible before I . . . *we* . . . kill him. And I want the ssssister of the king to view his demise, so that it will be burned into her memory for the rest of her life."

As she spoke, the humming of the druids intensified. The small portion of Laylah's mind that remained lucid could sense someone coming. She heard a commotion near the opening of the chamber. And then the inside of the tree filled with fire.


WHEN TORG, Rathburt, and Elu walked into the clearing, it appeared at first as if the druids could not see them. Rathburt clasped his hand to his mouth and gasped. Elu's eyes sprang wide open. Even Torg was dismayed. There were more druids here than he could have believed possible, jammed together like termites gathered around the base of a mound. Their humming caused the ground to tremble.

"Does Jivita realize the true extent of its peril?" Torg said.

"Jivita?" Rathburt said. "What about us?"

"Good point. We still have only two choices. Proceed or flee. I will go forward, but I'll force neither of you to join me."

"Elu will go where the great one goes."

"Good job, Elu. Show me up, why don't you? Oh, what's the use? A man's got to die some time, right Torgon? Who knows that better than you and I?"

When the trio stepped forward, the druids surged toward them like a rising tide.

Torg held Obhasa in his left hand and the Silver Sword in his right. Elu brandished the Tugarian dagger. When the first druids were just a few paces away, Rathburt lifted his own staff and waved it above his head. Blue fire crept along the shaft and then showered up and out like a fountain. When the magical fire struck the first of the druids, they burst into flames, running crazily about.

"Forward," Torg shouted. "They will shy before us."

As they proceeded, the druids gave them a wide berth, but it was a long walk to the tree, and the humming grew maddening. When Rathburt began to weaken, Torg touched his ivory staff to the wooden one, and the blue shower doubled in intensity, scorching hundreds of the creatures. Even so, their numbers were too immense to be depleted. They continued to swarm around the two wizards and the Svakaran, looking for any opening in their defense.

"Stay strong, Rathburt. We're almost there," Torg said.

"There? You mean that gigantic tree? And once we get there, what then? What hope have we against so many?"

"As you said before, a man's got to die some time. Once inside the tree, we shall see what we shall see."

"Don't worry, Rathburt," Elu said. "The great one will think of something."

"That is *so* comforting."

When they reached the opening, several large druids attempted to block their way, but Torg and Rathburt chased them off with the power of their staffs. The trio entered the tree and strode through foul-smelling mist. Elu seemed to be the first to see the druid queen, revealed in all her hideousness by the illumination of the wizards' fire. Jākita stood beside the queen, along with a powerful vampire. The Warlish witch's skin glowed eerily in a way Torg had never before seen, reminding him of the aura of Mala's chain.

As if Torg's presence tantalized her, the druid queen's pale flesh throbbed and rippled. He could sense the extent of her malice.

"Where is Laylah?" Torg asked the witch. "Deliver her to me, and I will spare your life."

Jākita cackled. "Such bold words from such a small man. Why don't you asssssk Urbana?" She gestured toward the vampire, who had grabbed a torch and was clambering onto the druid queen's back. Then she lowered the fiery tip and illuminated a portion of the queen's oily hide. Laylah's head and neck protruded from a fold of the creature's flesh. The rest of her body was obscured.

"If Laylah is harmed, I will kill *all* of you," Torg said. "Do not doubt it!"

"You will do no such thing," said a raspy voice that came eerily from Laylah's mouth. "If you attempt to harm me or any of my children, I will squeeze the life out of this tiny body and drink its blood."

The queen's body convulsed, causing Laylah to cry out—in her own voice.

"Youuuu are in a bit of a mess, Torgon," Jākita purred. "I don't believe you are in a position to make threats. In fact, if you want your precious Laylah to live, then you will do as I ssssay."

As if in resignation, Torg handed Obhasa to Elu. As he did, he whispered two words that the Svakaran could barely hear. "To Laylah."

Then he turned back to the witch. "What is it you would have me do, Jākita?"

"Queen Jākita."

Sigh. "*Queen* Jākita."

"Hmmmmmmmm. What issss it I would have you do? Let me see. For a sssstart, you shall bring back to life all those you killed at Kamupadana."

"Such an act is beyond me."

The witch became enraged, transforming from beautiful to ugly. Even in her hideous state, her mottled flesh continued to glow. From far above, the vampire screeched, prompting Laylah's head to speak again.

"Nor can you bring back my mother," it said. "Did you think I would not seek revenge?"

Then the druid queen directed all her psychic power at Torg's mind. His knees buckled, and he started to collapse, but before he lost control, he whispered one last word to Elu. "Now."


TO LAYLAH'S mind, existence was a nightmare. She floated in a soupy darkness frequently interrupted by dazzling but painful bursts of energy, as if a lightning storm blasted all around her. She could not move her arms or legs, and her head flopped about like a baby's. At one point the darkness closed around her so intensely she screamed. But just when she was about to give up hope, a veil was removed from her eyes, and she could see more clearly.

Kneeling next to her and shouting frantically was the cute little Svakaran.

"Elu. What brings you here?"

He still shouted, his face flushed, eyes bulging. And then he held up Obhasa. "The great one told Elu to give this to you. Torg needs your help. And so does Rathburt. The witch is going to kill them."

Laylah had no idea what Elu was talking about, but she heard a curious moaning. With great effort, she turned her head in the direction of the sound. Lying near her face on an odd-looking carpet was Urbana, with a Tugarian dagger driven into her belly. Black blood gushed from her stomach, staining the carpet.

"Elu?" Laylah said slowly. "Would you please tell me what's happening?"

But the Svakaran wasn't listening. Instead he yanked on her head, which hurt her neck. She lowered her eyes and saw in amazement that she had somehow fallen through the carpet and was stuck inside it.

"Huh?"

"Help them," Elu continued to shout. "Laylah, take the staff and help them!"

Then the Svakaran pressed the rounded head of Obhasa against the side of her face.


LOST AMID THE madness was Rathburt. He felt the druid queen's will sweep past him and crash down upon Torg. Then Elu ran off, but not before grabbing Obhasa. The Svakaran's disappearance had amazed Rathburt, but things were happening too quickly for him to react.

Torg collapsed to his knees and lowered his head, as if preparing for an executioner's strike. He even dropped his precious sword. And then the witch was coming toward Torg with murder in her eyes, her body aglow.

This terrified Rathburt, but not even a coward of his proportions could stand by and watch as a helpless friend was butchered. Rathburt dropped his staff and picked up the sword. It was heavier than he expected and cold to the touch. He grasped the hilt in both hands and directed the point of the blade at Jākita.

"Come no closer, or I will skewer you," Rathburt warned, trying to act brave. Instead, his voice sounded shrill.

The witch laughed, but her eyes were full of menace.

"Step aside, ssssilly man," she hissed, boils erupting on her hideous forehead. "You are no match for me. Put down the sword and ssssit down. When all of thissss is over, I will come for you. Perhaps Invictus will have use in Uccheda for someone with your skills."

"I would prefer to stand aside. In fact, nothing would please me more. But, alas, I cannot. The Torgon is my friend. And I will not forsake him—now or later, no matter how painful it is for me."

Incensed, Jākita raised her arms and cast them forward. Blobs of golden light, laced with threads of crimson, leapt from the palms of her hands. Without thinking, Rathburt held up the sword in hopes of deflecting just a portion of the onslaught. To his amazement, the sword absorbed all of the wicked energy, and still its blade was cold.

Jākita howled and rushed forward, her gnarled fingers spread wide to throttle him with her bare hands. Rathburt stepped back and almost tripped over Torg, who remained kneeling with his head down.

Now that Rathburt had dropped his staff in favor of the sword, the druids also converged on him, no longer fearing his blue fire. Rathburt looked down at the staff and concentrated, willing it like a puppeteer to stand on its own and shower the enemy. The druids retreated. Emboldened by his newfound ability, Rathburt turned back to Jākita, who now was just a few paces away.

This time his voice was steady. "If you come any closer, I will pierce your foul heart."

Despite his new-found confidence, the witch was undeterred. She approached within a span of the point of the blade and stood there, unwavering. Rathburt's skinny arms trembled from the weight of the sword. Jākita laughed again, then slowly transformed back to her beautiful incarnation. Intoxicating perfumes swirled into Rathburt's nostrils. She smiled at him with the innocence of a virgin, but her skin, still glowing gold, betrayed her true intentions.

"You would stab me, ssssilly man . . . with that mean old sword? A sweet little thing like me?"

Then she glided even closer to the point, smiling all the while. "Do it, ssssilly man. Give it a try."

Rathburt's cowardice finally raised its ugly head. He could barely hold the sword aloft, much less stab the creature. Her radiance caused sweat to burst from his brow and stream down his face, burning his eyes.

"Ssssilly man. No sword can harm me."

Rathburt looked down at Torg, who remained on his knees, head bowed, as if ashamed. "Torgon, help me . . . tell me what to do."

But Torg remained silent. Instead, it was a cry from above that shattered Rathburt's paralysis. Soaked with goo, Laylah stood on top of the druid queen, waving Obhasa over her head like a lasso. Blue energy laced with white strands spat from its rounded head, illuminating the entire chamber. Rathburt could see the bloated body pulsate in response, its folds and curves heaving.

Without further thought, Rathburt took a single step forward and punched the point of the blade between the witch's breasts.


WHEN OBHASA touched Laylah's cheek, an explosion of blue and white lifted Elu off his feet and tossed him backward, causing him to roll off the druid queen like a boy tumbling out of control down a steep hill. Urbana also was thrown to the ground, the dagger still jammed in her belly. The searing energy caused the druid queen to spasm, spreading open the folds that had held Laylah in place.

Covered with foul-smelling goo, Laylah struggled to her feet and looked down to see Torg kneeling on the ground beneath her, while Rathburt attempted to fend off the advance of the Warlish witch. The sight filled her with rage, and she waved Obhasa above her head and screamed with all her might. Then she swung the fiery staff down, smiting the bulbous flesh. *Kattham* let out an inhuman screech. In response, every druid in the chamber swarmed over the queen, forming a protective barrier. Undeterred, Laylah wielded Obhasa like a stave, knocking dozens of druids aside with each swipe. But there were too many. She was overwhelmed and sent tumbling herself. She fell off the queen and hit the ground with a thump, momentarily losing her breath. Suddenly a strong hand lifted her above the tumult. She started to fight, then saw that it was Torg.

"Beloved . . ." she said in the sweet tone reserved only for him.

"My love . . ."

And then: "The danger is not yet past," he said. "We must flee."


TORG WAS LOST in his own nightmare world. He had been cast into a raging sea and was fighting with all his strength to remain afloat. Thunderous waves flung him about, threatening to submerge him. A small part of his mind was aware that he was under the druid queen's spell, but he was powerless to resist. It was all he could do to save himself from drowning, and he was growing weaker by the moment.

When Laylah screamed, the psychic assault dropped from his mind. Under threat from the sorceress and Obhasa, the druid queen became intent on her own survival, withdrawing her will and focusing it instead on her "children," whom she called in a panic.

In response, the druids swarmed over her in layer upon layer, forming a shield far stronger than armor. Torg shook the dizziness from his head and stood. To one side, he saw Rathburt step forward and punch the point of the Silver Sword between the witch's breasts. Her golden shield shied from the blade in the same way the flames had parted when Torg had slid it into a fire in the foothills of Asubha. The witch's eyes opened wide in surprise.

"What have you done?" she said to Rathburt, stepping back in bewilderment. She touched her hand to her chest and held it to her face. Blood dripped off her fingertips, sizzling on the dirt at her feet.

Rathburt had not driven the sword deep enough to kill the witch, but now she knew she was dealing with something more dangerous than she had realized, causing her to back away.

Torg reached over and took the sword from Rathburt's hands. "You've done well. I'm proud of you. But now it's my turn."

Jākita yelped and started to run, but a wall of druids blocked her and then cast her forward. She tumbled at Torg's feet and looked up, inadvertently transforming again. The act froze her in place just long enough.

"I've told you this before, but your kind never seems to listen," Torg said. "You are not my match."

In one swift motion he beheaded her. She died in the same way the demon had died, with flames and smoke bursting from the base of her neck. Then Torg turned just in time to see Laylah tumble off the queen. He forced his way through the druids, wielding his sword like a machete, and then lifted the sorceress to her feet. She was covered with putrid-smelling goo. He was amazed that she still held Obhasa.

# 38

AT THE SAME time Torg was slaying the witch, Rathburt was scrambling on hands and knees toward his staff, which had remained standing amid the druid horde like a living entity with a mind of its own. A lone druid charged past him and inadvertently kicked him in the ribs, sending him tumbling. But it turned out to be a lucky blow, rolling him right next to the staff.

Rathburt stood and grasped the shaft with both hands, willing more power into the ancient wood. Blue fire exploded from its head, arcing outward. Dozens of druids were consumed, and the rest shied from him. Rathburt strode forward, waving the staff in front of him while scanning every speck of the ground in search of Elu. Finally he saw the Svakaran crumpled in a heap just a few paces from the druid queen's body, where the stampeding creatures had stomped him into unconsciousness.

"No," Rathburt cried. "Not you! Not you!"

He rushed to Elu's side and barely was able to lift him onto one shoulder, the small man's weight amazing him. Rathburt staggered away from the queen, but it was difficult to manage both Elu and the staff. The druids, sensing weakness, closed in again.

"Torg, Laylah . . . *help!*"

A blast of blue energy laced with curling white tendrils blew a hundred druids to pieces. Then Laylah and Torg rushed forward. Torg sheathed the sword and took Elu from Rathburt, casting the Svakaran over one shoulder as easily as he would a child.

"He's hurt," Rathburt said, barely able to hear his own voice above the tumult.

"Follow me," Torg shouted back. "I can help him, but first we must fight our way free."

"He's trying to say something," Laylah said, leaning close to Elu's face. "The dagger. He doesn't want to leave the dagger."

Rathburt was incensed. "To hell with the dagger!"

But Torg lifted his free hand and spoke words from the ancient tongue. "*Kantaara Yodha tam!* (A Desert Warrior calls!)"

The air crackled above their heads, and then the dagger leapt into Torg's palm, leaving a trail of smoke in its wake.

"Come, now! No more delays. We must flee."


STILL DRIPPING goo from her hair and clothes, Laylah used Obhasa to lead the way, spraying blue-white fire in all directions and slaughtering druids by the score. But *Kattham Bhunjaka* drove her children forward with her psychic might, ordering them to attack with a madness that overcame any fear. Rathburt protected their rear, his own staff thrumming, as if eager to destroy. Though he still carried Elu on one shoulder, Torg was able to use the Silver Sword to hack apart any druids that came too near, cutting through them like parchment. The four of them managed to squeeze through the opening and into the blinding sunlight of the clearing. It was not yet noon.

Even though they were now outside of the tree, tens of thousands of druids still surrounded them. Laylah was disheartened. How could they possibly escape? Even if they made it to the forest, it would offer little protection. The druids would continue to hound them.

Then the druids suddenly halted their assault and tilted their pointy heads skyward. This puzzled Laylah. Was it another trick? She looked up as well and gasped. High above them all—circling the uppermost branches of the great tree—flew a crimson dragon, glittering in the bright sunlight. The enormous creature dove toward them, and when it neared the ground it spat molten fire from its gaping jaws.

"Bhayatupa comes," Torg said in a puzzled voice.

"But why?" Laylah said.

"Who cares?" Rathburt shouted. "What are we waiting for? We should make for the river."

"Rathburt's right," Torg said. "Cariya is our only chance."

Bhayatupa dipped down, soared just over their heads, and burned a wide path. They scrambled through it, stepping over the charred remains. The dragon swept around and flew low again. Laylah looked up and saw a gray-haired woman riding on his neck, cackling with glee.

The four of them made for the forest. A few dozen druids followed close behind, but dragon fire cut off the rest. Bhayatupa continued to pass low along the tree line, creating a blazing wall of flame that the druids could not breach. It didn't take Torg long to kill the few who had made it past the fire. Suddenly, they were alone in the forest.

The wizard dropped Elu onto a bed of needles. Rathburt knelt beside him.

"Don't let him die, Torgon. Please . . ."

"I'll do my best. But I need Obhasa."

Laylah passed him the ivory staff. The wizard waved it over Elu's broken body. "*Minta . . . Minta . . . Minta*," he whispered tenderly, as a blue-green glow emanated from the rounded head and flowed into the Svakaran's flesh.

"It's not as bad as it looks," Torg finally said to Rathburt. "Elu is small, but he is stronger even than I realized. When you rebuilt his body, a part of your magic must have remained in his flesh. He has some bruises and some injured ribs, but I believe he will recover."

Just then, Elu sat upright and shouted: "*Aalokadharana.*"

Rathburt yelped and fell back onto his buttocks. "Elu! Are you trying to stop my heart?"

The Svakaran remained dazed and said nothing, but Torg smiled.

"What does that mean, beloved?" Laylah asked.

"In the ancient tongue, *Aalokadharana* means 'container of light,'" Torg said. "It is a secret Tugarian name for Obhasa."

The wizard looked down at Elu. "Allow me to carry you a while longer, my friend. We still have a ways before we reach the river, and the druids will eventually find their way around the fire."

Elu nodded.

# 39

VEDANA COULDN'T remember the last time she'd had so much fun—probably all the way back to her sexual encounter with the The Torgon in the bowels of Asubha. She was so distracted that she failed to veil her presence from Invictus. Bhayatupa was putting on a great show of power, blasting the druids apart with ridiculous ease. And yet, he was being careful not to slay too many. After all, their goal wasn't to cause serious harm to the druid army—just to make it look like that's what they were trying to do. Their real goal was to provide enough distraction to allow Torg, Laylah, and Rathburt to escape. Elu mattered naught.

After the wizards and sorceress made it to the forest, Vedana leapt off the dragon's neck, transformed into her raven incarnation, and sped across the clearing to the great tree. Once inside, she cawed with delight upon seeing Jākita's headless corpse lying limp on the floor of the chamber, while the druid queen quivered with fright, her bloated body shrouded by her "children."

Urbana still lived, but barely. The vampire had suffered a severe wound to the abdomen but had managed to crawl over to the witch's body, leaving a trail of black blood in her wake. Vedana had half a mind to transform into her grandmotherly persona and give the druid queen a good tongue-lashing for attempting to betray her, but she saw with satisfaction that *Kattham Bhunjaka* was already suffering enough.

Vedana cawed once more and fled the chamber.

Bhayatupa continued to put on an impressive display, knocking druids over with the downdraft from his wings while fanning the fire just enough to keep the army pinned inside the clearing. She buzzed by the dragon and winked, thinking, "He's not such an old codger after all." Then she flew up and over the fire and zoomed down to check on the progress of the sweet lovers and their companions. To her delight they'd already jogged more than a mile, but then she noticed that a swarm of druids—returning in a rush from patrol—was approaching unseen from the south. That wouldn't do.

Vedana incarnated into a mountain eagle—she'd been practicing this ever since seeing the Faerie do it so well—and swept down upon them, intending to summon an army of *efrits* to destroy them, even though it would be a dreadful waste of her precious babies. But then she saw other creatures foraging nearby, and a better idea entered her devious mind.

Nine great apes in all: two large males, four females, and three youngsters. The males stood more than nine cubits tall and weighed a ton apiece. The females were about two-thirds that size, but still huge—and each of the six adults was many times stronger than a druid.

Vedana poised herself in the path of the approaching druids and transformed into an infant ape. Her incarnation wasn't anywhere near perfect, but it was believable enough to fool the adults. She began to make loud, panicked hoots. The druids—more than a score, all told—came forward to investigate, their senses already on hyper-alert because of the psychic cries of their queen. When they saw the infant ape, they chose to ignore it, attempting to rush past on their way toward the clearing. But by then, the adults had arrived, and the two males tore into the druids in a primal rage, thinking they meant to harm the orphan. Only two druids managed to escape the males, and they were killed by the females who hid nearby. Afterward, the confused apes spent a good deal of time trying to find the infant, which had mysteriously vanished.

Once again in the form of a raven, Vedana flitted from tree to tree until she found Torg and the others. Now they were less than five leagues from the river and would reach it before dusk. The demon rushed ahead to prepare their transportation, a boat strong enough to survive the rapids, if cleverly maneuvered. A pair of Mogol warriors, who had remained loyal to Bhayatupa, guarded the craft—but with orders to flee when the wizard and his companions approached.

Then Vedana returned to check on Torg and Laylah's progress. "Hurry up . . . hurry up!" she whispered from above. "The druids will catch you, if you're not careful. Do you expect me to do *everything?*"

THE FOREST thickened and darkened once again, and though it was midafternoon, it became difficult to see more than a few dozen paces. Despite being burdened by Elu, Torg was the quickest. Laylah did her best, but the physical and emotional severity of her ordeals among the druids had drained her. To make matters worse, the goo had dried all over her, making her clothes as stiff as a suit of armor. Rathburt was exhausted and could barely walk, much less jog.

Torg began to fear they would not reach the river in time. And even if they did, escape wasn't guaranteed. None of them were capable of surviving the rushing currents without some sort of craft.

"Rathburt, can you not walk any faster?" Torg said, no longer able to conceal his annoyance.

"I'm trying, Torgon, I swear," Rathburt said, his voice almost pitiful. "Maybe the rest of you should go on ahead. My legs don't seem able to hold me up."

"We're not leaving anyone," Laylah said. "Torg, maybe if you carry Rathburt and I carry Elu, we'll move a little faster."

"You're strong, Laylah, I'm not denying that, but Elu is a lot heavier than he looks. Believe it or not, I think he might be even heavier than Rathburt. He weighs as much as a boulder."

The Svakaran finally spoke. "Elu can walk now."

Torg stopped and set Elu down in the darkness against a tree. "We all should rest," Torg said. "But for just a short while." Then he knelt next to Elu. "I don't think it's a good idea for you to walk just yet. Your injuries are mended to some degree, but only time will heal them completely. It might be a week or more before you can move around like you did before."

"We don't have a week," the Svakaran rasped. "Elu can walk *now*. His *legs* weren't broken. The great one should carry Rathburt, instead. If the druids catch us, we'll have to fight again. Elu can walk, but he can't fight."

Meanwhile, Rathburt had collapsed onto his side and was breathing heavily, grasping his chest. Torg knelt down and placed his hand on his forehead. His fellow Death-Knower felt feverish.

"I'm old, Torgon," he managed to say.

"You may be old, but that's not what's causing this problem. I'm sorry, Rathburt, I should have seen this before. The reason we're struggling is all around us. The trees are assaulting us—and you worst of all—for they perceive you as the greatest threat among us."

Torg placed his hand on Elu's muscled shoulder. "I don't like it, but I'm going to have to take you up on your offer. We need to reach the river before nightfall. In full darkness, the strength of the trees will increase beyond our ability to resist."

AT ANY OTHER time in his life, Rathburt would have been humiliated by Torg carrying him. But now he was beyond caring. Rathburt suddenly understood that he *was* under assault, not just from one tree but from thousands of hectares of forest. Like the druids, the trees fought in a unified group—an interconnected organism with many bodies but a single mindset.

He could sense the trees groping inside his mind in an attempt to crush his will. They could not move about like druids, strangling and rending. They even lacked the ability—or desire—to trip with a root or crush with a fallen limb. The selfishness of their species, their desire to cover all of Triken, drove their single-mindedness. Eons ago, they almost had achieved their purpose, but now Dhutanga was all that remained of their kind.

Within their borders, they tolerated only what benefited them: the druids, who were the shepherds of the forest; the great apes, which ate the pesky shrubbery that managed to take root in the fallen needles; a variety of birds and rodents, which helped to control the insects; and several species of wild cats, which kept the birds and rodents under control. Otherwise, not much else lived in Dhutanga, except near its outer borders and along the banks of the Cariya River, where a variety of monsters, animals, and ordinary plant life still thrived.

The trees were encouraging Rathburt to rest . . . to lie down and take a nap. A *long* nap—until his body decomposed and enriched the soil. Could anything be more pleasant? Rathburt always hoped he would die in his sleep, now more than ever. Here was the perfect opportunity.

Rathburt fell asleep in Torg's arms, entering a darkness rivaled only by death, his dreams sweet with relief but sour with surrender.


LAYLAH COULD feel it too. Though it was a relief to be shielded from sunlight, her legs were rubbery, her mind drugged. Each step was more difficult than the last. Elu leaned against her more and more, and Torg was right. The little guy was heavy. She wasn't sure how much longer she could walk on her own, much less continue to support the Svakaran. Plus, she was finding it increasingly difficult to see what lay beyond.

She guessed it was late afternoon above the canopy, but here on the ground, there was only darkness, speckled with trickles of light that provided scant visibility. Even Torg appeared to be weakening. She wondered if it might be a good idea for all of them to lie down and take a rest. Surely, they had earned some sleep after all their travails.

*Use Obhasa, you idiot!*

The words tore through her mind like a bolt of lightning on a black night. She found that she had stopped walking altogether and was leaning against a tree, with Elu lying at her feet, snoring. Torg stood a few paces ahead of her, still holding Rathburt but otherwise not moving, except for a subtle sway.

*How many times do I have to say it? Are you deaf? Use Obhasa!*

*Stop it. That hurts.*

*I'll make it hurt a whole lot worse if you don't do what I say.*

*All right. All right. Just let me rest a little while longer.*

*Use it!*

Just to make the annoying voice stop, Laylah grasped Obhasa firmly in her right hand and willed it to glow. As always, it responded to her with gusto, lighting up the forest for a hundred paces or more in all directions. A pair of Tygers with drooping fangs had been stalking them just a stone's throw away. The sudden light startled them, and they snarled and fled. Laylah cried out. In a blur of motion, Torg dropped Rathburt and his wooden staff, drew the

Silver Sword, and spun around. But his eyes were glazed, as if he had been rudely awakened from a deep sleep.

Torg staggered toward her, growing stronger with each step, and he grasped Obhasa just beneath where her hand also gripped the staff. The two of them forced their wills into the ancient ivory, and the staff grew brighter, illuminating the forest as far as the eye could see.

"*Ossajahi no. Nibandhissatha ce, mayam sevissaama aggim. N'atthi samsayo.* (Leave us be. If you persist, we will use our fire. Do not doubt it)," Torg said to the trees.

It probably was her imagination, but the trees seemed to shiver.

In response, Elu sat up and rubbed his eyes. "Elu fell asleep. He is sorry."

Even Rathburt stirred. When he stood, his own staff glowed, as if taking its cue from Obhasa. "I feel much better now that I've had a nap," Rathburt said. "As the Vasi masters like to say, 'shouldn't we be moving on?'"


IT HAD BEEN a close call. They probably had been standing there for just a few moments, but it would not have taken much longer for all of them to succumb. If Laylah hadn't used Obhasa when she did, they would have become easy prey for the Tygers or druids. Torg had ventured into Dhutanga several times in his life, but never while so weary. And the last time he had fought a druid queen, Bhojja had been there to carry him out. The great mare somehow was immune to the will of the forest.

"The trees fear us, as they should," Torg said to the others.

"They no longer desire to kill us," Rathburt added. "They only want us to leave."

"Elu agrees with the trees. He also wants to leave."

"How far do you think it is to Cariya?" Laylah said. "I wouldn't mind washing this sticky stuff out of my hair and clothes with some nice, fresh water."

"I would guess no more than three leagues," Torg said. "But the druids move faster than we do, and they are probably past the fire and on our trail already. We must hurry."

"And what do we do when we reach the river?" Laylah said. "What I saw of Cariya didn't look swim-able."

"Despite the evil of the forest, a few people manage to live along some portions of Cariya," Torg said. "The will of the forest does not extend to its banks, on either side. If we are lucky, we'll find a craft."

"But even if we get a boat, isn't most of the river just a series of rapids?" Rathburt said. "We'll be drowned."

"There's no good way out of here," Torg agreed. "But Cariya is my choice. And look on the bright side, Rathburt. If we die, at least it'll be fast."

"Too fast. I'd rather die in my sleep," Rathburt said, remembering his dreams. "I'll leave the painful deaths to people like you."

Torg laughed. "Tell that to the Warlish witch you stabbed in the chest."

Rathburt had no response.

VEDANA CONTINUED to watch from above.

She had seen the four of them come to a complete stop, as if they had all day to lollygag about. It had taken a massive dose of her strength to jolt Laylah into using the wizard's ivory staff, but at least it had gotten them going again—and none too soon.

Several thousand druids had breached the dragon fire and were marching toward them with alarming speed. The demon believed the foursome would reach the river before the druids, but it would be close. Still, there wasn't much else she could do. There were too many druids to use *efrits*. And beneath the canopy, the forest was too dense for Bhayatupa to be of any help. All Vedana could do now was get the Mogols into position so that Torg would find the boat soon after reaching the river.

"Mother, may I go to them?" came a sweet voice from a bubble of darkness floating in the air beside Vedana.

The raven cawed, the disturbance annoying it. "How can you possibly help?"

"I can guide him, Mother," Peta said. "That's what I do."

The raven considered this. "I will be listening to every word you say. If you reveal one word of my plan, I will shut you up for good."

"I want your plan to work as much as you do," Peta said. "I am Father's best chance. I promise to do just enough to help him escape Dhutanga. Besides, it will be wonderful to breathe fresh air again. Except for a brief moment just before my . . . death, I have not done so for thousands of years."

"You will still be blind," Vedana said, taking pleasure in the proclamation. "You will always be blind."

"I know, Mother. But until you entered my life, it had never caused me pain."

# 40

LAYLAH NOTICED that the forest was thinning. Soon she no longer needed to use Obhasa to light their way. She also began to hear the distant sound of rushing water. But almost at the same time, she heard the druids approaching from behind.

"We have to move faster," Laylah said.

"I hear them too," Torg said. "Hurry . . . everyone! I believe they are many."

For once, it wasn't just Rathburt who was slowing them down. Elu was struggling.

"I might have to stay back and fight them," Torg said. "The three of you should go on ahead."

"No," Laylah shouted, with enough force to rustle the needles at his feet. "I will not allow you to leave us again. We succeed . . . or fail . . . together."

"She's right," Rathburt said. "Your wandering off is what got us into so much trouble to begin with."

Torg started to argue, but then Laylah noticed Elu pointing at something. "Who is that?" the Svakaran said.

Laylah turned. A young girl with hair the color of sand and a fluffy dress that seemed to glimmer stood nearby. She beckoned them with her tiny hand and then scampered toward the river.

"*Dhiite! Dhiitaake!*" Torg shouted. "We must follow. She will show us the way."

The wizard ran after her, with Laylah and the others in pursuit. The girl's surprise appearance gave them a burst of energy, and they ran faster than before. Laylah had no idea who the girl might be, but she remembered Torg using those same words when they had come too near Arupa-Loka. Was this child some kind of demon? An ally of Vedana? If so, why would she want to help them? But Torg seemed to know her, which was enough reason for Laylah to follow.

No matter how fast they ran, the girl maintained the same distance from them. She angled down the side of a steep hill and raced along a path that weaved through a misty bog, then down an even steeper hill laden with crusty boulders. They followed in her footsteps, and Laylah learned to trust the girl's judgment. Every decision she made seemed to be the right one. Without her guidance, they would have struggled mightily to traverse this area of the forest. But why and how would a little girl in a pretty dress know so much about Dhutanga? Appearance-wise, she could not have been more out of place.

Then the girl slipped through a wall of trees and momentarily was lost from view. Torg followed her and also disappeared. Laylah was next. Beyond the trees was another steep cliff. The river—wider and calmer than when Laylah had first seen it—lay fifty cubits beneath them.

Torg knelt in front of the girl and hugged her. Was he crying? From her vantage point, Laylah couldn't tell. But she could see the girl's face—as beautiful as a Warlish witch's—with full red lips that curled upward at the corners. She couldn't have been more than ten years old, yet her aura seemed almost ancient. Her eyes were closed, and she was hugging Torg with strong little arms. When she opened her eyes, Laylah was startled; they were pure white, with no iris or pupil. Obviously she was blind. But then how could she have led them so well?

"The druids come," the child said. "We have to jump."

"Jump?" Rathburt said. "*I'm* not jumping."

"It's not far, Rathburt," the girl said. "And the water is deep."

"How do you know my name? Are you a demon?"

"She is many things," Torg said, standing up and towering over the girl. "But our enemy, she is not. If she says jump, we jump. Besides, what other choice do we have? The druids are upon us."

Torg grasped the girl's hand and then Laylah's and stepped to the edge of the precipice. "Hold on tight to Obhasa," he said to Laylah. Then: "Are you ready, ladies?"

The girl giggled. Laylah found it charming.

They jumped.

Laylah hit the water hard. It was stunningly cold but plenty deep, and Torg never let go of her hand. They surfaced soon after, taking big gulps of air. The current was strong but not a problem for good swimmers. A moment later, Laylah heard a splash and twisted her head in time to see Rathburt and Elu coming to the surface. Rathburt had lost his grip on his staff, but Elu reached out and grabbed it. Even injured, he was tougher than the slumped wizard.

"What now?" Laylah said to the girl as they floated down river.

"There's a canoe up ahead," she said. "A couple of Mogols guard it, but they'll run when they see us."

"How do you know this?"

"I know many things."

Then she broke away and swam for the far bank, clambering onto a flat rock. The others followed, relieved to be out of the icy water. Laylah was pleased that quick dip had washed the troublesome goo almost completely out of her skin and clothing. Rathburt coughed and spluttered as though he had nearly drowned.

"You'll find them just around the bend," the girl told Torg. "They've been ordered to run without a fight."

"Ordered? By whom?" Laylah said.

Suddenly, a fist-sized rock whizzed past Laylah's head, missing her by less than a finger-length. Hundreds of druids had gathered on the other side of the river, their strange, round eyes aflame. They picked up more rocks in their bony fingers and hurled them with terrific force.

"We must reach the canoe," Torg said. "Stay behind me . . . and cover your heads."

The wizard drew the Silver Sword from the scabbard on his back and sprinted forward. Just around the bend, they came upon the Mogols sitting near a large canoe that was tied to a boulder at bow and stern. When they saw Torg's approach, they hooted and ran.

Torg cut both ropes with his sword, and the five of them leapt into the boat, Laylah in the bow, then Rathburt, Elu, the girl, and Torg. Laylah took one of the paddles, Torg the other. They shoved off and entered the current, rocks whizzing all around them. One struck Torg on the top of his head with such force that it split in two, but it didn't seem to bother the wizard. A few moments later, they were racing down the river, paddling hard and riding the current. The druids could not keep up.

"Here we go!" the little girl said, waving her arms excitedly.


SOON AFTER THEY left the druids behind, the river calmed and broadened, though its current remained swift. Peta watched Torg, who sat in the stern, steer them down the middle of the watercourse. Until then, the air temperature had been warm enough to dry their clothes and keep them from shivering. But as dusk fell, a chilly breeze raced along the surface of the water in the same direction as the current.

To Peta, however, being cold was just one of an array of exquisite experiences. She was *alive* again—and even though the majority of her essence still resided in the Realm of the Undead, a significant enough part of her was incarnated into the Realm of Life. And it felt magnificent. Now she fully understood why Vedana was so driven to find a way to enter this realm permanently. The glory of it defied description. Though her eyes were dead and saw nothing but darkness, her other senses reveled in every sensation: the sound of bubbly water, the smell of fresh air, the touch of lumpy bark, the taste of warm saliva.

It was all so fantastic.

She smiled.

"I'm hungry," Peta heard Rathburt say. Of all of them, he was the funniest, always moaning and complaining, but in a manner that she found attractive.

Peta reached between her legs and found a canvas bag in the bottom of the canoe, knowing, of course, that it would be there.

"Here's some food," she said, tapping Elu on the chest after sensing that he had turned and was watching her. She and the Svakaran were almost the same height, though he was far heavier and more muscular.

"Thank you, missus," Elu said timidly.

"My name is Peta," she said, "and yours is Elu. I know you well."

Peta could hear Elu searching through the bag. "There's salted fish, cornbread, hickory nuts, and berries," the Svakaran said. "Lots and lots."

"Then hand it over," Rathburt snapped. "In another moment, I'll be dead of starvation."

Peta threw her head back and laughed.


VEDANA WATCHED Peta from the branches above, listening carefully to every word the little girl said. Vedana had the strength to remove her from the Realm of Life at any time. The ghost-child's abilities as a soothsayer were unrivaled in Triken's history, but her other powers were minuscule in comparison to a master demon's. Vedana could toss her around like a doll, if she so chose. And if Peta betrayed her now, she might do just that.

After all, a bargain was a bargain. Vedana had invited the ghost-child's karma to enter her unborn child given life from Torg's seed, but only as long as Peta did what she was told when she was told. Peta had agreed, knowing better than anyone that the future of Triken hung in the balance. Vedana's plan was selfishly devised, but it was the only one with any legitimate chance of unseating Invictus from his throne.

The way Peta had guided the foursome to the river had impressed Vedana. Though the girl was as blind as a Mahaggatan bat, she had not once stumbled or tripped, despite a wicked labyrinth of trees, roots, rocks, and bogs. Peta knew, in advance, the location of most every impediment. In some ways her knowledge was as immense as a god's, but she had limited ability to control or change what she foresaw.

To Vedana, this was pathetic. What good was power if you were unable to wreak havoc with it? It had taken Vedana's brilliance to put Peta's knowledge to good use. If the damnable Death-Knower hadn't stuck his nose into things, Vedana already would be freed from the Realm of the Undead and ruling the Realm of Life, with Invictus as her pawn. Whenever Vedana thought about Torg's intrusion in the tower of Arupa-Loka, where he released Peta from the spell of the magical amulet and set her free, it galled her. Still, Vedana needed the Death-Knower for now, even though she despised him. When the time came, she would gain her revenge. But that would have to wait.

The wizard steered the craft toward the near bank, just a few dozen cubits beneath where she perched. He and the others—except Peta—left the canoe to relieve themselves in the woods. Would she, the mother of all demons, have to perform that grotesque act once she permanently entered the Realm of Life? The thought made her squirm. Even then, it would be worth it. When Vedana was queen of all, she would *make* it worth it.


USING HER PSYCHIC abilities, Peta watched them return to the canoe, each bearing a look of relief on their exhausted faces. Peta could not share in this; her incarnated body did not require sustenance or release. But her senses—except for physical sight—were delightfully alive and well. It was going to be torturous if Vedana forced Peta to return, in full, to the undead darkness. Still, she knew the time would come when she would be released from her torment and reborn in another place, far from this horror. Peta had foreseen it herself. She again would be blind, as the demon had taunted. But she would be alive in a human body in a peaceful world. And it would be a wonderful thing.

As they returned to their places in the canoe, Peta smiled.

"For the next ten leagues or so, the river is manageable," she said to them. "My powers are limited, but I do have the ability to steer the boat without the use of a paddle, as long as Cariya remains relatively calm. It will give all of you a chance to sleep for what remains of the night. That is, if you trust me."

"Elu trusts you."

"You don't even know who she is," Rathburt scolded. "She might be leading us into worse danger than we're already in."

Laylah started to speak, but Torg interrupted her. "I know who she is," the wizard said. "And I have already told you that she should be trusted—as much or more than any among us. But to alleviate some of your concerns, I will tell you her tale as I know it, though it must be done quickly. We are weary and need rest more than conversation."

When they again were on the river, Torg described his first meeting with Peta in Arupa-Loka, which had occurred more than seven centuries ago when he had visited the Ghost City during one of his wanderings. Then he told them about his drugged sexual encounter with Vedana in the cavern beneath Asubha, which had occurred just a few months ago.

"When we neared Arupa-Loka during our march to Duccarita, you heard me say, '*Dhiite! Dhiitaake!*'" Torg said. "In the ancient tongue, this means 'Daughter! Little daughter!' As the demons were assaulting me, Peta managed to slip through the cacophony and speak to me. It was then that I discovered that her karma had entered my child born of Vedana."

The wizard gazed at Peta, his blue eyes sparkling in the light of the quarter moon. "Is there anything you would like to say?"

"Only that you are my Father, and I love you. In past lives, you have been my Father before. And I your Mother. And Sister. And even Lover."

The last word seemed to upset Laylah greatly. "How can you know such things, child?"

"I am aware," Peta said. Then she smiled at Laylah. "Do not be jealous of me. Torg has always preferred *you* as the Lover."

Laylah flushed. "And what of Vedana? What role does *she* play? I also have spent time with the demon and have found her to be utterly despicable. Tell us what Vedana desires."

Peta recoiled. For a moment she felt like a child who had been slapped on the bottom for using bad language. "I . . . cannot," she said softly.

Once again, Torg interrupted. "Before all is said and done, Vedana's motives will become clear. As for Peta, it is not our place to ask who she is or what she is. Rather, it is our privilege to be in her presence. I say to all of you—even *you*, my love—that Peta is to be trusted. She has told us what she can, and that will have to suffice. Now we should sleep. The river is long—and by morning it will again grow angry. We will need all of our strength to survive its assault."

And then he lowered his head and fell instantly asleep. Rathburt and Elu soon followed. For a short while, only Peta and Laylah remained awake.

"Father is right," Peta said softly. "I am not your enemy. You know me naught, but I know you. And love you."

The sorceress sighed. "I believe you. I'm not sure why, but I do. I will sleep now, if you don't mind. I place our lives in your hands."

"I will not forsake you," the ghost-child whispered, "though even Father will come to distrust me before the end."

But Laylah did not appear to hear those last words.


AT DAWN, TORG woke first, his muscled body unusually stiff and sore. Their canoe had ridden the currents well, but it didn't make for much of a bed. The craft had been hollowed out from the trunk of a cypress and was just large enough for the five of them, though it contained only three seats: one in the bow, one midship, and one in the stern.

Peta sat stoically, facing the stern, her alabaster eyes aimed in the direction of Torg's. A cool breeze blew through her hair. She was as beautiful as ever.

"There is much that needs be said that cannot be said," Peta whispered. "But you must know that your strength will be tested to its limits . . . and beyond." Peta then grimaced. "I can say no more."

"I love you . . . and trust you," Torg said. "Do not fear. When the time comes, I will not fail."

"I know . . . Father. But you will doubt even me." Then she sighed.

"Shall we wake the others? The river will soon become difficult. You should eat and perform your ablutions."

Torg sat up and leaned over to wake Elu, but his daughter froze him with a wave of her hand. "There *is* one last thing I can say, but it is not pleasant. Before this day is done, one among you will be lost—for a time. But he will return."

"He?"

"She will not permit me to say more."

Torg grimaced. "When you are with Vedana, little daughter, are you in pain?"

Peta did not answer.

Soon after, the others woke in cheerful moods. It was a sunny morning and surprisingly warm. The rock walls that had encased Cariya farther north had sloped down to the river's edge, giving way to tumbled banks. They paddled into the calm of an eddy and left the canoe to relieve themselves. When they returned, they sat on a dry slab of rock and ate most of what remained of the fish, cornbread, nuts, and berries. Then Laylah lay next to Torg and nestled in his arms.

Rathburt yawned and stretched, quite pleased with the situation. "I have never traveled this far south in Dhutanga, but this area is rather pleasant, don't you think? Surely we've left the druids far behind. How far is it now to Jivita?"

"Just under twenty-two leagues to the White City," Peta said. "But little more than ten leagues to the edge of the forest."

Rathburt looked at her and arched an eyebrow. Then he turned back to Torg. "If we're so close, why do you look so concerned, Torgon?"

"The last stretch of Cariya, before it finally emerges from the forest, is the most difficult," Torg said. "Even the Mogols fear these rapids, and their boatmanship is superior to ours. In a little while, you will no longer believe that Dhutanga is pleasant."

"Then why don't we get out of the canoe and walk?" Laylah said, the side of her face still resting on Torg's chest.

"It would take several days to walk out of Dhutanga from here. By boat, we might be able to escape the clutches of the forest before sunset tonight."

"Elu likes that idea," the Svakaran said, grimacing as he stretched. "He doesn't like this forest—or this river."

"There is a Jivitan saying that goes, 'Nothing good ever comes from Dhutanga,'" Torg said.

At midmorning, they pushed away from the bank and re-entered the currents of Cariya. Soon the river dropped radically in elevation, churning, frothing, and roaring so loudly they could barely hear themselves speak. Torg steered from the stern while Laylah was responsible for quick turns of the bow. Peta shouted orders, warning them about submerged boulders, whirlpools, and holes.

"Maybe we *should* walk," Rathburt squealed.

"Too late now," Peta said.

After two leagues, they approached a stone island that rose from the middle of the river like a spire. The rapids roared past on each side.

"Steer to the right, close to shore," Peta shouted.

With Laylah paddling hard on her left, Torg was able to steer the canoe along the right side of the island, though the craft scraped a boulder. They shot through the narrow opening and back into the middle of the river.

Rathburt's eyes were clamped shut. "Is it over?"

"It's only just begun," Peta said.

As the channel narrowed, steep cliffs again rose on both sides. The river picked up speed, blasting around boulders, plunging over ledges, and surging through troughs. The canoe bounced and rocked like a bucking horse, and they were all forced to tuck their knees under the lip of the hull to avoid being cast overboard. Peta continued to shout orders. Several times her directions enabled them to avoid undercut rocks and twisted branches.

They approached another island, smaller than the first but no less dangerous. The massive trunk of one of Dhutanga's mysterious trees had fallen into the river and become hung up on the rock, leaning like a splintered figurehead.

"To the left!" Peta shouted.

They turned hard and sliced through a channel less than five cubits wide. Rathburt and Torg had to duck to avoid smacking their heads on the overhanging tree. When they shot past the rock, the canoe started to spin and would have overturned had Laylah not straightened it with several huge strokes.

"That was close," she shouted, glancing back at Torg. Even amid the tumult, Torg took a moment to admire the taut muscles of her arms. He was proud of her, especially considering she was performing so well in direct sunlight.

From there, the river picked up even more steam. Twice they barely skirted small waterfalls, and once they struck a submerged rock that lifted the front half of the canoe several cubits into the air. Soon after, they dropped over a ledge and immediately were forced into another trough.

"Left, right, left . . . like an S," Peta commanded as they wove between a nasty series of boulders before squirting through the trough into a violent whirlpool. It took all of Laylah's and Torg's strength to free them from the vortex.

"We're not going to make it," Rathburt said.

The water roared like an avalanche. At the worst possible time, the canoe started to spin again. Peta was shouting something, but Torg couldn't hear. They approached a narrow trough that curved to the right and dropped fifteen cubits into a thundering tumult of potholes and undercuts. Laylah paddled hard, attempting to position them for the steep descent. But they entered the sluice at the wrong angle, too far to the left, and the bow slammed into an outcrop and locked into place. The stern leapt upward, as if a dragon had reached down and plucked it from the river, and the canoe somersaulted. All five were cast into the chaos.

Torg was sucked under and pressed against the bottom, where he could feel the scabbard of the Silver Sword jamming hard against his back. For a panicked moment he was convinced he would drown. But then the currents spewed him forward, and he was able to struggle to the surface, gasping for air and looking about. At first he could see no one. Then he recognized Elu, face-down just an arm's-length away. He grabbed the Svakaran's hair and yanked his head above the water. He was unconscious.

"Laylah!" he screamed. "Peta! Rathburt!"

To his relief, Laylah shouted back, "Over here. I'm all right." And then he saw her a little ways ahead, swimming strongly.

"The others?" he called to her.

"I don't see them!"

"The canoe?"

"It's gone past us. I'm not sure how far."

And then, as if the river had decided it had done enough damage, they were flushed into a peaceful pool, enabling them to swim to the far bank and haul themselves onto a rock protruding from the cliff wall. Torg laid Elu on his back, forced open his mouth, and breathed essence into his lungs. The Svakaran's eyes opened wide, and then he coughed and heaved. Torg and Laylah stood and scanned the river in all directions, but they could see no one.

"Rathburt, my friend, where have you gone?" Torg shouted. "She warned me, Laylah. She warned me."

"Rathburt," Laylah screamed. "Rathburt!"

But he and his staff had vanished, along with Peta.

"Torgon," Laylah said. "We've lost them. And Obhasa, too. Only the sword was saved. It's still in your scabbard."

Elu, who had struggled to his knees, reached down and plucked something from from the surface of the river. He held up the ivory staff, whose length was more than twice his height. "Obhasa is right here," the Svakaran said weakly. "Like it was waiting for us."

Laylah sighed. "But the others are gone."

"Peta was never in danger, at least not from the river," Torg said. "Perhaps she has returned to her Mother. But Rathburt? He is lost to us . . . for now."

Elu burst into tears.

NOW IT WAS LATE afternoon, and the sun was setting beyond the gorge. Laylah and her companions clambered along the eastern bank, calling Rathburt's name. But they got no response.

About a quarter-mile down the river, they found the canoe snagged on a fallen tree on the western bank. She watched Torg swim across. The paddles were lost, so the wizard broke a thick branch off the tree and used it to angle the canoe to the other side. Beyond the eddy, the current again was swift, but now it was more manageable. Laylah and Elu climbed inside the canoe. The Svakaran would not speak, other than to call Rathburt's name. But at one point, he painfully leaned over the side and plucked one of the paddles from the river, handing it to Laylah.

"You're finding everything," she said, trying to sound cheerful. But his face remained grim.

Torg reached over and grasped Elu's shoulder. "Allow me to lighten your heart. This morning, before any of you woke, Peta spoke to me, saying that one of us would be lost on this journey, but not forever. It's obvious now that she was speaking of Rathburt."

"How could he have lived through that?" Elu said, pointing behind them.

"Peta *knows*," Torg said.

When the sun disappeared, it grew darker. Except for its swift current, the river became as smooth as a lake. Strange trees, different than the behemoths of the inner forest but still unrecognizable, hung over the water, trailing long streams of moss. A peaceful dusk ensued. They floated along steadily, and for a long time no one spoke.

Finally Elu broke the silence. "What's that smell?"

Laylah curled her nose. "It's terrible . . . like rotten flesh."

Torg pointed toward the branches of the overhanging trees. "Vultures."

Their eyes widened. Huge carrion eaters were perched upon every branch: thousands of them, black as night and reeking of death and decay. But they seemed to have no interest in the intruders.

"Are they dangerous?" Laylah said.

"Not to the living," Torg said.

"Will they eat Rathburt?" Elu said with alarm.

"Peta is rarely wrong," the wizard repeated.

In the early evening, the trees around them began to thin—and become ordinary. Cypress, oaks, and pines dominated both banks of the river, as if old friends had come to greet them. Then with shocking suddenness, Torg and the others emerged from the forest. In the moonlit darkness, a wide plain devoid of trees extended as far as the eye could see—east, west, and south.

One final time Elu called Rathburt's name. One final time there was no response.

After a period of silence, Torg said, "Jivita is not far."

"What then?" Laylah said.

"We shall see what we shall see."

# Tāseti's Journey

# 41

ON THE SAME morning that the Daasa first bowed to Lucius in the City of Thieves, Asēkha-Tāseti began her journey from Nissaya to Anna on horseback. She was still enraged at Kusala for ordering her to corral the noble ones and escort them to Anna, but she was outranked and therefore helpless to protest any further. As her Vasi master used to say, infuriatingly at times, "It is what it is."

Though Tāseti would have preferred to walk to the Tent City, it was almost two hundred leagues away from the black fortress. The Nissayans outfitted her with a desert gelding, shorter and thinner than their destriers, but much better suited for marathon distances, especially in warm weather. He also would need less food and water than the heavily muscled war horses demanded.

Tāseti set out from the fortress without fanfare, carrying little food or gear. Most of her sustenance would be found along the way. She knew how to live off the land as well as anyone, and the path she would follow was familiar—to the point of boredom. She could take it easy on the horse and still reach the sanctuary south of Dibbu-Loka in ten days, but from there to Anna would be a dreary march that could take weeks. By the time she and the noble ones arrived at the Tent City, the fate of Nissaya might already have been sealed. The thought made her angry. As she had told Kusala, she had trained for two centuries to fight the ultimate battle, only to be denied the opportunity.

"Damn you!" she screamed to no one.

The gelding looked back at her, his small ears swiveling.

She patted his long, arched neck. "Pay me no heed, handsome sir. I'm just a bitter old woman, alone in the world. Did I tell you that I'm two hundred years old? And another thing that's bothering me, I've never felt comfortable around Sister Tathagata. It's like she can look into your eyes and see your thoughts. And my thoughts aren't always as pure as they should be."

The gelding nickered, a gentle sound that prompted the warrior to smile.

"At least I've got one friend in the world. And I don't even know your name. I'll have to give you one. Let me see . . . I'll call you Chieftain. How's that? Perhaps you'll treat me better than your namesake."

The gelding nickered again. To Tāseti, it sounded like the horse was giggling.

She didn't expect to encounter enemies during her journey, at least not any she couldn't easily handle. This portion of the Gray Plains wasn't barren, but there still were vast stretches of uninhabited land, broken only by occasional farms, ranches, and homesteads, most of which would now be deserted.

The short gray grass, stunted by a consistent lack of rainfall on the eastern side of Kolankold, remained decent fodder for livestock, and occasional ponds and streams provided irrigation for modest plantings. But you could ride for leagues without seeing anything but birds, snakes, and rodents—though wild horses, antelopes, Buffelos, and tawny cats as big as Tygers weren't entirely uncommon.

Whenever she found fresh water, Tāseti stopped and allowed the gelding to graze. She was in no particular hurry. What was the point? The noble ones were champions of moving slowly. And Anna wasn't going anywhere that she couldn't find.

After traveling just seven leagues, she camped the first night within a palisade of boulders that seemed to have sprung from the ground of their own accord. She knew the terrain would become much bonier once she was beyond Lake Keo, but it was unusual to find anything but grass, shrub, and an occasional copse of stunted trees this far west. She slept without worry. Most of the evil in the world was concentrated north of Java, marching down Iddhi-Pada on its way to Nissaya. It would have little concern with a single Asēkha on a mission that would play a minor role, at best, in the fate of Triken.

She slept later than she should have. At first she couldn't find Chieftain, who had grown restless and wandered out of sight in search of better grazing. But when she called his name he rushed over, stomping playfully. He already seemed to like her, and she him.

She decided that morning to stop eating for several days—except for *Ciraya*, the green cactus prized by the Tugars. When a warrior relied exclusively on *Ciraya*, its therapeutic effects increased dramatically, cleansing the body and clearing the mind. While on long journeys, Tāseti and other Tugars often did this voluntarily, both for the physical enrichment and to eliminate the time and effort of meal preparation. Tāseti had once eaten nothing but the cactus for an entire month, and other than losing a little weight, she had suffered no negative side effects.

Chieftain was feisty for a gelding, several times breaking into a canter without prompting. In typical Tugarian fashion, Tāseti rode without the use of a bridle, preferring leg and hand pressure to direct the animal. She also disdained a saddle, yet she did not become sore or blistered even when riding long distances, the bodies of Tugars being immune to ordinary wear and tear. Still, for the horse's sake, she sat upon a camel-hair blanket, which was tied around Chieftain's barrel with cordage.

She and Chieftain covered six leagues before noon, finally resting by a small pond. While the gelding grazed, Tāseti meditated in an attempt to ease her frustrations, sitting cross-legged by the water, eyes closed and body motionless. There was little breeze, which was unusual in the open plains, and it was unseasonably hot. Tāseti noted this and then returned to the breath.

While she meditated, a pair of Buffelo, weighing perhaps three hundred stones apiece, lumbered within a few paces and lowered their boulder-sized heads to drink, appearing not to notice her presence. Tāseti opened her eyes and studied their immense bodies, admiring their muscular flanks and enjoying their pungent scent. The male of the pair had a long, black beard.

Suddenly Chieftain appeared and galloped over to protect her, stomping his hooves and snorting. The Buffelo paid the horse little heed, but in order to avoid a confrontation, Tāseti stood and went to the gelding. For the first time, the Buffelo noticed her—and they bolted, charging directly into the shallow pond and splashing away in a mad rush.

Tāseti laughed. "You scared them off, Chieftain," she said, patting his shoulder. "I don't know what I'd do without you."

Pleased that the danger had passed, the clever gelding nickered.

"Time to get going," Tāseti said, "though I don't know why. I feel like a deserter. I shouldn't, I know, but that's the way it is. As my Vasi master used to say, 'You have to take what life gives you.' I have to admit that what it's giving me right now doesn't suit me well. That's another Vasi saying, by the way."

She rode until midafternoon before taking another brief rest, then on until dusk. Though her stomach was growling from hunger, she was already feeling the cumulative effects of the *Cirāya*. She began to notice an increased vibrancy of colors: the velvety glow of violet petals, the bright-yellow under-parts of a meadowlark, the deepening blue of the sky, even Chieftain's chestnut coat—all so beautiful and mournful.

To her surprise she saw a lone human figure, large and dark, staggering toward her on foot. She urged Chieftain forward and rode to investigate. Though he obviously was injured in some way, he still looked dangerous. She drew her dagger and moved closer.

Then she gasped, leaped off Chieftain's back, and raced toward the stranger, though he was a stranger no longer. It doesn't take long for one Asēkha to recognize another. Rati collapsed just before she reached him. When Tāseti took him in her arms, she saw that his neck and chest bore bloodied scorch marks, as if he had been tortured with fire.

Rati's clothes were in tatters, but Tāseti was more concerned that his longsword, short sword, dagger, and sling appeared to be missing. Of all the Asēkhas, Rati was the most fastidious. He would never abandon his weapons—or allow them to be taken—unless under the most extreme duress. All he carried was a skin of water. But for now, at least, he seemed unable to awaken and tell her what had transpired.

Tāseti carried him to a nearby copse, laid him down beneath the stunted trees, and covered him with her blanket. She poured wine over his lips, forced him to swallow, and then pushed a square of *Cirāya* into his mouth. Though barely conscious, he began to chew. After a while, his facial muscles relaxed, and he fell into a restful sleep.

While he slumbered, Tāseti rubbed his wounds with salve pre-made from the crushed roots of a creosote bush. Then she let him rest through the night, occasionally placing fresh squares of cactus in his mouth.

Soon after sunrise, he opened his eyes for the first time since she had discovered him. "Tāseti, how came you here?" he said weakly.

"I could ask you the same question."

"My answer is long."

"Tell me all of it. But first, are you hungry?"

"*Cirāya* is all I require—and more water, if you please," he said. "But why are you here? And where are you headed? Surely you were not sent to search for me."

"I'll hear your story first," Tāseti said. "My guess is it will be far more interesting than mine."

"BEFORE THE witches struck me with their flame, I destroyed twelve barrels," Rati said while sitting upright against the base of a tree. "But three wagons remained—each containing six more. The fire hit my chest and also burned my neck. I have never felt such pain. Not even a cadre of witches should have wielded that much power. I fear the sorcerer has gifted them with magic that has strengthened them even further."

*The force of the magical bolt knocked Rati's uttara from his grasp. The hags fell upon him like a pack of wolves, snarling, clawing, and biting. Though still dazed, he relied on his finely honed instincts, drawing his short sword while still beneath the pile. He stabbed one hag in the stomach, cut another's throat, and crushed the bones between the eyebrows of a third with a swift kick. Three blows, three soon to die. Rati grinned crookedly.*

*The final two hags backed away, gesturing for the Mogols to take over. The savages were better-disciplined fighters than some gave them credit for and were especially proficient at ganging up on outnumbered opponents. They swarmed him all at once. Rati dropped to the ground and rolled on his side, stabbing two Mogols in the groin and knocking several others off their feet. Then he sprang up and attacked, not giving the savages a chance to regroup. Five strokes later, three more were dead or disabled, but two suffered relatively minor wounds.*

*Rati cursed himself. He hated wasted motion.*

*Another tendril of crackling fire struck him, this time in the ribs beneath his heart. He was thrown backward again, crashing against a boulder and banging his head. More flame leapt at him. He spun to the side, barely avoiding it. Where the fire struck the boulder, the stone exploded, casting razor-sharp splinters. One stuck in Rati's earlobe, an extraordinary occurrence. He threw his dagger, stabbing a witch—in her hideous state—between her sagging breasts. Her chest flared red and blew outward, casting burning gore.*

*In a fit of snarling rage, the final two hags leapt at him again. With his short sword, he killed them both with crunching plunges to the heart.*

*Rati's odds were slowly improving, but four witches and more than a dozen savages still lived. The largest Mogol—the lone Porisāda among them—approached next, bearing a glowing war club in his left hand and Rati's* uttara *in his right. The other Mogols backed away, as did the witches. Apparently this savage was their champion. But all it really did was make Rati angry. His* uttara, *the one hundredth of a special line, had been presented to him on the one hundredth day after he had turned one hundred years old. All in attendance at the special ceremony had laughed, knowing Rati's obsession with numbers. But he had been deeply honored. From then on, he adored this sword like no other. That a Porisāda dared foul it with his touch was the ultimate insult.*

"My anger got the best of me," Rati told Tāseti, who couldn't help but smile. She had been in attendance when Torg presented the *uttara* and had laughed as hard as the rest. "I broke his left wrist with a straight kick and hacked off his right hand with a single stroke. When I picked up my *uttara*, I had to pry his fingers off the handle."

*The battle continued. Betrayed by their own rage, all four witches transformed into their hideous selves, and rather than coordinate, as they had in the beginning, they acted as individuals and lashed out wildly, making it easier for Rati to avoid their attacks. Three more Mogols fell—with just three strokes.*

*He leapt onto one of the wagons, destroyed all six barrels, and then fought his way to another. The witches' chaotic assaults began to work against them, their own magic blowing several barrels apart. Only one wagon remained, but the surviving Mogols climbed into its bed to defend it. The witches joined them and formed a wall in front of the wagon, knowing that its precious contents were all that was left of their original cargo.*

"'Come, Asēkha,' their leader squealed. 'We await youuuu,'" Rati said to Tāseti, "And then, before my eyes, they all transformed to their beautiful selves, as if that would somehow seduce me. Though their artificial loveliness had no effect, their magic did. The wounds I had suffered from their earlier strikes began to fester, and dizziness overcame me. I was like a rodent bitten by a viper—and suddenly realized that I was beaten. My only hope was to escape and tell my story to others.

"Instead of attacking, I ran toward Ogha and cast myself into its currents, where I was tossed to-and-fro until darkness overtook me. When I woke, it was morning. I had somehow become entangled in the roots of a great oak that had fallen into the river. For this reason only was my life spared, for the oak had held my head above the water, but my *uttara* and other weapons were gone, as if the river had taken them as payment for my life."

"And how did you come to be here?" Tāseti said.

"With great effort I reached the bank, but I was wrought with fever. For days afterward, I wandered in the plains, hoping somehow to reach Nissaya—or at least, come upon a friendly face. In that regard, I succeeded."

"And the last barrels?"

"I can only assume their contents were dumped into the Ogha. The citizens of Senasana are in peril, but I was too sickened to warn them."

"Once the remaining barrels were dumped into the river, the damage was done," Tāseti said. "The *undines* multiply so quickly. The entire lower half of the river could have become contaminated in just a few hours. Ten thousand people live along its banks and many more that number in the city itself. You could have warned a bare fraction. Going to the city would have done you no good then, and it will do us no good now. We have no choice but to continue on our way."

"My mission failed."

Tāseti lifted Rati's right hand and kissed his palm. "Only The Torgon himself might have prevailed against such foes," she said. "Do not despair."

Rati smiled wanly. Then his face grew puzzled. "The odd thing is, in the tumult of the river I lost all my weapons, but my skin remained attached to my belt, though it was loosely tied. When I refilled it, it didn't even leak. How can something so delicate survive, while something so strong does not?"

"Such is the way of the world," Tāseti said.

# 42

AFTER RECOUNTING his tale, Rati slept some more. Tāseti waited until noon before waking him. The Asēkha stood shakily, took a few steps, and then sat back down. Chieftain loomed over both of them, neighing with a sense of urgency.

Finally Tāseti leaned over Rati and said to him what Kusala had dreaded to say to her. "You are too weak to continue on to Nissaya by yourself.

Instead, you must accompany me to Anna."

To her relief, Rati did not protest. After taking a long swig from his skin, he stood on his own and climbed onto Chieftain's back. "I will ride, and you will walk," Rati said. Then he collapsed upon the gelding's neck and fell asleep again.

Though they moved slowly throughout the day, the trio managed to cover another seven leagues before dusk. Chieftain had been bred for endurance and was capable of traveling long distances day after day, as long as the pace was reasonable and he was watered and well-fed. Rati dozed fitfully, sometimes crying out and startling the good-tempered gelding. Despite the Asēkha's erratic behavior, the horse never bolted, but he did appear to give Rati what Tāseti perceived to be dirty looks. She couldn't help but chuckle. Sometime during the afternoon, she made the decision to keep the horse as a personal pet.

When they finally camped, they were within ten leagues of the northwestern shore of Keo, the second largest freshwater lake in the known world. Chieftain led them to a spring hidden at the base of a hollow. A trio of large cats—called Lyons by the wild men of Kolankold—noticed their approach and scampered off. The horse would have made an excellent meal for the enormous predators, but they were obviously wary of Tāseti. Still, Chieftain was nervous and huddled near the Asēkhas, refusing to wander more than a few paces to graze.

Rati crawled on hands and knees to the spring and plunged his face into the water. Though there were many animal tracks in the vicinity, the spring was constantly replenished from deep beneath the ground and so remained potable. Rati drank until his stomach bulged, but rather than make him even more sluggish, it seemed to perk him up. After Tāseti rubbed fresh salve into his wounds, he sat up until midnight, drinking even more water from the spring and eating salted beef, brown bread, and raw carrots from Tāseti's pack.

She was relieved. The ill effects of the injuries and poisons from his battle with the witches seemed to be losing their grip on the powerful warrior. When he finally slept, his breathing was steady.

The next morning, they left without bothering to fill their skins, knowing that water would be plentiful over the next leg of their journey. Rati seemed as strong as when she had last seen him by Lake Ti-ratana. He even offered to walk, and though she refused at first, he insisted, saying that he needed the exercise. The pair ended up walking together. They spoke long about Anna's role in the war, and what they would do to defend the Tent City if both Nissaya and Jivita fell.

Eventually, they picked up the pace and broke into a jog. Chieftain joined the game, galloping far past, waiting for them to catch up, and then racing by them again. Tāseti and Rati laughed so hard they had to stop and slap their knees.

By late afternoon they were within a stone's throw of Lake Keo. Though trees were sparse throughout most of the Gray Plains, a mile-wide band of woodlands—mostly cypress, birch, poplars, and a few longleaf pines—surrounded the banks of Keo. The poplars were in spring bloom, coating broad portions of the grassy ground with pollen.

A young deer wandered within their range of vision. Rati borrowed Tāseti's sling and brought the doe down with a single bead. They built a fire by the water's edge and roasted the loins, fearing no assault. The nearest danger was the wild men of Kolankold, who lived in the eastern foothills more than twenty leagues away. Tāseti broke her fast and ate a little of the meat, but Rati devoured several times his normal portion, as if ravenous. Then he drank enough water from the lake for both of them. Afterward, he was chatty again before falling into another deep sleep.

They ate more of the deer for breakfast and then roped it to Chieftain's back, though the gelding didn't like that at all. For the next part of their march, the terrain was friendly. The woodlands came to a sudden halt about fifty paces from the lake, and the grassy banks sloped gently to the water's edge. They made good time again, covering almost twelve leagues by nightfall. After camping, they roasted more of the deer and slept well.

The next morning, Chieftain would not allow them to strap what remained of the doe to his back. Neither of them wanted to carry it, so they abandoned the carcass by the water's edge, where it would serve as a meal for a wandering bear or Lyon. By noon, they had come to the southernmost point of Lake Keo. Five leagues farther south lay the havens where the Asēkhas had sequestered the noble ones the previous summer.

A small band of Tugars had remained with the noble ones as guardians. Tāseti looked forward to seeing these warriors. Along with Rati, their presence would make the long journey from the havens to Anna far more tolerable. But the noble ones tended to move slowly, seeming to have no concept of what it meant to hurry. They would stop to examine anything that caught their eye: wildflowers, butterflies, termite mounds, even Buffelo dung. Their behavior endlessly fascinated The Torgon, but Tāseti found it annoying. She did not share her lord's wisdom or patience. He was beyond her. And so were the noble ones, apparently.

After Tāseti filled her skin, they continued on. Less than a mile south of the lake, Rati cursed himself for forgetting to do the same. His skin was about a fourth full, but the water had become old and bitter. He hadn't bothered to drink from it in quite a while, and there had been no need to refill it during their march along Keo.

"Should we go back? There's no more water between here and the havens."

"We'll be there before sunset," Tāseti said. "My skin has plenty for both of us. And Chieftain carries his own water. We'll be fine."

And so they were. In the late afternoon, a Tugarian scout greeted the trio enthusiastically. Even as Tāseti was clasping forearms with the large male warrior, she felt a strange rumble, as if the land was announcing their arrival. By dusk, the havens were within sight. Soon Tāseti would be face to face with Sister Tathagata.

"Kusala, I curse thee," she said out loud. "It's bad enough that I'm going to miss the battle at Nissaya. But making me put up with Tathagata all the way to Anna? I'll never forgive for this."


THE TERRAIN SOUTH of Dibbu-Loka was craggy and awkward. Even the stunted grass of the Gray Plains, which dominated an area larger than the forests of Dhutanga, Kincara, and Java combined, surrendered to the somber crumble of dust and rock. Limestone cliffs sprang from the ground with stunning suddenness. There were nooks within nooks and crannies within crannies—most too miserable to explore. It was a terrible place to live, but a clever place to hide.

Tāseti, Rati, and the Tugar scout marched southward along the ancient road that eventually plunged toward lands unknown even to the *Kantaara Yodhas*. They encountered little in the way of life, except for a pair of ostriches, a small herd of oryxes, and circling vultures, ever present. Otherwise silence surrounded them. They approached a towering escarpment, its sheer side speckled with scattered patches of vegetation. Slabs of rock lay about its base, long ago fallen and now dark with age.

They came upon a secret place known only to the Tugars. A curled lip of rock concealed a narrow crevice. From the outside, the crevice appeared to end abruptly just a stone's throw away. In reality, it angled sharply to the right and plunged into the thick wall before ascending to a rounded tunnel with a sand floor.

Tāseti went first, then Rati. The scout did not follow. Instead, he climbed onto the gelding and rode farther south to a pen shaded by a rock overhang, but not before the second in command told him to take especially good care of Chieftain. The warrior laughed heartily at the name.

Tāseti and Rati crawled through the tunnel for a distance of one hundred paces, eventually spilling into a torchlit chamber tall enough even for a Tugar to stand. Two more desert warriors greeted them, bowing low to their Asēkha superiors and then grasping forearms.

Tāseti and Rati continued down a wide passageway, also lighted by torches, before finally arriving at a cavern as large as the inside of a castle.

A dozen more Tugars trotted forward and bowed. The defenders of the haven had been hard at work, preparing another meal for their guests. Since Torg's encounter with Mala at Dibbu-Loka the previous summer, the five hundred monks and nuns of the holy city had called this cavern their home, sharing it with their Tugarian guardians as well as a few rats, scorpions, and rattlesnakes. Almost anyone but the noble ones would have gone stir crazy, but they saw it as just another opportunity to learn the value of patience.

The floor, walls, and ceiling of the cavern were smooth and polished. In the center of the main chamber stood three long stone tables set low to the floor. Next to these tables lay an unquenchable spring that rose from the bedrock, only thirty paces in circumference but immeasurably deep. Rati knelt down, pursed his lips, and drank his fill. After that, he rinsed out the stale contents of his skin and refilled it with fresh water.

Dozens of other chambers fed off the main one, some as large as houses, others as small as bedrooms. From many of the ceilings, natural shafts wound their way to the high plateau that formed the roof of the haven. In one large room, the shaft vented enough air to enable the Tugars to cook with fire.

"Where are they now?" Tāseti said to a Tugar warrior known as Appam.

"They are meditating in the darkest cave they can find. Other than eat, sleep, bathe, and relieve themselves, meditation is all they do. We even feed them and clean their robes. They're not the greatest at pitching in with the chores, but otherwise they are easy to shepherd. I've heard not a single complaint, and I've been here since you and the Asēkhas first brought them in the wagons."

"And where is *she?*"

"Sister Tathagata leads them in meditation," Appam said. Then he chuckled. "I would rather be in Nissaya or Jivita, but I must admit that being here with her has not been as bad as I expected. My own meditation has never been as peaceful, and my thoughts never as clear. It's enough to make you want to cast down your sword. The *Perfect One*, as they like to call her, has little use for violence. And she has ways of winning you over."

"I've listened to her lectures," Tāseti said. "Lord Torgon adores them, but they always make me feel guilty. What's the use of warrior training if the skills you acquire are considered harmful? It's not as though Tugars seek violence for its own sake. But neither do we shy from it. She would have us lay down our arms and surrender to Invictus? Bow our heads and allow them to be separated from our bodies? No matter how hard I try, I cannot see the wisdom in that."

"She seeks *Abhisambodhi* in this lifetime," the warrior said. "Nothing else, or I should say, anything less holds little interest for her. She says, *'Jaati pariyaadinnaa. Me kato aakankhito. N'atthi punaagamano.* (Birth is exhausted. I have done what was needed. There is nothing more).'"

Tāseti started to respond, but Rati came forward and interrupted. "What's for dinner?" he said, his hair dripping wet.

Tāseti looked at Appam. "Does the *Perfect One* permit us to dine?"

"The High Nun will not eat the flesh of animals," Appam said. "She and her noble ones survive on cholla berries, ground mesquite, flower buds, seedpods, and cactus juice. That must be how they stay so slender."

Tāseti snorted. "As my Vasi master used to say, 'Tugars cannot live on bread alone.'"

"Shhhh!" Rati said harshly. "They come." And then in a whisper, "She leads."

Tāseti cursed Kusala under her breath before turning and forcing a smile.


WHILE RATI and the Tugar guardians sat at their own table and feasted on the carcass of a roasted pronghorn antelope, protocol of rank forced Tāseti to join Sister Tathagata at one of the long tables. The noble ones always ate in silence, paying mindful attention to every morsel of food, even counting how many times they chewed.

Tāseti had a warrior's habit of devouring all her meals in a hurry, as if the enemy might attack at any moment. But she had to admit that eating slowly did increase her pleasure. Mesquite bread had never tasted so good, and the tang of the cactus juice made her tongue tingle. Though she was uncomfortable in the sister's presence, she enjoyed the meal, even without roasted meat as the main course.

Afterward, the Tugars gave them herbal tea and biscuits made of ground wheat and honey. Tāseti allowed herself the luxury of service—a reward for being the only one sitting with Tathagata. When the meal was completed, the sister stood and grasped the Asēkha's muscular bicep with her slender fingers. Then she dragged her toward the haven's exit.

"Dark caves are excellent for meditation," she said to Tāseti, "but fresh air's better for talking. Walk with me beneath the stars."

"Of course, High Nun," Tāseti said uncomfortably.

"No need to be so formal," Tathagata said. "Call me Sister. In fact, just call me Sis." Then she laughed. Lord Torgon often spoke about how much he loved the High Nun's laugh, and it surprised Tāseti to find that she also found it pleasant.

The crescent moon had not yet risen, but the clear sky was ablaze with stars. The last time Tāseti remembered rain was the night she and the Asēkhas attacked the enemy camp in the Gap of Gamana.

*Just two weeks ago. It feels like two months.*

"Where are your thoughts?" the High Nun said, startling Tāseti, who wasn't used to being startled.

"I was thinking about rain. This time of year, we get so little east of the mountains . . . especially in the heart of Tējo, where it rarely rains except in early winter."

"A person of my attainment isn't supposed to become attached to things. But in this instance, at least, I can't seem to help it. I *love* rain. In a past life, I must have lived somewhere where it was always wet. Dibbu-Loka and this place"—she pointed in the direction of the haven—"are too parched for my tastes."

"I have journeyed through much of the world, but I was born in Tējo, and the desert is where my heart remains."

"The quiet of the desert is a good place to spend the present moment," Tathagata agreed.

"I'm glad you feel that way . . . because it is my assignment to take you there."

If this stunned the High Nun, she did not show it. "I had assumed we were to be returned to Dibbu-Loka," she said calmly.

"War is at hand, Sister. In a very short time, Anna will be the only safe place left."

"That depends on how you define the word *safe*. Surely, Invictus has lost his interest in Dibbu-Loka. It offers him nothing of value, other than a few sculptures and paintings."

"You and the noble ones have value," Tāseti said. "The Tugars must not allow your welfare to be compromised again. It almost cost us our king."

"But it did not?"

"You haven't heard?"

"Little news comes this way. Yet I know The Torgon still lives. I would have sensed his passing."

"Then why play games with words?"

"Games? You mistook my meaning. I wasn't referring to his life or death."

Tāseti grunted. "We leave for Anna in the morning."

"And if I refuse to accompany you?"

"You will be roped onto the back of a camel."

"You would do such a thing to a fragile old woman?"

"You are old, but not fragile. Regardless, don't blame me. This comes straight from Torg."

"That doesn't surprise me. The Death-Knower is the only one who would even care."

"You underestimate us, Sister. The Tugars care about a great many things."

"The Tugars feel it is their duty to protect the weak. But do you understand the true meaning of strength? If Invictus imprisoned us, tortured or killed us, we would view it as just one more learning experience. The cycle of birth, death, and rebirth ends only with the attainment of enlightenment."

"I do not doubt your ability to withstand torture. I witnessed your courage firsthand in Dibbu-Loka," Tāseti said, with a touch of sarcasm.

"Aaaaaaah, Asēkha . . . you have quick wit. You refer, of course, to my cowardly reaction to the appearance of Mala. I must admit that such a thing has never happened to me before. There was something in the monster's eyes that unsettled me. I could see Yama-Deva trapped behind them, begging me to save him. But I knew then, as I do now, that I could not. Only Yama-Deva himself can perform this miracle."

"When I looked into Mala's eyes, I saw only evil. He is a bane that must be eradicated, not coddled or cajoled."

"There is no mercy in your heart?"

"For Mala? None."

# 43

BENEATH A FIERY sun, they set out the next morning: two Asēkhas and fourteen Tugars adorned in black, five hundred monks and nuns wearing white robes with white head cloths, fifty camels, and one horse. Each camel carried almost twenty stones of baggage, including flour, rice, and dates. But most of the weight was in water—a dozen goatskins per beast filled that morning at the spring in the haven. Chieftain carried his own needs: ten skins of water and a bulging sack of grain.

The Tugarian drums were too cumbersome to haul on such a journey, so their ability to communicate over far distances would be limited. Therefore, Appam was sent ahead on his own to spread the word of their coming among any allies he might encounter before arriving at Anna. This would increase the likelihood of their receiving aid before they reached the Tent City. Tāseti was counting on it.

From here on, water would be a precious commodity. Tugars were excellent at finding it in the least likely of places, but they were even better at rationing what they already had. The noble ones, though much smaller in stature, still would require a good deal more than their warrior companions, especially once they passed through Barranca and entered the true desert.

A short time before noon, they reached the trail that angled up to the vast mesa. Even for Tugars, it was a difficult ascent. Loose rocks and crumbly soil made it even more hazardous. The camels snarled and roared as they climbed—a hot, sweaty business that took half the afternoon. The Tugar warriors saved more than one life by grabbing a handful of white robe just as a monk or nun was about to stumble off the side of the trail. Tāseti was relieved when everyone was safely on the mesa.

The afternoon grew torridly hot. Tāseti ordered a halt, and they rested on sheepskin rugs within an abundant stand of mesquite, the only significant shade for several leagues. They would journey on the mesa for two more days—during daylight, regrettably. Along this stretch, there were too many dangers to risk stumbling along in darkness. Once they descended to more easily traversable terrain, they would reverse their habits and travel mostly between dusk and dawn.

The mesa extended halfway to Barranca, and though Tāseti had traveled it frequently on her way to and from the rest of the world, it was one of her least favorite places. Giant sagebrush choked most of it, concealing thousands of depressions in the limestone perfectly sized and shaped to trap a foot and sprain an ankle. Few animals lived on this area of the plateau, but most that did were dangerous to the unwary: scorpions, rattlesnakes, Gila monsters, and fist-sized bats that fed on blood. Several varieties of poisonous plants were capable of causing anything from a small rash to a painful death. The Tugars knew all these things and walked freely among them without concern, but the noble ones had far less knowledge and physical immunity. Tāseti had chosen this route only because there was no better one.

After a brief rest, they marched until dusk, moving at an agonizingly slow pace and covering less than a league before stopping to camp. The Tugars led them to a bare area of stone covered with brown sand. The bald would not be a comfortable place to sleep, but at least it provided protection, giving the poisonous creatures fewer places from which to stage an ambush. Anyone stupid enough to sleep within the sagebrush would wake up "worse for wear," as Vasi masters liked to say.

While the Tugars built several fires, the noble ones pitched a slew of camel-skin tents, each large enough to sleep six. The sand was just deep and dense enough to hold the stakes in place.

The Tugars dropped cakes of kneaded dough on the fires, quickly searing the outsides and then burying the dough in the sand beneath the embers. It was no easy task to feed so many, especially when they refused meat. To Tāseti's dismay, the noble ones drank far too much water before and after the meal. When they camped the next evening, she would have to lecture them. But it had been a rough first day, so this time she permitted it.

Though the heat of the day had been uncomfortable, the chill night air was worse. The dramatic contrast in temperature caused the noble ones to shiver. After their meal, most of them either huddled by fires or went directly to their tents. In contrast, neither the heat nor cold affected the Tugars, and they needed little sleep, standing silently beneath the clear sky and watching the crescent moon rise at midnight.

Before first light, the Tugars roused the noble ones and gave them rice for breakfast before breaking camp. In the coolness of early morning, the band made better progress, covering almost two leagues by noon. As feared, one of the monks hurt an ankle and could no longer walk. Tāseti spread some of Chieftain's load among the camels and put the monk on the gelding's back.

In the early afternoon, they ate lightly again and then marched until dusk, covering two more leagues despite the afternoon heat. They found another bald, its location well-known to the Tugars, and camped at dusk. Before sleep, they ate buttered bread and a thin vegetable stew flavored with salted sardines. The noble ones would not eat the fish, but they tolerated the broth only because it provided them with much-needed nourishment.

The next morning, they came upon a dry bed gouged out of the limestone by a long-dead river. The arroyo was shallow at first, but it deepened to fifty cubits or more below the surface of the plateau. Huge slabs of rock had broken off its sides and tumbled into its bed. Tea plants, thickets, and prickly cactus clung to the remnants of the ancient landslides, which swarmed with spiders and scorpions feeding on mice and other insects. The arroyo, which was about thirty paces wide in most places, would have been impossible to traverse except for a natural path down its middle, as if an ambitious giant had cleared away the rocks. Though they were forced to proceed in single file, they made the best progress of the journey thus far, despite the dreadful heat.

The arroyo eventually spilled off the side of the mesa, descending upon a lower range of flat land. By nightfall, they had left the dreaded highlands behind and were within sight of the western border of Barranca.

Tāseti could not have been more pleased. It would take their slow-moving band a week to cross the rocky wasteland, but they would have little to fear while doing so. And beyond Barranca lay the desert.

Her beloved Tējo was so close she could taste it.

AT THE CAMP that night, Sister Tathagata felt strangely lightheaded—and she had never been so thirsty. Though none of the ordinary Tugars dared chastise her, Tāseti found the courage to complain about her excessive consumption of water. But Tathagata couldn't stop herself. The evening after they'd left the haven, her mouth had become constantly dry, more so even than the exertions of the journey should have demanded. She became concerned that she was coming down with a fever, which would make the march to Anna far more difficult. She found a quiet place on the rim of the camp and tried to meditate. Normally, she would be able to view her discomforts with detached concentration, watching them rise and fall in wave upon wave of impermanence. But this thirst was different.

When she watched her breath, it only made it worse. She found herself literally sneaking behind Tāseti's back to drink. She noticed several others doing the same, their normally placid faces flushed and agitated. Did she look that way, too? Sister Tathagata, the *Perfect One?* This was the kind of behavior for which she had lectured others. Never before had she felt so out of control.

The Tugars gave them bread, dates, and berries. She ate mindfully but did not enjoy the small meal. She would have preferred the stew with the sardines. This time, she would have eaten the fish along with the broth.

After feeding the monks and nuns, Tāseti, Rati, and the desert warriors had roasted a bighorn sheep they had brought down earlier that day with a bead from a sling. The warriors were tearing into it with gusto, relishing the greasy meat and washing it down with Tugarian wine.

The High Nun stood silently off to the side and watched, her mouth watering. She almost felt like she could take a bite herself, an especially juicy bite—and she hadn't eaten the flesh of an animal since she was a child almost three thousand years ago.

To somehow quench her newfound desires, she snuck over to the water-skins and drank until her stomach bloated. Then she staggered to her tent and slept. The nuns by her side smelled like raw meat.

# Lucius' Transformation

# 44

"HOW FAR to Jivita?" Lucius said to Bonny as they huddled together beneath the stars on the border of the forest Dhutanga, still only a couple of leagues south of where the druids had ambushed them earlier that day. They did not dare a fire.

Bonny lay on her side and placed her head on his lap. "I have never been to the White City, but I know the maps. It's close to eighty leagues. With the Daasa wandering about as much as they do, it could take two weeks or more."

"The druids will easily reach the White City before us, if that's their desire—though it's probable they'll wait until Nissaya is under siege before they attack Jivita. But I can't help but worry about Laylah and the others. What hope do we have of ever seeing them alive?"

"I believe the great wizard will save Missus Laylah. And if they can escape to the river, they will be in Jivita long before us."

Lucius looked down at her face and stroked her short red hair. "I hope you're right."

The corners of Bonny's mouth turned downward. "Do you love Missus Laylah?"

Lucius smiled. "Yes. But don't worry, not in that way . . . anymore. I've fallen in love with someone else."

Her face brightened. "Me?"

"No . . . Ugga." Then he laughed, leaned down, and kissed her on the mouth.

The next morning, while the Daasa grazed, Lucius focused his attention on Ugga and Bard. Something about their behavior seemed odd. They were more sluggish than before, which was understandable considering everything they had been through the past several weeks. But they also acted as if they were as sore and stiff as worn-out old men. Come to think of it, they *looked* older, their beards flecked with gray. Had they been that way before?

After their encounter with the druids, Bonny, Ugga, and Bard wanted to head toward the foothills of the Mahaggatas, thereby staying as far from the forest as possible. But Lucius argued against it.

"For one thing, I don't think the druids are much interested in us anymore," he said. "For another, the Daasa always seem hungry, so we need to keep them near a steady supply of food. There'll be more here on the edge of the forest than in the foothills. And we've reached a point where we'll need to start fending for ourselves, even if it's just wild berries, like Elu said."

"I wishes the little guy was here with us now," Ugga said. "I misses him."

"I misses all of them," Bard said. "Especially Jord."

In low spirits, they began the tedious march toward the White City. The Daasa, however, seemed anything but downcast, charging about frenetically, climbing trees, tearing through shrubs, and splashing in streams. When they came upon large ponds, the Daasa squealed with delight and dove in by the hundreds. Lucius was amazed to see that they were excellent swimmers, almost more comfortable in water than on land. He wondered what they would do if they encountered a lake the size of Hadaya. How far and deep would they swim? And how long could they stay submerged? Lucius wished he could see for himself.

"The Daasa are cutesy," Bard said. "But they make loud noises that scare everything away. Pretty soon, we'll need to hunt. Maybe Ugga and I should go on ahead and see if we can get us something."

"I've been thinking about that too," Lucius said. "But I'm worried about how the Daasa will react if they see us eating a dead animal. As far as I can tell, they feed on only nuts, berries, and leaves."

"Only when they are in their nicey state," Bonny said. "When they turn mean, they eat almost anything. I have seen it up close . . . very close."

"We have to eat," Ugga said. "And more than just berries. I don't know about ya guys, but I is not feeling so good. I needs something hot in my tummy so that I can get strong again. I is so hungry . . . I thinks I smell something cooking right now."

"Me too," Bard said.

"So do I," Lucius said. "It can't be all our imaginations."

Without warning, Bard and Ugga took off in the direction of the delicious aroma, though the handsome trapper was limping, and the crossbreed was as hunched over as Rathburt. The Daasa charged after them, squealing and whistling in their peculiar manner.

Bonny shrugged. "Let's go see what it is. If it tastes half as good as it smells, then I'm all for it."

They approached a broad hill. Despite their new infirmities, Bard and Ugga were the first to surmount and then disappear over the crest. The Daasa poured after them, kicking up a cloud of grass and dust. Lucius jogged and then ran—and still he was losing ground. Even Bonny was outdistancing him.

"Come on," she shouted back at him. "Run!"

Then Bonny disappeared, and for a few disconcerting moments, Lucius was alone, as if his companions had vanished from the world. When he finally reached the top of the hill, he stopped and stared down. At its base, a dozen oaks—huge and ancient—encircled a longhouse. A trail of white smoke poured from a hole in its roof. Apparently, Bard and Ugga already were inside, while Bonny was charging toward the door. The Daasa, meanwhile, lay outside the cabin like well-trained pets waiting patiently on their masters.

Lucius panicked. *How have you gotten so far ahead?* "Wait!" he screamed. "We don't know who's there. Wait!"

And then Bonny was gone also. Lucius stumbled down the hill, shouting and cursing. But he didn't seem able to make any progress.

*What's happening? Where am I?* His face was hot and swollen, his vision blurred. Rage and turmoil consumed his thoughts.

And the pain . . . such terrible pain.

Such angry pain.

Such sweet pain.

Then darkness.

WHEN LUCIUS woke inside the small room, it really *was* dark, but a merry fire blazed a few paces from his mattress, which smelled like pine needles. For the first time since Duccarita, he noticed that his magically healed arm no longer throbbed. Bonny sat beside him, caressing his brow with a damp cloth. He bolted upright, his eyes wild.

"Shhhhhh! Shhhhhhhhhh!" she said soothingly. "Lay back, sweety. Everything is all right now, though you had us worried. It was Jord who finally found you and helped us bring you back here, safe and sound. Where did you think you were going? You were wandering around the woods like a madman."

"Jord . . . the eagle-woman? I thought the dragon killed her."

Bonny laughed. "If he did, then a ghost is taking care of us now."

Lucius sat up again, more deliberately this time, and looked around the room. In addition to the hearth, he saw a roughly hewn table, several chairs, and some small barrels by the door. Otherwise the chamber was empty, as if whoever lived here did so sparingly.

"Where is everyone?"

Bonny laughed again. "They are outside with the Daasa. Do you want to go see? I think Jord wants to talk to you, anyway. She seems to think you are important or something. I can't imagine why."

Bonny leaned forward and gave him a wet kiss on the mouth that tasted like beer. Then she leaped up and rushed to the door. "Come on, sleepyhead. There's some good eating out here—the food's still hot. And some good drinking too—the beer's still cold."

Lucius remained confused. When he stood up, he felt nauseated and dizzy but determined to follow. Bonny had left the door ajar, and he pushed it slowly open. About fifty paces away, a skinned and spitted deer was suspended above a crackling fire. Bard and Ugga stood next to it, drinking with gusto from large pewter mugs. Beside them was a woman with long white hair that hung past her waist. She wore a white gown that nearly matched the color of her skin.

"Master Loo-shus!" Ugga bellowed. "Come and have some beer. It is ex-cell-lent. I had almost forgotten how much I loves it. And we roasted a deer while ya were sleeping. We've eaten a lot of it, but don't worry, there's plenty left."

Jord turned to him. When she spoke, her voice was strong and clear. "You are safe in the house of Jord. Now is the time to build your strength for the difficult times ahead."

Ugga handed him a mug of beer.

Lucius sniffed it, almost suspiciously, and then took a sip. Not since the inn at Duccarita had he tasted anything so delicious.

Ugga and Bard were already several mugs ahead of him—Bonny, too, for that matter. The pirate woman gave him a wooden trencher with chunks of sizzling venison, white cheese, boiled cabbage, and stewed berries. He picked at it with his fingers, amazed to discover that he wasn't particularly hungry. But he was thirsty and soon downed second and third helpings of beer. The others watched him with amusement, their eyes sparkling in the firelight.

Finally he quit drinking long enough to speak. "Where are the Daasa?"

"They are just a little ways away, fast asleep," Bonny said. "They ate too many of the young berries, I think. It made them drunk and tired."

"I must be a Daasa because I is drunk and tired too," Ugga said. "I thinks I will go inside the cabin and lie down."

"I'll join ya," Bard said.

Bonny yawned. "I must be a Daasa too," she said to Lucius. "Would you mind if I went with the boys, sweety? Just to sleep, I mean. I promise I will behave myself."

"I trust you," Lucius said.

"A *little* jealousy would be nice," she said, before leaning down and kissing him on the cheek. Then she staggered to the cabin, barely making it inside the door. After she was gone, Lucius looked up at Jord, whose hair swirled as if in the midst of a magical maelstrom.

"I thought you were dead," he said at last.

"Dead? Alive? I am neither."

"I don't know what that means. Who are you, really?"

"I am a friend . . . to you and the others. Will you walk with me?"

"Where? Why?"

"There is something I must show you. Do you not trust me?"

"I neither trust nor distrust you."

Lucius stood and brushed off his breeches. It was only then that he noticed he was wearing a different outfit than before he arrived at the cabin. "What happened to my clothes? And where did you find these new ones?"

"You ask many questions, firstborn."

"That's what Torg always says. And—like you—he gives me few answers."

Jord threw back her head and laughed. It was a rich and pleasant sound. "Sometimes the wise don't answer because it takes too long to explain all that they know. But we must delay no longer. The night grows old. After what you've been through, you need sleep even more than the others."

"After what I've been through?"

Jord took his hand and led him into the dark forest. The gibbous moon glowed in a clear sky, providing enough light to see for about a hundred paces. The Daasa were all around him. Though they were quite large, even in their gentle state, many of them had managed to climb into the trees and were asleep in the branches.

Then Lucius stopped and gasped. A few paces from where he stood, the trunk of a thick pine had been split in two near the base, splinters of wood jutting skyward. The upper portion of the tree had been dragged more than a stone's throw away. And beyond that, there was more damage: other trees gashed and scarred, bushes uprooted and shredded, and most disturbingly, a Tyger the size of a mountain wolf mangled and partially devoured. Lucius stared in dismay, especially at the ruined carcass of the wild cat. What could have done such a thing? And would it return?

"I don't . . . understand," Lucius said. "Why are you showing me this? Shouldn't we go back and warn the others? Something this dangerous could harm even the Daasa."

"What makes you so sure the Daasa didn't do this? You've seen what they're capable of. Yet it did not even enter your mind?"

He slapped his forehead with the palm of his hand. "You're right, you're right . . . of course it was them. When they saw the Tyger, they must have transformed and killed it."

Jord shook her head. "Your first inclination was correct, firstborn. It was not the Daasa. Do you not remember?"

"Remember what? This?"

Jord did not answer, but her eyes glowed green. She walked over to the broken tree and pulled something off it . . . a torn piece of cloth.

"Do you not remember?" she repeated.

There *was* something; he couldn't deny it. He was running. Feeling lost. And then pain. And a blazing rage.

Jord placed her hand on his shoulder, startling him. "You were born of the Daasa. Their flesh is your flesh. Their way is your way."

"I don't know what you mean."

"I think you do."

Lucius backed away from her . . . slowly.

"Listen, nothing like *this* has happened before. I've been angry many times in my life. And afraid, too. If you're saying what I think you're saying . . . why now?"

"The *Mahanta pEpa* no longer exists," Jord explained. "But even that is not the true reason it has taken so long for your first transformation. That being's power had little effect on you. Instead, it is your recent proximity to so many of the Daasa that has awakened a part of you that before had lain dormant."

Lucius became so dizzy, it was a struggle to stay on his feet. "Then . . . I'm a monster?"

"You were born of the Daasa . . . a creation of great magic. Are you a monster or a miracle? That will be for you to decide."

Lucius lowered his head. Tears fell from his eyes. "What about Bonny? She's falling in love with me . . . and I with her. What will she do when she finds out about . . . this?"

"She already knows. She saw."

"She *saw*?"

Jord nodded.

"She saw me *change*?"

Jord continued to nod.

"And she wasn't sickened?"

"Do not underestimate her. She is strong. There is a reason she has grown to love you so quickly. For you see, she is also not fully human."

Lucius' jaw dropped. He could think of nothing else to say.

Jord smiled compassionately. "This is enough for one night. We all have endured sorrows. The mountain eagles are dead. What could be worse than that? Return with me to the cabin and sleep without fear. Over the coming days, there'll be plenty of time to talk—for I will be with you. At least for a time. If it is within my power, I will see you safely to Jivita."

# 45

THE MORNING after his transformation, Lucius still wasn't hungry. While Bonny and the others gorged on deer meat, blackberries, white cheese, and brown bread, Lucius wandered back into the woods to study the destruction in daylight.

The Daasa followed him, almost ten thousand in all, squealing and leaping about excitedly in his presence. Lucius ignored them, concentrating on the task ahead. The carcass of the Tyger had been dragged away, presumably by something large. Another Tyger? A bear? One of his own Daasa?

Lucius walked over to the trunk of the tree that had been split in two. How much strength would it take to perform such a feat? Far more than he contained. Or believed he contained. Now he was no longer sure. If Jord's assertions were correct, a beast lurked within him that could knock down trees and kill Tygers with its bare hands. If so, he really was like the Daasa. The thought filled him with horror—but a part of him was tantalized. While living in Avici, he had been pushed around far too often. Did the monster within give him powers that would enable him to seek revenge?

When he returned to the cabin, Bonny ran out to greet him, her face flushed with pleasure. When she tried to hug him, Lucius looked at her distrustfully and nudged her away.

"What?" Hurt echoed in her voice.

"What? All you have to say is 'what'? After what happened to me last night?"

"Oh . . . that."

Lucius felt an urge to slap her. How dare she act so nonchalant. His world had been forever changed, yet she barely seemed to care. "It's obvious *I'm* not human," he said, his voice mean-spirited. "But Jord mentioned something about you. What have you been hiding from me?"

Now it was Bonny's turn to get angry. "I wasn't hiding anything. I was just waiting for the right time to tell you. I didn't want to scare you away, until you knew more about your own self. Now that I see how mean you can be, I wish I *had* scared you away."

"Tell me *what*?"

"It's not such a big deal, you know . . ."

"*What* isn't? Tell me *now*."

"All right, I'll tell you, though I'd prefer it if you asked more nicely. The truth is my mommy was a pirate . . . but my daddy was a newborn just like you. There, are you happy? Oh, and one other thing: I can change into a monster anytime I like. I don't even have to get mad.

"It's why Rakkhati and the Jivitans found me so *valuable* in Duccarita. When I'm that way, I can fight real good. The scar I showed you on my tummy back at the tavern? A cave troll got a slice of me with his axe. Afterward, I killed him myself with a bite to the neck. And I enjoyed it. So you can see now why I didn't get all scared when you changed last night. Sorry to disappoint you."

"You could have saved us when the Porisāda attacked us in the alley."

"Maybe. I was tempted to try. Instead, I called the Daasa."

"You called? I didn't hear anything."

"I spoke with my mind, just like you did when they came to you in the open square."

"I'm not like you," Lucius said, backing away.

"That's true," Bonny said. "Half of me is human, while you are a purebred, which makes you even stronger. That's why the Daasa follow you. They love you. As do I—if you will let me. Who could make you a better wife than me?"


LUCIUS CALLED everyone together later that afternoon. It had become a beautiful day, breezy and warm. They sat facing each other on a pair of fallen logs, the firstborn and the Faerie on one side, Ugga, Bard, and Bonny on the other. The pirate woman sat with her pretty face buried in her hands. All around them were the Daasa, looking silly and pleased.

"I need to talk to the four of you, not as a leader, but as a friend," Lucius finally said. At the sound of his voice, many of the Daasa chittered. "We have decisions to make, and we need to make them soon. Our plan all along has been to go with the Daasa to Jivita, and Jord now tells me that she will accompany us. Still, as I've said before, I have no desire to force any of you to follow me. You are free to go elsewhere, without feeling shame or betrayal."

Bonny looked up sharply, her eyes red and puffy. "How can you even ask? You know full well we're all going with you—any of us who are welcome, at least."

Lucius sighed, then looked at the crossbreed and his companion. "Do the rest of you agree?"

Ugga and Bard smiled. Lucius was stunned to see how young they looked again. Their recent sprouts of gray hair were gone, and they held their backs erect. Had Jord's presence rejuvenated them?

"Of course we will go with ya, Master Loo-shus," Ugga said. "Me, Bard, and Miss Bonny are going to help ya fight the war. Jord says that's what we're supposed to do, but we'd have done it even without her saying it."

"All right, that's settled. My next question, then, is to Jord."

Lucius turned and gazed at her. The first time he had seen her by the cabin, she was dressed in a glowing white gown that had been perfect to the point of surrealism, but now she wore an ordinary-looking green coat, baggy brown trousers, and a brown shawl that concealed her hair. She had supplied similar clothing for Lucius and the others, including brown leather boots. They continued to look more like Duccaritans than Jivitans, but these new outfits would be comfortable in most any temperature. Though it was becoming unseasonably hot during the day, it still was chilly at night, especially this far north, only a few leagues from the Gap of Gamana.

"I am at your service," the Faerie said. "What do you want to know?"

"I want to know *everything*," Lucius said, chuckling. "But I'll settle for a few things. For instance, are our other companions still alive?"

"That's a good question, Master Loo-shus!" Ugga said.

"I don't know how they fare," Jord said sincerely. "But I believe at least some of them will make it to Jivita."

"Some . . . but not all?"

"That's up to fate," the Faerie said with a shrug of her slim shoulders. "What are your other questions?"

"I has one," Ugga said. "Can the meanie Daasa beat up In-vick-tuss?"

All of them laughed, even Bonny.

"We shall see what we shall see," Jord said.

"And the druids?" Bonny said. "Where are they now? When will they attack Jivita? And will some of them come after us?"

"Those were my next questions," Lucius said, smiling at Bonny. In response, the pain in her face seemed to melt away.

"But I have no answers," Jord said. "I have been with the four of you since yesterday afternoon—and I was waiting for you even longer than that."

"Ya could turn into a big birdie and look around," Bard said hopefully. "We knows ya can do it."

"For the time being, my place is with you and the Daasa," Jord said.

Lucius sighed again. "I'm unsure whether the druids consider us enough of a threat to even bother to attack, but our plan still should be to continue south and reach Jivita as quickly as possible. Bonny believes it will take at least two weeks—and that's if we do not encounter unusual difficulties along the way. Traveling with the Daasa is like marching with a slow-moving army.

We'll be lucky to average six leagues a day—and we have almost eighty to go."

"Two weeks will be soon enough," Jord said. "And when we arrive, Jivita will be the better for it."

# 46

THEY ATE another meal at dusk, which Lucius skipped again. He still didn't feel hungry, and it made him a little nauseous when his mind pondered why. A large portion of the Tyger carcass had been devoured, and his stomach still wasn't as flat as usual.

After their meal, Lucius and the others left Jord's cabin and began their long march. When the mood struck, the Daasa slept like babies, but when awake they were bundles of energy, darting to and fro in search of food, water, and entertainment. Though they were capable of running almost as fast as horses while in their nicey state, they spent as much time scampering sideways and backward as they did forward. They dove into ponds, splashed in streams, climbed trees and mounds, rooted in piles of dead leaves, and wrestled friskily with each other. Bonny even pointed one time to a pair that appeared to be mating.

The look she gave Lucius caused a certain area of his body to tingle. Then she took his arm. "Everything's going to be all right, sweety," she said in a cheerful voice. "I don't love you because you are a monster. I love you because you are not. Who we are right now is who we really are. But being able to change into something different is a blessing from the *One God*, not a curse. Nobody wants to be weak, especially when it comes to war. And believe me, sweety, you and I are not weak. You will see, when the time comes again."

Lucius swiveled and hugged her. "I'm sorry for what I said before. I was scared and angry. You've been wonderful to me since the moment we met. If not for you, I'd still be obsessing over a woman who loves someone else."

"You are not obsessing anymore?"

"I still love her. And wish her well. But I no longer want to be her lover. It's you I want, if you'll still have me."

"I'll still have you . . . on one condition."

"What's that?"

"Soon, sweety," she said. "I want to have you soon."

THEY HALTED THEIR march before dawn, ate bread, cheese, and berries, and then began to prepare for sleep. Though the Warlish witch had destroyed his *uttara*, Lucius still carried the Mogol war club, and his arms were sore despite switching it frequently from hand to hand. The Daasa settled down wherever they could make themselves comfortable: soft grass, a bed of leaves, the crook of a tree. Bard and Ugga cast themselves upon deerskin blankets and were asleep in moments, the crossbreed hugging the staff of his axe like a favorite toy.

Jord walked over to Lucius and placed her hand on his chest. "I do not need sleep," she said. "I will keep the watch." Then she smiled knowingly and strode away.

"She's telling us it's all right," Bonny said from behind him.

"What's all right?"

"*You* know."

"Aaaaaaah . . ."

In some areas, the gap between Dhutanga and the foothills of Mahaggata was less than a mile wide. Bonny grabbed a blanket and then took Lucius' hand, leading him eastward, away from the woods. At first, some of the Daasa who were still awake started to follow, but Bonny hissed at them with surprising vehemence, causing them to hunker down and back away, clearly intimidated.

This impressed Lucius. "You even scared *me* a little."

"Maybe you *should* be scared," she said, but the look in her eyes said otherwise.

Soon they came upon a jumble of low hills, the tallest of which were no more than fifty cubits. They passed over several before finding a hidden hollow.

"This is the best we can do," she said, spreading the blanket on a patch of grass. "If someone sees us, good for them."

By now the sun had started to rise, filling the hollow with yellow light. It was not a time to be shy.

"Bonny, there's one other thing I have to tell you," Lucius said timidly.

"What else could there be, sweety?"

"Believe it or not, I've never done this . . . had . . . I have witnessed every form of sex you could imagine, but I've never . . . I know that sounds absurd, but it's the truth."

Bonny laughed, but gently. "I knew there was *something* weird about you."

She removed her coat and undershirt. Her breasts were small but lovely, in contrast to shoulders packed with muscle. Her stomach also rippled. The pirate woman was less feminine than Laylah, but she was beautiful in her own way.

Though his heart was thudding, Lucius felt a strange calmness, enabling him to take his time and enjoy his newfound treasure. He kissed her mouth, then her neck and breasts. He paused at the long scar on her belly and nibbled it. When he did that, she moaned and reached for his breeches.

"Hurry, Lucius," she whispered. "I *want* it."

"No . . . let's not hurry."

But he allowed her to remove his clothes and the rest of her own, and he pulled her naked onto the blanket, both of them gasping and moaning.

*So much for going slowly.*

When he entered her, she screamed so hard it hurt his ears. She clawed at his bare back and buttocks with enough force to draw beads of blood, while wrapping her muscular thighs around his waist and squeezing the breath out of him. He pumped faster. Never had he felt such pleasure or experienced such passion. It made his infatuation with Laylah seem like a childish crush. This was real—for both Bonny and him. Everything about her wild, squirmy body filled him with lust.

Sometime during their lovemaking, his face grew strangely hot and his arms and legs thick and heavy. A relentlessly building dizziness blurred his vision. Yet it only seemed to empower him. He felt terrible pain. But not all pain is bad. Lucius pounded into her harder and harder, as if trying to tear her apart. But within the clouded veil of his desire, he could hear her screaming, "Yes! Let it happen! Don't *stop!*"

Then he was growling.

And she was growling.

Spittle flew from their mouths.

When he transformed, she did the same.

Afterward they lay in each other's arms and slept. When they woke in the early afternoon, their bodies had returned to normal. They made love again, in a more traditional fashion—though they still managed a little more growling.

When they returned to the camp, most of the others were already awake. Ugga and Bard had made a cream soup flavored with strips of deer meat to enjoy with bread, fruit, and cheese. To Lucius, it seemed like a feast. For the first time since the bizarre night at the cabin, he felt hungry. Being with Bonny had taken a lot of energy. Afterward, the four of them drank some wine. Jord was nowhere to be seen.

"Jord has been gone for a long time," Bard said. "She left while we were sleeping."

"Kinda strange," Bonny said. "Where would she be off to now?"

"Maybe she took Bard's suggestion and went on a scouting mission," Lucius said.

"I hopes she hasn't run off again," Ugga said, his small eyes darting about. "I was wishing she'd stay around this time."

"Don't you worry your big ol' head!" came a voice from off to the side. Jord appeared, as if out of nowhere. "I won't be leaving you for a while."

"Where'd ya go?" Bard said.

"I can't tell you all my secrets."

"Did you learn anything more about the druids?" Lucius said hopefully.

"I have seen them," Jord admitted. "They are far away. Not a one is on our side of Cariya. In fact, this whole area is clear of *any* enemies—not even a wolf or Mogol. We've chosen a good place to take a walk. But there'll be plenty of fighting for us once we reach Jivita."

The news seemed to please all of them. The dreadful battle that loomed in their future felt unreal. Just to be cautious, they continued to walk mostly at night, but they encountered nothing threatening—not even a Tyger or a bear, much to Ugga's chagrin. Occasionally Bard went off by himself and returned with game. The Daasa showed no interest in it, but neither were they offended. Whenever they were hungry, they fended for themselves.

Lucius and Bonny made love every morning, then slept naked beneath the hot sun. It was the best time of Lucius' life. After seven marches, they covered about forty leagues and were halfway to Jivita. The closer they got, the more Lucius dreaded it. He felt like someone who dreamt he was in heaven but knew he would wake up in hell.

Would the Daasa be slaughtered in the war?

Ugga and Bard?

Bonny?

Please, not her. He even found himself praying to the *One God* to spare her. For that, he gladly would sacrifice himself.

During the late afternoon of the tenth day since they left Jord's cabin, a squadron of Jivitan horsemen—three hundred strong—caught sight of them and approached rapidly from the south. Lucius feared this moment. If the Daasa saw the horsemen as a threat, would they butcher them? To Lucius' relief, the squadron halted half a mile away. Only a single rider came forward.

It was the first time Lucius had ever seen an armored Jivitan. The rider and his destrier impressed him. If there were thousands more of such men, women, and horses, would it be such an impossible task to defeat the druids?

The horseman dismounted, walked directly to Lucius, and bowed. When he straightened and stared at the Daasa, they chittered playfully, appearing to approve of the white-haired man.

"I am Worrins-Julich, senior captain of the *Assarohaa*," he said in a clear voice. "I ride in search of General Lucius Annaeus. You match his description. Are you that man?"

"I am."

"And you have proof?"

"If you know of me, then you know of my companions. What more proof do you need?"

Bonny stepped forward and handed Julich the scroll that Ditthi-Rakkhati had given her. The captain read it carefully, then respectfully handed it back.

"Rakkhati was my wife's brother," he said to Bonny. "His death is a great loss to me and to all who hold Jivita dear. We have long been aware, missus, that you assisted his brave efforts in Duccarita. Let it be known that your years of toil on behalf of the White City will not go unrewarded."

Then he turned to Lucius. "It is said you are a traitor."

"True enough."

Julich smiled. "A traitor to Invictus is a hero to the world. It would be my honor, General Lucius Annaeus, to escort you and your companions to Jivita—if you will have me."

"And what will we find when we arrive?" Lucius said.

"The most beautiful city in the world. Will you help us defend it?"

"That is my desire," Lucius said.

# The White City

# 47

ON THE SAME night that Tāseti and Rati camped on the shores of Lake Keo, Laylah finally closed her eyes, the side of her beautiful face resting against Torg's heart. It was midnight, and Elu had been long asleep, curled in the bottom of the canoe like a little boy, his healing body needing rest more than anything else. Torg remained awake.

His long journey from the Tent City to the White City would soon come to an end. He had left Anna in the summer and had arrived at the southern border of Dhutanga in early spring. In between, he had surrendered himself to Mala at Dibbu-Loka, come face-to-face with Invictus at Avici, endured the agony of the pit on Mount Asubha, destroyed the spider Dukkhatu, battled witches in Kamupadana, aided in the destruction of Duccarita, escaped the druids in the heart of Dhutanga, and ridden the rapids of Cariya to where he now sat.

He was lucky to be alive. Then again, perhaps luck had little to do with it. The overwhelming tide of karma had been set into motion, with Torg as one of its many agents. He believed he would survive this lifetime for as long as was needed and no longer—which was true for everyone who ever lived.

Torg tilted his head down and sniffed Laylah's hair. There was a foul smell to it, faint but detectable. Though their impromptu swim in Cariya had washed most of the dried goo away, shreds of the druid queen's mucous fluids still clung to Laylah's scalp. He lovingly combed her blond strands with glowing fingers, vaporizing the residues from the druid queen, along with naturally accumulated dirt and oils. When he finished, her hair was luxuriously clean. He then swept over the rest of her body and clothes with the palm of his hand while she slept. Afterward, he slipped out from under her and did the same for Elu—and then himself.

*At least we'll be presentable when the white horsemen find us, though it will still be nice to take a hot bath once we reach Jivita. I won't turn down a little luxury.*

Torg pondered what might happen next. Since leaving Anna, his goals had been twofold, save the noble ones and reach Jivita. He had achieved the first at great sacrifice, and now the second appeared close at hand. He knew that within a month, Mala's army would besiege Nissaya while the druids were attacking Jivita. If the fortress fell, the Chain Man would march west and assail the White City.

With a sudden shiver, Torg realized that no matter the final outcome at Jivita, the Sun God would still be in command. He had tasted Invictus' power, if only briefly, and it had dismayed him. What good did it do any of them to defeat Mala, when the specter of Invictus remained? Torg had no answer, other than his trust in fate. Something would intervene, a solution would arise, help would come from an unexpected source. His selflessness at Dibbu-Loka demanded it; his suffering in the pit and beyond could not have been in vain. There were forces at work greater than he. Would they eventually prove more powerful than Invictus? That was yet to be seen.

As the canoe drifted steadily southward, Torg again took Laylah in his arms, slipping so delicately beneath her that she did not awaken. Then he began to cry. If her brother came for her, as he surely would, how could Torg stop him? If she were again enslaved, how could Torg rescue her? He considered sending her with a Tugarian escort to the Jivitan havens by the sea, but what good would that do? Invictus would find her, sooner or later. Even if Torg and Laylah sailed across the ocean, the sorcerer would follow. They could outrun him for a year, or a decade, or a century, but not forever. Flight was not an option. Torg had to draw the line at Jivita—and hope that karma provided him with the means to defeat the Sun God. It was either that or suicide . . . and not the temporary kind. Torg did not discount that option for both him and Laylah, especially if it meant saving her from a semi-eternity of suffering at the hands of a lunatic.

Torg must have been crying harder than he thought. Laylah's eyes opened, and she looked up at him. "What is it, beloved?"

Torg lifted her and kissed her full lips. She wrapped her arms around his neck and kissed him back. When they finished, she asked him again. "What's wrong?"

"I can't bear the thought of losing you. I'm sworn to protect you, but I'm not sure I can. What if I fail?"

Now tears sprang from Laylah's eyes. She hugged him so hard it rocked the canoe. "We can't think that way. We have to enjoy every moment we have together. No matter what happens, he can't steal our love from us. It's too strong. If he does take me again, our love is what will keep me sane. In some ways, it's what kept me sane before you and I ever met. Somehow, I knew you were out there . . . and one day would find me."

"That will be true even beyond this lifetime."

Then they both cried, until sleep took them in its dark embrace. The canoe stayed its course for a remarkably long time, but eventually it wandered off the river into a creek and gently came to rest nose-first upon a sandy bank.

Soon after, night completed its final bow and then stepped aside, surrendering the stage to the rising sun.

BEFORE DAWN, a Jivitan squadron rode through the north gates of the city and halted outside the walls. Three hundred white horsemen dismounted, laid their weapons at their own feet, and knelt in a thick circle around their captain as he led the morning communion.

"There is but *One God*, all powerful and all merciful," the captain said. "In the name of *Ekadeva*, we pray. Dear God, please grant us the strength to prevail in arms against our foes, as well as the good fortune to return to our loved ones when the battle is done. We are forever your loyal servants. May any who die in your service this day ascend to your magnificent heaven and reside with you in eternal bliss. So shall it be."

"So shall it be," the horsemen responded.

They mounted their destriers and followed their captain along the west bank of Cariya, one of fifteen squadrons assigned to patrol the Green Plains. Their orders were to follow the river for ten leagues to the southern border of Dhutanga and explore the outskirts of the forest. If they encountered the enemy, they were to return to the city in haste. Therefore, they were lightly attired by their standards, wearing only knee-length hauberks over their quilted undergarments, as well as mail leggings and sollerets, all made of a special white iron smelted by the skilled metallurgists of Jivita. They displayed no armorial bearings and wore no helm, allowing their long white hair to flow freely about their shoulders. Their only weapons were two-edged swords and crossbows, discarding the long bows and lances they used more frequently in the open field. Their horses bore no armor, but beneath the high saddles they wore white silks that matched their alabaster coats. The squadron was built for speed, though even then it was formidable by ordinary standards.

Captain Worrins-Julich rode in front with several sergeants. Even before the sun rose over the plain, Julich and his men surveyed the terrain, searching for anything unusual. War was at hand, but the enemy had yet to show itself. Though reports indicated that Mala's army was on the march, the more immediate threat to Jivita was the druids, the White City's longtime nemesis. How many were they and when would they attack? No one knew for sure, not even the necromancers in the employ of Queen Rajinii. More disturbingly, the usually reliable mountain eagles, which often were used to spy on the druids, had left the White City several weeks ago and not returned. But despite a lack of information, it was widely believed that the druids were stronger—and angrier—than ever.

Between Jivita and Dhutanga, the river was wide and powerful, though not nearly as tumultuous as it was farther north. Numerous creeks, streams, and fingers wandered beyond its banks, some too deep to cross on horse. Captain Julich and his men encountered one of these and rode westward in search of shallows. But before they reached the ford, they found something else: a canoe, with passengers.

A quarter-mile away, Julich and a dozen of his sergeants dismounted and crept as quietly as they could toward the craft, but their hauberks and leggings scraped and clinked, making enough noise to wake the dead. Even then, the occupants did not stir.

"Perhaps they *are* dead," Julich said. "Who are these people, and what brought them here? They appear to be dressed in the raiment of Duccarita, but they do not have the feel of pirates. This is indeed a puzzle."

Then all three sat up at once.

Julich's sergeants readied their crossbows, but when the largest of the strangers leapt from the craft, the horsemen lowered their weapons and bowed.

Though he was oddly attired, there was no doubt: Lord Torgon, leader of the Tugars, had found his way to Jivita. The long hoped-for miracle had occurred. The great wizard was among them. Blessed be *Ekadeva*, in all his glory.

THOUGH SHE had been in a deep sleep born of exhaustion, Laylah sensed the approach of the white horsemen long before they drew near. She slit her eyelids against the painful rays of the sun and looked at Torg's face. Elu also stirred.

"Stay still and allow me to greet them," Torg whispered to both his companions. "These men know me."

Laylah did as the wizard asked, resting the side of her face against his thick chest. Elu huddled on the bottom of the canoe.

Suddenly Torg sat up, moved her aside and leapt out of the canoe, splashing through knee-deep water to the sandy bank. Laylah watched him approach the white horsemen. To her amazement, they lowered their weapons and knelt before him. Soon after, several hundred others rode up, dismounted and also bowed, placing their weapons at his feet.

"*Maranavidu!* (Death-Knower!)" said one who appeared to be their leader. "Though I am but a child to you, we have met before, several times. I am Worrins-Julich, senior captain of the *Assarohaa* (white horsemen). I rejoice in honoring you. How came you here?"

Torg bowed. "Well met, Captain Julich. Of course I remember you and am pleased to once again be in your presence. My companions and I have journeyed far, and we are weary. But we must ride with you in haste to the White City. I have urgent news for the queen."

"My stallion shall bear you," Julich said. "He is ill-tempered with anyone other than me, but I can see in his eyes that he loves you already."

Torg laughed. "Any mount will do, as long as he or she is large enough to carry both myself and my lady," the wizard said, gesturing toward Laylah and causing her heart to flutter. "As for my third companion, I ask that he ride with you—for though he is small, he is as stout as any man and is well-deserving of the highest honors the White City can accord. Plus, he is recovering from injuries and is in need of gentle treatment."

From his knees in the canoe, Elu bowed.

Julich returned it. "It will be as you say, Lord Torgon. Come. Let us make haste."

They presented Laylah and Torg with Julich's white destrier, which was as large as any horse Laylah had ever seen. She had heard much about the ways of Jivita, but her first meeting with the white horsemen left her thoroughly impressed. Each man had pale skin, gray eyes, and long white hair that matched the color of his armor. Only their belts, scabbards, and crossbows were other than white. There also were at least twenty women among them, smaller in build but otherwise similar in appearance and attire. Laylah felt as if she had encountered an army of snowmen.

Captain Julich, who now rode with Elu, seemed to read her thoughts. "Believe it or not, we do not melt," he said with a grin, "even in the middle of summer."

She smiled. "Your soldiers look as strong as iron. It is an honor to be in your presence. I thank you for treating me so kindly."

Julich's face grew serious. "Kindness is the least you deserve, my lady. I would give my life for you, if Lord Torgon but commanded it."

"There will be enough lives lost in the coming days," Laylah said. "Please save yours for the battles to come."

"Wise words," Julich said. "Lord Torgon, you have chosen well."

"Without doubt," Torg said, causing Laylah to blush.

*I grow faint if he but looks at me.*

As if in response, the wizard spun in the saddle and smiled at her. "I hear your thoughts, my love, and they fill me with bliss."

Laylah hugged him from behind. Captain Julich and Elu were grinning at them mischievously.

"What are *you* looking at?" Torg said.

All four of them laughed.


JIVITA HAD LONG been the most heavily populated city in the known world, housing more than a quarter million people, including its ceaseless and magnificent military, which was as well-maintained in peacetime as in war. Now, only Avici had more inhabitants. Jivita also was the wealthiest city in the world, surpassing even the current version of Avici. In the ancient tongue it was called *Jutimantataa* (City of Splendor), and for good reason. Its beauty and extravagance astounded all who experienced it.

Unlike Nissaya, Jivita was not a fortress. The concentric bulwarks of Nissaya were huge and impenetrable, while only a single low wall less than ten cubits tall protected the White City, forming an almost perfect circle around it. The wall was for show more than defense. The city was huge—almost ten leagues in diameter—and the wall was more than thirty leagues in circumference, making it almost impossible to defend properly in many places at once. But the Jivitans weren't concerned. If the main pitch of the battle were ever to reach the wall, it was likely they were already defeated.

The white horsemen were masters of the open field, which is exactly what surrounded Jivita. The Green Plains, a level expanse of lush grass, wildflowers, and fertile farmland, extended for at least thirty leagues in all directions except the north, where Dhutanga loomed, and even the forest was a full ten leagues distant.

When the city was under attack, the white horsemen didn't cower within its walls. Instead, they rode out to greet their enemies, and for as long as history had recorded their deeds, they had always prevailed. The horsemen—and their destriers—wore heavy armor, as close to impenetrable as any that existed. They carried lance, axe, and sword, and their archers were proficient either mounted or on foot. In addition, the Jivitans were highly disciplined fighters, attacking from a variety of intricate formations. None could withstand them, not even the black-hearted druids, though they often were greater in number.

But the Jivitans' military brilliance was not the main reason they were superior to their enemies. The *One God* was their true general, providing them with the strength and courage to succeed against any foe. Without *Ekadeva*, their exploits would be meaningless. All victories were due to God, he who did not sleep.

*So shall it be.*


LAYLAH CARED little about *Ekadeva*.

The bulk of her religious indoctrination had been formed during her brief time with the Ropakans and had clung to her for the rest of her life. The Great Spirit, the ruler of nature who reigned from the sky, was supreme in her world, but there were other gods representing animals, plants, rocks, and soil that also played important roles in the affairs of mortals.

As she and Torg approached Jivita, she pondered these thoughts and realized that she didn't yet know much about Torg's beliefs. But she didn't care. It had to be something good, or he couldn't have become who he was.

By the time they reached the wall encircling the city, tens of thousands greeted their squadron of three hundred. Some were mounted horsemen, some infantry, and some civilians who had chosen not to evacuate to the havens by the sea. But all were cheering as if the *One God* had come down from the sky for a personal visit. For the first time, Laylah gained a full appreciation of Torg's stature among the free peoples of the world. She looked at Elu and saw that the Svakaran was also impressed.

"I guess it's a good thing Rathburt isn't here," she yelled at Elu, trying to make a joke. "You know how angry *this* would make him." She regretted the words even as she spoke them.

"Elu still wishes Rathburt was here. He misses him."

"We have not seen the last of Rathburt," Torg said. "Do not doubt it."

Elu did not respond, as if he somehow knew differently.

The company rode in pairs through an open set of wide wooden gates, entering a grassy field much like the one they had left behind. Though the field was hundreds of hectares broad and long, Laylah could easily see the great expanse of the city spread out before her in the distance. Castles, cathedrals, and manses dotted the horizon as far as the eye could see, while immense clusters of buildings dominated the interior. In terms of area and opulence, it dwarfed even Avici, though no single structure rivaled Uccheda, her brother's wretched tower.

As impressed as Laylah was with Jivita, the field directly in front of her was even more captivating. Spring wildflowers bloomed all around her, and a thousand horses—white as the clouds above—pranced delicately among the flowers, their alabaster coats every bit as beautiful as the petals. Some of the horses approached near enough for Laylah to see their eyes, which were as multicolored as the blooms. Laylah gasped with pleasure. Other than Torg's face, it was the most beautiful thing she had ever seen.

"We love our horses more than ourselves," Julich said to her. "We believe they hold a more sacred position in heaven than we."

"Seeing how graceful and beautiful they are, I can understand why."

The captain seemed pleased. "There are many fields like this inside the wall. For every horseman, there are at least three steeds. Jivita has never been so strong. Every soldier, including infantry, has exquisite armor and weaponry. How can the druids—or even Mala himself—expect to defeat such might?"

"You have done well, as has Nissaya," she heard Torg say. "Nonetheless, whatever victories you attain will be hard fought."

"Only the *One God* can determine victory or defeat. Our strength is due to his grace. Even Invictus must bow to his will."

"As you say," Torg responded.

A wide gravel road meandered through the fields toward buildings beyond. They passed several manses with lawns as broad as pastures. Soldiers and civilians continued to greet them. Laylah noticed a group adorned in black, perhaps three dozen all told, sprinting toward them on foot with astounding speed and grace.

"Tugars come," Julich said.

Beneath the palms of her hands, Laylah could feel Torg's back muscles tense. The wizard urged their stallion into a canter. As they grew near, the Tugars began to shout.

"*Maranavidu! Maranavidu!* (Death-Knower! Death-Knower!)," they cried in unison, each drawing a curved sword that glittered in the bright sunlight. "*Nandaama te garukaatum!* (We rejoice in honoring you!)"

"Well met, *Kantaara Yodhas!* (Desert Warriors!)" Torg said. "*Nandaami te garukaatum!*"

Laylah watched with fascination as Torg dismounted and hurried to greet them. The Tugarian males were mirror images of Torg and the Asēkhas. But despite being tall and heavily muscled, they moved with stunning fluidity. Even the females among them were taller than any of the white horsemen.

Torg grasped forearms with a Tugar who appeared to hold special rank.

"How came you here, lord?" the warrior said. "The last we heard, Kusala and the Asēkhas had gone in search of you, but there has been no word from the chieftain, and we have not been in contact with our other sisters and brothers for several days. So we know little of the world outside the White City. To make matters worse, the eagles have quit making appearances, causing much grief. Even the pigeons seem hesitant to fly."

"Kusala and the Asēkhas found me, but I was forced to take a different route than they. I journeyed through Dhutanga, while Kusala was to travel east of the mountains en route to Nissaya. If all is well, the Asēkhas are already at the fortress."

"I see that you did not journey alone."

"Seven were with me at one point, but only two remain," Torg said, nodding toward Laylah and Elu. "For various reasons, I was separated from the rest. But these two must be treated with the highest honor. They have survived great perils, and each fought bravely. The lady, especially, is dear to my heart. Defend her above all else."

"Thy will shall be done," the warrior answered. "And what of the Tugars at Hadaya? More than five thousand are camped on its shores. Will you call them here?"

"Of this, I can say no more until I speak to Rajinii," the wizard said. "Make it known that I have returned. War is at hand. The druid queen has birthed a mighty army. Jivita is in peril."

The Tugar nodded, turned away, and trotted down the road, followed by the others.

Torg climbed back onto his horse and urged him forward. "To the queen," he told Julich.

"As you command," the captain responded. "But I would know the answer, as well. Will you call the rest of the Tugars here?"

"I cannot yet say."

Meanwhile, Laylah leaned forward and spoke in Torg's ear. "I am dear to your heart?"

"More so than all things."

They rode on toward the palace of Queen Rajinii. Torg told Laylah that it had been constructed within sight of the bustling business district of Jivita, though there were still more than forty hectares of manicured lawn separating it from that massive tangle of stone and wood buildings. Most of the land on which Jivita stood was as flat as the surface of a pond, but a few low hills sprouted from the ground in various places. The palace stood upon one of those.

A moat, purely for show, surrounded the base of the hill. Several wide bridges spanned its indigo waters. Dozens of white marble fountains, arrayed between the spans, spewed foam high into the air. Laylah was especially impressed by a sculpture off to her right: a partially submerged chariot driven by a single rider and drawn by four horses poised on the water's edge, as if in the process of rising from the depths. While most of the other fountains and statues were white, this one was made of gold. The complexity and perfection of its design were astounding.

During the ride to the palace, the squadron that had accompanied them since midmorning had declined in number, peeling off here and there to attend to other duties. Now just Captain Julich and a dozen horsemen remained with them. Before crossing the moat, they dismounted and marched over one of the bridges onto a paved walkway lined with tulip poplars. A battalion of guards carrying banners mounted on poles as tall as the trees met them. The guards wore white plate armor, mail skirts and flowing green cloaks. Suddenly Laylah felt like a servant girl.

As if sensing her discomfort, Torg took her hand.

Julich approached the guards and bowed. "I bring honored guests to greet the queen."

The master of the guards also bowed. "Queen Rajinii is aware of King Torgon's arrival. She will address you at the main entrance, but she commands that afterward, the wizard be brought to the Throne Room alone. Guest suites have been prepared for his companions."

Torg started to protest, but Laylah squeezed his hand. "It's all right, Torg. I'm not much in the mood for company anyway. What I'd love more than anything right now is a hot bath."

Julich also looked perturbed, as if an insult had been issued that Laylah did not fully perceive. They continued on in silence, except for the clanking of armor and the snapping of iron shoes on the concrete pathway. As they approached the front entrance, Laylah looked up at the palace in amazement.

The five-story edifice—constructed with white limestone, sandstone, and marble—was only a tenth as tall as Uccheda, but it was several times broader at the base, containing more than nine hundred rooms. A pair of massive columns supporting a pointed arch framed the main arcade. Within the arcade were the two largest windows Laylah had ever seen—as tall as the poplars and filled with monochrome glass. Between the windows were the main doors, which were carved from rare white oak found only in the heart of Kincara, fifty leagues south of the city. While still Invictus' prisoner, Laylah remembered reading about these very doors during one of her visits to his library.

"Do you like it?" Julich asked her.

"The palace is magnificent."

"It was built by the queen after the death of her husband, King Avikheppa X," Torg said.

"How long ago?"

"More than fifty years," Torg said.

"Jivitans are not like Tugars," Julich said. "Our life spans rarely exceed one hundred springs. But the queen is much older than that, and yet has retained her youthful beauty. There is magic in her veins. You will see for yourself. Like all true-blooded necromancers, her skin is white, but her hair is black."

As they spoke, the doors swung open. Henchmen clad in white robes emerged, formed an aisle, and fell to their knees. Laylah could see a well-lighted foyer and beyond that a majestic staircase with a banister of green marble. Standing on the bottom stair was the queen.

She wore a belted, V-necked gown of white samite with silver speckles, its collar, hem, and cuffs trimmed with green velvet. She held a tall staff of white oak with a fist-sized square of jade on its head. Her black hair was unadorned, hanging freely past her waist, but she had donned a magnificent crown made of white ivory studded with emeralds. She was a tall woman, though not quite as tall as Laylah, and she moved with long-practiced grace. When she approached, Laylah saw that her gray eyes were as sparkly as the silver in her gown.

A woman who also had black hair accompanied the queen. The severe contrast of white against black caused Laylah to shudder. The woman reminded her of Urbana.

Everyone bowed, including Torg, though his was less pronounced.

The queen appraised Laylah with a glance, then focused her attention on Torg.

"Welcome, King Torgon, to Jivita. It has been long since we last spoke."

"Five years," Torg said. Laylah sensed wariness in his voice.

"Five years . . . yes," the queen purred. She glanced at Laylah again, her eyes smoldering. Then she smiled at Torg.

"War is at hand," she continued. "My army is prepared, but it is always *nice* to add one more soldier to the fold. I am sure you're in a hurry to change out of your pauper's attire and into something more presentable, but you and I—king and queen—have much to discuss first. Will you join me in the Throne Room for refreshments? After that, you can bathe—and then enjoy a proper meal. By the grace of the *One God*, the White City is well-provisioned."

"I will join you," Torg said. "As for 'something more presentable,' Tugarian raiment will do. One of my warriors will bring it to me, if asked politely."

"Anyone within our walls is under command of the queen," the eerie aide said to Torg. "She need not *ask*."

Rajinii hushed her. Then she turned to Julich, her voice stern. "You heard him, Captain."

"Yes, your highness." He bowed again and marched away.

Rajinii glided over to Laylah and stared into her eyes. The jade on the head of her staff sprang to life, tossing out brilliant green beams laced with pale yellow. Laylah increased her grip on Obhasa, which glowed blue-white in response. For a moment the beams clashed, but blue-white proved stronger.

Rajinii winced and stepped back. "Take them to their chambers," she snapped at the henchmen. "And bring refreshments to the Throne Room."

Then she stomped into the foyer and up the stairs, with her strange assistant scampering behind. When Torg did not immediately follow, Rajinii turned and glared.

"Are you coming?"

"In a moment," he said. Then in full view of the others, he kissed Laylah on the mouth. "Will you continue to take care of Obhasa for me, my love? I'll join you shortly."

"When you do, I'll be sure to be more 'presentable.'"

"You can look even better than you do now?"

"Oh . . . yes."

# 48

THE THRONE Room of Jivita was one of the most opulent chambers in the palace. Its walls were white, but its chandeliers were gold and its wood floors laden with lush green rugs. Five stairs led to the platform that contained the three-legged throne, which had been sculpted from a core of white crystal and studded with emeralds, diamonds, and rubies. The throne was wide enough for three to sit upon, but of course only Rajinii was allowed, her pride rivaling King Henepola X of Nissaya. Both had been born with magic, and it had made them precocious.

Rajinii ascended to the throne, placing the tail of her staff in a narrow basket. Manta, her dark-haired assistant, took her assigned place beside the queen. The Jivitan necromancer was no stranger to Torg. Like Indajaala, Manta pretended to be devious and mean-spirited but in reality was in his employ.

Servitors entered the room bearing goblets of wine and trays of white cakes. A single chair and small table were arranged at the foot of the stairs.

"Bring me wine," Rajinii barked at a cupbearer.

Torg sat down. "No cakes for you?" he said to the queen. "Watching your figure?"

"How dare you!" Manta snapped, but the queen only snorted.

"I have already supped."

"As you say."

Torg had not enjoyed a true meal since Duccarita. The cakes were but a trifle to his massive frame, but they were moist and fluffy. He devoured several. The wine was delicious, rivaling the nectar of Tējo.

"You should have taken me up on my offer," the queen said. "If you had, your recent travails would have been avoided. I hear that Invictus imprisoned you. How unpleasant. And why? Just to save the helpless Dibbu-Lokans?"

"*Unpleasant* is not the word I would choose. As for the noble ones, does not your *One God* believe in defending the helpless?"

"Your highness, enough is enough," Manta said. "How dare he speak to you this way in your own chambers? We should have him chained and dragged from the room."

The queen snorted again. "That would not be so easy." Then she smiled sweetly at Torg. "If you and I had married, as I suggested the last time you were in this room, I would have counseled against your visit to Dibbu-Loka. It was a fool's errand."

"As my Vasi master liked to say, 'fool to one is wise to another.'"

"You insult her highness in her own palace?" Manta said.

"I do as I please."

Rajinii did not respond, turning her attention to her goblet, which she drained. "The girl is cute," the queen said, changing the subject. "A diversion to ease the rigors of your travels?"

"If you had trodden in her shoes, you would say no such words. She is no girl, nor is she a diversion. Her name is Laylah, and she is Invictus' sister."

With a sharp inhalation, Rajinii stood and hurled the goblet across the room. "And you bring her here? To my city? How dare you! The wrath of Invictus will fall upon us."

"And if she were elsewhere, it would not?"

Rajinii growled. "More wine!" she shouted to no one in particular.

"I grow weary of this," Torg said. "A marriage between you and I would not have been wise. Some of the reasons are obvious. You prefer carpets of grass, not sand between your toes. And I could not have lived here. I enjoy my visits to Jivita, but it is not my home. My heart remains in Tējo." Then Torg sighed, his voice barely a whisper. "And there are other reasons you and I were not meant to be."

"But the girl . . . Laylah. These reasons do not apply to her?"

"They do not. And as I said before, she is no girl. She is a woman, both in age and experience. Besides, she is the love of my life. All else pales."

Then he drew the Silver Sword and punched the point of the blade into the wooden tabletop. "If you attempt to harm her, I will kill you," Torg said.

"Guards!" Manta screamed.

Several raced forward, drawing their swords, but Rajinii waved them off. They backed away, eyeing Torg suspiciously.

"Torgon, Torgon, Torgon . . . I have no plans to *harm* your precious Laylah. But as far as you and I are concerned, you know naught what you have refused. As husband and wife, we could have ruled the world. Imagine the might of Jivita and Anna combined. Even Nissaya would quail before it."

"I thought our might was already combined," Torg said. "And Nissaya? Are the black knights not also our friends? I have no desire to see them quail. Invictus is our enemy. And the druids. Or have things changed since I last sipped wine with you?"

"One thing has changed," Manta said in a menacing tone. "This very morning, we were informed that Chieftain Kusala ordered the Tugars at Hadaya to march to the aid of the black fortress. It has become obvious who the desert warriors prefer as their allies."

For that, Torg had no answer. He sheathed his sword and then bowed at the foot of the stairs. "I am weary, your highness. Forgive me, but I must retire."

"Very well," she said. "We'll speak more at dinner."

"I have little else to say. For what it's worth, I will fight at Jivita's side until the end of all things. Is that not the behavior of an ally?"

As he was leaving, Torg strode past a wall decorated with elaborate paintings of past kings, queens, and military heroes. He stopped in front of a portrait of a famous captain whom Torg had befriended almost nine centuries before. Torg was amazed by how clear his memories remained of the last full-scale war between Jivita and the druids.

Rajinii came up quietly beside him. Manta remained near the throne, her face strangely placid.

"You always pause before Ditthi-Sagga," Rajinii said.

"I spoke at his funeral. He died peacefully of old age, and yet still there was grief among the Jivitans."

"I forget sometimes just how long you have lived. I feel so old myself, and yet I am just a child compared to you." She leaned against him and took his arm. "I am a spoiled and wicked brat," the queen whispered. "But I love my God and my people. When the druids come, I will not shy from battle. Instead, I will ride in the front as their commander."

"Your courage is beyond question, Rajinii. As is your strength. When the druids come, I will be at your side—if you will have me. But Laylah must be allowed to join us. For she also is strong."

Then he broke from the queen and fled the room. Rajinii did not follow.

BEFORE GOING TO Laylah, Torg first checked on Elu. A henchman led Torg to a chamber on the third floor of the palace, where he found the Svakaran fast asleep on a large cushioned bed, bathed and freshly clothed. Torg laid his hand on Elu's cheek. He loved him dearly. Would the Svakaran ever see Rathburt again? Torg wasn't sure.

"I'm glad that you are sleeping, my friend," Torg whispered. "It will speed up the healing." Then he left the room.

"Your chambers have been prepared," the henchman said.

"Take me to the lady," Torg said.

"My lord? The queen arranged for three separate chambers."

"Take me to the lady . . . or I will break down every door in the palace to find her."

"As you say, my lord."

Before Torg went into Laylah's room, a Tugarian warrior approached from the shadows, startling the servants. He bowed low to his king.

"May I take your sword?" the warrior said. "It would be my honor to polish and sharpen it, and you also appear to need a new scabbard."

"Excellent," Torg said, handing him the sword. "But don't waste your time trying to sharpen it. This blade is beyond improvement of any kind. And be careful, for it will cut even a Tugar."

Then Torg turned and entered the room, finding Laylah dozing in a copper tub filled with steaming water. Next to it was a tall wooden table with towels and several cakes of perfumed soap. No servants were in the room, not even a chambermaid. Whoever had prepared the bath must have only recently departed.

Torg leaned down and kissed her forehead. Her eyes opened slowly, and she smiled at him, her perfect teeth as white as the spring blooms of a dogwood.

As if reading his thoughts, she said, "The servants were doting over me, so I asked them to leave. It reminded me too much of Avici. I prefer to take my own baths and wash my own hair."

Torg chuckled. "As do I."

"Will you join me? There's room in the tub, even for you."

"There's nothing in the world I would rather do at this moment. But I'm afraid."

"Afraid of me?"

"No. Afraid that if I get in that tub, we'll end up destroying half the palace."

Laylah laughed. "I'll behave, I promise."

Torg undid his breeches and lowered them to his knees. Laylah gasped.

"As deeply as I love you and lust for you right now, I dare not share your bath," Torg said, quickly pulling up his breeches. "It would be better if I went to my own chambers, for now. The queen has arranged a dinner in our honor. I'll join you there. Afterward, I will take you to a place where you and I can be alone. Once there, we shall see what we shall see."

"If I have anything to say about it, there'll be plenty to see," Laylah purred.

# 49

TORG FOUND several henchmen waiting outside Laylah's door. When he asked them to lead him to his own chambers, they seemed relieved. A bath had been prepared for him, and he soaked in it alone, enjoying it immensely.

He already missed Laylah, but he knew that their attraction had become too supercharged for them to be together without something happening. Their mutual lust would have to wait until later—perhaps at midnight, after the moon had risen. And Torg knew just the place where they could make a lot of noise without attracting attention.

To calm himself, he relaxed in the bath. But even as his eyes grew heavy, he noticed that he wasn't alone. Something slithered through his window and moved toward him along the floor. A normal person would have mistaken it for a wandering shadow cast by the windswept curtains. But Torg recognized the necromancer.

Manta stood and scampered toward his door, barring it as quietly as possible. Then she came forward and stood over him, unabashed despite his nudity. Tugars held no shame with their bodies.

"Lord Torgon," she said softly, "it is a great honor to be in your presence again. I apologize for invading your privacy, but the queen is not easily fooled. After your meeting in the Throne Room, she rushed to her chambers, so I took this opportunity to visit you for a short time without notice."

"You're as good at scaling walls as Indajaala," Torg whispered.

Manta chuckled. "Almost."

"What have you to report?"

"The queen has been acting strangely," Manta said, quickly adding, "more strangely than usual. She has always been petulant, but this is worse. I fear the pressures of an impending war are wearing on her more than she might admit.

"She says the *One God* comes to her chambers and speaks to her in person about the glory of death in battle and how it will propel us all to the kingdom of heaven. It is as if she does not believe victory possible, not so much against the druids but against the army that is now said to march on Nissaya."

"Are there reasons for this, other than the obvious?"

"None that I am aware, but she spends a great deal of time alone in her chambers. What goes on there is beyond my knowledge. I'm sorry, my lord. I have failed you as a spy."

"You have told me all that I need know," Torg said. "I'll begin my own investigation shortly. Thank you, dear friend."

Manta smiled, bowed again, and unbarred the door. Then she left the way she had come, slithering out the window like a demon incarnate.

Afterward, Torg pondered her words, his powerful mind considering every aspect. After washing, he stepped out of the bath, dried himself, and lay on the bed, still naked. Though he was tired, he didn't expect to be able to sleep. But when he closed his eyes, exhaustion overcame his thoughts, and he drifted off immediately.

He later awoke to a tapping on his door.

"Enter."

Several henchmen poured into the room, bearing a new outfit and boots. After setting these items on a dressing table, they waited for instructions.

"When is dinner?" Torg said.

"The queen requests your attendance in the banquet hall as soon as you are able," the chamberlain said. "Your companions are already en route."

"How long did I slumber?"

"It is past dusk, my lord."

"Leave me. I will dress myself."

"Very good, my lord. We shall wait outside your door and escort you to the banquet hall at your leisure."

"Fine."

After they departed the chamber, Torg put on the new outfit, a kind that Tugars wore during ceremonies and other special events. His underclothes were black and skin tight, stopping above the elbows and knees. His loose trousers also were black, matching a full-length robe of brocade that was closed at the side and belted. He also wore ox-leather slippers with blue stitches, and a silk cap with a blue streamer.

Along with the outfit, the Silver Sword had been returned to him, sheathed in a new scabbard fashioned of Jivitan white steel ringed with gold and studded with diamonds and rubies. Usually Torg didn't care much for such extravagance, but in this case he was pleased. The straight, double-edge blade slid in and out of the scabbard with a crisp ring.

"You finally have a home worthy of your beauty," Torg whispered. "I can only hope to prove worthy of you as your wielder." Torg pressed the flat surface of the blade against his cheek. It was cold as ice, though his chamber was quite warm.

A short time later, when Torg entered the banquet hall on the first floor of the palace, it was already crowded to capacity. More than one thousand filled the cavernous room, which was lined on three sides with huge arched windows framed by green-silk curtains. Torg saw white horsemen dressed in embroidered doublets with jade-colored hose, noblemen and women of high society displaying the finest fabrics and jewels, and clergymen wearing white albs beneath green chasubles. Fifty Tugars were among the guests, adorned all in black, and they moved toward Torg and threw themselves at his feet.

The room grew quiet, save for Torg's deep voice. "*Kantaara Yodhas, titthatha. Tumhe na koci puujetha.* (Desert Warriors, please rise. You bow to no one.)"

The Tugars greeted him, one by one, each clasping his forearm.

Afterward, Queen Rajinii came forward with Laylah and Elu at her side, each bearing pewter goblets filled with fine red wine. The queen wore a spectacular white gown embedded with diamond chips and a green veil beneath her white-crystal crown.

"Our honored guest has finally arrived," Rajinii said, with a mixture of enthusiasm and sarcasm. "Laylah and I were running out of good things to say about you. Our little friend Elu, however, has an endless supply of tales of your derring-do."

Elu hobbled over. "Did you have a nice rest, great one?" the Svakaran said. "Elu slept well. He's feeling better already."

"*Great one?*" Rajinii quipped. "Is that your latest title?"

Torg did not hear her words. His eyes had seized, along with the rest of his senses, on Laylah. She was dressed far simpler than the queen—a crimson cloak over a pale-green gown—but she far outshone Rajinii or any woman in attendance, including the female Tugars. Her gray-blue eyes sparkled like the chandeliers suspended high above.

Torg walked over to her, leaned down slightly, and whispered in her ear. "You are perfect . . . your face, your hair, your body. I don't deserve to be in the same room with you."

"I swear that I was about to say those exact words to you," she whispered back.

Torg laughed. "No matter what happens from here, this moment will have made my existence complete."

"You stole my words again."

"My, my . . . but aren't we the sweetest couple," Rajinii said in an exaggerated tone. "Someone bring The Torgon some wine before he drinks poor Laylah instead."

Torg turned to the queen. "Wine would be excellent."

Trumpeters announced the start of the meal.

The queen and her guests sat at a table that was only two arm lengths wide but five hundred paces long. Rajinii was at its head, Torg and Elu on her left, Laylah across from the wizard on the queen's right, Manta the necromancer to Laylah's right. Five harpists provided soothing background music for the feast, which began with beef stew dusted with spices, onion soup with cubes of pork in a goat-milk broth, and grilled hare basted with lemon and garlic.

After the first course, a dozen jugglers put on an entertaining show, tossing swords back and forth the length of the table and catching daggers with their teeth.

The second course consisted of white fish caught on the shores of the Akasa Ocean, roasted venison, and stuffed pigs.

The jugglers returned for an encore, but this time they dressed like druids skewered with flaming arrows, and they tossed and juggled branches and pine cones. This was greeted with outrageous laughter from the Jivitans.

Butter cakes, glazed eggs, fritters, and spiced wine made up the final course. It was Torg's best meal since leaving Anna the previous summer.

"I don't believe I have ever seen you eat so much," the queen said. "Nonetheless, Elu surpasses you."

The Svakaran looked up and burped. But this did not offend Rajinii. Whatever anger she felt over Laylah did not seem to extend to the Svakaran. The queen laughed sincerely. "I must say, Elu, that you lighten my heart."

Then she turned to Laylah, and her smile grew devious. "And you, as well. Seldom has such beauty graced my halls."

"I find that difficult to believe," Laylah said. "From what I've seen, all Jivitans are lovely . . . and you the loveliest of all."

"Ahhhh, sweet words," the queen said, her smile becoming a leer. "But old age has tempered my true beauty. When I was a child like you, I was more deserving of your compliments."

"I'm not as young as I appear," Laylah said.

"Elu has never seen two such pretty ladies in one place."

Torg watched all this with amusement, but eventually he grew impatient, standing and slamming his fist on the table. "A toast!" he shouted, startling the queen and Laylah. The entire room went silent, including the servitors. "I come to you from far away—with evil at my heels," he said, raising his goblet.

"During a long period of peace, Jivita has wisely chosen not to rest, growing stronger than ever," he continued. "But the blessed times are past, and your strength will soon be tested."

Now there was complete silence—not a cough or a cleared throat. "There is no evil greater than hatred . . . and make no mistake, our enemies hate us. They will attempt to take from us all that is dear, and they will show no mercy in doing so. Against such might, we cannot avoid loss. There will be death and disaster, murder and mayhem. But we fight for a worthy cause."

The silence ended in an explosion of cheers, whistles, and applause. When it finally grew quiet, Torg turned to the queen. "Queen Rajinii is great and proud. We must all unite beneath her banner." Then he drew the Silver Sword and whipped it through the air with speed so great it left a trail of sparks and crackles. "I offer my strength to you, Queen Rajinii of Jivita," he shouted. "Do you accept?"

*Accept* boomed like an explosion.

The queen stood. There again was silence. "Yes," she said softly.

The room erupted again.

The Tugar who had first greeted Torg when they arrived at the White City then stood. "The *Kantaara Yodhas* offer our strength to you, Queen Rajinii of Jivita. Do you accept?"

"I accept."

Captain Julich followed suit. "The white horsemen offer our strength to you, Queen Rajinii of Jivita. Do you accept?"

"I cannot accept what has already been so loyally given," the queen said. "But I will be honored to ride with you into battle, *Assarohaa*."

Torg smiled at Julich, then turned back to the queen. "We stand united in the face of our enemy. Let no heart quail!"

All in attendance stood and raised their goblets.

"Let no heart quail!" they repeated.

When they finally sat, more wine was poured, raising everyone's spirits another notch.

Rajinii leaned forward and whispered to Torg. "You have bested me again, Death-Knower."

"It was not my intention to best you—but to join you. Enough of bickering and jealousy. It is beneath you. If we are to prevail, you and I must stand as one—our combined strength against the strength of the enemy. Anything less would make us fools."

"You are wise in most ways, Torgon, but not in the ways of the heart," Rajinii said. "Unrequited love is a painful burden." Then she stood and fled the room.

Manta glanced at Torg before following the queen.

Afterward, Laylah leaned across the table and spoke to Torg. "Let no heart quail. I like that. Did you just now think that up?"

"My father used to say that to the Tugars when he was chieftain of the Asēkhas," Torg responded. "But that was a long time ago."

"When all this is over, you'll have to tell me more about him," Laylah said.

"If only you could have met him."

The Svakaran tapped Torg on the shoulder. His eyes were weepy. "Elu wishes Rathburt and our other friends were here. Will we ever be reunited, great one?"

"Whatever happens will happen," Torg said. "But I believe we have not seen the last of our companions. Perhaps Captain Julich will be able to help us."

A tall figure loomed behind Torg. "Did I hear my name mentioned?"

Torg turned and greeted Julich. "You did, indeed. I will have need of you. Has there been word yet of a meeting of the Privy Council?"

"The queen has made no order, but I believe a council headed by her highness will be arranged for tomorrow. However, our generals and bishops are anxious to speak with you informally this evening. Will you join them in the library?"

"I will . . . but only briefly. In the meantime, I need a favor."

"Anything, my lord."

WHILE TORG spoke to Julich, Laylah found that the Tugars had begun to surround her. One handed her Obhasa. Each warrior was almost as tall as the Death-Knower, and even the females were a full span taller than she. The women among them were not as thickly muscled as the men, but they still appeared powerful and even more graceful, if that were possible. The Tugars treated her with a great deal of respect, asking polite questions about her comfort and needs. They also paid considerable attention to Elu, making sure not to exclude him from the conversation, though he barely came up to their knees.

The *Kantaara Yodhas* enthralled Laylah. A chill ran up her spine when the thought entered her mind that she might one day be their queen, assuming they survived the war.

Suddenly, the Tugars parted, allowing Captain Julich to approach her. She had no doubt that any one of them—male or female—easily could have stopped the Jivitan had they considered him a threat, though the captain was no weakling himself.

Julich faced her and bowed. "Lord Torgon asks that you walk with me in the gardens. A Tugar of your choosing may come with us as an escort, if you so desire. The Torgon has been called away to the library for an informal meeting, but he promises to join you shortly."

"No escort, other than you, will be necessary, Captain."

She feared the Tugars might protest or take offense, but instead they respectfully backed away.

Elu looked up at her and yawned. "Elu drank too much wine, and his body is still sore. Would you mind if he went to bed, pretty lady?"

"Not at all," Laylah said. "I'll look forward to seeing you tomorrow."

Elu smiled and bowed so low his forehead almost brushed against the marble floor. Then he yawned again and limped off.

"My lady?" Julich said, offering Laylah his arm.

"Lead the way, Captain."

They left the banquet room and strolled down a hallway that led to the west wing, its walls lined with white-marble busts depicting Jivitan war heroes. The wing was adjoined to the Gallery of Mirrors, a magnificent chamber with seventeen arched windows—each several times as tall as a man—looking over the gardens. Opposite each window was a matching mirror framed with gilded bronze.

A pair of grand doors opened into the gardens, which were laced with torchlit walkways weaving through green lawns decorated with evergreens, spring wildflowers, and sophisticated arrangements of rock, stone, and sand.

Laylah was entranced. "Invictus believed that his gardens were the most beautiful in the world," she found herself saying. "But these are far grander."

"Your time spent in Avici must have been terrible," Julich said, quickly adding, "Forgive me if I say too much, but word travels fast in the White City."

Laylah sighed. "There's nothing to forgive."

Julich nodded. "I would ask you much about the sorcerer and his ways, but now is not the right moment. I believe, however, that you will be requested to speak tomorrow at the Privy Council."

"I have nothing to hide. If I can add anything of value, I will do so."

"That is all any of us can ask in these difficult times."

They walked a while longer in silence. The quarter moon began its late-evening rise. Laylah felt an immediate surge of strength flow through her sinews.

"My lady," Julich said, amazed. "Do my eyes betray me? You are aglow."

"I take pleasure in moonlight."

In the rear of the palace, the gardens opened onto a sloping green lawn many hectares in size and dotted with spectacular groves of wildflowers. White horses wandered freely, grazing beneath the starlight.

Julich let out a shrill whistle, and a heavily muscled stallion thundered playfully toward them, neighing as it approached. It came to Laylah and nuzzled her, then also nuzzled the head of Obhasa, its ears relaxed and eyes calm.

"He likes you . . . and the ivory staff," Julich said.

"It matches his coat," Laylah said. "Does he have a name?"

"He needs a new one," came a voice from behind, startling Laylah and Julich but not the stallion. "This horse you shall name, for you shall ride him into battle at my side."

Laylah's heart pounded.

Torg's presence always made her dizzy, especially when she had been separated from him for even a short time. "I shall name him Izumo, in honor of the dracool that gave his life to save mine."

"An excellent choice," Julich said softly. Then he leaned forward and whispered in the stallion's ear. "He knows now, my lady, and will come when called. Izumo will not betray you. He ranks among the greatest in our stables. The queen's mare is his only superior."

"I am honored beyond words," Laylah said.

Torg carried a folded white blanket, and he cast it over Izumo's back. "Leave us, Captain."

Julich bowed again. "As you command, Lord Torgon. Until tomorrow."

# Sorcerer and Wizard

# 50

AT THE APPROACH of midnight, Invictus continued to lean over his magical basin. He had remained in his upper chambers long past the usual time when he descended into the bowels of Uccheda to avoid the darkness. Earlier that day, he had done his best to ruin Henepola's mind. That had been so much fun. Scrying had an addictive effect, even on a god. He couldn't seem to pull himself away.

Invictus suspected, but did not yet know for certain, that Torg and Laylah had escaped the druids and reached Jivita. Once they had entered the forest, he had lost sight of them.

*The two of you must be so proud of yourselves. You imagine that you are safe, protected by the pitiful white horsemen and their dried-up queen. But you are safe only because I allow you to be. For now.*

He'd always found Rajinii easy to manipulate and infiltrate.

As he swept over Jivita, the glow of her power shined like a star, making it ridiculously simple to locate her. His gaze slipped through one of her bedroom windows and into her personal chambers, where he discovered her lying naked on her bed, clinging to a strange jacket of Duccaritan make. The queen pressed it against her face with her free hand and sniffed it as she masturbated.

*How interesting!*

After the queen climaxed, she cast the coat on the floor and fell asleep.

Invictus considered entering her mind and tormenting her—which he had done so many times in recent weeks—but instead he grew bored and left her, making another aerial sweep of the White City.

From high above, Jivita resembled a tangle of bonfires. He had to admit that its immensity impressed him. Once Mala's army crushed the white horsemen, he would spend a considerable amount of time exploring the city. It would hold his interest for several days, at least. It was worth conquering Jivita, just for that.

At the last moment, something caught his eye, a streak of blue, green, and white light emerging from the shimmer of the city and entering the darkness outside its walls, passing quickly along the western bank of Cariya, before finally settling in an open field a league or so away. Invictus focused as best he could, but it was too dark for him to see clearly. However, the glow seemed to halt in a dense field of multicolored wildflowers.

He watched with frustration as the light expanded and contracted, firing mysterious tendrils through the flowers that resembled bolts of lightning. Suddenly there was a magnificent explosion, as if a volcano had vomited in his face, and even Invictus was thrown back, the cataclysm temporarily blinding him. When he was able to focus again, thousands of flower petals—many of them aflame—fluttered in the air and obscured his view. The glow beneath them had diminished but remained vividly warm.

His suspicions filled him with anger. He considered climbing onto the back of a Sampati or dracool and flying to Jivita right then, but that would be too much work for too little reward. He knew he needed to be patient and let everything play out. If he did, the end result would be all the sweeter—and more interesting. Already his plans for Torg's demise were taking root.

When he reached the inner chamber far below the base of his beloved tower, he masturbated to orgasm, melting every candle in the room. Servants rushed in, cleaned up what little remained of the gooey wax, and brought in new candles, their fingers trembling as they lighted each wick.

Invictus paid them no heed. His thoughts were on his sister and the wizard.

The time would come when the Death-Knower would receive his proper punishment. When Laylah would again reside in Uccheda as queen of Avici. When his sister would give birth to a son so much like himself.

The time would come!

Can a god be prevented from achieving his desires?

# 51

BENEATH THE roaring currents of Cariya, at a spot where the rapids were particularly violent, boulders had been cast together in such a way as to form a small cavern beneath the surface that was filled with a bubble of stale air. No living being larger than a grain of sand had ever inhabited the cavern. Nothing of size could reach it from above or below. Now Rathburt lay there motionless, his eyes closed, appearing deeply asleep or dead.

Two ethereal figures huddled over him, one resembling a gray-haired woman dressed in translucent robes, the other a girl-child in a glowing dress. They stared at Rathburt, debating his condition.

"If he dies, my plan will be ruined," the gray-haired woman said. "And if that happens, we'll *all* die."

"Mother, have you forgotten what I have foreseen? He is a Death-Knower. He will perish but return, which will give him the strength to perform his final duty."

"This one is not like your Father. He is too pathetic for such a feat. If he dies, he will not have the courage to return."

"When he dies, I will follow—and bring him back."

"I know that's what you've been saying, but I still don't trust you. Instead of coming back, you'll run off with him to your next life and leave me here to fend for myself."

"I would not betray Father in that way. I'm not like you."

"*I would not betray Father in that way. I'm not like you.* And thank the demons for that! You're so icky-sweet you make me nauseous."

"Will you allow me to follow or not?"

"If you don't return, your Father will suffer a fate far more terrible than anything I could devise."

"I know that, Mother, better than you."

"Tccch! Children these days. Such smart alecks. Very well, follow him. I'll be here to welcome you both back with open arms."

"What a warm and wonderful thought."

# 52

RATHBURT HEARD all of this, but he paid it little heed. Though he sensed it was chilly and damp, he did not feel cold. Though he sensed there was a constant roaring noise nearby, he could not hear it. The air that whistled into his nostrils was odorless.

He spoke, but the words that emerged from his mouth made no sound.

"Am I dead? Not quite, but close. How pleasant it will be to die. I'm sick of this life, every bit of it. The only thing I'll miss is my plants. Maybe in my next life, I'll be a gardener in a place where there are no sorcerers and no wars. And no Tugars to make me feel guilty."

Just then, something emerged from above and floated toward him: a little girl, glowing like a candle in the darkness. Or was she an angel? Rathburt didn't believe in angels. But there was a first time for everything. Then he recognized her as Peta, the ghost-child who had led them out of Dhutanga.

When she spoke there again was no sound, but Rathburt could hear her voice inside his head. "You are damaged and will not live much longer. But it is not yet time for you to permanently depart this body. You must achieve *Maranapavisana* (Death Visit). It will give you the strength to heal your body and return to life."

"Why should I want to do that? There's nothing here for me. I've always been an outcast. The future holds more promise."

"The Torgan needs you."

"Ha . . . that's a joke! Since when has Master Showoff needed me? He'll be much better off without me around. And so will everyone else. In fact, *I'll* be better off without me around."

"You are Torg's only hope. You are Triken's only hope. If you die and return, there is a chance. If you die and do not, there is none."

"Rubbish. What possible role could I play in all this?"

"Your vision at the waterfall was not a lie."

Instantly Rathburt began to cry, though he could not hear his sobs. Tears sprang from his eyes, though he could not feel them course down his cheeks. "You ask too much."

"Courage builds positive karma. Cowardice does the opposite. The choice you make now will follow you to your next life and beyond. As a Death-Knower, you know this better than I."

"Even so . . . you ask too much."

"I will go with you—and guide you back."

"That's not my concern. It's what will happen when I return that frightens me."

"The choice is yours. I cannot force you."

With immense sadness, Rathburt relented and allowed himself to die.

Peta followed and watched him feed. The force of her will lent him the strength to return to his body. A few moments later, he sat up and screamed, causing the physical incarnation of Vedana to yelp and tumble back on her haunches.

"You could have given me a little *warning,*" the demon demanded, glaring at her daughter, who again stood within the chamber.

"Warning is all I've ever given you, Mother."

Rathburt knew exactly what she meant.

# Epilogue

AS TORG LAY atop Laylah, his lips pressed against hers, he felt flower petals fluttering down onto his back, buttocks, and legs. Thousands of them. Tens of thousands. The sorceress moved her delicate hands along his back side, brushing them off.

Torg rose on his elbows and looked down at her lovely face. Her eyes glistened with tears, and when one of his own tears dripped onto the tip of her nose, he realized that his eyes also glistened.

"Laylah. I love you. I *love* you!"

"Torgon. You are my king."

"And you my queen, if you'll have me."

"Are you asking me to marry you?"

"Yes . . . as I have asked you countless times before, in our past lives. Will you marry me, my love?"

"The answer is the same as it has always been. Yes . . ."

Afterward, they slept—but a while before dawn, Torg awoke. Something startled him: a far-off cry. Just a dream? Perhaps. But his thoughts drifted to Rathburt. And it was then that he made his decision. Torg would attempt his third Death Visit in less than a year, an unprecedented frequency, but a necessity—for he needed the extra strength for the trials ahead. He stood quietly. Even in the darkness, he could see that the ground surrounding where they lay had been scorched for several hundred cubits in all directions, forming a charred circle amid the grass and flowers. He could see Izumo's silhouette a quarter-mile away. The stallion appeared to be watching Torg with wary curiosity. Their clothes and the white blanket lay unharmed in a ball only a few cubits beyond the destruction.

Torg wandered several paces from where Laylah slept and sat cross-legged on the ground, his back straight, head held high, body otherwise relaxed. Then he began *Sammaasamaadhi*, the supreme concentration of mind that led to temporary death. At least, he hoped it would be temporary. There was never a guarantee.

Torg's first task was to focus on the present moment by achieving *Parimukhap Satip*, which meant *mindfulness in the front* in the ancient tongue. He did this by breathing—observing each inhale, exhale, and slight pause in between.

Torg focused his awareness on the rims of his nostrils, paying mindful attention to the beginning, middle, and ending of each breath. When thoughts inevitably arose to distract him, he noted their impermanent existence and then returned his attention to his nostrils. Torg had performed this act millions and millions of times over the course of his long life, so it was relatively simple for him to gain intense concentration. His thoughts were tamed, ceasing to hold any power over his awareness. Meanwhile his breath grew subtler, almost unnoticeable, until it eventually became a single perception.

There was no inhale, exhale, or pause. Just breath.

His great heart slowed. From fifty beats a minute.

To thirty.

Ten.

One.

When he died, his body remained in the cross-legged position, but his head sank slowly until his chin rested against his chest. He could not have looked more peaceful.

Torg saw this from above. His mind/karma entered a place he had visited more than a thousand times in this lifetime alone. Silence was all about him, as relentless as it was limitless. He could not smell, taste, or touch. All he could do was see. But that was enough. Once again he had become a broiling ball of karmic energy, leaping great distances across time and space. Countless other spheres streaked along beside him, gazing at him and each other like old friends.

But as he journeyed toward the future, Torg's mind/karma noticed a slight difference. Glints of green followed the spheres, urging and nudging. How was it possible he had never seen this before?

When he reached the deep-blue ball of Death Energy, he settled just above its enormous surface and fed. But again there was a difference. When the blue tendrils leapt up to imbue him with power, brilliant flashes of green emanating from his own sphere greeted them.

Which wasn't so amazing.

Except for one thing.

For the first time in all his experiences with death, Torg *heard* something.

Barely audible.

But unmistakable . . .

*Voices.*

So Ends Book Three.

# Coming Next by Jim Melvin

# Torn By War

## The Death Wizard Chronicles
## Book Four

# 1

THOUGH TORG knew it naught, Laylah woke soon after he peeled himself off her naked body. She lay still as a fawn and watched through the slits of her eyes as the wizard wandered a few paces away and then sat down in a cross-legged position on the grass. She had witnessed him in meditation one other time, in the rock hollow near Duccarita, and had been curious then too. Everything he did pleased her, but this was especially fascinating.

Immediately his body became motionless—except for the rise and fall of his chest. Soon after, even that steady movement ceased, and when his head fell forward she became puzzled and then frightened. It dawned on her how little she knew about his abilities. He was a Death-Knower; she could surmise what that meant. But to consider it psychologically and to view it physically were two different things. Suddenly her heart pounded, and her breath came in gasps. Beyond belief, Torg was *dead*. The reality of it struck her like a blow from a war hammer.

Laylah didn't know what to do. Should she cry for help? Or rush to Torg and shake him? Even as she sat up, the great stallion she had named Izumo came up silently behind her and nuzzled her on the ear, startling her so much she nearly joined the wizard in death. Her scream caused the horse to bolt, spin around, and snort. It took Laylah what felt like a very long time to regain her composure.

When she again could breathe semi-normally, she crawled toward Torg on hands and knees, her arms and legs trembling so much she could barely support her own weight. The night was so quiet she could hear herself shuffling through the scorched grass, which was carpeted with wilted petals. She also heard a strange thudding sound—and finally realized it was her own heavy tears striking the ground. Her beloved was dead! She could see it, sense it, *feel* it.

Laylah crept within an arm's-length of her lover's lifeless body. She wanted to grab him and hold him. Sob and shout. But she was afraid to touch him. If his death became that real to her, she might go mad.

Without warning, Torg's head jerked up, his eyes sprang open, and his mouth opened so wide she could see the back of his throat. Blue-green energy roared from his body and battered her face, lifting her off the ground and casting her several hundred cubits. She landed on her naked rump in a cushiony patch of wildflowers just beyond the scorched circle. Obhasa came to rest beside her, but she noticed in her daze that the Silver Sword remained where she had left it. The blast would have killed almost any creature on Triken. But other than feeling dizzy and stunned, Laylah was unharmed. As if concerned for her welfare, Izumo trotted forward bravely and nuzzled her cheek; this time, she didn't shout, which regained his trust. The stallion backed a few paces away, lay down, and rested his muzzle on the ground like a loyal dog. Soon after, Torg came over and took her in his arms.

"My love! What have I done? Are you hurt? *Tell me you're all right!*"

"I'm . . . fine, beloved." Then she looked into his eyes, where she again saw life. "In fact, I'm better than fine."

Torg squeezed her so hard she grunted. Then he released her, sat back, and leaned against his hands.

"I'm sorry, Laylah. You appeared to be sleeping so deeply . . ."

"You frightened me."

Torg chuckled ruefully. Then he took a deep breath and sighed. "With all the running we've done since Kamupadana, we've never had a chance to fully discuss *Maranapavisana*, my visits to death. They are brief in duration but appear unnatural to those unprepared. I apologize again. I made a severe mistake in judgment. But when the mood comes upon me, it's safer and easier for me if I succumb to it quickly."

"Succumb to what?"

"To the desire! My magic comes from *Marana-Viriya* (Death Energy). I have lived a thousand years—and died a thousand deaths. Only a Death-Knower is able to fall—and rise. When I return from death, I am renewed."

The wizard leaned close to her face, speaking now in a whisper. "At this moment, I am greater than I have ever been. But the trials that lay ahead will require all my strength. Will it be enough?" Then Torg lowered his head.

Though Laylah had been with him for just a few weeks, she already knew him well enough to sense that he was holding something back. "This time was . . . different?" she said.

The wizard appeared surprised. "I will never be able to deceive you. In our future together, that should work to your advantage."

It was Laylah's turn to chuckle. "You don't strike me as the lying type."

"I have weaknesses, but lack of truthfulness is not among them," Torg agreed.

Then he described to Laylah what it felt like to die and what he witnessed while in the Realm of Death. He also told her about seeing the green energy for the first time—and hearing the disturbing voices. By the time he finished, it was almost dawn.

"Did you understand anything the voices were saying?"

"Whoever, or whatever, it was spoke in no language in which I am fluent," Torg admitted. "I sensed neither friendship nor hostility. But I was stunned, nonetheless. After more than a thousand visits, I was arrogant enough to believe that I knew everything about death and its accoutrements. Apparently, I could not have been more wrong. I have been humbled."

As if in response, Izumo nickered. They both laughed.

"Maybe Rathburt is speaking through the horse," Laylah said. They laughed even louder, though afterward they fell into mournful silence that lasted until the first fingers of dawn crept across the plain.

# Glossary

**Author's note:** Many character and place names are English derivatives of Pali, a Middle Indo-Aryan dialect closely related to Sanskrit but now extinct as a spoken language. Today, Pali is studied mainly to gain access to Theravada Buddhist scriptures and is frequently chanted in religious rituals.

*Aarakaa Himsaa* (ah-RUH-kah HIM-sah): Defensive strategy used by Tugars that involves always staying at least a hair's width away from your opponent's longest strike.

*Abhisambodhi* (ab-HEE-sahm-BOH-dee): Highest enlightenment.

*Adho Satta* (AH-dho SAH tah): Anything or anyone who is neither a dragon nor a powerful supernatural being. Means *low one* in ancient tongue.

**Akando** (ah-KAHN-doh): Eldest brother of Takoda.

*Akanittha* (AHK-ah-NEE-tah): A being that is able to feed off the light of the sun. Means *Highest Power* in the ancient tongue.

**Akasa Ocean** (ah-KAH-sah): Largest ocean on Triken. Lies west of Dhutanga, Jivita, and Kincara.

**Ancient tongue**: Ancient language now spoken by only Triken's most learned beings, as well as most Tugars

**Anna**: Tent City of Tējo. Home to the Tugars.

**Aponi** (ah-POH-nee): Biological daughter of Takoda. Younger sister of Magena.

**Appam** (ah-PAHM): Tugar warrior.

**Arupa-Loka** (ah-ROO-pah-LOH-kah): Home of ghosts, demons, and ghouls. Lies near northern border of the Gap of Gamana. Also called Ghost City.

**Asamāna** (ah-sah-MAH-nah): Senasanan bride of Invictus.

**Asava** (ah-SAH-vah): Potent drink brewed by Stone-Eaters.

**Asēkha** (ah-SEEK-ah): Tugars of highest rank. There always are twenty, not including Death-Knowers. Also known as *Viisati* (The Twenty).

*Assarohaa* (ASS-uh-ROW-huh): White horsemen of Jivita.

**Asthenolith** (ah-STHEN-no-lith): Pool of magma in a large cavern beneath

Mount Asubha.

**Avici** (ah-VEE-chee): Largest city on Triken. Home to Invictus.

**Avikkhepa** (ah-vih-KAY-puh): King of Jivita during the war against Slag.

***Badaalataa*** (BAD-ah-LAH-tuh): Carnivorous vines from the demon world.

**Bakheng** (bah-KENG): Central shrine of Dibbu-Loka.

**Balak** (BAH-luk): First wall of Nissaya.

**Bard**: Partner of Ugga and Jord, trappers who lived in the forest near the foothills of Mount Asubha.

**Barranca** (bah-RAHN-chuh): Rocky wasteland that partially encircles the Great Desert.

**Bell:** Measurement of time approximating three hours.

**Bhacca** (BAH-cha): Chambermaid assigned to Laylah.

**Bhasura** (bah-SOOR-ah): One of the large tribes of the Mahaggata Mountains.

**Bhayatupa** (by-yah-TOO-pah): Most ancient and powerful of dragons. His scales are the color of deep crimson.

**Bhojja** (BOH-juh): Mother of all horses. Magical being of unknown origin or lifespan.

**Black mountain wolves:** Largest and most dangerous of all wolves. Allies of demons, witches, and Mogols.

**Bonny:** Female pirate from Duccarita who has joined the forces of good.

**Broosha** (BREW-shah): Female vampire from Arupa-Loka. Daughter of Urbana.

**Bruugash** (BREW-gash): Pabbajjan overlord.

**Bunjako** (boon-JAHK-oh): Stone-Eater; son of Gulah, grandson of Slag.

**Cariya River** (chah-REE-yah): Largest river west of Mahaggata Mountains.

**Catu** (chah-TOO): Northernmost mountain on Triken.

**Cave monkeys:** Small, nameless primates that live in the underworld beneath Asubha.

**Chain Man:** Another name for Mala.

**Chal-Abhinno** (Chahl-ahb-HIH-no): Queen of the Warlish witches.

**Che-ra** (CHEE-ruh): Svakaran name for a fat possum.

**Chieftain:** Desert gelding befriended by Tāseti.

**Churikā** (chuh-REE-kah): Female Asēkha.

**Cirāya** (ser-AYE-yah): Green cactus that, when chewed, provides large amounts of liquid and nourishment.

**Cubit**: Length of the arm from elbow to fingertip, which measures approximately eighteen inches, though among Tugars a cubit is considered twenty-one inches.

**Daasa** (DAH-suh): Pink-skinned slaves captured on the western shore of the Akasa Ocean.

**Dakkhinā** (dah-KEE-nay): Sensation that brings on the urge to attempt *Sammaasamaadhi*. Means *holy gift* in the ancient tongue.

**Dalhapa** (dal-HAH-puh): Tugar warrior.

**Death-Knower**: Any Tugar—almost always an Asēkha—who has successfully achieved *Sammaasamaadhi*. In the ancient tongue, a Death-Knower is called *Maranavidu*.

**Deathless people**: Monks and nuns who inhabit Dibbu-Loka. Called deathless people because some of them live for more than one thousand years. Also known as noble ones.

**Death Visit**: Tugar description of the temporary suicide of a Death-Knower wizard.

**Dēsaka** (day-SAH-kuh): Famous Vasi master who trained *The Torgon*.

**Dhutanga** (doo-TAHNG-uh): Largest forest on Triken. Lies west of the Mahaggata Mountains. Also known as the Great Forest.

**Dibbu-Loka** (DEE-boo-LOW-kah): Realm of the noble ones. Means *Deathless World* in the ancient tongue. Originally called Piti-Loka.

**Ditthi-Rakkhati** (DEE-tee-rack-HAH-tee): Current-day Jivitan who is a spy within Duccarita.

**Ditthi-Sagga** (DEE-tee-SAH-gah): Jivitan captain who battled druids during war against Slag.

**Dracools** (drah-KOOLS): Winged beasts that walk on hind legs but look like miniature dragons. Taller than a man but shorter than a druid.

**Druggen Boggle** (DROO-gun BAH-guhl): Druid representative from Dhutanga.

**Druids** (DREW-ids): Seven-cubit-tall beings that dwell in Dhutanga. Ancient enemies of Jivita.

**Duccarita** (DOO-chu-REE-tuh): City of slave traders, pirates, thieves, and rapists in the northwestern corner of the Gap of Gamana.

**Dukkhatu** (doo-KAH-too): Great and ancient spider that spent the last years of its life near the peak of Asubha.

**Dvipa** (DVEE-puh): Asēkha left in charge of Anna.

*Efrits* (EE-frits): Invisible creatures that dwell in the Realm of the Undead. When summoned, they voraciously devour the internal organs of living beings.

*Ekadeva* (ay-kah-DAY-vuh): The *One God* worshipped by the Jivitans and many other inhabitants of Triken.

**Elu** (EE-loo): Miniature Svakaran who is an associate of Rathburt.

**Eunuch** (YOO-nuk): Castrated male slaves who reside within the fifth wall of Kamupadana.

**Fathom**: Approximately eleven cubits.

**Gap of Gamana**: Northernmost gap of the Mahaggata Mountains.

**Gap of Gati**: Southern gap that separates the Mahaggata Range from the Kolankold Range.

**Golden Road**: Road paved with a special golden metal that connects Avici and Kilesa.

**Golden soldiers**: Soldiers of Invictus, mass-bred in his image.

**Golden Wall**: Oblong wall coated with a special golden metal that surrounds Avici and Kilesa.

**Gray Plains**: Arid plains that dominate much of the land east of the Ogha River.

**Green Plains**: Lush plains that surround Jivita.

**Gruugash** (GROO-gash): A representative of the Pobbajja.

**Gulah** (GOO-lah): Stone-Eater who became warden of Asubha. Son of Slag.

**Gunther**: Son of Vedana, father of Invictus and Laylah.

**Hakam** (huh-KAM): Third wall of Nissaya.

**Harīti** (huh-REE-tee): Kojin rumored to be in love with Mala.

**Henepola III** (HEN-uh-POH-lah): King of Nissaya during war against Slag.

**Henepola X**: King of Nissaya during war against Invictus.

**Hornbeam**: Ancient trees whose twisted lust for life causes madness. Called *Pacchanna* in the ancient tongue.

**Ice Ocean**: Ocean that lies northeast of Okkanti Mountains.

**Iddhi-Pada** (IDD-hee-PUH-duh): Series of four roads that leads from Jivita to Avici, passing through Lake Hadaya, the Gap of Gati, Nissaya, and Java.

**Indajaala** (inn-duh-JAY-la): Powerful Nissayan conjurer.

**Invictus** (in-VICK-tuss): Evil sorcerer who threatens all of Triken and beyond. Also known as *Suriya* (the Sun God).

**Izumo** (ee-ZOO-moh): Dracool from Mahaggata.

**Jākita-Abhinno** (JAH-kih-tuh-uh-BHEE-no): Successor to Chal-Abhinno as queen of the Warlish witches.

**Jākita-dEsa** (JAH-kih-tuh-DAY-suh): Hag servant of Jākita-Abhinno.

**Java** (JAH-vah): Dark Forest that lies east of Nissaya.

**Jhana** (JAH-nah): Father of Torg.

**Jivita** (jih-VEE-tuh): Wondrous city that is home to the white horsemen. Located west of the Gap of Gati in the Green Plains. Also called the White City. Known as *Jutimantataa* (City of Splendor) in the ancient tongue.

**Jord**: Mysterious partner of Ugga and Bard, trappers who lived in the forest near the foothills of Mount Asubha.

***Kalakhattiya*** (kah-lah-KHA-tee-yuh): Black knights of Nissaya.

**Kalapa** (kuh-LUH-puh): Powerful Asēkha chieftain during war against Slag. Grandfather of Kusala.

**Kamupadana** (kuh-MOO-puh-DUH-nah): Home of Warlish witches and their lesser female servants. Also called the Whore City.

***Kattham Bhunjaka*** (kuh-TAM boon-JAH-kuh): Most powerful druid queen to ever exist.

**Kauha Marshes** (COW-hah): Deadly marshes that lie between Avici and Kilesa.

**Kilesa** (kee-LAY-suh): Sister City of Anna.

**Kincara Forest** (KIN-chu-ruh): Large forest, though not as large as Dhutanga, that lies south of the Green Plains.

**King Lobha** (LOW-bah): Sadistic king who built Piti-Loka.

**Kithar** (kee-TAR): Tugar warrior.

**Kojin** (KOH-jin): Enormous ogress with six arms and a bloated female head. Almost as large as a snow giant.

**Kolankold Mountains** (KO-luhn-kold): Bottom stem of the Mahaggata Mountains, located south of the Gap of Gati.

**Kuruk** (KERR-uck): Traitorous Ropakan who desired Magena.

**Kusala** (KOO-suh-luh): Second most powerful Tugar in the world next to Torg. Also known as Asēkha-Kusala and Chieftain Kusala.

**Lake Hadaya** (huh-DUH-yuh): Large freshwater lake that lies west of the Gap of Gati.

**Lake Keo** (KAY-oh): Large freshwater lake that lies between the Kolankold Mountains and Dibbu-Loka.

**Lake Ti-ratana** (tee-RAH-tuh-nah): Large freshwater lake that lies west of Avici.

**Laylah** (LAY-lah): Younger sister of Invictus.

**Long breath:** Fifteen seconds. Also called slow breath.

**Lucius** (LOO-shus): General of Invictus' legions before the creation of Mala.

**Madiraa** (muh-DEE-rah): Daughter of Henepola X, king of Nissaya.

**Magena** (mah-JAY-nah): Name given to Laylah by the Ropakans.

**Mahaggata Mountains** (MAH-hah-GAH-tah): Largest mountain range on Triken. Shaped like a capital Y.

***Mahaasupanno*** (mah-HAH-soo-PAH-no): Mightiest of all dragons.

***Mahanta pEpa*** (mah-HAHN-tah PAY-pah): Great Evil that resides within Duccarita.

**Mala** (MAH-lah): Former snow giant who was ruined by Invictus and turned into the sorcerer's most dangerous servant. Formerly called Yama-Deva.

***Majjhe Ghamme*** (Mah-JEE GAH-mee): Means midsummer in the ancient tongue.

**Manta:** Jivitan necromancer in the service of Queen Rajinii.

***Maōi*** (muh-OYUH): Magical black crystals found in caverns beneath Nissaya.

**Maynard Tew:** Duccaritan pirate.

**Mogols** (MAH-guhls): Warrior race that dwells in Mahaggata Mountains. Longtime worshippers of the dragon Bhayatupa and the demon Vedana. Ancient enemies of Nissaya.

**Moken** (MOH-kin): A chosen leader of the boat people.

**Mount Asubha** (ah-SOO-buh): Dreaded mountain in the cold north that housed the prison of Invictus.

**Nagara** (NUH-gah-ruh): Central keep of Nissaya.

***Namuci*** (nah-MOO-chee): Magic word that summons the *efrits* from the Realm of the Undead.

**Nirodha** (nee-ROW-dah): Icy wastelands that lie north of the Mahaggata Mountains.

**Nissaya** (nee-SIGH-yah): Impenetrable fortress on the east end of the Gap of Gati. Home of the Nissayan knights.

**Noble ones**: Monks and nuns who inhabit Dibbu-Loka. Also called deathless people.

**Obhasa** (oh-BHAH-sah): Torg's magical staff, carved from the ivory of a desert elephant found dead. Means *container of light* in the ancient tongue.

**Ogha River:** (OH-guh): Largest river on Triken. Begins in the northern range of Mahaggata and ends in Lake Keo.

**Okkanti Mountains** (oh-KAHN-tee): Small range with tall, jagged peaks located northeast of Kilesa.

**Olog** (OH-lahg): Ogre from the interior of Mahaggata.

**Orkney**: Cave troll.

**Ott**: Second wall of Nissaya.

**Pabbajja** (pah-BAH-jah): Homeless people who live in the plains surrounding Java. Little is known of their habits.

**Pace:** Approximately 30 inches, though among Tugars a pace is considered 36 inches.

**Palak** (puh-LUCK): A senior commander of the *Kalakhattiya*.

**Paramita** (puh-ruh-MEE-tuh): Magnificent sword made by a Tugar master. Contained a dragon jewel on its pommel.

**Peta** (PAY-tuh): Ghost girl of Arupa-Loka. In life, she was blind.

**Pisaaca** (pee-SAH-kuh): Female demon from Arupa-Loka.

**Piti-Loka** (PEE-tee-LOH-kuh): Original name of Dibbu-Loka. Built by King Lobha ten thousand years ago as his burial shrine. Means *Rapture World* in the ancient tongue.

**Podhana** (POH-dah-nuh): Asēkha warrior.

**Porisāda** (por-ee-SAH-dah): Most dangerous of all Mogols. Are known to eat the flesh of their victims.

**Raaga** (RAH-gah): Magic word from the Realm of the Undead that causes humans to experience orgasmic lust.

**Rathburt** (RATH-burt): Only other living Death-Knower. Known as a gardener, not a warrior.

**Rajinii** (ruh-GEE-knee): Queen of Jivita during war against Invictus.

**Rati** (RAH-tee): Asēkha warrior.

**Ropaka** (row-PAH-kah): One of the large tribes of the Mahaggata Mountains.

**Sakuna** (sah-KOO-nah): Eagle incarnation of Jord.

**Salt Sea:** Dead inland sea south of the Okkanti Mountains.

***Sammaasamaadhi*** (sam-mah-sah-MAH-dee): Supreme concentration of mind. Temporary suicide.

**Sampati** (sahm-PAH-tee): Giant condors crossbred with dragons by Invictus. Used to transport people and supplies to the prison on Mount Asubha.

**Sāykans** (SAH-kuns): Female soldiers who defend Kamupadana.

**Senasana** (SEN-uh-SAHN-ah): Thriving market city that lies north of Dibbu-Loka.

**Short breath:** Three seconds. Also called quick breath.

**Silah** (SEE-luh): Female Tugar warrior.

**Silver Sword:** Ancient sword forged by a long-forgotten master from the otherworldly metals found among the shattered remains of a meteorite.

**Simōōn** (suh-MOON): Magical dust storm that protects Anna from outsiders.

**Sister Tathagata** (tuh-THUH-guh-tuh): High nun of Dibbu-Loka. More than three thousand years old. Also known as *Perfect One.*

***Sivathika*** (SEE-vah-TEE-kuh): Ancient Tugar ritual. Dying warrior breathes what remains of his or her *Life Energy* into a survivor's lungs, where it is absorbed into the blood.

**Slag:** Stone-Eater defeated by Torg outside of Nissaya. Father of Gulah.

**Snow giants:** Magnificent beings reaching heights of 10 cubits or more that dwell in the Okkanti Mountains.

**Sōbhana** (SOH-bah-nah): Female Asēkha warrior.

**Span:** Distance from the end of the thumb to the end of the little finger of a hand spread to full width. Approximately nine inches, though among Tugars a span is considered 12 inches.

**Stēorra** (STAY-oh-rah): Wife of Gunther, mother of Invictus and Laylah.

**Stone:** Equal to fourteen pounds.

**Stone-Eater:** Magical being that gains power by devouring lava rocks.

**Svakara** (svuh-KUH-ruh): One of the large tribes of the Mahaggata Mountains.

**Takoda** (tuh-KOH-duh): Adoptive father of Magena.

***Tanhiiyati*** (tawn-hee-YAH-tee): Insatiable craving for eternal existence suffered by some long-lived beings.

**Tāseti** (tah-SAY-tee): Most powerful female Asēkha in the world.

**Tējo** (TAY-joh): Great Desert. Home of the Tugars.

**Tent City:** Largest city in Tējo. Home to the Tugars. Also known as Anna.

***The Torgon*** (TOR-gahn): Torg's ceremonial name. Also Lord Torgon.

**Torg:** Thousand-year-old Death-Knower wizard. King of the Tugars. Means *Blessed Warrior* in the ancient tongue.

**Triken** (TRY-ken): Name of the world. Also name of the land east and west of the Mahaggata Mountains.

**Tugars** (TOO-gars): Desert warriors of Tējo. Called *Kantaara Yodhas* in the ancient tongue.

**Uccheda** (oo-CHAY-duh): Tower of Invictus in Avici. Means *annihilation* in the ancient tongue.

**Ugga** (OOO-gah): Human-bear crossbreed who was a partner of Bard and Jord, trappers who lived in the forest near the foothills of Mount Asubha.

**Ulaara the Black** (uu-LAH-ruh): The supreme dragon before the rise of Bhayatupa.

***Undines*** (oon-DEENS): Creatures of the demon world who—when summoned—can infect living bodies and turn them into flesh-eating zombies.

***Uppādetar*** (oo-pay-DEE-tar): The God of Creation worshipped by the Nissayans.

**Urbana** (oor-BAH-nah): Mistress of robes assigned by Invictus to attend Laylah. A vampire.

**Ur-Nammu** (oor-NUH-moo): High priestess of Kamupadana.

***Uttara*** (oo-TUH-ruh): Specially made sword wielded by Tugar warriors and Asēkhas. Single-edged, slightly curved.

**Vasi master** (VUH-see): Martial arts master who trains Tugar novices to become warriors.

**Vedana** (VAY-duh-nuh): One-hundred-thousand-year-old demon. Grandmother of Invictus and Laylah. Mother of King Lobha.

***Vijjaadharaa*** (vee-jhad-HUH-rah): Mysterious guides.

**Vinipata** (VEE-nee-PUH-tuh): Central shrine of Senasana.

**Warlish witch** (WOR-lish): Female witch who can change her appearance between extreme beauty and hideousness.

**Wild men:** Short, hairy men who thrive in the foothills of Kolankold. Their women do not fight as warriors and are rarely seen. Longtime enemies of Nissaya.

**Wooser:** Wild man from Kolankold.

**Worm monster:** Nameless beast with more than a thousand tentacles that lives beneath Asubha. Largest living creature on Triken.

**Worrins-Julich** (WAR-ins-JOO-lich): Senior captain of the white horsemen of Jivita.

**Wyvern-Abhinno** (WHY-vurn-ahb-HEE-no): Powerful Warlish witch.

*Yakkkkha* (YAH-kuh): Magic word from the Realm of the Undead that brings corpses and skeletons temporarily back to life.

**Yama-Bhari** (YAH-muh-BAR-ee): Snow giant. Wife of Yama-Utu.

**Yama-Deva** (YAH-muh-DAY-vuh): Ruined snow giant that became Mala.

**Yama-Utu** (YAH-muh-OO-too): Snow giant. Brother of Yama-Deva. Husband of Yama-Bhari.

**Ziggurat** (ZIG-guh-raht): Nine-story temple located within the first wall of Kamupadana.

# Acknowledgements

Any and all descriptions of meditation in this volume were based on the Buddha's enlightened teachings in the *Mahasatipatthana Sutta*. May all beings one day share in this wisdom.

Dennis Chastain continued to enrich this work. Margo McLoughlin legitimized the ancient language; any flaws or inconsistencies are not of her doing. Timothy Spira helped to inspire certain aspects of Dhutanga. Jack Wise guided me through the rapids. And thanks to my sister, Robin Brethwaite, and my best friend, Rick Humphrey, for their ongoing support.

Much thanks also to Bell Bridge Books, for reviving the series and giving it new life. Pat, Debra, Deb and crew . . . you are truly awesome people, both in talent and in character. And you have vastly improved the product.

And of course, much love to my wife, Jeanne Malmgren, who always sweetens the pot.

# About Jim Melvin

Jim Melvin is the author of the epic, six-book epic fantasy *The Death Wizard Chronicles*. He was an award-winning journalist at the *St. Petersburg Times* for twenty-five years. As a reporter, he specialized in science, nature, health and fitness, and he wrote about everything from childhood drowning to erupting volcanoes. Jim is a student of Eastern philosophy and mindfulness meditation, both of which he weaves extensively into his work. Jim lives in Upstate South Carolina in the foothills of the mountains. He's married and has five daughters. Visit him at:

www.jim-melvin.com
and
www.deathwizardchronicles.blogspot.com.

CPSIA information can be obtained at www.ICGtesting.com
Printed in the USA
LVOW120309060613

337145LV00002B/3/P